SISTERS WHITE

The Complete Series

SUNNY MACKENZIE

2021

ISBN: 978 0 6451429 1 4

Published by Sunny Mackenzie
www.sunnymackenzie.com.au
Email: sunny.mackenzie@outlook.com

Cover Designer: TRC DESIGNS

TABLE OF CONTENTS

DEDICATION

To Sisters:

The ones who fight

and know exactly where to aim the sharpest of arrows;

The ones who care

and know exactly what to do to comfort the best;

The ones who share a bond like no other

and will love you for a lifetime,

no matter what.

WHITE SAILS

SISTERS WHITE SERIES: Book One

SUNNY MACKENZIE

2020

Sea Fever

I must go down to the sea again, to the lonely sea and the sky,
And all I ask is a tall ship and a star to steer her by,
And the wheel's kick and the wind's song and the white sail's shaking,
And a grey mist on the sea's face, and a grey dawn breaking.

I must go down to the seas again, for the call of the running tide
Is a wild call and a clear call that may not be denied;
And all I ask is a windy day with the white clouds flying,
And the flung spray and the blown spume, and the sea-gulls crying.

I must go down to the seas again, to the vagrant gypsy life,
To the gull's way and the whale's way, where the wind's like a whetted knife;
And all I ask is a merry yarn from a laughing fellow-rover,
And quiet sleep and a sweet dream when the long trick's over.

John Masefield

Chapter One

'No! And I'm sick of talking about this, Jane. No more!' Ginny slammed the skillet down onto the table with force. 'You do what you want! I'll do what I want! Stop interfering in my life!'

I watched the Mediterranean Chicken slip across the skillet, almost sliding off one side.

'Be reasonable, Ginny,' I tried to placate her, although I was rapidly losing my cool. It had been a crappy day at school – the Year 10 boys had refused to work, even though I'd tried to make learning Geography skills as interesting as I possibly could for them – and I was tired and frustrated. 'You need to be responsible –' I didn't get far with that, as Ginny cut me off.

'Responsible! That's your middle name!' Her voice rose and I watched her face twist in anger, her nose scrunching and her eyes narrowing. 'You're so busy being *responsible,* you've turned into the most boring person on Earth!' She turned away, grabbing a chef's knife and the bunch of fresh oregano resting beside the wooden cutting board. 'Stop trying to control everyone else's life,' she muttered, attacking the poor herb with furious chops.

'She's right, Jane.'

That's just what I needed: Charli getting involved. I sighed, dropping my head. Raising my left hand to my face, I briefly pressed my fingertips into my closed eyes.

'Charli, don't...' I implored, looking up at her. This had the potential to turn into a nightmare argument if the others bought into it. 'This is between Ginny and me.'

'Except it's not!' Charli stepped closer, standing right in front of me, and pulled her shoulders back in a challenge. 'I didn't want to go to university, either. But no! You were on my back until I caved in.' She shook her head in disgust, contempt entering her eyes. 'So, here I am... Off to uni every day, doing a course I'm not really interested in because,' she spread her arms wide, 'Saint Jane, the boss of us all, decreed it.'

'Stop being so dramatic,' I countered, and I could feel my eyes tearing up. *I refuse to cry in front of them. I refuse to cry in front of them*, I chanted in my head. 'Someone's got to manage things.'

'Well, actually... Seeing as you've raised it... *I'm* the one who manages everything, not you, Jane.' And so, with Daphne's comment, it became a whole-family fight. Well – not quite – as Lou hadn't said anything, but then, she never did.

'Daph, I know that you take care of the house and finances, but this is different. And you *must* agree with me that Virginia *should* get some formal education. She can't just loll around the house all day until all the restaurants and bars open again – if we *ever* get over COVID. I don't care if it's *hospitality*, but she could at least get some TAFE qualification. Instead, *nothing*. Just the mandatory Responsible Service/Conduct stuff. Nothing!'

Yes, I could hear the disdain in my voice. Yes, I could hear me getting worked up, stressing words like a 15-year-old girl instead of the mature, twenty-eight-year-old woman that I was. And calling Ginny "Virginia" didn't help. She hated being called that. But this was *so* not the day for this argument. I just wanted to sit alone with a cider, away from noise and loud voices and petulant females, and chill. Not talk to anyone. Not deal with the pressure and responsibility of my family. And a part of me knew that I was being a bit unreasonable. I wasn't stupid!

'I'm sick of uni. I want to be a jillaroo,' Charli cried out, caught up in the moment. 'And you can't make me stay.'

'And I'm *not* going to do what you want, just because you're the eldest,' Ginny chimed in. 'If I want to be a barmaid, that's what I'll be. If I don't want qualifications, then I don't have to get them. Plenty of places employed me before the pandemic. I'll get work again once all the restrictions are lifted.'

I thought, for a moment, that she was going to poke her tongue out, as the unvoiced "so there!" reverberated around the kitchen.

'You know, not *everyone* gets to do what they want!' Okay, I was losing it. '*I* don't especially like dealing with teenagers every day!'

'Then bloody-well don't!' Charli yelled, 'but don't keep holding it over our heads.'

8

'Daph,' I said, turning to her and speaking as calmly as I could, 'can you talk sense into them?' *C'mon, Daph*, I wordlessly implored. *You've been with me through all of this…*

'No, I don't think I will. I think it's time that you stopped trying to control us all. I think you need to let Ginny and Charli make up their own minds about their lives.'

I was stunned. I stood there, silently staring at each of my sisters in turn. The sisters that I'd had to raise when our parents had died that afternoon, six years ago. The sisters I'd had to take responsibility for, so we hadn't been split up amongst well-meaning relatives who came out of the woodwork while we were still all numb with grief.

I watched as Louisa – quiet, placid Louisa, who never, *ever* entered a disagreement – slinked out of the kitchen, most probably heading towards her room.

And as Daphne – steady, calm Daphne, who usually had my back in all my decisions – gazed right back at me, unblinking and unmoving.

And as Ginny – a rebel from the time she'd been born, a flame-haired, doll-faced baby with a shriek that could deafen, when I was four years old – glowered, animosity emanating from her in waves.

And as Charlotte – the baby of the family – stared back, a defiance that only someone barely out of her teens could successfully carry off.

And I'd had enough!

'I'm out of here!' I yelled, not proud of myself but … I didn't care anymore. 'You can all take care of yourselves!'

I stormed to my bedroom – the room that had once been our parents and that, three years after their death, I'd taken as my own so that Lou and Charli didn't have to share a room any longer – and grabbed the bag that I'd stashed there when I'd arrived home from a shocker-of-a-day teaching high-school Geography. Or, more to the point, *attempting* to teach Geography, I grimaced to myself. I snatched my all-weather jacket from the back of the chair near the window because I knew I'd need it where I was going.

As I stomped – yes, I was as capable as the others of behaving like a child – towards the front door, Louisa came out of her room.

'You know, she's right,' she said, in a quiet voice, her tone conciliatory. 'We're not children anymore. You can, if you want, do what *you* want to do. You don't have to be responsible for all of us anymore.'

I was floored. Did she not understand? Did she not get just how stressful it was, all those years ago? She must have read my thoughts from my face.

'Jane, it's not that we don't appreciate what you've done for us. But it's time to let us be grown-ups, too.' She looked down, her head tilting. This was a common trait of hers – a slight swoop – not looking at us directly in the eye. It had the effect of being supplicating, as though she didn't want to upset anyone, but she was making a point. 'Think about it, Jane.'

'Oh, I'm going to *think* about it!' I retorted, beyond reason at that point. 'I'm *definitely* going to think about it! Why should I rock up to school every day, teaching a bunch of entitled kids who have *no* interest whatsoever in the amazing geographical wonders of the world, when I get *no* respect whatsoever from my own *sisters*? Oh, I'm going to *think* about it, alright!'

And with that, I behaved like one of those entitled brats and stormed out of the house, slamming the front door for effect.

And tried – unsuccessfully – not to cry.

Chapter Two

The sway was soothing…

I'd burnt off most of my boiling emotions when I'd marched along the road to Greenwich Wharf. The rocking motion of the ferry released the residual hurt and anger, as the vessel left the Lane Cove River and swung around to join the Parramatta River before merging into Sydney Harbour. I could feel the afternoon sea breeze flitting across my cheeks as I sat, my eyes closed, my head flopped back, my face turned upwards, on the outer deck of the boat. My breathing slowed as I calmed down.

Riding the ferries always soothed my stresses, no matter the cause. Dad used to take us when we were little: he'd had a free pass with his work. When our mother wanted time to herself, he'd drag us all down to the wharf and we'd go somewhere – anywhere – on the ferries. Louisa didn't like them much – she'd be green with seasickness – and it wasn't long before she'd stayed home with Mum, promising not to disturb Mum's "quiet time". But I loved being on the harbour. I loved the ferries. Especially the big older ones.

I didn't want to think about the fight. Incidents like that were becoming more and more frequent and I suppose it should be expected: five girls – no, we were women now – all living in one house. And, for all that we were sisters, we were so different. Five distinctive blends of our parents' characteristics, with highly personalised responses to the suddenness and circumstances of their deaths. I knew that I had become much less impulsive and more responsible – ugh! There was that word, again. But it was true. I'd had to not only *be* responsible (blah!), but I'd had to *appear* to be a sensible, mature adult at the ripe old age of twenty-two. Or – and this was the threat – we'd all be split up. Charli had only been fourteen and Louisa just two years older and, between the hovering relatives and the threat from the authorities of foster care, I knew I couldn't put a foot wrong. And I hadn't.

And now they were holding this against me! As if I were *enjoying* this! As if this were how I'd *wanted* my life to be...

'Do you mind if I sit here, dear?'

The soft, quivery voice interrupted my indignant thoughts. I opened my eyes to see an elderly woman, her beige overcoat pulled tightly closed with one hand, gesturing to the seats next to me.

'No. Not at all,' I responded, shifting slightly to make room for her to position two shopping bags on the seat beside me. A quick glance revealed that we'd already passed the Greenwich Point Wharf: a sure sign of how distracted I'd been that I hadn't realised we'd stopped. I sighed, heavily.

'Are you alright, dear?'

I looked towards my new companion, taking in her concerned look. 'Sure. I'm fine.' I paused. 'Just tired.' I attempted a smile, before turning away and closing my eyes again.

'Oh, I find the sea breeze very refreshing. Wakes me right up,' she said, satisfaction in her voice.

'Hmm, yes,' I felt obliged to reply. 'Usually does with me, too.'

'But not today, dear?'

'Not yet. Maybe in a while.' And with that, I burrowed into my bag and retrieved the latest copy of *Earth Today*, my favourite magazine. It was a move designed to discourage her conversation – I really didn't want to talk – but, more importantly, because I was dying to read an article in there. I'd bought it on the way home from school and I knew there was a feature from my favourite writer. Okay, not *just* my favourite: I was a total fan! I could give those teenage girls I taught at school a run for their money, I was such a fangirl! And, at my age!

It was a sexy blend of my two loves: incredible sites from around the world, just waiting for me to explore them – even if it was only by reading – *and* Jackson McGee!

Jackson Alexander McGee. Yes, I'd looked him up on the Internet: Wikipedia ... Instagram ... The *Earth Today* site. You name it. I've done more research on Jackson Alexander McGee than ... pretty much anything! And I have four years of uni!

He's so gorgeous! I could look at his photo for ages, reading into his beautiful blue eyes all sorts of adventurous escapades and thoughts. He had only one dimple – his naughty dimple, I imagined – just to the left of his mouth. And his mouth... His full lips upturned in a satisfied smirk, as though he knew secrets and magical places that other people could only guess at.

But he wasn't all sun-streaked, dark blonde hair and well-defined muscles... He travelled! Everywhere! He sailed the world, sending to duty-bound mortals, like myself, all manner of tales and images of amazing places. He'd written stories from Alaska and Madagascar and Tahiti and the Galapagos Islands. He'd eaten exotic foods with indigenous peoples from *all* around the world.

He was Jackson Alexander McGee. And he was my hero.

My secret, secret hero.

I was sure that my sisters had seen the magazines in my room and knew I had a stack of them on the bookshelf near the door. But they didn't know *why* I had them. My guess was that they just thought they were for school – teaching Geography and all. But I never mentioned Jackson's articles to the kids at school: they would have spoilt it. Knowing them, they'd just ridicule the article, the adventure or him in some way and ... *Nah! Not giving them the chance!*

But there I was. The cooling breeze, salty with the sea, whipped away the last turbulent emotions from the squabble at home and I had the latest *Earth Today* in my hands, just waiting for me to dive into Jackson's latest adventure.

The article was about White Island, the site of the volcanic eruption in New Zealand which killed all those tourists in 2019. Jackson didn't go into detail about the incident: the text was more about the volcano itself. How the island is really the summit of the volcano, most of which is underwater. And, for the geography-nerd in me, he expanded on the structure of the volcano, the number of explosions, especially in the late 70's and early 80's, that had occurred. And how volatile it is.

And, most of all, what an *incredible* geological wonder it is!

The article was littered with fantastic photos: of crooked and cracked crannies left from the cooling magma; stunning shots of the marine creatures, swimming around the lichen-covered rocks just below the surface of the surrounding sea; the green tinge of sunlight filtering through the branches of trees that, somehow, still manage to grow on such an unpredictable place.

Yes, I could have downloaded the magazine and the article – it's not like I don't have a subscription – but there was something more substantial about holding it in my hands; about the heft of the magazine; and the smooth, silky texture of the paper.

'Oooh, isn't he a hunk!' My neighbour's voice interrupted my daydreaming. She was leaning over the seat that separated us, her bony finger pointing to the photograph of Jackson standing on the deck of a cruise boat, the ocean and volcano a backdrop to his image. 'I wouldn't mind *him*. He'd be a handful, wouldn't he! Look at that cheeky dimple! He could get up to no-good, I'm telling you,' she chuckled, delightedly.

I turned to glance at her, a little shocked at her words. I mean, she looked like someone's *grandmother*, for crying out loud! But she sounded like any of the younger teachers in the staffroom, or the girls in the classroom, giggling over someone on Snapchat.

She raised her eyebrows suggestively, her eyes widening with invitation. 'Don't say you haven't noticed! Why, I'd even *read* the article!' And then she laughed out loud, a chortle that suggested she might have been "a handful" herself when she was young.

I imagined Ginny seeing Jackson's photograph. She'd be sure to make some inappropriate remark: something lewd and dirty. And then I thought of Lou, who wouldn't comment at all. And Charli, who would make some innuendo about 'riding him' or stud services. And Daphne, who would probably remark about the practicalities of living on a yacht.

'You know, dear, he looks a lot like that handsome young man there. The one who's been watching you for most of the trip.' I followed the direction of her pointy finger and ...

'Although it's not surprising, I guess,' she continued, filling the silence left by my speechlessness. 'Your hair *does* look pretty. The setting sun seems to bring out all the colours. Is it 'tawny'? Is that what they call that colour? Girly?' she prodded. 'Are you listening to me? Oh, you're distracted by the hunk!' She chortled again. 'Wel-l-l-l, if I were twenty years younger, I'd be going there myself.'

Her voice continued to ramble on, but I didn't really hear her.

Because, on a Sydney Harbour ferry, today of all days, was *him*!

Jackson Alexander McGee!

My secret, secret hero!

Sprawled on a bench seat, not two metres away from me, within hearing distance of our conversation.

And he'd heard it, I could tell.

Because he was looking directly at *me*, smiling a very knowing and wicked smirk, self-satisfaction oozing from his relaxed demeanour.

Chapter Three

Oh. My. God!

Earth Today slipped through my trembling fingers and clattered to the deck. I jolted, self-consciousness washing over me. My face felt hot, the blush blooming on my cheeks, as I looked down, trying desperately to disappear from his sight. My hand rose to my face, my fingers splayed across my eyes. I could see my magazine – the same one alerting Jackson Alexander McGee, of all people, to my reading preferences – lying listlessly open on the deck, "White Island? It's More Shades of Grey!", splashed across two pages in bold black lettering. As if I needed that extra dollop of mortification.

Earth, swallow me now!

The familiar sounds of the surging water as the ferry's engines slowed signalled our arrival at Circular Quay. Bending down, I snatched up the incriminating magazine, hastily shoving it into my bag and stood, readying to leave the ferry.

And, yes, I was darting quick peeks in his direction. Not directly at him – I didn't want to appear *too* obvious. But I was still trying to absorb the idea that he was *really* here! In Sydney! On a ferry! In the harbour!

It made sense, in a global sort of way. He *had* just written an article about New Zealand, so he must have been there, and his parents did live in the outer western suburbs of Sydney. He was "just in the neighbourhood and thought he'd drop in!" But what were the chances! Jackson on *my* ferry! Right there!

My mind was spinning – thoughts in a spiral – as I processed his presence and, simultaneously, tried to appear normal. Or at least, not look like a lunatic.

Yep, he was still there. Lounging languidly on the bench-seat, a lazy grin gracing his face. Totally comfortable and relaxed. *He* wasn't all flustered. *His* hands weren't shaking. *He* didn't look like he felt faint, panting quick gulps of air. No, he was all casual sex appeal, his legs long and lean, stretched out, a slight bend in the knees, his loafer-clad feet at an angle to the deck. The denim of his jeans, sun-bleached white in patches, soft from wear. His cranberry-coloured Henley highlighting the blonde streaks of his hair, sexy in its windblown disarray, and the sailor's muscles of his chest and arms, one draped across the back of the seat, the other resting on his thigh.

And then I realised that his gaze, covered as it was with his aviator sunglasses, hadn't moved from my face the entire time I was studying him. So much for a quick peek! In my defence, what woman alive would only give him a glance? He *commanded* a longer look. He bloody-well *deserved* an extended examination. My hand lifted towards my head, which had flopped forward in my mortification. I felt like a child – *If I couldn't see him, he can't see me!*

I was all over the place. My thoughts were swirling at speed, even though I hadn't moved from where I stood. I turned and noted that my elderly companion was still gathering up her shopping bags, but it appeared that she'd been slowed down by her attention to Jackson-OhMyGod-McGee and me.

'Oh, he *does* like you, doesn't he, dear?' she teased.

'Can I help you with your bags?' I returned, pointedly. And then I ruined it all by looking back at my hero.

'That would be nice, dear,' she said, 'and then you can get back to eyeing off that gorgeous hunk of manhood!'

I didn't groan, then – but I thought about it.

The bump of the docking ferry reminded us that we needed to concentrate on making our way to the exit and, with one last quick – okay, it was lingering – look back at the man that I had fantasised about for most of my adult life, I assisted my elderly friend along the passageway and off the boat.

Get your head on straight, Jane! I reprimanded myself. *Focus on where you're going. Do NOT look back!*

Tapping my Opal card against the reader, I noted that the next ferry scheduled to leave was heading towards Manly. *Yes!* I thought. *A long round trip to calm myself down again.* What a rollercoaster! Who knew that the emotions stirred up in the argument at home would be *nothing* compared to the tsunami of nervous jitters I now had!

But I wanted to look back. So badly. That was Jackson McGee – and I might never get the chance to see him in the flesh again!

I was just reaching out, Opal card extended towards the reader for the Manly ferry, when my composure was shaken again.

'You're going my way.' His voice, just behind me, was better than I'd imagined: kind of rough and salty, but deep and dark. Midnight voice, with a touch of brine.

And with that, my fingers fumbled, the Opal card falling to the concourse.

'Let me,' he murmured, as he leisurely leant down and plucked the card from the concrete. I watched as he tapped the reader and then held it out to me. I stared at it, as if I didn't know what it was. *Jane! Pull it together! Stop behaving like an idiot!*

Carefully, as though my fingers might get burnt, I reached out to take the card. 'Ah... ahh... Th-thank you.' *Jane, get a grip!* I could feel myself blushing, all over again, the heat flaming my face. I turned, as quickly as I could without tripping – by then I was really getting flustered – and hurried to the ferry gangplank.

'We can sit together,' he said, from just behind me.

'Uh... no. No, it's alright.' I stuttered. I kept moving. Fast.

I know it sounds strange, but I felt like I was caught in a storm – my thoughts and emotions swirling every which way. I *wanted* to sit with him. I *wanted* to just look at him – forever, if I could. This was Jackson, my hero. He lived the life that dreams were made of – adventures in far-off lands, meeting people and seeing places, and experiencing ... *everything*! He was Jackson McGee! He was world-famous! And I might never get the opportunity to see him again. That thought kept spinning in my head.

But this was also Jackson. The subject of my fantasies. He lived the life that dreams – *my dreams* – were made of. This was Jackson McGee, my secret fantasy hero. And I didn't want to spoil my fantasies. Once he met me, talked to me, he wouldn't want to know *me*. Why would *I* be of interest to him? And it would hurt me – being ignored by my fantasy hero.

'So, are you going to tell me your name?'

I was stunned. Whilst I'd been musing, he'd slid onto the bench-seat next to me, ignoring any appropriate social distancing. I was speechless. I just stared at him. He'd removed his sunglasses, so his blue eyes stared right back at me, only there was a mischievous twinkle in his and I'm sure that mine were just ... amazed!

'What?' I managed to say.

'Your name, sweetheart. What's your name?' Added to the twinkling eyes was a cheeky little grin.

'Umm... Jane. It's Jane,' my voice growing stronger.

'So, Janey, why are you heading to Manly?'

'What?' I stumbled again.

'Manly. Going home? Meeting friends?'

'Ah, no. No. I'm not really going to Manly.'

'Wel-l-l-l,' he drew it out, 'you *are* on the Manly ferry. It's going to Manly. Did you make a mistake?'

I was starting to feel like a fool. Oh, forget that! I'd been out of control for hours by then. I had the feeling that he was laughing at me. This was the stuff of nightmares! This was why I wanted to avoid him. I started to rise, clutching my bag closer to me.

'No. No. No. I'm sorry,' he said, leaning away from me, his hands raised in front of him in the unspoken gesture that he meant no harm. 'Sit. It's okay. I can move, Janey.' I sat back down as he stood, his hands patting downward, placatingly. 'It's just that we have so much in common.' He smiled gently, without the smirk. 'And I thought we could talk.'

Well, I felt like a heel. It hadn't occurred to me that he might be starving for conversation. I mean, he was Jackson McGee. People must be queuing up to talk with him. Although, I thought wryly, I hadn't been. Suddenly, I felt calmer. More in control.

'It's okay.' I motioned to the seat next to me. 'I'm sorry, too. You can sit.'

I was the one with the smile as I noticed how much space he left between us.

'I'm Jane. And no, I'm not really going to Manly. I'm just riding the ferry.'

'Again?' he frowned, his one word a request for further explanation.

'When I'm upset about something, I ride the ferries. And this afternoon, my sisters and I all had a huge fight. So,' I waved my hands around, indicating the ferry, the harbour, the evening – whatever else. 'Here I am.'

He nodded, as though what I'd just said made absolute sense. Then he held out his hand.

'I'm Jackson.'

'I know.' I nodded slightly, feeling the heat flood my face again.

He lowered his head slightly, in a tilt, and peered up at me. 'I know you know.' His tone was soft and intimate, a husky growl that vibrated along my nerves, and awareness flashed through me.

If I'd blushed before, I was sure I was now flaming red. My eyes widened with shock… and arousal. Breath filled my lungs as I inhaled, probably more deeply than I ever had before. His scent, a combination of citrus, salt and *him*, was intoxicating. I think I was melting. My underwear was becoming saturated with … Jackson-meltwater.

He was so damned *sexy*! I'd known that for years, but up close and personal? It was overwhelming.

And all the time, he watched me. He stilled. And he studied me. I didn't know if I liked the sensation of being so thoroughly observed: it was disconcerting, yet somehow, enlivening. I could feel the throb of my heart, my heated blood pulsing through my body, and was sure he could hear it, too.

I exhaled. And he watched that, too.

'Have dinner with me.' His invitation was uttered in that same devastating voice, his tone a little gruffer.

'Why?'

'Because we have so much in common.'

'No, we don't,' I argued, confused.

'Oh, Janey. Yes, we do.' He leaned in, his voice dropping an octave, if that was at all possible. 'We both head to the water when we need to chill. We're both into earth science. And,' he paused, as a slow, seductive smile softened his face, '*I* like to write … and *you* like to read what I write.'

And then he gave me a leisurely, deliberate wink.

And I was melting, all over again.

Chapter Four

'C'mon, Janey. You know you want to.' Jackson's tone was playful and cajoling. 'C'mon, Jane-ey.'

The truth was: I did want to have dinner with him. Jackson Alexander McGee had asked me out! My mind was being blown!

'I'm not dressed to go out for dinner.'

'Sure, you are!'

'Jackson, -'

'Jack, Janey. Call me Jack. And it's just fish and chips. You're dressed fine.'

'Fish and chips?'

'Yeah. Just fish and chips at Manly. You don't need fancy clothes for that.'

'Jack, I hardly know you!' Which wasn't totally the truth, but he didn't need to know that.

'You know, Janey,' his eyes narrowing, as his head tilted, 'I think you know more about me than you're letting on.' Okay, the man wasn't silly. It was a mistake to think that he could have attained the success that he had without his being quite astute. 'But...' his hands out in front again, the I-mean-no-harm-and-I'm-backing-off gesture from before, 'no pressure. It's only fish and chips.'

And then he sat back and said nothing, giving me plenty of space and time to make up my own mind.

'Okay. I will. Fish and chips.'

He smiled – a huge, beaming smile – and I was overcome. This was *Jackson McGee*, in the flesh! Tears welled in my eyes and I forced myself to take another deep, calming breath. I was awash, again, with the salty, clean scent of his skin. His smile had crinkled the skin around his eyes and revealed his teeth, so white against his tanned skin. He seemed delighted. When was the last time that anyone had looked at me with such … *pleasure* … that I had agreed to something? When was the last time anyone had looked at me like *that*?

Never, I answered myself.

As if he realised that something momentous had occurred, he stretched, leaning back again. Giving me space, I thought. Deliberately not crowding me.

'So-o-o-o,' he drew out the sound, as I became fascinated with his mouth, the shape of his beautiful lips as they formed the word, 'I take it you don't want to talk about the fight.' He said it as a statement, but there was a query buried in there.

'That would be a no!'

'Ok-a-a-a-y. Then let's talk about me!' His tone matched the mischievous expression on his face. Oh, I could look at that forever.

I laughed. 'Sure. Let's talk about you. So, were you planning to go to Manly for dinner?' I could hear the scepticism in my voice. 'I mean, how come *you're* on this ferry?'

'Nah. Like you, I was just riding the ferry.'

'Really? I was running away from home, but you …'

'Me, what?'

'Nothing.'

'No. Me, what?' There was a sharpness to his words. 'Why couldn't *I* have been running away from home?'

I didn't know what I'd stumbled into, but there was a real edge to his voice, and that relaxed, I'm-so-comfortable-in-my-own-skin demeanour of his? It was gone. I watched him, then, as he took a long deliberate breath – so deep, it was even *visible* – and carefully lowered his shoulders, rolling his neck and releasing tension as he exhaled.

'It's just… Well, it's just that … You haven't been home in so long,' I blurted. 'Wouldn't you want to spend time at home, with your parents? And Manly is a long way from them.'

He chuckled, and I was mesmerised all over again at the sheer gorgeousness of his slow smile. 'Well, well, well. I'm honoured,' he teased, his eyes bright with pleasure. 'So, Janey *does* know more about me than she's let on. I'm humbled.' He chuckled again, merriment in his gaze. 'How about we put my family with yours? The two of them together, in the we're-not-talking-about-it box?'

'Sure,' I said, relief at his good-humour warring with embarrassment that I'd revealed what a fangirl I was. I could feel the heat in my cheeks again and was astounded at how many times I'd blushed in his presence. I was a high school teacher, for crying out loud! We didn't blush, anymore. Except, obviously, I still did. It just took Jackson McGee to make me.

And he knew! I could tell by the sparkle in his eyes and the self-satisfied smirk on his face. He knew the effect he had on me and this evidently pleased him. Twisting his body slightly, he raised his arm and rested it on the back of my seat. It was a languidly lazy move, all seductive sensuality. And it affected me. I could feel my pulse, throbbing through me, my muscles relaxing, my body softening and heat pooling in my belly. He hadn't touched me at all, but I was incredibly aware of him. I felt like he'd created a little bubble, cocooning us from the other passengers on the ferry. There was an intimacy, even though there was still space between us.

'I was going to Manly because they're about to decommission these old Freshwater ferries.'

'Oh, I know! I hate that! I heard about it on the news!'

'I pitched to my editor today –'

'Pitched? You threw a ball?'

'No. A story. When you come up with an idea for a story, you pitch it first. If it doesn't take – if the editor doesn't like it and you don't think you can sell it – you don't waste your time researching and writing it.'

'But what if it's an important story? Like the ferries? What if it *should* be written and your editor doesn't agree?'

I tried to sound intelligent, and I warmed at his mellow smile and the warm appreciation in his eyes. Jackson McGee thought I was smart!

'Depends on the story. If I think it's worth it, I'll let my editor – Trish – know I'm going ahead. She gets first dibs and, if she doesn't want it, I offer it to another magazine. Usually, Trish backs down. I've been doing this awhile … as you know.' His voice lowered at this last bit – a deeper, teasing rumble. 'She trusts my judgement, most of the time. It's not often she won't take my stories.' He shrugged, a little self-consciously, I thought. For all he joked before, there was a touch of humility to him. As though what he did was nothing much at all.

Which, of course, was totally wrong. He was my hero. Jackson did *it*! He lived the life I fantasised about – the one I imagined when I was younger and thought the world was my oyster. Jackson went to all the incredible places and saw all the amazing wonders of the world. I'd read his article about the hot springs in Iceland; seen the awesome photos from Ha Long Bay in Vietnam. The sunset shots from the pyramids in Egypt were beyond imagining. Jackson had got up close with *whales!*

And his writing … It was as though I was there! The way he put words together – he captured a place: the smells and sights and sounds and sensations. What he did – week in and week out – wasn't nothing much at all.

'You know, you have a *very* expressive face, Janey. I can tell exactly what you're thinking,' he teased. 'What do you do for a living? I'm guessing you don't work for ASIO,' he said, referring to the Australian Security Intelligence Organisation. 'And I'm thinking you're not a doctor. You could be a model,' he mused, his tanned fingers stroking his chin, 'but I doubt that.'

I must have looked crushed. I certainly felt crushed. I knew I wasn't model-worthy, and I was dressed in sensible, school-teacherly clothing, but I thought I was still reasonably attractive.

'Stop! Stop thinking whatever you're thinking, right now!' Although his voice was soft, his tone was sharp. 'Janey, I didn't mean it that way. You *could* be a model. Look at your hair. So beautiful, that dark, tawny russet. It's gorgeous! And your eyes. I'm still deciding if they're green or aquamarine. I may have to keep looking a while longer, just to make up my mind.'

I stared at him. Stunned. I was speechless.

'But, Janey,' he leaned towards me, his warm breath brushing across my flushed skin, his low-pitched voice vibrating against my temple, 'you don't come across as contrived. You're real. Not fake.' He eased back, relaxing again, and a gentle smile tilted his mouth. 'So, no. Not a model.'

'I'm a teacher!' I blurted.

'Yeah. I can see that.' He nodded. 'You've got that no-nonsense, intelligent look about you. But Janey…' I waited, whilst he tilted his head, his dimple flashing with his cheeky grin, 'how do you cope in the classroom with that tell-tale blush lighting up the room every five minutes?'

'I don't blush normally. I'm very composed.' I patted both of my hands on my thighs in an effort to appear calm – and *not* touch my burning cheeks.

I watched the play of emotions cross his face. So much for *my* being the one with the expressive features: his disbelief at my words was clear to see, his brows drawn and his head tilted. And then, his face clearing with a triumphant expression, he almost fist-bumped the air, looking like a five-year-old boy who'd found a new lizard.

'Then it's me! I bring it out in you!'

I laughed. I couldn't help it. I was definitely going to have to watch myself around Jackson Alexander McGee!

Chapter Five

'Fish and chips, you said.'

'That's what we're having. Fish and chips. And, of course, salad, because you insisted.' He flashed that irresistible grin of his. And yes, I did melt a little more. Let's face it, I'd been in different degrees of meltdown since he'd sat next to me on the ferry.

'Jackson,' I started.

'I told you,' he interrupted, 'call me Jack. Every time you say Jackson, I feel like I'm in trouble with my mother or – and this is worse, if that's at all possible – my editor is going to tell me that what I've written is crap!' His cute little dimple appeared as he smiled again, his head dipping self-deprecatingly. I wasn't falling for it. He had probably never written anything that his editor hadn't gushed over.

'*Jack*,' I said, emphasising the shortened name, 'a seafood platter in a fancy restaurant does *not* constitute fish and chips. And check out these serviettes! Is this a swan?' I was enjoying teasing him. It was fun. '"Have dinner with me", you said. "It's just fish and chips", you said. And then you bring me to a swanky place with linen napkins and heavy silverware.'

I wasn't really upset. Well, maybe just a little. I felt out of place. When I'd left home, I was still in my "school clothes": sensible, practical outfits that students couldn't "see through, see over or see under" – the mantra for buying clothing for teaching. No visible bras or bra straps; no glimpses of belly skin or underwear elastic. So, whilst all the other women in this posh restaurant were dressed in stylish finery, I was trying to pretend that I wasn't wearing inexpensive grey pants and a floral cotton shirt. My hair was windblown from the ferry and, although I'd tried to tame it, I wasn't as well-groomed as the beautiful women around me.

But – and this was a big "but" – I'd never been in a restaurant like this before and I was determined to enjoy the experience. I kept telling myself to savour the adventure; it might only happen once in my lifetime.

'Shhh! Don't let the wait staff hear us arguing. They'll think you don't like me.' His dimple reappeared, as he nodded towards a wine waiter that I hadn't seen approach from behind me. Flashing that devilish smile again, he relaxed back into his chair, a picture of easy-going confidence. I watched them perform the wine-tasting ritual, a formal dance between the two men, each impressing the other with their sophisticated moves. Like a tango from olden times. Seeing him like this, so self-assured and comfortable in this classy environment, was sexy all by itself. Jackson was being seductive without even trying.

As the waiter poured the approved wine into my glass, Jackson lazily slid his gaze back to me and flicked me a wink, as though sharing a little joke between us: a moment of intimacy sparking across the table, joining us together. I no longer cared about my inappropriate clothes or my sensible shoes or my dishevelled hair. I was with Jackson and that old lady was probably right: perhaps he really did like me!

'To Freshwater ferries!' he toasted, tapping his glass against mine.

'To Freshwater ferries!' I intoned, smiling back at him.

'What do you know about them? You ride them all the time.'

'I don't know much, I'm afraid to admit. I know I've been *on* them a lot. Not as much as people who live in Manly, but I do like my ferries.' We shared wide grins at that. 'But a ferry has always just been a ferry, to me. I know that the Manly ferries are big and they're slower than the other ones, but … other than that, not much.' I grimaced. It seemed sad to have spent so much time on Sydney Harbour, undoubtedly the greatest harbour in the world, and I knew so little about its most iconic vessels.

'You should come with me tomorrow.'

'Come where?'

'On the ferries. Tomorrow. I'm doing research. You should come.' I could hear his growing enthusiasm, excited at his idea. 'You'd love it.'

'Jackson – Jack,' I corrected, 'I have to work tomorrow. It's a school day.'

'*It's a school day,*' he mimicked, and I could feel the sting of irritation at his mocking tone.

'Well, it is,' I said, crossly. 'I have classes to teach.' Lifting my glass, I took a healthy sip of my wine, turning away as I swallowed. I heard, rather than saw, Jackson sigh.

'You're right. Sometimes I forget that people have commitments.' He sighed again – ruefully, I thought.

'Well, what do *you* know about the Freshwaters?' I asked.

'So far, just the basics. There are four of them still in operation. All launched between 1982 and '88, making the *Freshwater*, the oldest of them, almost forty years old.'

'Hang on. Is the boat named the *Freshwater* or is it the type of boat named the Freshwater?' I was confused.

'Both. They're a class of boat – all about 70 metres long and with a capacity for 1100 passengers, give or take a few. But the first one launched, back in '82 was also called the *Freshwater*, after Freshwater Beach.' I nodded, whilst he sipped his wine, his body relaxed in his chair at an angle, his forearm on the chair's arm. 'The others are named after the Queenscliff, Narrabeen and Collaroy Beaches.' He paused, taking time to swallow some more wine, before gesturing with his glass. 'You know, it was the *Collaroy*, the youngest of them, launched in '88, that carried the flag for the Sydney Olympic Games.'

'I didn't know that. But then, I was only a child at the time.' I cautiously sipped my wine: I still had to get home and didn't want to get drunk. *What was I thinking!* Just being with Jackson was intoxicating enough, all by itself! I tried to stay on topic. 'Honestly, it's a little sad that I know so little about my own city.'

'Oh, I wouldn't let that bother you. If there's one thing I've learnt from travelling around, most people take their own environments for granted. It's a rare person who sees something every day of their life and is still amazed by it. Have you ever played "tourist" in Sydney?'

'What do you mean?'

'Exactly that. Have you ever treated Sydney as though it were a foreign city? Explored it? Pretended to be from somewhere else?'

'Well, no. I've never thought about it. I've visited The Rocks,' I said, naming the area just beneath the southern pylon of the Sydney Harbour Bridge, which dated right back to the first European settlement, 'and, of course, I've been to the Opera House to see a concert... But, no. I've never really explored the city as though I were a foreigner.'

'So American tourists probably know more about your town than you do,' he teased.

'Maybe.'

'We need to fix that. Tomorrow. We'll fix that! I've got research to do and you can come, too.' He was all excitement and enthusiasm again. Like a runaway train.

'Jackson...' I began.

'Oh, come off it, Janey. We've been over this. You *know* you want to. I can see it on your face. You're so damned *tempted*. What's stopping you? And don't say "school". When was the last time you played hookey and took the day off?'

Leaning on my left arm, I dropped my face into my hand. He was right. I *was* so tempted. A day of adventure. A day with no responsibilities: not to my school; not to my students; and not to my sisters. I was *so* tempted.

But ... I did have responsibilities.

And ... *Jackson Alexander McGee*! I'd idolised him since I was a teenager and bought my first copy of *Earth Today*. I *wanted* to spend time with him.

But ... I was also scared.

When he left – and he would leave soon, I knew – I'd crash. Hard. Like I'd never crashed before.

Like my parents did ... when they had their big adventure. Their crash killed them. Mine wouldn't physically kill me, but ... I wouldn't ever be the same again.

Yes, I was scared.

But ... *oooohhh, sooo tempted.*

I looked up to see Jackson's eyes upon me. Silently watching me. He'd backed off, but he wasn't backing off. It was as though he knew to stop talking and let me mull it all over.

And, while we wordlessly looked at each other, his face softened as he gazed at me and I knew that I'd most likely capitulate.

Because I *wanted* to cut free of my responsibilities.

And I wanted the adventure.

And I wanted it with Jackson, my secret, secret hero.

And this was one of those moments in a woman's life – which didn't occur very often – when you just *had* to go with the excitement and the thrill *and* the scariness ... and just go for it!

Chapter Six

Where are you? Are you at Sez's? Answer your phone, dammit!

The said phone had been buzzing in my pocket, on and off, throughout dinner. I'd ignored it. I hadn't wanted this meal with Jackson to be spoiled by any conversation with my sisters. They'd all ganged up on me – even Louisa, who never entered arguments. I was still feeling raw about that! So, I'd ignored them.

And what an incredible dinner! I'd eaten oysters, prawns and fish before. Hadn't everyone? But I'd never tried mussels, scallops, bugs and crab. And lobster! I knew that when my parents dined out, they'd had seafood platters, but we were too young to join them. And since their deaths, I'd been careful about our spending.

But I was with Jackson and … I'd had it all! He knew exactly how to get the crabmeat from the claws, and what buttery sauce to dip the lobster in so it tasted … oh, so sinfully good! And, when I was squeamish about the mussels, he patiently waited, the fork extended towards my lip, his eyes never leaving mine as he slid the soft, juicy morsel into my mouth.

We hadn't talked about my sisters or his parents or whether I was going to go with him the following day. We hardly talked at all; instead savouring the 'fruits of the sea' and watching each other eat, our only conversation, light banter, as we engaged in an exciting game of foreplay. And, for all his complaints, he ate his fair share of the salad – a healthy combination of leafy greens, aromatic fennel and tart citrus fruits.

He ate like he did everything else, with a lazy enjoyment in the way he surveyed the platter, making his selection with an air of satisfaction, casually reaching over to the chosen titbit, and pausing slightly, before gently plopping it into his mouth. It was as though the food gave him physical pleasure – the taste of it, the smell of it, the feel of it in his mouth –

his eyes half-closing as he savoured every bite. It wasn't obvious, in that sleazy kind of way that some men had: you had to be paying attention to notice.

And I was paying attention. I was totally captivated by him. Watching him eat was almost an erotic experience and I wanted to memorise every little move. Every single action. I was committing all of it to memory, to replay this evening when this was over, and he'd gone, and I was alone again. There was a sensuousness about him – probably why I loved his writing so much – and I wondered what he'd be like in bed.

What was also seductive – in a panty-melting way – was the way he watched me. I was the focus of his attentions: there may as well have been no-one else in the restaurant. It was just like it had been on the ferry, us in our own little cocoon. There was a stillness, as though he were *absorbing* me and memorising me, the same as I trying to memorise him. And it was hot!

Nope, we may not have spoken many words during dinner, but that didn't mean we weren't communicating.

Oh, and we were communicating! I'd been to dinner with men before – usually other teachers from school or conferences. Sometimes, I'd date someone I'd met in a bar or at a friend's party. But I'd never had a dinner like this!

And things were effortless. He made it so. When I returned from visiting the Ladies', the bill had magically been paid. I didn't bother arguing. This place was out of my league, anyway. I could have paid my share, but ...

We were standing on the outer deck of the ferry, both of our hands on the rail as he stood behind me – not touching me, but I could feel the heat of his body. And, finally, I decided that it was irresponsible of me to ignore the phone, buzzing in my pocket, any longer.

'Who's Sez?'

'My best friend. Sarah. My sister, Daphne, obviously thinks that's where I am.' I sighed. 'I should let Daph know I'm on my way home. She's probably worrying.'

'Tell her you're safe and that you won't be home tonight.' His voice was soft and low, a dark whisper in the night.

'Jackson, – '

'Janey, tell her you won't be home tonight.' There was a pause – neither of us speaking – both of us just breathing. My back was still to him and he had yet to touch me. 'Come home with me, Janey. Come back to my boat.' It was a rough murmur. Chocolate-seduction. Temptation, itself.

And he waited. Neither of us moved. The salty, evening breeze from the harbour ruffled my hair and cooled my cheeks that had heated. I swallowed and he was stillness, waiting for me.

I shifted my weight on my feet – just slightly – just enough to lean into his warm body.

'Okay.'

Such a little word. Not nearly big enough to cause the surge of excitement electrifying me. *I was going to do this!* I hadn't felt this *alive* in … forever.

He exhaled. A long breath. And I smiled, realising that this had been important to him, too.

Not at Sez's. Won't be home tonight. I'm safe. Austin

As soon as I clicked Send on my text, I felt the pressure of his body, pushing into my back. 'Austin?' he queried, a soft caress in my ear.

'Hmmm?' I think my brain cells had fried. I was overwhelmed by him: the warmth of his breath against my cheek, the hint of lemon in his aftershave blended with the scent of *him*, the solid feel of his chest along my spine, and the hum of his voice vibrating across my skin.

I quivered. I'm sure he felt it. I heard his groan.

And all we were doing was standing on the deck of a ferry.

What would happen when we got naked?

I shivered, just thinking about it.

'Austin?' he repeated. 'What's with the Austin?'

'Nothing.' I said, quickly. I trusted Jackson. Or I felt that I could. But … not with that.

'Janey?' A pause. 'Oh! *Jane Austin.* Is that it?' I didn't say anything, although I felt myself stiffen. He turned me in his arms, so that I was facing him. 'Is that your name? *Really?*' He sounded – and looked – incredulous. 'Is that your surname? Austin? Did your parents really name you Jane?'

'No,' I said, irritated – at him and my parents. 'My surname is White.'

'White,' he repeated. 'Jane White.' He paused, as his eyes narrowed, his eyebrows lowering. 'So, what's with the Austin? Is it a code, or something?'

I remained silent, hoping he'd let it go. He stared, waiting. And then, with a small knowing nod, he turned me back around, his arms enveloping me again, his body warming my back. His hands covered mine on the railing.

'It's okay, Janey. You're safe with me.'

The gentleness of his tone, the timbre of his voice, the strength of his body – I melted, my body softening against his, my head cushioned against his shoulder. I inhaled, deeply, and relaxed as I let the breath escape, a long sigh.

'However, when I get you home,' his voice dropped, a deep, gravelly sound, 'you won't be quite so safe at all.' His chuckle was low and wicked, as his hands tightened over mine, a slow, deliberate squeeze. 'I may have kept my hands to myself all evening, but ... once I get you on *Hobo's Flight*, I'm not guaranteeing anything.' I shivered as he paused. 'That glorious mane of hair is going to get totally mussed. You thought the wind wrecked it? That's nothing to what I'm going to do with it. I've fantasised all night about your hair. And that mouth of yours – I'm planning on spending *hours* exploring it with my tongue. That is, when I'm not tasting you all over. And Janey?'

'Hmmm,' I breathed, grateful that my jacket covered my nipples, suddenly hard at the images he painted.

'Then I'm going to ravish you. *All night.*' I gulped. 'I'm going to take my time, Janey. I'm going to discover all your wonders ... all your secret places.' I realised that I was holding my breath, waiting for his next words. I couldn't believe he was saying this to me. Right there. On the deck of the Manly ferry. With people all around.

I was so turned on.

I heard his chuckle in my ear at the same time as he gave my hands another quick squeeze. When he spoke again, the dark sexy purr was gone – in its place, a light-hearted merriment that caught me by surprise.

'And Janey, we're going to have fun. Lots of it. Together. You and me. Because I think Janey really needs to come out and play. And you *are* going to come. Lots of times.' This last bit was an arrogant purr.

'So, Janey,' his voice bright and bouncy, 'are you still coming home with me?'

And being totally incapable of any other response, I nodded.

Chapter Seven

'Here, take my hand.' It was at this moment that I felt the effects of the wine that I'd drunk at dinner. The wake from a passing boat caused Jackson's to bob on the water, making it more difficult to step across from the mooring. He'd held my hand from the moment I'd agreed to stay with him, letting go only when he'd boarded his vessel, and I was happy to anchor myself back to him.

'Would you like something to drink? I've only got cider. Or water.'

'No, I'm good. Show me your boat.'

'It's a yacht, Janey. Not a boat,' he admonished gently, smiling amusedly, before leading me across the stern deck towards the cabin stairs. 'Tomorrow, Janey. It's safer in daylight to walk around an unfamiliar deck. You can explore the cabin tonight, though, if you want.'

It was amazing. I hadn't known what to expect, but it was all glossy dark timber and light fabrics. Jackson rested against a wall, his arms crossing his chest, an indulgent smile on his face, as I ran my hands along the polished wood, enjoying the smoothness against my fingertips. Giving Jackson a sideways look, I gestured towards a cupboard handle.

'Knock yourself out, Janey. Satisfy your curiosity.'

He was patient, as I opened little doors, peering in to see the contents of his cabinetry. I investigated the little three-burner gas cooktop, the small fridge under the countertop, the dual-tapped sink. I admired the computer monitor suspended from a wall and brushed my hands over the seat cushions and curtains, tied back to let in light from the marina. And I tried not to focus too much on the double bed, visible through the doorway.

'I'm nervous,' I said, turning and looking back at Jackson, who was still leaning against the same wall, not having moved at all.

'I know. Take as long as you like, Janey. I'm right here.'

And, with that, my nerves disappeared. I *could* trust him, I realised. He wasn't going to rush me or pressure me or make me do anything I didn't want to do. A smile stretched across his face as I approached him. A slow, seductive smile. His dimple deepened. He straightened, opening his arms to receive me and I stepped up to him.

'You good now?' he murmured, his fingers gentle as he raised my chin, his eyes studying mine.

'Hmm. I just needed …'

'I know, Janey. You needed to feel comfortable here. It's okay.' His nod was just barely a movement.

And then, stretching my chin up even higher, he lowered his head, a gradual slide towards mine, and kissed me. Not really a kiss. A brush of our lips. His against mine. I released the breath I hadn't known I was holding as we both stilled. And then he touched his mouth to mine again. Softly, gently, patiently. The air I inhaled was all him: the scent of his skin, the lemon of his aftershave, the salt of the sea. When he deepened the kiss, his tongue gently delving into my mouth, I could taste the fennel of the salad, its aromatic flavour darkening the tenor of our embrace.

And I wanted him.

Ohhh, did I want him!

His hands left my face, smoothing down my sides to cup the cheeks of my bottom, pulling me closer to the length of his body, allowing me to feel *his* want. I opened my arms, wrapping them around his shoulders, my hands meeting at the nape of his neck, as I drew him closer to me. I pressed myself against him, wordlessly voicing *my* need.

He responded immediately, scooping me up and carrying me in a few long strides to the bedroom.

'I want to take this slow, Janey, but I don't know if I can.' He sounded pained, almost regretful.

'It's okay, Jack. Whatever happens, it'll be perfect,' I whispered back at him.

It was as though a dam broke. The intensity of his kisses, the grip of his hands, the tempo of his movements – they were all heightened. He laid me gently on the navy-and-cream quilt, his fingers going straight to my jacket, pulling it apart and lifting me to ease my arms through the sleeves. He then went to work on my shirt, leaving me in my plain white bra. I was too busy trying to pull his Henley up and over his head to worry too much about my uninspiring underwear, although the thought of acquiring black lacy lingerie in the near future did cross my mind. Jackson's attention returned to my mouth, his lips smashing against mine, our bare bodies pressed together, the soft hair on his chest tickling my skin.

Pausing, he lifted his head, his eyes gazing into mine with a piercing intensity. He inhaled and, for a brief moment, that seductive smile slid across his face, before it disappeared again, his potent focus returning to removing my pants. I lifted, wriggling, trying to help him, and my hands went to the waistband of his jeans. He stopped, capturing my hands in his.

'No, Janey. Not yet.'

'But –'

'Just wait. Let me take care of you first.' He lifted my hands, placing them above my head. 'Just let me…' he trailed off, as his face hovered over mine, his eyes closed and his breathing slow. Two long inhalations later, I realised that he was breathing me in. Smelling me. I closed my eyes and slowed my breathing, too. I felt a blissful smile break across my face. And then I felt his lips on mine and … *oh*, I had missed his mouth! His kisses were slow and deep, his tongue unhurriedly lapping against mine, his lips sucking softly.

He shifted, his tongue tracing a line along my jaw, drifting down my neck and licking languidly along my collarbone. His teeth nibbled at my earlobe, the sound of his deeply drawn breath resonating in my ear. I was boneless, a melting mass on the bed, heavy with want. I felt drugged and made no resistance as his fingers unfastened my bra, before smoothing the straps down my listless arms.

'Janey,' he murmured, 'look at me.' His face was mere inches from mine, his eyes dark with desire. 'You are so beautiful,' he breathed. 'Do you *know* how beautiful you are?'

I don't know if he expected an answer. I do know that I felt overwhelmed at that moment. Heat burned my eyes as they welled with tears.

'Shhh. I didn't mean to make you cry. Shhh.' I scrunched my eyes closed, embarrassed. His mouth touched mine again – softly, gently, supplicating – whilst his fingers trailed down to caress the tender flesh of my breasts. Slow circles, gradually closing in on the tight bud of my nipple. Lazy, teasing strokes. Driving me crazy.

Well, that sure dried up my tears. 'Now, Jack! Stop taunting me!' He laughed, a wickedly joyful sound, making me laugh, too. 'You're *bad*,' I said.

'I know, Janey. But you love it.' With that, he lowered his face to my breast, my nipple disappearing into the warmth of his mouth and, without warning, he sucked me – hard.

'Ooooohhhh!' I moaned.

He looked up, watching me, as he lightly licked across the sensitised skin. 'More?' he asked, his grin naughty.

I nodded, greedy, and he gave me more. Hard and soft, fast and slow. Until I was squirming beneath him, my body on fire with need.

'J-a-a-a-ck,' I begged.

'Getting there,' he said, as he moved his way down my body, his tongue trailing a track around my belly, creating goosebumps across my skin. His fingers grazed along my hips as he eased off my underwear, wet with want, and tossed them over his shoulder. His hands travelled the length of my legs, smoothing them open as he moved between them. My discomfort at being so exposed vanished when he whispered, 'You're so beautiful. And you smell amazing.'

Mindlessly, instinctively, I lifted my hips, offering myself to him. Without hesitation, he dipped his head, leaning down to lick my heated liquid centre, and I felt myself spasm with longing. He growled, the sound reverberating along my sensitised nerve-endings, and my fingers clenched with intensity.

He raised his head. 'More?' he queried again, a satisfied smirk on his face.

'Oh, God, yes!' I cried, my hands grabbing at his head, holding him to me.

'Shhh,' he whispered, 'other boats.' He tipped his head towards the window.

'Just don't stop, Jack!'

And he didn't.

At least, not until I exploded. My moans had been muffled by biting down hard on the corner of the quilt that was mashed into my mouth. *Volume control*, Jack had called it, somewhere in my ecstasy.

'Good?' he queried, rising above me.

'Hmmmm.'

'It'll get better,' he promised, reaching across me to a bedside drawer. He glanced back at me, his dimple flashing, as he removed the condom from its packet.

'I don't know if it can,' I said, my head rolling heavily towards him, my eyes half-shut.

And then I saw him. My eyes opened. Wide. My mouth fell open.

'Ooohhh!' My gaze swung up, then, to his face and – there it was. That self-satisfied smirk.

'Hmmm. You were saying?'

'I don't know if *I* can,' I almost stuttered. 'I mean … It's been a while… and you… That's impressive!' I finished, on a gush.

He winked. 'Janey, I have total faith. Leave it up to me.'

And I did.

And he was right.

It did get better.

Chapter Eight

'What time is it?' His voice was rough and grainy. The early morning light was just filtering in between the gaps in the curtains.

'A quarter to six. Go back to sleep,' I whispered.

'What are you doing?'

'Calling in sick.'

'At this hour?'

'You have to call in sick before seven o'clock. Preferably the night before.'

'But you're not calling. You're texting.'

'Jackson,' I said, irritation lacing my words, 'go back to sleep. I'm trying to concentrate.'

'To do a text? What are you writing?'

'You know, Jack, you can be painful.' I sighed. 'It's a simple text. It's just that my eyes are all gritty and I've hardly had any sleep.'

'Yes,' he said. 'That would be my doing.'

'No need to sound so proud.'

'Are you finished yet?'

I nodded, taking the time to turn off the alarms, permanently set for six o'clock and a quarter after six, before putting the phone back in my bag on the floor.

As I turned, Jackson lifted the covers, an unspoken invitation to return to bed which also provided me with a glimpse – alright, a long glance – at his body, his nudity allowing me to see that he was, indeed, awake.

'I see you're ready for the day,' I said, wryly.

'I know.' Yep. That satisfied smile.

'No need to be smug.'

'You don't think so? C'mon. I'm getting cold.'

We spooned. I snuggled in, letting him warm my back, his arms wrapped around my waist, one hand on my breast. I could feel his length nestled against the curve of my bottom, but he seemed content just to cuddle. My left cheek rested on the pillow next to his shoulder and his face was just above mine.

'Hmmm. This is nice,' he murmured, his fingers lightly skimming little circles on my skin.

'Hmm,' I agreed, drowsily.

'I knew you'd take the day off to come with me.'

'Don't gloat. And who said I was coming with you?'

'Of course, you are, Janey. You want to.'

I didn't respond, enjoying the gentle stroke of his fingers along my skin. They weren't soft hands: no part of him was soft. It was obvious that he spent a *lot* of time in the sun, his skin roughened with exposure, and his hands had calluses from working the sails.

'I can't believe I just did that!'

'Did what?'

'Called in sick when I wasn't. And … I haven't left any work.'

'What d'you mean?'

'When you're sick, you're supposed to either leave work for your classes – if you know in advance that you're going to be away – or you have to send it in, so the kids have got something to do.'

'What? If you're sick, how can you be putting work together?'

'You just have to. Teachers have to. It's the job.'

'But you're not going to?'

'Nope. And I don't even feel guilty about it.' I giggled. Also, *not* like me. 'How many times have I had to find work for other teachers? Well, today – they can find work for my classes.' I chuckled. 'Oh, I'm so *bad*!'

'Why, look at you, Janey! Being corrupted!' His fingers tickled along my side and I squirmed.

'Stop! Jack! Stop!' He didn't let up as I wriggled and squirmed, giggled and laughed.

Rolling me over onto my back, he rose above me. He leant down, intent on his face.

'No, Jack! I haven't brushed my teeth.'

'Ohhhh, Janey. You're about to be corrupted some more. Responsible Jane is about to be kissed without first brushing her teeth!' he teased. 'And a whole lot more!' he promised.

It was after eight when we rose.

'You want first shower?' he offered. 'It'd be good to share, but the shower's a little small,' he added, ruefully.

'I'll have to go home and get clean clothes. I can shower at home.'

'No, Janey. Shower here. We can swing past your place and get you clothes – not a problem – but shower here.'

'Why?'

'I want you to come with me today, Janey. It's important to me.' He paused, running his hand through his hair. 'If you have to be at your place long enough to shower, you might change your mind.'

Wow! I hadn't expected Jackson to be that vulnerable. Although, thinking about it, he had appeared humble on the ferry the afternoon earlier.

'If I'm first shower,' I conceded, 'you have to make me coffee. White, with one.'

'Done,' he said, his dimple flashing.

Who knew that Little-Ol'-Me could make my secret, secret hero, Jackson Alexander McGee, so happy – just by showering on his boat? I mean, *yacht*.

'I wondered where they were.'

'Hmmm?'

'Your cameras. I didn't see them around. I wondered where they were.' I watched him as he carefully removed two expensive-looking cameras from a locked cupboard in the cabin.

'I was out last night, Janey. I don't leave these lying around. They're valuable. I don't want them to go missing.'

'These boats – yachts – are safe, though, aren't they? In the marina?'

'Sure. Reasonably safe. But it doesn't hurt to be careful.' He nursed one of his cameras, as though it were a small animal. 'I can't replace this. I could buy another camera, but this one's been everywhere with me. I started with this camera.' He actually *stroked* the camera.

He looked up and caught me watching. 'You ready?'

'Sure.'

'Is there going to be anyone at your house when we get there? How many sisters did you say you have?'

'Four – and no. Well, maybe. I'm not sure.' His left eyebrow rose in query, so I explained further. 'Daphne will be on her way to work, if she's not already there. Charli *should* be at uni. Ginny's most likely at home, but she won't be awake yet. And Louisa? Not sure. She works in a bookstore and I don't always know her shifts. Louisa just sort of … she's quiet and doesn't cause any waves.'

'Can't wait to meet them all.'

'Not now, Jack. I'll just duck in – get changed. You can wait outside.'

'What?' His tone – his whole demeanour – was incredulous.

'Just let me go in and get out again. If you come, it'll turn into a *thing* and … Please, Jack.'

'Well, don't forget your swimmers and a towel. If we're going to Manly, we may as well go to the beach,' he grumbled. 'And bring a hat. We're going to be on the harbour most of the day.'

It was an amazing day … and an eye-opening one. Watching Jack in action was very revealing. I'd been such a fan of his for so long, but I hadn't really thought about what it took for him to write the stories he wrote, and how he took the photographs to accompany his words. By Friday's end, though, I had developed a whole new appreciation for his work.

There'd been no-one at home when I'd stopped there, changing into navy shorts, a light summery shirt and sandals, and gathering my beach gear. I also – just in case – slid a change of underwear into the side of the beach bag, together with essential toiletries. You never knew. Jack and I had Uber'd from his marina in Woolwich to my house in Greenwich, so we walked down to the wharf to catch the next ferry to Circular Quay.

First stop: the Australian Maritime Museum in Darling Harbour. Or so Jack said.

We caught the ferry around to Darling Harbour and, as soon as we arrived, he headed straight to the Blackbird Café, leading me along with him. I'll admit, I was a bit peckish. The coffee on the yacht had only held off hunger for a bit. After last night's dinner, though, I was surprised when Jack ordered The Ultimate Breakfast: the menu described a *lot* of food. I settled for avocado on Tuscan flatbread and a cappuccino. It felt decadent, sitting in the sun, eating breakfast made by someone else, when I was supposed to be at school.

I grew suspicious when our trip to the museum itself only lasted about twenty minutes: a quick wander around the exhibits; a short conversation with the librarian, which didn't provide any substantive research on the Freshwater Class ferries. Then we were out in the sun again, admiring the submarine, patrol boat and *Endeavour* replica, normally available for tourists to explore, but closed because of the pandemic.

'Are we going on board?' I asked, a bit confused.

'Nah. Not today. Don't really have time.'

'Then what was that?

'What do you mean?'

'Well, we hardly spent any time in there. And you could have asked more in-depth questions of the librarian. If we're not going to see the boats over there… Well, it's hardly worth the price of admission.' I stared up at him, even though his eyes were shielded by his aviators.

'Oh, I just like to visit whenever I'm in Sydney. This place was … Well, when I was a kid, I almost lived here. I just like to come back every so often.' He turned away and started back to the ferry terminal.

'That's it?' I got no answer. 'Jack, I think you only came around here so we could have breakfast!'

That got a response. He grinned back at me, his dimple flashing, as he tipped his head to the side. 'You may be right. C'mon. We've got to get back to Circular Quay. We've got ferries to catch.' And then he winked … and I melted, smiling back at him.

If Jack'd been fudging it at Darling Harbour, he became all serious once we were back at the Quay. Whilst passengers were boarding the Manly ferry, he stood back and chatted with the maritime officer overseeing the gangplank. Both of their eyes were fixed to the people moving into the ferry, but I knew that Jack's attention was really on what the man was saying. As we criss-crossed the harbour, on multiple journeys, Jack talked with passengers, asking them about their experiences on the ferries: how often they travelled, what they knew about the boats themselves, if they had favourite memories or stories to tell. Sometimes he took notes, right there in front of his interviewees; other times, he waited and made notes when they'd disembarked. He took photos – lots and lots of photos. Of the passengers, after having asked their permission; of the ferry's structure, from all different angles and perspectives; of the harbourside and its iconic attractions: the Sydney Harbour Bridge, Opera House, and Botanical Gardens. The Taronga Park Zoo, Fort Denison and The Heads. He spoke with the personnel at the Manly Wharf and at Circular Quay, including cleaning staff. When I asked about this, he said that often the best information he got came from those people who were at a site, day in and day out. They observed things; got the "feel" for people, places and event.

And they were usually more than happy for him to photograph them, doing their important work for the people of Sydney.

And then we were off to the Port Authority offices. Jack had lined up a ten-minute interview with the newly-appointed Harbour Master for the Port of Sydney and Botany Bay. It was incredible to watch Jackson work his sailor's charm on the veteran of the merchant navy, and the ten minutes stretched to half-an-hour. I'm not sure what he got from the exchange – other than a new friend – but Jack seemed happy, especially with the images he captured on his fancy camera.

'At the end of the day, you two are just boys on boats, aren't you?' I teased, as we walked along the corridor to the exit.

His blue eyes sparkled. 'You bet, Janey. One thing that all seafaring men have in common is a love of conversation, especially when it's about boats or the water. Doesn't matter about the size of the boats or the water. Seas, oceans. Even rivers will do.' He rolled his shoulders and almost swaggered out of the building. I had to laugh.

'C'mon, Janey. Time for a swim.'

'You're kidding! We're heading back to Manly?' I was incredulous. 'What will this be? Our fifth round-trip?'

'Are you piking?' he goaded. 'Have you had enough of the ferries?' he teased, his face tilting sideways, his eyes squinting in challenge.

'Ja-a-a-ck!' I whined.

'Nah. We'll head around to the ABC Pool. We could do with the stroll.'

'The what?'

'The ABC. You know – the Andrew Boy Charlton Pool. In the Botanical Gardens. You haven't been there?'

'Well, no.'

'Then you're in for a treat. We'll cut straight across and, on the way back, we'll go past Mrs Macquarie's Chair. I'd love to take some photos of you in the late afternoon light. I can capture the sun filtering through your hair. It'll look amazing.'

The pool was fabulous. I couldn't believe that I'd lived in Sydney all my life and never ventured to "The ABC", as I could now call it. Floating on the surface of the water, watching the ships across the bay, was magical. After Jack had stashed his cameras into one locker and my beach bag into another, we'd scampered like kindergartners to the crystal-clear water of the pool, holding hands as we jumped in – all splash and no style. I'd swum a few laps and then sat on the infinity edge, watching as Jack swam lap after lap. He was like a machine, his arms cutting through the water in metronome time, the kick of his feet making only a small wake behind him.

It was erotic, watching his shoulders and arms rise above the surface. Today, though, I was finding pretty much everything erotic. I was mesmerised by Jack. I had to keep pinching myself to believe that, here I was, hanging out with a man I'd idolised since I was sixteen years old.

'C'mon, Janey. Get back in the water.' He was right in front of me, his hand reaching up to grab mine to pull me in. Although I protested, I slid down into the pool and was immediately captured by Jack's arms encircling me. He tugged me closer and our legs tangled together. His happy smile was infectious and, our eyes sparkling at each other in pure joy, we moved together and kissed. What started as an exuberant celebration of good times quickly slowed into a sensual exploration: heated and sultry.

Until the rain of water droplets, cool from the pool, stunned the skin of my face, forcing my eyes to open in shock.

'What the...! J-a-a-ck!' I wailed.

'Race you, Janey! To the other side.' And he was off.

There was no way I was going to catch him – he was far too strong a swimmer – but I gave it a red-hot-go. We spent the next half-hour playing in the water, like a couple of teenagers skipping school – which, to be honest, was how I felt. No obligations. No responsibilities. Just young and carefree. I supposed that this was just how Jack lived his life. All adventure and accountable to no-one.

Chapter Nine

'See? *This* is what is meant by "fish and chips"!'

We were sitting on a wooden bench-seat at Circular Quay, having walked around the harbourside through the Botanical Gardens, and we *did* stop and relax for a while at Mrs Macquarie's Chair, as Jack had promised. Spread between us – white butcher's paper as our tablecloth – was our takeaway battered fish and a pile of golden chips, with lemon wedges and a large red blob of tomato sauce on the side. We ate with our fingers as we lazily watched the ferries come and go, and the larger container ships being tugged towards The Heads, and we studied the vacant terminal where huge cruise ships usually berthed as passengers disembarked and new ones swapped in.

Other than my teasing comment, we were content to sit and eat in companionable silence. Both of us were tired from our exertions. We'd had little sleep the night before – I wasn't complaining! – and had walked, talked and swum a lot throughout the day. We were both happy to people-watch and, every so often, our eyes met and we exchanged slow smiles. Satisfied smiles. Jackson-McGee-smiles.

Now, I understand where they come from, I thought. *Contented exhaustion.*

The ferry trip back to Woolwich was uneventful. I rested against him, comforted by the heat of his body, as the afternoon wore itself out and a cool onshore breeze ruffled my hair – unkempt from my day's adventures. But I didn't care about how I looked anymore. No-one else was noticing and, from the warm approval in his eyes whenever he glanced at me, Jack wasn't bothered at all.

It was unspoken: that I didn't get off at Greenwich. As the ferry approached the wharf, I stilled, waiting to see if Jack made a move – any move. But … no. There was no change to his relaxed posture, no shift in his body, no movement in his hands. He could have been asleep, for all he noticed that this was my stop. But he wasn't.

As I eased back, slightly more heavily, against him, the arms that encircled me tightened – just a slight squeeze – but I felt it.

And I think I felt my heart, deep in my chest, squeeze too. A sudden sadness swamped me. I would miss him when he was gone. I knew that. And so did my heart, spasming in my chest.

'Uber or walk?' Jack said, as we clambered off the ferry onto the wharf. 'I'm easy, either way, but an Uber sounds good.'

I smiled up at him, a dopey smile, and nodded. I felt tired and happy: drugged with contentment. A wonderful day, physical exercise, a full belly, a gorgeous man. I wanted to hang onto this feeling for as long as I could.

Jackson held my hand as we walked along the wharf, as we waited for the Uber, as we rode in the back, and as he helped me board his boat … *yacht.* I noticed its absence when he left me on the deck whilst he stashed my beach bag and gathered two ciders and a throw blanket for us to snuggle on deck and enjoy the twilight.

Our lovemaking was lazy and languid and easy and sensual. Long slow caresses, tender touches, our mouths melting, our bodies moulding together. His rope-roughened fingertips skimming across the planes of my face. My palms tickled by the scratch of his unshaven jaw. I felt like I was drowning in sensation. The thump of my heart echoed the throb between my thighs. By the time Jackson lifted me in his arms and carried me to his bed, I was a molten mass of want, limp with need. Unhurriedly, our mouths explored our skin, gradually exposed as our hands shed our clothing. And I took enormous pleasure in the seductive act of smoothing protection over his pulsing length, before he rose above me, his eyes never leaving mine, his gaze hot and sultry, and he joined us. We groaned, together, the sound reverberating in the semi-darkness.

And I knew.

And I think he knew.

This wasn't just sex.

This wasn't casual.

This wasn't just two people sharing a day together.

This was *more.*

And I was going to hurt when he left. Lots.

And so was he.

It was inevitable.

But ... I was going to enjoy this while it lasted.

He took me sailing. On Saturday. We spent the entire day sailing. I'd never been before and it was *amazing!* We went out of the harbour, out through The Heads. Ocean all around. Yes, we were still in sight of land, but ...

It was *amazing!* The sound of the sails slapping in the wind. The bite of the sun and the wind on my cheeks. How many times I'd slathered sunscreen on my face! And my hair... I'd tied it back, but that made no real difference – it was just a tangled mess!

I spent most of the day laughing with sheer exhilaration!

I *loved* it.

I totally understood the call – the addiction – to this life. It reminded me of that poem we studied in high school: *I must go down to the sea again ... it's a wild call and a clear call that cannot be denied ... a windy day with the white clouds flying ... wind's song and the white sails shaking.* "Sea Fever". That's it. I remembered that it had appealed to me: I'd liked it. Well, now I knew why!

And watching Jackson...

So hot and sexy! His sun-bleached hair blown this way and that. His tanned skin stretched over his lean muscles as he worked the sails and ropes – no, *lines*, as he told me often. And those shoulders... He was so deliciously *hot* as he scampered, barefooted and long-limbed, over the deck and up the mast.

I spent the day in a daze, exhilarated in the present and eagerly anticipating *later*, when I could rip his clothes off and devour him. And I knew it was mutual. Every time I laughed out loud – joyfulness bursting from me – his smile would widen, his dimples deepen, the heat from his gaze intensify.

I couldn't *wait* for later!

It was worth the wait, I thought drowsily, as I lay in Jack's arms late on Saturday night. Or was it early Sunday morning?

Earlier, we'd returned to the marina and moored *Hobo's Flight* – I'd even helped with tying the lines – before we snoozed on the deck, exhausted from the excitement of the day. It had quickly become a ritual, tiring ourselves out all day and then lazing around, sipping a cider, and watching the sun sink to the horizon, while we dozed off, gently rocked by the harbour swell.

The loud blast of a ship's horn had echoed across the water and we were both jolted out of our nap. Rising, we ventured to the galley to forage through his fridge and cupboards, putting together a platter to pick at for our dinner. We laughed at the combination of food: two different cheeses – one of which we had to trim the mould; an apple we sliced; stuffed green olives; cured ham; cherry tomatoes and salty biscuits.

'I need to shop for supplies,' Jack said, grimacing. 'The worst part of preparing for a trip.'

'I would have thought you'd like that.'

'Nah. Do you like grocery shopping?' he asked, as he sliced the ham.

'Well, I don't do it, actually,' I admitted, pausing for a moment to reflect that Ginny did all the shopping for my family. 'Ginny does it.'

'Which one's she?'

'The middle one. It was Ginny who started the argument the other night.'

'Oh. What did she say?' It was the first time he'd pushed me for information about my sisters and I could tell he was curious. He was that sort of guy: interested in people, as I'd seen the day before; and interested in why and how things happened.

'Well, I brought up the subject of her doing some formal study, at university or even TAFE, and she said she didn't want to,' I said.

'Say that again,' he instructed, his expression quizzical.

'Ginny's the only one who hasn't enrolled in formal qualifications. All the rest of us have university degrees. Well, except for Charli, but she's studying now. But Ginny's so damned stubborn. I've been trying for years to get her to commit to her education and she just refuses. Anyway, it's that time of year when people enrol in courses for the next semester and I raised the issue again. And she went off!'

Jack stared at me incredulously, as though I'd said something strange.

'Let me get this right,' he said, at last. 'You brought up a topic that you knew Ginny would baulk at, and when she did, you considered that she'd started a fight?'

I nodded.

He burst out laughing.

'It wasn't like that!' I protested, not finding the situation funny at all.

'Oh, Janey, the red in that tawny hair of yours does sneak through every so often, doesn't it?' His chuckles grew into laughter again, and his merriment became infectious. I smiled at him and then the absurdity of the situation grabbed me, and I joined him in his laughter.

'It's serious, Jack. I worry about her. She's twenty-four years old and she doesn't have a permanent job, and no qualifications to help her get one.'

Jack sobered. 'I don't have a permanent job, Jane. Nor do I have any formal qualifications.'

'But it's different for you,' I protested.

'How? Maybe Ginny will find something that she's passionate about, like I am with my work, and she'll make lots of money. More than you.'

'As if!' My tone was pure disbelief.

'Let's eat, Janey. And we'll talk about something else.'

'Like what?' I asked, as he carried our platter to the table, and I slid onto one of the little bench seats.

'What a great day we had? Two great days! You had fun today, Janey. I could tell.'

'Yeah, I did,' I said, smiling, my face softening. 'Yesterday was interesting, but today … That was just *thrilling*, Jack! I loved it!'

'You fit here, you know.'

'Fit where? What do you mean?'

'Here. On the yacht. With me,' he said, softly, his tone tentative.

'Oh, *Jack*,' I sighed. 'We both know this is just for the weekend. I've got work and you'll go sailing off into the wide blue yonder.'

'It doesn't have to be that way. And the wide blue yonder can be pretty lonesome, sometimes. I meet lots of people, but they're all strangers. And you … We fit together, Janey.'

'Eat some apple, Jack. Let's not spoil our last night together.'

And Jack, being Jack, had backed off. He just shook his head at me and changed the subject. We talked about Mount White and the people he met, and his favourite places in the world.

We didn't mention again whether or not I fit into his life.

Chapter Ten

It was Sunday afternoon and I had to go home. I'd texted on Friday in response to Ginny's text so everyone knew that I was okay. But I knew I'd face a barrage of questions when I got home. This – this weekend … It was so totally unlike me. I'd never been so *irresponsible* in my life. Well, at least not since that horrible day six years ago. So, yes, there would be questions. A lot of them.

And I didn't want to go home. Not really. I wanted to put this weekend in a time-capsule and live it, repeatedly, for the rest of my life. I'd *never* been so happy! Ever!

But I did have to go home. I had responsibilities: a family that needed me; a school that relied upon me; and students to teach. I had to go home … and face the music.

'Stay with me.' Jackson stood right behind me. I ignored him as I attempted to shove my things into the beach bag. I was wearing the shirt I'd bought yesterday – a touristy T-shirt with "Sydney" splashed across the front in a loud lime green, against the golden colour of Australian wattle. We'd laughed when we'd bought it. Well, *Jackson* had bought it for me. *You've been playing tourist; you may as well look like one,* he'd said at the time.

'Stay with me, Janey. Come with me. I planned to head up the coast tomorrow. I want you to come with me.'

When I remained silent, busy pulling my grubby clothes and towel out of the bag to try again to get them all to fit, he tugged on my arm, turning me around to face him.

'You know you want to.'

'Jack, it doesn't matter what I want.'

49

'Sure, it does, Janey. You want this. I saw you. Yesterday. You love this. I told you last night that you fit here with me. I see you, Janey. I see that you crave adventure, almost as much as I do.'

'Of course, I'd love to go with you. But I have *responsibilities*, Jack. Responsibilities.' I was getting agitated. I wanted to cry and rage and hit out at something. And it was going to be Jack. 'You don't get it! You sail off, into the wide blue yonder. No consideration for anyone else. Just doing what *you* want to do, all the time. Well, I can't!'

'It's not like that, Janey.' His voice was quiet. Low. Very calm. 'It's not like that. I have responsibilities, too.'

'Sure, you do, Jack! To yourself.' I could hear myself – my voice getting ugly, sounding spiteful, whilst I really wanted to cry at the thought that Jack was going to leave.

'Of course, to myself. All of us have a responsibility to ourselves, Janey. That's what life's about.'

'What about your parents, eh? What about them? You don't want to *talk* about them. But they're here. I know that they're right here in Sydney. Did you even bother to go and see them?' I was getting louder, losing control. I had to get a hold of myself.

'Yes,' he said, his voice ominously dark. 'I saw them. I see them every time I come to Sydney. But, Jane, this is what you need to know. *They* don't want to see *me*. *I'm* not the son they expected. *I'm* supposed to be a builder, like my father. Not an *irresponsible vagrant wandering around the world.'*

The way he spat out these last words told me he was repeating what he'd been told, probably hundreds of times, and this chilled me, cooling my anger and frustration.

'Oh, Jack,' I soothed, reaching my hand out to him.

'Don't! Just *don't*, Jane!' He pulled away. 'You think I'm not responsible? Really?' He glared at me. 'I sail the *ocean*, Jane. By *myself*! How much preparation do you think goes into that! How much careful *planning* do you think that takes! And this yacht was not bought with *peanuts!* How much *work* do you think I had to do? To get people to buy my articles? To get contracts with magazines? Do you know how much money I had to make to buy this yacht? Do you have any idea how much each of these cameras is worth? And, Jane,' the volume of his voice lowered again, 'I had *no* encouragement from my parents. None!' He shook his head, turning away from me. 'So, don't you *dare* talk to me about responsibility!'

'Jack, -' I began.

'No. I thought that you, of all people, would understand. I love what I do, but it comes at a cost. I told you last night that it can be lonely, travelling on your own all the time. It's great, but it's got its downside. And once – just once – I'd like to hear something positive from my parents about the life I've carved out. Some *pride* in the success their son has become. But, no! Not a skerrick of pride. Not one word of – *anything!* So, when you're busy criticising your sister for the choices she's making, how do you think that makes her feel? How do you think that makes *me* feel?'

'Jack, – ' I reached out to him again, trying to narrow the yawning space between us.

'No, Jane, let me be.' He stormed off, crossing the cabin and climbing the stairs two at a time. I saw him, out the cabin window, as he strode away from me along the pontoon mooring.

I collapsed onto the bed, overwhelmed. Tears ran down my face. Remorse flooded me. I'd had no idea about Jack's parents, about how they'd let him down. And continued to do so, from the sounds of it. My parents had died. They didn't *choose* to leave me, nor Daph and Ginny and Louisa and Charli. We hadn't been *rejected*.

And I'd just rejected him, too.

I felt the bed dip, unaware that Jack had returned. He pulled me into his side and I twisted into him, my face burying itself into the nook between his neck and shoulder. I took a shuddering breath, inhaling the scent of his skin.

'I'm sorry, Janey,' he murmured, his voice quiet, his tone gentle and apologetic. 'I didn't mean to yell at you. I'm sorry,' he repeated.

'I'm sorry, too, Jack. I didn't know. I didn't understand.' I hiccupped, making us both laugh, the tension easing. 'I can't come with you. But Jack,' I paused, my hands drawing his face to me, my eyes searching his, 'you *are* right. I *do* want to. I don't want to leave you. I …' I didn't want to say the words first. And I didn't know if they would make things better or worse.

'Then don't, Janey. Don't leave me,' he implored.

'I'm scared, Jack. My parents …' I began, before pausing, moving away from him, needing to be disconnected if I were to say this. 'My mother … she was – not flighty, but – Mum read a lot. Lots of books. She was *fanciful*, I guess you'd say. She wanted adventure. She wanted to do things … lots of things. Dad was more stable. He was a manager in the public service. Transport. How's that for irony! Anyway, for her birthday, he bought her – them, really – tickets to go for a joy-flight in a small aircraft. Just a little four-seater. Mum was over the moon. So excited. "Such an adventure", she said.'

I paused, focused on his face, making sure he knew what I was trying to tell him. 'And it crashed, Jack. The plane crashed. On her birthday. On her big adventure. It crashed. And I had to identify their bodies. And I had to take care of my sisters. Because – suddenly – we had *lots* of relatives that thought they'd have one or two of us, but not *all* of us. And there was the will. And the house. And the bills. And the insurance. And the funeral.'

I was crying. Ugly sobbing. My face grotesque in my agony, reliving the horror and the hurt and the confusion, all over again. Jack pulled me to him, his arms holding me close, strong around me, as though attempting to absorb my grief.

'Shhh. It's okay, Janey. Shhhh.' His voice was a soothing murmur as I hugged him tight. 'Shhh. It's okay. I get it. I understand. It's okay, Janey.' We rocked together, slow gentle movements, barely discernible. 'It's okay. I'll take you home.'

Chapter Eleven

'They'll all be here,' I said, as we walked up the pathway to the front door.

'Really? All four of them?'

We were both in a post-storm calm, too exhausted from our emotional outbursts to inject much energy into our words.

'It's Sunday night. Everyone's got to be home for Sunday dinner, even if we go out later. It's a rule.' I paused. 'I made it. When everyone started getting out and about at night. It's the one night when we can all be together.'

'What? Don't you do dinner together other nights?'

'Well, yes. But it doesn't matter on other nights. Sunday night it does.' Inserting the key into the lock, I turned to him. 'Jack, you don't have to stay. I mean … it's not that I don't want you here – exactly – but … They can be a lot to handle and … There'll be a lot of questions …' I trailed off.

'Janey, you've been gone all weekend. I *know* they'll have stuff to say. I'll see you home. All the way home. Now, open the door and let's get this over with.' He smiled at me. I know it was supposed to be reassuring, but it just looked sad. As though he knew we were about to say goodbye to each other. And I felt sadness, too. A strange sort of emptiness.

'Where have you been?' Ginny must have heard the key in the lock. 'You give *me* grief over being irresponsible, but where the hell have you been all weekend?' And then she squinted, finally noticing Jack behind me. 'And who is *that?*'

'Ginny, language, please.'

'Is Jane home?' I could hear Daphne's voice and footsteps as she approached the hallway. 'So, you *are* still alive.'

'C'mon, Daph! I sent you texts.'

She stilled, studying Jack. His attention was caught by Charli, barrelling into the hallway, Louisa sidling out of her room and leaning against the back wall.

'Well, this is crowded. Can we please go into the living room? We don't all need to be in the hall like this,' I said, trying to give Jack and me some space.

They moved, but Ginny kept glancing back and forth at Jack, whilst Daphne remained where she was standing, until she, too, followed us into the larger space.

'You look familiar,' Ginny probed. 'Who are you?'

'He's Jackson McGee,' Daphne answered her, before Jack or I could say anything.

'Who?' Charli asked, her face scrunched in confusion.

'Jackson McGee,' Louisa repeated. 'From *Earth Today* magazine.'

I was stunned. And I could see that Jack was, too.

Who knew that my sisters had paid so much attention to my reading material? Although I really shouldn't have been so surprised. Daph was only two years younger, and she and I had spent a lot of time together, especially since our parents died. And it was hardly surprising that Ginny had noticed a photo of a good-looking man. Let's face it, photos were her main source of reading pleasure. And Louisa – well, quiet Louisa just silently observed. *Every*thing.

'Like ... are you famous? Or something?' I could tell that Charli was still trying to catch up.

'Handsome catch, I will say that for you!' declared Ginny, deliberately eyeing him off and making sure that I noticed her. 'What are you doing with our Jane?' she asked, provocatively.

I watched Jack narrow his eyes at her, his face tilting slightly to the side.

'Not really your business, Ginny – is it?' he drawled, his hand reaching for mine, silently showing that, in a disagreement between Ginny and me, he'd side with me.

I saw Louisa's eyes follow the gesture, slide to my overstuffed beach bag – still in Jackson's other hand – and then to my gaudy T-shirt. A subtle smile flitted across her face before it disappeared again.

'So, who is he, again? Is he a star or something?' Charli brought attention back to her.

'He's a photojournalist for *Earth Today*. The geography magazine that Jane reads,' answered Daphne. 'He travels the world, taking pictures and writing stories about different places. And people.'

'So-o-o,' Ginny drew the word out, 'how did you two get together? Has Jane been sending you fan mail?' She was being a bitch.

'Ginny!' I snapped, embarrassed.

Jackson squeezed my hand and gently tugged me towards him. 'I'm going to go, Janey.'

'Ooooh, *Janey!*' Ginny mimicked.

'See me out,' Jackson said quietly, his voice calm and soothing to my fraught nerves.

'So, should we be asking for his autograph? Or will he take our picture?' Charli interrupted the moment.

'No, Charli. Let's go into the kitchen,' Daphne said, and I sent her a look of gratitude. 'Ginny, you come, too. Louisa?' Daph glanced around, but Louisa had already returned to her room.

'C'mon,' I said to Jackson. Whilst I didn't want it to be the time to say goodbye, I also didn't want to expose him to my sisters, any more than I'd already done. 'Let's go on the porch.'

Dropping my beach bag on the lounge, he followed me out, his hand still clasped in mine.

'Will you be alright?' he asked, as soon as we were standing in the privacy of the banksia rose, climbing along the trellis in the front garden.

'Yes,' I said, my despondent tone contradicting my words.

'You've got my number, Janey. You can ring me anytime.'

'You'll be overseas, though. I won't be able to get you.' I knew I sounded pathetic. After all, *Whatsapp? Messenger?*

'I'll still be in Australia for another couple of weeks,' he reassured me. 'I'm probably doing a story on the Barrier Reef. There's a spot where the coral has bleached, but there are reports that it's rejuvenating. Thought I'd look into it.'

I felt my eyes burning, hot tears filling them. 'I don't want you to go,' I whimpered, feeling bereft and he hadn't even left yet. And then a wave of remorse washed over me: after all, he wanted me to go with him. It wasn't *his* choice that we were saying goodbye; it was *mine*.

'I don't want to leave you, either.' His arms tightened around me and I hugged him right back, as hard as I could.

He eased back and his mouth lowered to mine. It was such a sweet kiss, a gentle kiss, a goodbye kiss. My lips clung to his as he raised his head again.

'I'll go now, Janey. Best not to draw this out.' He stepped away from me, turning towards the street.

'Jack...'

'Take care, Janey. I …' He glanced back at me, his face tortured. 'It was only a weekend … Three days … Too soon really to say this.' He looked down at his feet for a long moment. 'You're important to me, Janey. If you change your mind …'

He turned away again and walked towards the gate.

'Jack…' I cried and he turned. 'Me, too. You are to me, too.'

'I know. I see you, Janey. I know you think that your sisters don't, but I see you. I know who you are.'

And he left.

I watched him until he was out of sight, his head down as he walked out of my life.

I went straight to my bedroom. I didn't want to talk to anyone. I especially didn't want to see Ginny, the catalyst for all that had happened over the last three days.

I sat on my bed, silent tears sliding down my face, my nose dribbling. I felt empty. Like a gigantic hole had gaped open inside me. *Had I done the right thing?* Jack's face in those last few moments kept flashing through my mind, like a photograph stuck on repeat.

The soft knock at the door startled me.

'Are you alright, Jane?' It was Daphne, her face furrowed with concern.

'I don't know.'

'Is he going away?' she probed.

'He asked me to go with him,' I confessed, my shoulders hunched, my voice small.

'Where?' Daph asked gently.

'Just go. He's heading up to Queensland.'

'So, you could go.' This was Louisa. I hadn't heard her enter the room. She was standing near the door; her usual place. 'You could try it out. It's only Queensland,' she persisted. 'If you don't like it – if you're not happy – you can come home.'

'But what about all of you? I'm needed here.'

'No, you're not,' Ginny said, pushing through the doorway. 'You *were* needed here, Jane, when we were all young, but you're not anymore.'

'Virginia!' Daphne roared, turning on her. 'Stop it!'

'I'm not being a bitch, Daph. I'm not!' Ginny yelled back. 'Don't you see? Don't any of you see?' She swung around, glaring at all of us in turn, and I saw that Charli was just inside the room, hovering near the doorway.

56

'Jane did what she had to do when Mum and Dad died. She did. She dropped everything! She didn't want to be a *teacher!*' Ginny sneered. 'She was studying geography and geology, sure! But the only time she even *mentioned* a Diploma in Education was *after* Mum and Dad died. She's only in a school because she feels *responsible* for all of us.' She paused, gulping in air after her outburst.

'She's right,' Louisa murmured from her place near the wall. 'Ginny's right about Jane becoming a teacher so she could support us. And she's right about it being time for Jane to go do her own thing. We're all adults now.'

'Is she?' Daphne directed her question to me. 'Did you never really want to teach?'

'Daph, it's not that simple.'

'Why isn't it?' Charli demanded. 'Why can't you do what you want? Why can't all of us?'

'Because we have to be careful,' I almost screamed, shocking them all and even myself.

'Why?' Charli screamed back at me.

'Because Mum and Dad died,' Louisa said, softly. 'Because Jane's afraid. Aren't you, Jane? You're afraid of what can happen.'

'Is that it?' Daphne queried. 'Are you scared for us?'

'Of course, she is,' answered Ginny. 'That's why she's been so damned *controlling* all of these years. She's had all of us wrapped in cotton wool. Well, not cotton wool, exactly. *University degrees.*' The derision was apparent. 'Her way of keeping us all safe.'

'It wasn't just that,' I argued. 'I knew that Mum – especially – but Dad, as well, would want all of us to be educated and financially independent. *That's* why I've been pushing you and Charli to get degrees.'

And then I deflated. Like all the strength in me just dissolved. It was all too much.

'I want to be alone. Leave me alone.'

'Jane,' Charli began, but was stopped by Daphne.

'Let's go. Ginny, did you make dinner?' And my partner – all these years – ushered our younger siblings from the room. 'I'll bring you a plate, Jane.'

'Don't. I'm not hungry.'

Flopping onto the bed, I hugged my pillow to me, and closed my eyes. *Sleep*, I thought.

Chapter Twelve

The jarring sound of the bell irritated me. Let's face it: everything was irritating me. The snide remark from Emily that I hadn't sent in classwork on Friday – Emily, a second-year teacher giving *me* criticism, when I'd been teaching for five years. The gossipy prattle of the senior students who really *should* have been more focused on their assessment task. The closeness of the staffroom – teachers squashed in there with the little crappy desks that teenagers would reject if their parents provided them for home study; the constant chatter curtailing any sustained concentration on coursework. The head teacher reminding me, again, about the reports due at the end of the week. Seriously, I'd had them finished last week. When had I *ever* needed reminding of my professional responsibilities?

I felt heavy and sluggish. Lacking in the energy and verve with which I usually approached my work. My eyes were still swollen from crying, even though I'd risen early and pressed an icepack to my face for fifteen minutes. The makeup I'd slathered on wasn't helping and I'd received a few curious glances. *Not well,* I'd mouthed, shutting them up and justifying Friday's sick day in two words.

And I hadn't slept well. Was it possible to get used to the rock of a boat – *yacht* – in only three nights? Or had I just, very quickly, become accustomed to the gentle pressure of Jack's body stretched out against me? Or his warmth in the night, redolent with his special blend of citrus, sea salt and skin? Or the husky purr of his breath in my ear, his long inhalations and sighing exhalations?

'Miss,' the whine interrupted my musings, 'why do we hafta write this stuff in our books? Why can't we just cut-and-paste it in a Word document?'

'Because.' I really wasn't up to this.

'Because why? No-one uses a pen, anymore. What's the point?'

Could I be bothered to say that writing by hand allowed students to learn and memorise information better? Or that the exams were still handwritten, not typed? Or that handwriting was a valuable skill that students should still be learning?

Nope. Not really. I just wasn't up to this.

My mind wandered again. I wondered if Jack had left yet, or if he was still moored at the pontoon. We'd used up all his eggs yesterday for breakfast. Would he go shopping before he left?

I guessed so. He'd been looking after himself for a long time. I felt sad for him. I knew that, in his way, Jack was lonely.

'Miss, can I go to the toilet?'

'What?'

'Can I go to the toilet?'

'May I. It's "May I go to the toilet?"' I corrected automatically.

'Oh, whatever!' Did they teach that in sixth class? Before students came to high school? Did they teach them how to shrug, just like that, and invest so much derision into their voice?

'Yes, you *may* go to the toilet.'

This was what my life had come to. Twenty-eight years old and I was giving permission to teenagers to go to the bathroom.

I'd left my toothbrush in his bathroom. Before we'd climbed into the Uber, I knew I'd done it. I could have gone back and got it. But I didn't. It wasn't much, but I'd wanted to leave something of me there.

Maybe I had. Just not something physical.

Would he remember me? He said I was important to him. And I'd said it back … sort of.

But it was only three days. Could people really make that strong a connection in only three days?

'Miss, my pen's leaking. Are you sure we can't use our devices?'

It wasn't like I had any long service leave available to me. I'd only been teaching for five years – well, almost six. I'd have to take Leave Without Pay. How would I manage with no money coming in? How would my sisters? Although… they were all working, except for Charli. But the others would take care of Charli. And we owned the house, outright. It was just the bills. Not like we had to pay a mortgage.

'M-i-i-i-s-s-s!' A long whiny plea. 'Do you have a spare *pen*? I've asked you three times.'

I stopped and looked at her. I looked around the room. At a whole class of students, none of whom probably had the foggiest idea of how *incredible* the geography of the earth was. How *amazing* the landscapes around the world were. How *fascinating* the geology of our planet was. And they really weren't that interested in finding out.

'Sure. Have this one,' I said, handing over my own pen.

I used the remainder of the period to apply for Leave Without Pay online. And, when the bell rang again – music to my ears this time – I went straight to the Principal's office.

'Jane,' he said, in greeting.

'I've just applied for Leave Without Pay, starting tomorrow,' I said, getting straight to the point. 'I know you can cover me. Please approve the leave,' I almost begged.

'Why? What do you need it for?' He wasn't going to make this easy.

'A family emergency,' I lied – sort of. It was family – me. And it was an emergency – Jack was leaving today.

'For how long?' he queried, getting down to business.

'Three months.' I figured that would give me enough time to see if Jackson and I would work out.

'Let Bradley know,' he dismissed me, referring me to the teacher who organised replacement teachers.

'Oh, and Jane,' he called, as I was about to leave, 'make sure your reports are completed before you go.'

'Will do,' I said, trying desperately hard to contain my excitement, fearing he would see it and query the "family emergency".

The adrenalin was surging through me and I had to dial the numbers three times before I got them right. I waited, listening as his phone rang, hoping he was still in Sydney. I told myself that if he'd already left, I could always meet him somewhere up the coast.

'Jane?' I melted, relief flooding through me, just at the familiar sound of his voice.

'Have you left yet? Have you gone?'

'No. Are you alright?'

'Yes. Don't go without me, Jackson. Don't leave me behind.'

There was a long pause and then his laughter boomed down the phone.

'Oh, Janey, there's *no* way I'll go without you.'

He laughed again and I started laughing, too.

'Have you gone already?'

'Nah. I spent all weekend with this gorgeous red-head and I haven't written my Freshwater article yet. Thought I'd spend the day finishing that before I headed out.'

'Good.'

'When will you be ready to go, Janey?'

'Tomorrow, Jack. I'm coming tomorrow.' I stopped to think. 'Can you come 'round tonight and help me get organised?'

'Sure, Janey. Whatever you want.'

'It's going to work, isn't it, Jack?'

'Janey, we're going to work. And you're going to be safe. And you and I, we're going to have a lifelong adventure. All around the world.'

I smiled.

WHITE SEDUCTION

SISTERS WHITE SERIES: Book Two

SUNNY MACKENZIE

2020

Chapter One

They had to be joking!!

This was what I was greeted with at the end of a crap-awful, shitty day? I came home to *this*?

It had been bad enough at work, with that imbecile of a Dominic – the bane of my existence – goading me all day, whilst he charmed the pants off most of the other people in the unit! Well, I don't know if he ever got them *off*, exactly, but I knew there were women at work who would definitely go there … And those damned *problems* with the Metro! *I* was the person who solved difficult problems! Me! It was *my* speciality! But … nah, couldn't fix this one. And then that damned Dominic prances on in, all smug smirk and self-satisfied saunter, and – sure enough – puts his damned finger on the issue in seconds.

Aaaaagggghhhh!

And then I had to stand, all the way home, on that damned train! Whatever happened to men standing for women? Or even, children standing for adults? Oh, I missed the good old days. Old-fashioned courtesy. Old-fashioned respect. I'd heard about it, but I'd never *seen* it in person.

All I'd wanted – all day – was to come home, sneak into my room and steal a shot of good Scotch whiskey, before sliding into a just-warm bath with a glass of merlot – nectar of the gods.

But I've walked into *this!*

Ginny was screaming at Jane, slamming the frypan in which she was cooking dinner – chicken, by the looks of it – down onto the table with enough force to waken the dead. Definitely enough to ratchet up the throb of my headache!

Jane was doing nothing to stop things from escalating. As soon as we heard Jane's "placating" voice, the rest of us wanted to smash something. *Reflex action*, I called it.

And then Jane said the magic words, guaranteed to detonate a bomb! "Be *reasonable*" and "you need to be *responsible*".

Ginny went *off*! Like a firecracker! It was to be totally expected. Ginny's face twisted in anger; her voice rose a couple of decibels – yep! really helping my headache – and she attacked some herb with the chef's knife. *Better the oregano than Jane*, I thought wryly.

And then, just to make matters worse, Charli chipped in her two-bobs-worth. Oh, this was going to be a doozey! Jane, in her defence, did try to get Charli to stay out of it, but …

I could see it all slipping away: the soothing balm that was sinking into a cool bath, floating on the surface with just my face above the water, my eyes closed, sound muffled by the liquid covering my ears, the taste of fruity red wine on my tongue. Nope! Not likely to happen any time soon. Not with the War of the Whites being waged around the kitchen table. Talk about domestic terrorism!

Charli's button had been pushed: if there was one thing the youngest of my sisters hated, it was being excluded from something. Or, *feeling* that she was being excluded from something.

So, it was on! My only older sister was battling on two fronts: Ginny and Charli. I knew that Louisa would stay out of it; she never engaged in fights. She never really engaged in much at all, except reading her novels.

And then Charli pushed Jane's button. If there was one thing that five sisters living together were very, very good at, it was knowing *exactly* where everyone had their weakness. 'Saint Jane,' Charli said, 'the boss of us all…'

I held a certain sympathy for Jane. I knew that she had everyone's best interests at heart. The problem was that it was *her* interpretation of what everyone's best interests were. It was not unreasonable: I knew that Jane had worked hard all these years, since our parents died, to keep us all together and that she'd had to forego her wants to do so, but…

And then, just to irritate me, Jane pushed *my* button: 'Someone's got to manage things,' she said. Okay, she probably hadn't intended to irritate me, but … I saw red! I'd had a shit of a day and Jane was *now* making out that *she* was the one who managed everything!

'Well, actually… Seeing as you've raised it… *I'm* the one who manages everything, not you, Jane,' I said, leaning back slightly and crossing my arms over my chest. I tilted my head and squinted my right eye, challenging her.

'Daph, I know you take care of the house and finances, but this is different. And you *must* agree with me that Virginia *should* get some formal education. She can't just loll around the house all day until all the restaurants and bars open again – if we *ever* get over COVID. I don't care if it's *hospitality*, but she could at least get some TAFE qualification. Instead, nothing. Just the mandatory Responsible Service/Conduct stuff. *Nothing.*'

O – Oh! Them's were fighting words! All the "musts" and "shoulds" and "Virginia" and "loll" and the *disdain* on the word "hospitality". Not only had she relegated the hours and hours of work I put in to managing the household to 'take care of the house', but she'd pretty much dropped missiles on every one of Ginny's soft spots. And Ginny *hated* to be called Virginia.

And Charli butted in again, despite all my mental efforts to keep her quiet. Nope! Telepathy didn't work. Anyone who said so was just whacky.

A couple more inflammatory exchanges – twenty-year-old Charli screaming like a toddler; twenty-four-year-old Ginny, her body rigid with mutiny, like a feisty teenage girl ready to belt a bully at school – and Jane attempted to get me on side.

'Daph,' she said, turning to me, 'can you talk sense into them?' I could see her silently begging me for help. But … not this time.

'No, I don't think I will. I think it's time that you stopped trying to control us all. I think you need to let Ginny and Charli make up their own minds.'

Well, that shut her up! It shut everyone up. There was a part of me that felt a bit sorry for her. I watched her face each of us in turn, silently staring. And I watched the play of emotions across her face: that she was stunned, speechless; and then disbelieving; followed by hurt. It crushed her face, her mouth trembling and her eyes welling with tears, making them appear like sparkling aquamarines.

But then she stiffened. It was fascinating, watching her pull herself together, her stance straightening, her back stiff, her face set.

'I'm out of here!' she yelled. 'You can all take care of yourselves!' And she stormed off to her room. Moments later, I heard the front door slam.

Ginny stood silent, staring at the skillet on the table, her shoulders dropped in defeat. Charli was near the sink, her rolled fist in her mouth, her eyes wide. She looked stunned – and scared – as though she didn't really understand what had just happened.

And then Ginny looked around as if confused. I could see the hurt in *her* face, as well. There'd been no winners in this fight. There never was. And these fights were becoming more frequent. Ginny picked up the skillet, looked at it, and then put it down again. She wobbled on her feet, balancing from one foot to the other, restlessness vibrating through her.

'I'm outta here,' she growled, and strode out of the kitchen. I heard her door open, the sounds of cursing coming from her room, before it, too, was slammed. As was the front door.

Nothing like slamming doors to release some pent-up tension.

'Are we still having dinner?' Charli asked, her voice like that of a child. 'Will they come back?'

'Sure, Charli. It'll be alright. Just give me a minute and I'll finish cooking this.' One shot of Scotch? You've got to be joking! Two nips, here I come!

'It's alright, Daph,' Louisa murmured, quietly re-entering the kitchen. 'Go have your bath and I'll take care of dinner. I'll save you a plate.'

Chapter Two

Rolling over, I thumped my pillow again. I needed to get to sleep – especially as I had to deal with Dominic the next day – but Ginny's text had bothered me.

If Jane were here …

And where *was* Jane? I'd tried her number countless times: after my blissful soak; half-way through eating the slightly overcooked chicken and vegetables; when I'd finished the dishes and cleaned up the kitchen; and before I brushed my teeth. No answer.

I understood that Jane was upset, but she knew the rules. You couldn't just go radio-silent, no matter what you were doing or how steamed up you were! We only had ourselves to look out for each other, so the rules were the rules. And Jane was the one who'd created them. Queen Responsibility, herself.

My frustration was warring with my worry. Was she okay? She'd left the car at home, so I assumed she'd hit the ferries, which was what she always did when she was upset about something.

Had she drowned?

Had she been attacked, walking down the road?

Where *was* she?

I punched the pillow again – and then sat up, my fingers fumbling with the fury coursing through me.

Where are you? Are you at Sez's? Answer your phone, dammit!

Still no answer. I could feel the headache – relieved a couple of hours ago by the paracetamol swallowed with the red wine chaser – return, a dull pulsing across my skull.

And then, thank God, my phone buzzed.

Not at Sez's. Won't be home tonight. I'm safe. Austin

Well, at least she'd signed off so that I knew she was okay. I still had no idea where she was, but I knew she was safe.

Not like with Ginny. When I hadn't heard from Ginny, I'd sent her a similar text: *Where are you? When will you be home?*

And she'd answered promptly. Almost immediately. What was bothering me – worrying me – was her text. She'd only written *I'm fine. Staying with a friend. I'll see you in the morning.*

That was it! Nothing else!

If Jane were here, we could talk about it. But she wasn't. So, it was up to me to decide what to do.

I sent another text: *Ginny, are you okay?*

And – again, so promptly, it was scary – there was the reply: *Sure. Had too much to drink, but I'm fine. I'll see you in the morning.* And a smiley face!

I mulled over her texts. Maybe she was too drunk to sign off properly. Maybe she was still so angry, she was deliberately torturing me. Maybe she'd been drugged by some sexual predator and she wasn't writing her own texts.

I could feel, though, in the second text – the repetition of *I'll see you in the morning* – a sense of exasperation, and *that* was like Ginny.

I knew if I rang the police, they'd laugh at me. *What? Your sister is a grown woman who has been missing for five hours and has texted you twice to say she's okay, and you're bothering us?*

Yep, that would go down really well! But they didn't understand our rules…

If I don't hear from her in the morning – say, by nine o'clock – I'll ring the police, I thought. She should be awake by then, even for Ginny, who didn't like to rise too early.

I felt better once I had a plan. Planning and solving problems was what I did. And then Dominic's smirking face flashed into my mind. Damn him!

Don't think about him, I said to myself. *Get some sleep.*

I turned to arrange my pillows – again – carefully and purposefully. I smoothed the crisp cotton covers and, taking a deep soothing breath, I eased my body back down to the sheets, my head finding its place on the fluffed-up cushion. *Take a breath*, I told myself, rolling my shoulders. *My neck is relaxing, my shoulders are relaxing, my back is relaxing*, I intoned, sliding my head back and forth across the pillow. My eyes drifted closed as I inhaled, deeply. Exhaling, I let my body sink into the mattress, becoming heavy.

And, drowsily, my mind slowing down, the meditation techniques working their magic, I thought of … Dominic.

Damn!

Start all over again…

I knew that I shouldn't let him get to me. I knew that!

I wanted to ignore him. But … he was hard to ignore.

I could admit it – but only in the privacy of my bedroom. Well, okay – in the bath, as well.

Dominic Northcott was gorgeous! He was mouth-wateringly, jaw-droppingly, panty-dampeningly gorgeous!

He was also as irritating as all hell.

He was the stuff of every woman's fantasies … and all my nightmares.

At twenty-six, I was the youngest senior manager in my section of Transport for NSW, the public service for buses, trains, ferries, ports, and all other modes of getting from one place to another. I'd been *recognised*, dammit, for my management skills and my ability to solve the most complicated problems, untangling the trickiest of debacles. I was good at my job. My dad would be proud of me!

And then along came Dominic. The bane of my existence. Sure, I wanted to be like the other women and just ogle him – there was a *lot* to ogle. He was tall. Not that tall that it was freakish, but tall enough that he commanded attention as soon as he entered a room. It could have been the way he stood that gave him that extra sense of height. He *never* slouched. Didn't matter how long a day it had been, or how deadly boring a meeting was, or how casual everyone else was. Dominic *never* slouched.

And even when he was relaxed – or pretending to be relaxed – he was always very alert to what was going on around him. You just knew that he was aware of conversations three cubicles away. Or who had entered the room. And when he turned that focus on you … When his grey eyes were staring directly at you… *Oh My God!* It was like high voltage electricity charging through you.

So, yeah – I wanted to ogle him. His thick dark hair – always just so. There was no evidence of product, but he *must* use it. It was finger-running hair.

And his mouth … Yep, I could gaze at his mouth. His full lips, easing into a slow, seductive smile, parting to reveal his even white teeth. I could fall into a lazy daydream just fantasising about what that mouth could do to me…

Get your mind out of the gutter, Daphne!

But then he'd speak – and ruin the whole effect.

Sure, his voice was beautiful, too. Dark. Molten chocolate. The deep voice that could turn you to jelly if he whispered in your ear in the middle of the night. A panty-wetting voice.

But he used it to torment me. He was constantly needling me. Questioning every decision I made. Poking fun at the way I operated. Calling me *Snow!*

Snow! As if I needed him to undermine me at work. In front of my staff. In front of the director.

I *hated* him. *Loathed* him. *Despised* him.

But – he was just *so* damned attractive. And sexy. And ...

Go to SLEEP, Daphne! I mentally berated myself. *Stop thinking about him!*

I rolled over, punching the poor pillow again. Jane ... Ginny ... the house ... the problems with the Metro. And Dominic. It was all too much!

Chapter Three

'Jasmine,' I said, having called my executive assistant on her mobile phone, 'did Brad get back to you on the projections for the station completions?'

Jasmine, like most of the clerical grades, was working from home three days a week. If I'd wanted, I could have worked remotely, but then I would have had to contend with Ginny's taste in music and Charli's comings-and-goings. Much easier to come into work each day. And, yesterday afternoon notwithstanding, there was a lot fewer people travelling to the city, making the commute more enjoyable. Okay, well … not necessarily *enjoyable*, but definitely less stressful. And, although I'd never admit it to my colleagues, I *liked* travelling on trains. There was a difference, though, between peak hour commuting and a journey on the *Indian Pacific*.

'Not yet. I meant to give him a ring, but I haven't got to it yet,' came the breathless reply, dragging me from my musings. I wasn't sure what Jasmine was doing at home: probably loading laundry into the washing machine. It wouldn't surprise me if she were multi-tasking like crazy. Her energy was boundless and I'm sure she was taking advantage of the current situation.

'Send him an email,' I instructed. 'That way we have a record of the fact that we've requested the projections. Oh, and cc me into it.'

'Sure. I'm on it!'

'Oh, and Jasmine?'

'Yes.'

'Cc Dominic Northcott into it, as well. He may as well earn his money and chase up his staff.'

Snide much? I thought to myself, before I heard Jasmine's response. 'Oh, I can *call* Dominic, if you'd like, Daphne. I don't mind. I'm sure I can get a quicker response that way.' *Gushing much, Jasmine?*

'Thank you, Jasmine. That won't be necessary. Just the email.'

After carefully placing my favourite leather tote on my desk, I removed my Surface Pro and sank into the highbacked office chair. Eight o'clock. I was going to need coffee. No way was I going to survive today without coffee – preferably delivered intravenously. I still hadn't heard from Ginny. Nor Jane, for that matter, although Jane would have been on her way to work at this time. I guessed that she'd returned to the house after I'd left: there was no way that Jane would go to school in yesterday's clothes or someone else's. There weren't too many people around who dressed as conservatively as Jane did.

Like you can talk, I said to myself, smoothing my hand down the crisp neatness of my black, pencil-slim skirt and letting my right foot ease out of its matching, kitten-heeled pump, the shoe rocking back and forward on my big toe. I took a moment to admire the glossy red polish on my toenails – "Queen of Tarts", my favourite colour – through the sheerness of my stockings.

'So, you decided to show! What? Slept in?'

And there he was, leaning against the door frame, that smug smirk – *there's some alliteration,* I thought snidely – detracting from his otherwise handsome face. Oh, who was I kidding! *That* was the expression that had most of the office females running after him, eager to please. What ever happened to feminism!

He had this trick of being totally motionless, whilst his eyes took in everything and, to my horror, I watched them zoom in to my shoeless foot, his smile softening slightly, before they rose to meet mine. 'Nice colour, Snow!'

What was I supposed to address first: that he'd implied I was late? I wasn't really; it was just that I was usually early. That he'd visually assaulted me? Alright, I was taking that a bit too far, but there *was* an electrical charge wherever his eyes scanned my body and I just *knew* he did it to get a rise out of me. And it was *totally* unprofessional behaviour in an office. That he'd mentioned my toenail polish? Making personal comments *could* be considered sexual harassment. He wouldn't say that to a male colleague. *Although he might,* I mentally conceded, *if that male happened to be wearing bright red nail polish.* Or that he'd called me "Snow" again? That dreaded nickname! And I *knew* that he did it to get me going!

Take a breath, Daphne, I instructed myself. *You're overreacting. Calm down!*

'Nothing to say?' he goaded, and I felt the steam starting to rise from my face, it was burning so hot! The hide of that man!

Take a damned BREATH, Daphne! I mentally screamed to myself.

I was just about to respond when my phone beeped. Glancing down, I saw Ginny's name on my screen, with a one-word text: *Woolf.*

'Dating animals now, Snow? Is that your boyfriend?' His voice was grating on my raw nerves, especially frayed as I realised that he'd approached without my noticing. 'If it is, he can't spell.'

Nothing else – just "Woolf" – but, as relief flooded through me, I felt the firm control, that I'd managed to maintain all morning, slip. My hand, holding the phone, started to shake. I stared at it – that shaking hand – in disbelief. And then I felt the hot flood of tears in my eyes. *What the …!*

I had to get a hold of myself. I could feel Dominic's piercing attention focused on me and I was mortified that I was almost crying. Dammit! *Take a breath, Daphne!* But it wasn't working.

'Snow? Are you alright?' He moved closer, his voice lowered in concern. *Huh, as if Dominic would be concerned about me!*

'Snow…' He was right there, but not touching me. 'Daphne, what's wrong? Talk to me.' There was a gentleness in his voice I hadn't heard before. It made the tears worse and I felt my eyes overflow, a long, slow slide of salty water down my face.

Oh! My! God! I was *mortified*! My nemesis was standing – right there – in front of me and I was *crying!*

'Daphne,' he said, his voice coming from deep in his chest, 'Look at me.' A pause. I saw his index finger slowly approach the underside of my chin. There was ample time for me to pull away, but – for some unknown reason – I didn't. I *let* him *touch* me! 'Look. At. Me!' he repeated. It was a command and – again, for some unknown reason – I did.

'What – is – wrong?' The words were quiet, but distinct. 'Tell me what's wrong,' his tone commanding, authoritative. I just stared into his eyes, that steely-grey gaze that was intent on my face. 'Talk to me, Daphne.' Again, a command – not a request.

'It's nothing,' I began, feeling foolish, whilst also a bit mesmerised at the energy passing between us and the intensity of his eyes. 'I'm sorry,' I faltered, 'it's nothing…'

'No, Daphne,' he corrected me, 'whatever it is, it's not *nothing*. You don't do this …' he paused, his free hand wafting in front of me, 'without a good reason. You're not that type of woman. You're tougher than that. So, what's wrong?'

How was I supposed to react to that? Not only had he used my real name – four times, even – without anyone else around to notice, but he'd also *complimented* me. Twice! It was overwhelming! And I felt the tears well up again. *Dammit!*

'I don't know what the problem is, but you can't stay here.' I started to protest. 'No, Daph, we need you out of here until you pull yourself together.'

Well, that stopped me cold! Was he going to take advantage of my weakness? The bastard! I *knew* he was a weasel!

'I'll create a distraction and you go down the elevator,' he instructed, ignoring that I'd pulled away from him, crossing my arms in front of me. He paused, his eyes narrowing. 'Don't argue, Snow. You need to take time to regain your composure. Go get a cup of tea. Or coffee, although that'll probably wind you up more.' At my expression of outrage, he grinned. 'See! That's more like you!'

And then he did something shocking!

He reached out and ran his finger, feather-soft, down the side of my face. From just beside my eye to my jaw. And – don't ask me how or why – but my face kind of … leant *in* … to his touch. I could feel my eyes widening with surprise.

'Go, Snow!' he urged, gently but firmly. 'I'll cover for you. Go get your nails done – your fingers can match your toes. Or get a shampoo and blow-wave, or whatever it is that you women do to make yourselves feel better. And, when you're back to being *you,* come back. Take an hour. Or two. Nothing disastrous will happen while you're gone.' Then he grinned, a devilishly playful smile. 'I won't wreck any of your projects whilst you're not here. I'll wait until you're back again!'

I watched him open my office door and stride to the far wall of the open-plan clerical space, drawing eyes to him as he loudly greeted those staff already in the office. 'So, tell me,' he cajoled loudly, capturing the attention of all present, 'what's been happening up here whilst I've been working my magic downstairs?'

And I stunned even myself!

I took advantage of Dominic – or, rather, his ploy. Moving slowly, out of the line of sight of the others, I snuck around to the stairwell. Our eyes met over the heads of the clerical assistants and, just before I disappeared behind the fire door, his right eye twitched in a discreet, but wicked, wink.

Chapter Four

'How'd your meeting go, Snow?'

I couldn't believe it! That man was still hovering around my workspace when I arrived back from my "break". I'd been gone for well over an hour and I was sure he would have been busy in his section, solving issues that were none of his business, engendering hero worship amongst his male subordinates and making female colleagues swoon and forget one hundred years of the quest for female equality.

I had to admit, though, I felt infinitely better after the soothing Chai tea I'd enjoyed in a small café at Central Station, before ducking down to my favourite little Chinese herbal medicine shop, where my feet were pleasantly tortured with forty minutes of reflexology. I *loved* the delicious relief that came hot-on-the-heels (pardon the pun!) of the steadily increasing pressure on the sensitive sore spots on the soles of my feet. It was one of my guilty pleasures. Like my baths at the end of stressful days.

Before I could formulate an appropriately snitty response, Melissa, one of the clerical support officers, piped up. 'Why do you call her Snow, Dominic? Her name's Daphne and she lets us call her Daff.'

I watched as, without moving his head – how does he do that? – his gaze slid to Melissa, his expression going completely blank. And puffing up – no doubt ecstatic that she had his attention – she continued, 'She *hates* it. She says so after every time you call her that.' She finished with quite a deal of aplomb, as though she'd just released high-security government secrets. I almost vomited in my mouth when I saw the fawning gaze she was bestowing on Dominic, her rapture evident to anyone even briefly glancing at her.

My eyes turned back to Dominic – maybe, I *could* learn this technique of his – just in time to see his attention return to me. And, in a long quiet moment, both of us completely motionless, we communicated: our disbelief that Melissa could be so obtuse as to not recognise the reference that 'Snow' was; our dismay at her unprofessional revelations, when she should have kept my office secrets; and our mutual appreciation of the fact that we weren't quite so … I didn't want to say "stupid", but that was the only word that came to mind. There was a warmth in his eyes, the steel grey darkening to a molten metal colour, before he nodded, a barely-there tilt of his head.

'Oh, and by the way, Snow,' he said, his back to me as he walked towards the elevator, 'I scheduled our five o'clock meeting in your calendar.' I stiffened. There *was* no five o'clock meeting – and what was he doing anywhere near my calendar? 'Oh – and try to be early. I don't have time to waste.' Pausing, his hand just touching the call-button, he glanced back over his shoulder and … yep! Just the *suggestion* of a wink!

'He's *sooo* yummy!' Melissa's sugary simpering brought me back to earth.

'Haven't you got any work to do?' I did feel a little jolt of guilt as I watched her face fall just before a flash of dislike crossed her features. *Yep, I thought, winning friends and influencing people here, Daphne!*

The day sped past: emails, text messages, phone calls, meetings. In the back of my mind, though, was Dominic's "five o'clock meeting". I was irritated by his high-handedness, his sheer arrogance that allowed him to not only schedule it into my calendar – and he had! I checked – but also that he could dictate to me that way. But … he'd been right about my leaving the office. If I'd stayed, I probably would have snapped at people, which wouldn't have helped me, or – worse, yet – I might have *cried* in front of someone else! And totally ruined my professional image; an image I'd spent years cultivating. And I had felt better after my time-out. Much, *much* better.

But – oh! I hated that he'd been right! Almost as much as I hated that he'd seen me in a weak moment.

I thought about what my father would say. That had guided me through most of my university studies and working life: What Would Dad Do?

Well, for starters, he wouldn't have cried at work. No going back and changing *that* now. In my defence, I had spent most of the night worried about Ginny, hardly getting any sleep. And the fight the previous evening hadn't helped. There would have to be a circuit-breaker sometime soon:

all of us living in the same house, with different goals, the tensions were rising. It had been alright when Charli and Louisa were younger, but we were all adults now. It was different.

And Dad had only had to concern himself with work: Mum had taken care of the house and us kids and the garden, and birthdays, Christmas, and all that fluffy stuff that involved *family* and *people*. Now, it was all back on me. Well, except for the cleaning – that was Louisa. Oh, and except for birthdays and Christmas and the rest – that was Jane. And except for the cooking – that was Ginny.

But *I* had to worry about the garden and the house – the bills, the maintenance and keeping everyone clothed and financed, so they could do the things they wanted to do. As well as work in the public sector, where the construction of the Metro infrastructure was not going to plan and there were hundreds of ambitious people just waiting to take my job, if not the promotion I was trying to win. Okay, maybe not *hundreds*. But the public service was much more competitive than it had been in his day.

So, Dad, I'm allowed to get overwhelmed every so often!

I knew I had to honour the "five o'clock meeting". I owed Dominic, as much as I hated to admit it. Because I assumed I could go home immediately afterwards, I gathered my jacket and laptop bag, and headed down to his office. The *ding!* of the elevator announced my arrival on the floor and, as the doors opened, I watched as Dominic, his office directly across the open-plan work space, looked up.

Again, the stillness. There was no discernible movement. His face didn't change; nor did his posture. And yet … There was a difference. I'd sound like Ginny if I said that the energy changed: I could *feel* his smug self-satisfaction from the elevator!

His eyes didn't waver as he watched me traverse the space between us. Feeling self-conscious and strangely vulnerable – a sensation he often evoked – I slowed my pace, keeping my shoulders back and my head high. He wasn't going to intimidate me!

'On time,' he smirked, as I entered his office.

Don't react, Daphne! Don't let him rankle you.

'It was on my calendar,' was my cool response, as I draped my jacket on the visitor's chair and placed my bag on his desk.

'No. Don't get comfortable,' he said, shutting down his Surface Pro and rising from his chair. 'Put your jacket on. We're leaving.'

Frowning, I reached for my jacket, fumbling when I attempted to slide my arm into the sleeve. I couldn't help it. He distracted me. Not deliberately, I knew, but …

He had a unique way of putting his jacket on and, when his arms were raised above his head, his body was on full display. Dominic wasn't a skinny man. His chest was solid. Firm muscles covered his rib cage. There was no excess fat on him, but there was nothing fragile about him, either. And his abdomen was cut. It was covered by his white shirt, which still appeared crisp at the end of a work day! How did he *do* that? And, there was no other way to describe it: he had more than a six-pack. An *eight-pack*?

And my mouth watered. It really did! And here I'd thought that *that* was just some expression in torrid romance novels, but – no! Saliva could really flood your mouth when confronted with such a – a – *delectable* example of the human male.

Pull yourself together, Daphne! It irritated me that I found him so … *attractive,* when I didn't want to like him.

He'd paused, watching me. His right eye half-closing as a slow smile curved his mouth. He knew! He knew what I was thinking! I could feel my cheeks flame with mortification. *Oh My God!* Twice in the same day!

'C'mon. Let's go,' was all he said, shrugging to ensure that his jacket sat properly. As if it *dared* not to fit perfectly! He lifted a duffle bag – what's with the duffle? – off the floor and loaded his Surface Pro into it. 'Time's a-burning.'

I followed him out, standing to one side whilst he locked his office, and walked beside him to the elevator. Neither of us spoke as we waited for the car to arrive and the doors to open. With so many people working from home, the lift wasn't full, but I was still aware of him beside me – a pulse of energy emanating from him, despite his stillness.

Once outside the building, I hurried to keep up with him, his steps much longer than mine, especially in my heels. He paused and turned, watching me as I covered the space between us, and I was relieved when he slowed his pace to mine once we started walking again.

'So, where are we going?' I finally asked. I'd held off for as long as I could, feeling that he was playing a game with me: a control game where he knew the answers and I had to guess or play catch-up.

'For a drink, Snow. It's Friday afternoon.' He didn't even turn to face me when he said this – just kept looking straight ahead. *Damn him.*

'I can't have a drink!' I blurted and stopped, right there on the path, blocking the people behind me.

'Of course, you can.' He, too, paused and turned towards me.

'No. I haven't eaten anything since last night – if you don't count the Chai tea I had this morning. I can't drink on an empty stomach!'

'Snow, there *is* something called soft drink – and juice – and water.' He grabbed my hand as he changed direction.

'Now where are we going?'

'I could go an early dinner and you definitely need food. You eat Chinese?'

'People?' I queried, drolly.

His only response was an equally droll raised eyebrow. And we kept on moving, this time with my wrist captured in his warm hand.

Who knew I could be so … docile!

Chapter Five

It was a little restaurant, tucked down a side street, away from the passing pedestrians, scurrying either to their favourite Friday afternoon watering-hole or the nearest bus stop or train station, in the hopes of a quick trip home.

'I didn't know this was here,' I commented, smoothing my skirt after sitting down at a small table positioned against the outside wall. It was like eating al fresco, but with the protection of the building and the tantalising aromas from the kitchen. A perfect spot.

'Hmmm. Most don't. It's where the Chinese eat.'

An older woman approached the table, her greying hair twisted into a knot on the top of her head, her bright red satiny dress tied in at the waist, menus in hand. And, interestingly, she greeted Dominic by name, only hesitantly offering him the menus, which he waved away.

'What'll you have to drink, Snow? A green tea?'

'What are you having?' I asked, curious.

'Jack Daniels, Single Special.' As he said this, he nodded to the woman. And – shut the gate! – he *smiled* at her. Not his smug smirk that he so often directed at me. Not the derisive twist that his mouth made when he was being particularly obnoxious. Nor the panty-melting bit of seduction that he flashed to the fluffy girls at work, designed to get him whatever he wanted, as soon as they could do it. No. A full-blown *smile*. An I-like-you-and-I-think-you're-great smile. And she grinned – one of her top teeth missing, just to the side of her mouth – right back at him!

'I'll have a Scotch – neat. Glenfiddich, if they have it,' I spluttered, desperately trying appear unaffected.

He nodded again, and then rattled off our food order: a platter of mixed appetisers, special fried rice, honeyed beef, some vegetable dish, and spicy chicken and mushroom dumplings. 'Oh, and water, please, Chuntao.' Smiling and nodding at him, she – Chuntao? – backed away, ready to do his bidding.

'Do you mind?' I queried, my tone and raised eyebrows suggesting incredulousness. To be honest, though, I'd quite enjoyed sitting back and watching him be all masterful and domineering. It had been a change, not having to make any decisions. And his menu choices *did* sound yummy!

'You're hungry. I could eat. It saved time to just order.' He inhaled slowly before sipping the golden liquid placed before him. I reached for my drink and followed suit, pausing to savour the first sip. The distinctive bitterness chasing the sweet fruity taste of my favourite Scotch. My special treat at the end of a long day.

My eyelids closed in sensual appreciation and I could hear my own exhalation as I swallowed. When I opened my eyes, Dominic was watching me. Scrutinising me, really. There was a quiet intensity to his gaze. It was direct – and focused. Feeling flustered, I asked, 'I take it you come here often?' and then I blushed self-consciously at the cliched inanity of my question.

'Hmmm.' He hummed – more a low growl. 'My go-to place for Friday dinner. So,' he murmured, leaning back in his chair, his eyes on mine, 'are you going to tell me what caused your little … outburst … this morning?'

I knew this was coming. Just a matter of time.

'No.' I sipped my whiskey, staring straight back at him. Two could play this game, I thought.

'Rare behaviour for you, Snow. You're usually much more contained.' He sipped his bourbon.

'Hmmm,' I murmured, non-committally, taking another taste of my drink.

'Check,' he chuckled, a rich dark sound, as he mimed moving a chess piece on the table. 'So, how long have you been with Transport?' he asked, changing the subject.

Just the topic to rile me up, again. I'd been there since I finished university, four years before. I'd been working my way up the ladder, one step at a time. And then, in came Dominic. From the Department of Health. Straight into the same grade as mine. What did he know about Transport? Sure – he was obviously a few years older than I was. I picked him at around thirty. And, sure. – he was a good operator. I couldn't deny that. I'd seen him in meetings – lots of them, unfortunately. Everyone else would be busy offering their opinions and saying everything they knew, which – let's face it – for most of them, wasn't much. There'd be lots of movement and people rising from their seats to make a point, or requesting something – a glass of water, a new notepad, copies of reports or emails – and Dominic would be silent. Still and silent. His eyes taking in … *every*thing.

And when everyone else had finished posturing and gesturing; when they'd run out of words and opinions; when their thoughts had been loudly and boisterously expressed – he'd open his mouth and, clearly and succinctly, sum up all the pros and cons, before very precisely stating the solution to whatever the issue had been. All those in the meeting would sit, stunned, and then bounce in enthusiastic agreement. As though he were some Messiah! So, yeah… It irritated me.

'A few years. You?' I fake-queried. I knew *exactly* when he'd arrived, but I wasn't letting him know that.

'Oh, Snow! I'm sure you could tell me the precise date,' his voice, smooth and dark, curled around me. 'Transport special? Or would any department do?'

'My father worked for Railcorp, before it got renamed,' I admitted, not quite sure why I told Dominic this.

'Did he retire?' he asked, moving his glass to allow the dishes of mini spring rolls, steamed dim sims and prawn toast to be placed on the table.

'No.' Looking down, I picked up the chopsticks, removing them from their protective wrapper. When I glanced up, Dominic was placing a spring roll in my bowl, and nudging the soy and sweet chili condiments towards me.

There was silence for a time, each of us sampling the food, and studying each other. When the plates were removed, Dominic ordered another round of drinks.

'My father worked for Railcorp,' he offered. 'Drove the trains. All my life, that's what Dad did. He wanted me to do the same.'

'Did he retire?' I asked, breaking the silence that had developed.

'Nope.'

A young girl brought our fresh whiskeys and – bonding, strangely, over our missing parents – we clinked glasses. 'To fathers,' he intoned.

'To fathers,' I responded. And we exchanged weak smiles, sadness in our eyes. And … was that *regret* in his?

The arrival of the rice, dumplings and beef provided the perfect distraction and we ate, only commenting on the food, which *was* excellent.

'I like your bag,' Dominic said, as the plates and bowls were cleared from our table. 'Ashwood?' he asked.

'How'd you know?' I was stunned. Only a couple of people had ever commented on my bag – it wasn't a proper laptop case; rather, a large vintage tote. I loved it! I'd bought it for myself as a reward for my last promotion, and I enjoyed the sensation of the soft, luxurious leather in a beautiful brandy colour. It was the perfect size for both my Surface Pro and personal items, and I carried it everywhere!

'Well, the tag was a dead giveaway,' was the dry reply. 'But I bought my mother something similar in their range for Christmas last year. She doesn't use it much, though. Says it's "too good" to use. Women!'

'Good present. You've got taste, at least,' I teased.

'At least,' he agreed.

'So, what's with the duffle?' I asked, nodding towards the worn tan leather bag at the side of his chair. 'Going somewhere?'

'Hmmm. Down the coast for the weekend.' He sipped the last of his bourbon.

'What for?' I was curious.

'I go home most weekends.'

Well, this was interesting. I thought he lived in Sydney. 'Where's home?'

'Wollongong.'

'I thought you lived locally.'

'I do. I've got a one-bedder in Kirribilli,' he said, mentioning the area just to the east of the northern pylon of the Sydney Harbour Bridge. 'That's for midweek. Most weekends, I prefer to be down the coast. Get away from the crowds and the rat-race.'

Who knew? This last tidbit fascinated me. Let's face it – *he* fascinated me. But, after the week I'd had – and I was still mad at Ginny, *and* Jane, over their antics last night – the *idea* of a weekend away, Down The Coast, as he put it, was tantalising.

'Take me!' I blurted, before I could censor my words.

I felt the instant flame in my cheeks – which *must* have been bright red – as his lips slowly curved upwards into a seductive smile, his eyes gleaming dirty messages at me.

'Oh, Snow,' he drawled, the two words drawn out into a growl, a truly decadent depth in his voice, 'you have *no* idea!'

'That wasn't what I meant – and you know it!' I fired back.

'Hmmm. Then how about you tell me what you meant,' he almost purred.

'Forget it! It was a stupid idea!'

'No, Snow. You brought it up.' He sat up, all business. 'What is it that you want? A weekend away? Do you, Miss I-Can-Take-Care-of-Myself-and-Everyone-Else, want to run away from home? Is that it?'

I sat mutely, crossing my arms in front of me, wishing that I'd kept my big mouth shut.

'Okay. We want to make the 7.22 train and it's just after six now. Can we do that? Where do you live?'

'What! Are you taking me?' And … another flame lit across my cheeks.

'Sure, Snow. Let's get your stuff! What's the quickest way to your house?'

I watched him reach for his wallet and, even before his credit card was between his fingers, the older woman – Chuntao – was there to take it.

'Snow. Focus. How do you normally get to work?'

'Train. But there's a ten-minute walk at Wollstonecraft.'

'Then let's hot-foot it! We'll grab an Uber when we hit the station. You'll need your swimmers – don't bother with towels. And runners, Snow.'

'Are we really doing this?' I asked, stunned into incoherence.

'Sure. Why not?' was his reply, as he reached across and draped my bag over his shoulder, on top of the duffle. 'C'mon. Time's a-burning.'

And then he winked.

Chapter Six

I'd amazed myself with how quickly I'd managed to get my overnight bag packed. I'd followed Dominic's instructions: swimmers, shorts, a couple of shirts, underwear and bras, and runners. I knew how to pack light and I figured he'd have towels, or there'd be towels where we were staying. I hadn't even asked him about that... I probably should have been more concerned, but – for some reason – I wasn't.

I was excited – like I hadn't been in a long time. Maybe this little adventure was long overdue. I fed Charli's cat, Clancy, and wrote on the miniature whiteboard beside the fridge – our "communication system":

Fed the cat. Going down the coast. Back for Sunday dinner. Daph.

Short and sweet. There was no-one at the house, but I was sure that someone would be home soon.

And then I was back in the Uber that Dominic had held out the front, and we were on our way to the station. We had to change trains at Central: the South Coast Line departed from a separate platform than those frequented by the city trains. Our connections, though, worked and we were sitting in the carriage ahead of time, waiting for our departure.

'We could have sat in the Quiet Carriage,' I said, referring to the two carriages on the train where there wasn't the incessant ring and chatter on mobile phones, and no loud conversations between passengers, or the audible sound of all manner of music leaking from earbuds. 'That would be more peaceful,' I added.

I felt, rather than heard, Dominic chuckling beside me, his arms and body shaking with his mirth. 'No, Snow. That would never do. You'd spend the entire time in your own head, overthinking this little escapade, and regretting your decision to come. Not happening.' He leaned back, stretching, before settling himself – more comfortably, I assumed – into his seat. 'So, let's get to know each other. We'll be here for a while.'

These words – and the suggestive tenor in which they were delivered – didn't reassure me. 'Why? So you can use the information against me at work?' I asked, snidely. And then I shut my eyes – instant remorse! He didn't deserve that. He'd been only good to me all day. But, before I could say anything to withdraw them, I felt his body shift – followed by the sizzle that heated my skin whenever he directed that grey gaze to me.

'No, Snow,' he drawled. 'It's what people do when they're travelling together. Or when they work together. They make conversation and they learn about each other.' He paused, his body still. He was waiting – for what? I wasn't sure. Curiosity got the better of me, though, and – embarrassment flooding through me – I turned my head to look at him. 'But, Daphne … If you aren't comfortable … if you don't feel safe, we can get off the train and I'll see you home.'

'What?'

'This is your choice, Daphne. If you honestly think that I can't be trusted … that I'll sabotage you at work with anything that you tell me… Well, frankly, I'm a bit offended. So, if you'd like to go home, I'll see you safely there.'

'But … you'll be too late to go down the coast, won't you be?' I asked, confusion robbing me of rational speech.

'No. I can go later tonight. I can go tomorrow. It doesn't really matter.' He shrugged, as though it was inconsequential. And I felt stupid. Like a child that didn't know its own mind. But, in my defence, I really didn't know him… He exuded an aura of competence and trustworthiness, but …

'Where are we staying? Are we going to a hotel?'

'Nope. We're going to my mother's.' He smiled at my look of incredulity, and then winked. 'That stopped you, didn't it, Snow! You weren't expecting that!' He chuckled again, a warm self-satisfied sound, that wasn't as obnoxious as I'd like to pretend. 'Close your mouth, Snow.'

I will admit, it wasn't just because of his words that I was stunned silent. The twinkle in his eyes, the merriment on his face, the sheer … *cockiness* of the man! It was captivating. And I had to swallow the saliva that filled my mouth. Oh! I was going to have to be careful. For all that I hated to admit it, he was one *yummy* man.

'And,' he continued, obviously enjoying my shock, 'there'll probably be a little plate of cake and biscuits waiting for me.'

'You still live with your mother?' I could hear astonishment in my voice, my pitch rising to a squeak. *Daph, you sound like an idiot. Get a hold!*

'Not quite.' He straightened, his body tensing beside me. 'But the point is, Daphne, you're safe with me.' He paused. 'If you don't feel that, though, we can get you home.' I glanced at his hands as they spread, openly, before me.

'No. It's alright. I'm good.'

He nodded – once – and settled back down. 'Sooo,' a teasing glint in his eyes, 'I guess talking about work is out of the question? What's your favourite colour, Snow?'

I could play this game. He was probably expecting me to say "blue", like almost every other person on the planet. After all, it *was* the most popular favourite colour. 'Blood red!' I stated, baldly.

'Aahhh! Of course! Like your toenail polish.'

Did he have to sound so smug?

I could feel the warmth in my face, not only because of the delicious deep rumble of his response. He *knew* about my secretly-painted toes. I wondered if he guessed about my lingerie. *Snap out of it, Daphne! He probably hasn't even given it any thought at all.* But, studying him, I noticed the narrowing of his eyes – a gleam catching the light – and his head subtly nodding, a tiny movement, a barely-there rocking on his spine. And the soft fullness of his lips, his mouth relaxed. *Yeah, he's given it some thought*, I thought. The man *oozed* wickedness.

'Mine's green,' he declared, snapping me out of my thoughts.

'Green? What sort of green? There are hundreds of green,' I exaggerated.

'The green of your eyes, Snow.'

And there he went again … stunning me into silence.

'Close your mouth, Snow.' That deep purr was becoming addictive.

Change the subject, Daphne.

'So, what will we be doing this weekend?'

'Whatever. I've got a few things to do around the house, but after that …' He shrugged his shoulder. 'Anything in particular you want to see?'

'I don't really know what's there. Oh, except for the Kiama Blowhole. Can we see that?'

'Sure. I'll give you the ten-cent tour. All the sights of the Illawarra,' he said, referring to the low-lying area spreading from just south of Sydney all the way to the Shoalhaven River and including the escarpment that rose to the Southern Highlands plateau.

It turned out that we were both avid fans of the ABC – the public national broadcaster – and, specifically, the Monday evening panel program, Q-and-A, where viewers asked questions of politicians, authors, experts in their fields, and other commentators. We chatted about the previous week's episode until, the gentle sway of the train and the long, emotional day, took its toll and I nodded off.

'Snow. Wake up. We're almost there.' Dominic's low voice disturbed my drowsy state. 'C'mon, Daphne, we're the next stop.'

'I wasn't asleep,' I mumbled. 'Just resting my eyes.'

'Yeah, and the dribble on my suit jacket says otherwise,' he taunted, dryly. 'C'mon, Snow, get with the program.' Slinging the strap of his duffle over his left shoulder, he reached for my overnight bag, before putting his hand out to help me up.

'I can manage.'

'Let me take your laptop bag.'

'No, you're not getting your hands on this. I'll take it.' I softened my words with a quick grin. 'No one touches my computer.'

After the train stopped and the doors slid open, we stepped onto the platform, both of us reaching for our Opal cards.

'I usually walk from here, but we'll get a taxi,' Dominic said, as we each scanned our travel cards.

'No. We can walk. If you normally walk, it can't be that far. And it's a nice night.'

'You sure? I like the exercise after a week in the office, but … Are you sure, Daph?'

'Yeah. Don't make a big deal out of it,' I said, waving my hands at him, still a bit embarrassed that I'd fallen asleep on the train. 'Lead on, MacNorthcott!'

'You know that's wrong, don't you?'

'Nah. Just depends on whom you're quoting,' I teased. 'Show me the way to your mother's house.'

Chapter Seven

'This is nice. I wasn't expecting this.'

We'd walked down a cobbled pathway on the side of his mother's house and Dominic had unlocked the door to a self-contained living area under the main floor of the dwelling. It was an open-plan design with the kitchen, dining room and lounge all in one large space, and two closed doors along the opposite wall. Curtained windows lined the long side to our left and I imagined, in the daytime with the drapes drawn, there'd be lots of natural light and a garden view.

'A granny flat!' I teased him. 'Dominic's got a granny flat!'

'Did you really think that, at my age, I'd still live with my mother? Really, Snow? That's what you expected?'

'To be honest, Dominic, I didn't know what to expect. This whole evening has been … a bit of surprise. If you'd told me at eight o'clock this morning that I'd be in Wollongong this evening with you, I wouldn't have been able to contain my laughter. And yet … here I am! It's all a bit …' I tapered off.

'Drink? I can offer you tea or coffee? There'll be milk in the fridge.'

And that was when I noticed them. Three iced cupcakes, covered with clingwrap, on a dainty little plate. Bone china, a floral pattern, gilt-edged. And I tried – really, really hard – not to laugh. Especially when I glanced back at Dominic and saw his eyes narrowed in warning.

'What are you having?' I asked, watching him drop both of our bags near what I assumed was the bedroom door. He shrugged out of his jacket, draping it on the back of a chair, and I was reminded of how damned attractive he was. The muscles of his back rippled beneath the cotton of his shirt, his shoulders and arms flexing fluidly with his movements.

'Jack Daniels, but I don't have any Scotch. I do, however, have wine,' he offered, interrupting my trance.

'Shiraz?'

He nodded and prepared our drinks. It was fascinating, watching him being domestic in his own space. I was so used to thinking of him as the "arch enemy" – the "usurper come to threaten my domain", or as the domineering sex-god over whom women swooned and demeaned themselves to get his attention, and whom I *had* to resist – that I hadn't really thought of him as just a person. A man who knew his way around a kitchen. And whose mother who baked him cupcakes.

But then he turned back to me, the drinks in his hands and I forgot any ideas about his being domesticated. I didn't know whether it was the comparative fragility of the delicate wine glass in his hand, or the controlled way he moved – no wasted shuffles or fidgets; or the strength in his posture: Dominic's spine was always straight, his shoulders back, his head perfectly balanced atop his neck. Or it could have been the energy that shot across the room as soon as his eyes met mine. But I knew – Dominic was not tame.

'Sit, Snow,' he said, gesturing towards the three-seater leather lounge that dominated the room, facing the long windows. Sinking into its cushioned comfort, I stroked my hands along the surface, enjoying its supple softness.

'Nice lounge,' I commented, accepting my drink. *Did our fingers just touch?* I thought I felt a zap, but ... not so much his skin. Was it just energy flashing between us?

'Hmmm,' was his only response as he sipped his bourbon. I tentatively tasted the shiraz and grinned. 'What? Were you expecting something bad?' His eyebrow quirked. 'It's Pepperjack. A good wine, priced reasonably enough for quaffing.'

'Quaffing?' I teased. 'Do people still use that word?'

'You know what I mean, Snow. Drink your wine.'

And I did, savouring the fruity nectar as I surreptitiously ogled him as he first bent forward, releasing the laces on his polished black shoes, before easing his feet from their confines and resting them on the edge of the coffee table in front of us. All with minimal movement. Quiet and controlled.

Taking a deep breath, I followed suit, sliding off the chocolate brown ballet flats I'd changed into at home and propping my feet on my end of the table. I relaxed back into the softness of the lounge and snuck another look in his direction.

His head was back and his eyes were closed. *Permission is granted*, I assured myself. *Feel free to ogle!* And I did. I let my eyes laze over his profile, the length of his neck with the bump of his Adam's apple clearly visible; the sharp ridge of his chin, jutting upwards; the fullness of his lips and the straightness of his nose. His high forehead, his thick dark hair brushed back. Was that a bit of a receding hairline there at his temple? *Ooohh! Bet he didn't like that!*

And then my gaze travelled down to his chest. His solid chest. The type you could rest your head on and you wouldn't feel like you were stopping someone from breathing. Defined. Not an ounce of fat. And, stretched out as he was, the line of his abdomen, interrupted only by his hands, relaxed and holding the old-fashioned glass against his belly. A black leather belt threaded through the waistband of his suit pants ... and his long legs extended to the coffee table. His feet looked somehow vulnerable in only socks, as though without shoes, they were defenceless.

'Are you done yet?' His warm tone, humour leaching through, jolted me out of my perusal. I'd thought he'd fallen asleep. Obviously not!

'I think so,' I said, sipping at my glass to recover my composure. 'Why am I here?' I asked, curious.

'What do you mean?' His head turned slightly towards me, one eye open.

'Why did you bring me here? To have your wicked way with me?' I tried to make the last bit sound like a joke, but it fell flat.

'No.' Both eyes were on me now. 'You asked me. That's why you're here.'

'I asked you? That's it! I *asked* you?' My voice rose on this last bit.

'Yes, Snow,' he said evenly, patience personified. 'You asked for something that I could give you or do for you. That's it.'

I reared back, trying to take this in. 'And you don't want to sleep with me?'

'W-e-l-l-l, I didn't say *that!*' He shot me an evil grin. 'But, Snow, that's not why you're here.'

'Then – again – why did you bring me here?' I persisted.

'Because you asked me and it seemed like you needed a break from ...' he flickered his hand in the air momentarily, 'whatever is bothering you.' He drank from his glass. 'Daphne, don't read too much into it.' With that, he settled back into that uber-relaxed pose and shut his eyes again.

My mind spun. He'd really said that he brought me because I'd *asked* him to? As though that was all it took? I just had to *ask* him for something and he'd give it to me? Really?

I tried to think of the last time someone had done that to me… For me… Even if I asked Jane for something, there was usually a third-degree. *What do you want it for? Do you really need it? Can you do without it? When do you have to have it by?* That's why I always looked after things for myself. I very seldom asked anyone for anything.

And he wasn't expecting sex? He had said, on the train, that I was safe. That I could trust him. But, *really*? He wasn't expecting *anything* from me?

And how did I feel about that? I mean, he *was* drop-dead gorgeous. And he *did* give off that vibe that said, "Women have a great time in bed with me!" I was sure he'd know what he was doing.

But I worked with him. And I'd have to see him every day… It really wouldn't work. *No, Daphne. You can't go there!* Damn the voice in my head!

'Stop it, Snow.'

'What?'

'Stop tying your brain up in knots. I can hear you thinking from over here. Take a breath, settle back and enjoy your wine. Just relax.'

And I did. Which shocked the hell out of me. *Who knew I was this docile!*

I remembered I'd had this exact same thought as we'd gone to dinner. And that shocked me all over again!

I was almost asleep when I heard Dominic's deep voice close to me. 'C'mon, Snow. You use the bathroom first.' I opened my eyes to see his hand out in front of me, ready to help me up. 'I've put your bags in the bedroom. Grab what you need and I'll get you a towel.'

When I finished in the bathroom and walked out, wearing my most demure cotton pyjamas, I noticed that he'd created a bed on the lounge – sheets, a blanket and pillow. Assuming it was mine, I moved in that direction, only to be stopped by his voice. 'No, Snow. You sleep in the bedroom. The sheets are fresh. I'll sleep out here.'

'I'm not tossing you out of your bed,' I protested. 'I can sleep on the lounge. And, anyway, you're bigger than I am. You won't be comfortable on the lounge.'

'Snow, don't argue. I don't like it.' Well, that popped my eyes open! 'I bought this lounge because it was perfect for a Sunday afternoon snooze. It won't hurt me to sleep on it for a night or two. Now, go to bed. I'll see you in the morning.' He strode into the bathroom, clothing in his hand, and shut the door.

Conversation closed!

Hrrhhmmph!

I stomped into the bedroom and, pulling back the covers, I flung myself down onto the mattress, before dragging the bedlinen over me.

I tried to sleep. I really did. But I was wide awake.

I could hear him ... in the shower. Well, it was the water splashing and gurgling down the drain that I could hear. But I knew he was in there. Naked. Probably lathering up with that sandalwood-scented soap. Suds sliding down his body. I could picture him lifting his face up to the warm spray of the water as it burst from the showerhead. And that same water sliding down his back. Over his butt.

Did he *really* not want to have sex with me?

He hadn't exactly said that ...

But we *worked* together. And he was my *competition*.

This weekend was a truce, of sorts, though... And he'd been nice to me. Undemanding. I supposed we *could*. If we both agreed that it was only this weekend ...

I heard the water stop in the shower. And silence. Followed by the sound of the vanity tap running... And the door opening. And the click as it was shut.

Then there was darkness, as the strip of light under the bedroom door was extinguished.

And silence.

Did I dare?

What if he didn't want to? If he'd wanted to, he would have said – surely! He wasn't the sort of man not to do what he wanted...

W-e-l-l-l, I didn't say that! His words flashed through my mind again, accompanied by that evil grin. And the number of times he'd directed that hot, intense stare at me. And how often he got in my face, being an obnoxious pain.

I supposed that, if I made things awkward by propositioning him, I could always go home on the train in the morning. And ... would it make *that* much difference at work if he knocked me back?

Dammit, Daphne. Either fish or cut bait!

Chapter Eight

'Snow?'

I guessed that he'd heard the door open. Either the door or my stumbling around in the dark.

'What's up? Is something wrong?'

'No,' I answered. 'I just thought … that …' I didn't know how to phrase it, exactly.

'No, Daphne.' His tone was firm, brooking no argument.

'Don't you want me?' I argued, ignoring his unspoken command.

'Don't play coy, Snow. You're a grown woman. A highly intelligent, capable woman. And you would know – *should* know – that no grown man in his right mind would not want you.' He paused. 'But it's been a long day – an emotional one for you – and you don't know what you're playing with. You'll regret it tomorrow.'

'No, I won't!' My mind was still absorbing the "highly intelligent, capable" bits, though. I was thrilled. The third compliment today … and from Dominic, of all people! 'And what do you mean I don't know what I'm playing with?'

'Sit down, Snow.'

And I did, perching on the edge of the coffee table, facing him as he sat on the lounge.

'Daphne,' he paused, looking up at the ceiling as though for inspiration. I realised that he was choosing his words; that he didn't want to offend me. Maybe I'd read all the signals wrongly. He really wasn't interested in me...

I swallowed hard, feeling a little nauseous.

'Daphne,' he began again, dropping his head to look directly at me. I looked away, embarrassed, but he reached out and gently tugged my chin so that I couldn't avoid his gaze. 'Sex with me is probably not like anything you've had before. And I don't know that it's something you'd want.'

'What do you mean?' *Is he into kink?*

'I like to be in control, Snow. And I'm not talking about being on top.'

'Oh!' The penny was dropping. 'Are you – like a – dominant?'

He was still. And silent.

'Are you like – Dominant Dominic?' I joked, laughing at the ridiculousness of the name.

He looked away to the side and then, after drawing a deep breath, his gaze returned to mine. 'Not quite, but in the bedroom, I'm in control. And I'll admit, I've never put those two words together like that,' he added, grimacing.

'So-o-o,' I tried to remember everything from the erotic romance novels I'd read, 'are you into the whole sex-slave thing? With "sirs" and "masters" and all of that? And women kneeling on the floor giving you oral? And spanking? Is that what you're into?' I trailed off, not sure if I was appalled or … excited?

'Not exactly, but sort of,' was his response, his hands palming his face and swiping up and down. 'Listen, Daph. You don't want to go there, okay?'

Did I? Did I want to go there? What would it be like? I was sure, just as he'd said, that it would be different.

And I wanted to know what it was like…

'Yeah, Dominic, I do,' I said, leaning forwards and reaching for his hands. 'I do.'

He stilled, his eyes unwavering on mine. And then – it was as though a furnace had been ignited inside him, his gaze grew so hot. Scorching! And the hands that I held in mine clenched.

'Are you sure? Have you thought about this, Daphne?' Not a muscle moved. I'm not sure either of us breathed.

'Yes, I'm sure. I want this, Dominic.'

I thought that he'd pounce: that the tension that had built would be broken – shattered – with a sudden move. That he'd tug me to him. Or mindlessly kiss me. Or … something…

But nothing. Not so much as a twitch.

And then he exhaled, the release of air moving him – ever so slightly – towards me, his eyelids lowering. He drew a long, slow breath and rocked closer to me, almost as though he were breathing me in. His hands twisted in my grip, and I felt the gentle squeeze of his fingers on mine.

Again, I thought he was going to kiss me – but he didn't.

Instead, he rose and pulled me up, one hand still in mine, and led me back to the bedroom.

'Dom,' I started, as he switched on the bedside lamp, but he turned to face me, raising a finger in front of my face.

'Don't speak.'

'Wh-wh-at?' I stammered.

'Don't talk, Daphne. You're not to speak.' He was serious. I could tell by the unyielding expression on his face and the firm tone of his voice. 'Do you understand?'

'I – I...' I nodded.

'Good girl,' he said, a slight smile softening his mouth.

Good girl? Really? While my mind was still trying to comprehend this, he sat on the side of the bed and, with me standing between his spread legs, he coaxed me to sit – perch, really – on his left thigh. And, before I could process any of this, his hands gently framed my face, turning it towards him as he drew my mouth to his.

A barely-there touch of his lips. Gentle. Soft. Not at all what I expected from a "dominant". Another tender kiss – lips on lips – a little firmer this time. And then the slight pressure of his thumbs along the side of my mouth, below my cheeks, coaxing it to open. The touch of his tongue on mine – just a slow caress.

It was all so slow… and delicate… Tantalisingly – teasingly – slow and deliberate.

I instinctively stretched upwards, towards his mouth, my spine elongating. A shiver rippled down my neck and my shoulders shook – a tremble that I'm sure he felt. He tasted of mint toothpaste, with the faintest shadow of bourbon. He smelled of sandalwood soap and some sort of woodsy aftershave. My hands were on his shoulders – a light touch. I needed the balance – my world was tilting – but I didn't want to ruin the fragility of this moment. The magic of our first kiss. The sheer eroticism of his seduction. And his mouth was so soft… His touch so gentle…

Until he growled – a low rumble from deep in his chest – and it was like a switch was flicked. He didn't pounce, push me down and have his wicked way! But his kiss – it became hungrier – more intense. It was as though he was *eating* my mouth, his tongue swiping through mine, exploring along my teeth, and the soft flesh of my inner cheeks, and the sensitive roof. His hands – the strong press of his fingers on my scalp as he tilted my head, this way and that – searched for the perfect angle, as his lips lapped at mine. His breathing deepened – his lengthy exhalations vibrating through his chest in grumbly groans. My fingers dug into his sturdy shoulders, clenching and releasing in the same heavy rhythm pulsing through me, as I hung on, desperately trying not to topple from his lap.

And I was on fire!

A lightening flash of pure hot *want* surged through me, leaving a wake of tremors washing over my skin. I was *melting* from the inside, out. The throbbing from the heated flesh between my legs was almost agonising in its intensity.

I wanted him! I wanted Dominic! *Right now!*

My fingers knotting the fabric of his shirt, I twisted my body, smashing my chest against his, desperately trying to get closer to him. To absorb him through my skin. I may have thrashed a little – I was so out of control. All I knew was that I *needed* him!

And then he was firmly pushing me away. Startled, my eyes flew open and I saw Dominic, his eyes closed, his face impassive, as he drew a deep breath. When my fingers grabbed at him, attempting to tug him nearer, he clasped both of my hands in his.

'What?' I spluttered, trying to wrestle my hands free.

'Shhh,' he hushed me, stroking the backs of my hands, still in his clasp. 'Shhh. Just give me a minute.'

'I don't understand,' I stammered. 'What's wrong?'

'Nothing, Snow.' His mouth twisted. 'I just need to slow us down.'

'Why?' I asked, totally confused. 'Don't you want...' I trailed off, uncertainly. *Did I do something wrong? Was I too ...?*

I struggled to rise, pulling my hands from his, dropping my feet to the floor. I felt jittery – frantic! 'Let me go,' I said, pushing at him, as he placed his hands on either side of my waist, guiding me back to sit on his thigh.

'Snow.' I didn't look at him. I *couldn't* look at him.

'Look at me, Snow.' I kept my head down. I felt his fingers under my chin, a light pressure, lifting my face. 'Look. At. Me. Daphne!' There was no mistaking the command in his voice, a command that I, surprisingly, obeyed. 'It's not what you think.' His eyes focused on mine. 'We just needed to slow down. *I* needed to slow down. Get back in control.'

'Oh!' The light came on in my mind. *It's not about me! It's about his need for control!* And this was quickly followed by the delighted: *He was losing control ... over me!* My eyes widened. I felt my cheeks stretch into a huge beaming smile. A giggle escaped. Really? A twenty-six-year-old woman – *giggling!*

A pained expression crossed Dominic's face. 'No need to look *quite* so gleeful,' he said, drolly.

I couldn't help it: he looked *so* put out, I reached around and hugged him. As tightly as I could. *Dominic Northcott was losing his cool ... over me!* The refrain kept bubbling in my mind. Who knew! I giggled some more.

And that must have been his tipping point because the next thing I knew, I was flat on my back, his body hovering over mine, and – yes. The look in his eyes was all dark wickedness.

I lifted to meet his mouth as it descended: the kiss was as flammable as the one before. Raising his head, he gazed down at me, studying my face. And then, leaning on his forearm, he grazed the backs of his fingers along the centre fastening of my pyjama top, from my neck to my belly, creating little sparks as he went. My nipples hardened into tight buds, and my whole body almost undulated with the sensations he aroused. I opened my eyes to see him watching me, his eyes hot and intense, almost black with desire.

His focus was on his hands, as he slid the buttons on my pyjamas through their holes, brushing the fabric aside and revealing my flushed skin as he went. Feeling self-conscious, I glanced towards the lamp, opening my mouth to speak, when he slanted his head, his eyes narrowed in warning.

'The lamp stays on, Snow,' he murmured, his fingers continuing with their task. 'It's my pleasure to see you.' I gulped. 'You are so beautiful.' His words were like a caress – a silky, seductive caress.

He slid his fingers down the length of me in one long stroke, passing the waistband of my pyjama bottoms and pressing gently – delicately – on the juncture at the top of my thighs. Again, my body rose, as though on a wave, as he touched me. That humming moan I heard? It was coming from me. The pressure of his hand between my legs increased as, watching me the entire time, he slowly leant down, his free hand cupping my breast, and sucked my nipple into his mouth.

'Oooh,' I moaned, the sound drawn from deep in the centre of me. He pointed his tongue, flicking it back and forth, back and forth, across my nipple, before he, once again, sucked the sensitised bud – *hard*! My body tensed and straightened, my legs squeezing his hand, as he twisted and rolled it along the heated core of me, the increase in pressure almost unbearably good.

I needed to touch him! My arms felt heavy, floppily spread out beside me on the bed, but I felt agitated. I *had* to touch him! Just as I lifted them, though, he stopped me, his hands coming up to take both of mine, placing them next to my head, my elbows bent.

'Don't move, Snow. Stay just like that.' Although he spoke softly, there was still that thread of command.

'But – '

'Daphne.' It was a warning, as he tilted his head sideways again. 'Do as you're told.'

I felt my eyes widen. Was it with amazement? Or excitement? Did I really *like* this? This being bossed around. *Me?*

Well, obviously I did. I didn't move a muscle.

Not when he kissed my mouth – gently, but deliberately; not when his tongue crossed over the flesh of my bottom lip and drew a line down to my chin, pausing momentarily to flick the tender crease just below the bone a couple of times.

Not when he continued down the length of my neck, as I stretched it out for his mouth to access more easily.

And *definitely* not when he trailed his tongue from the notch between my collarbones all the way down between my breasts to my navel, swirling around and around its rim, before plunging into its indentation.

And – my control almost slipping, my body twitching – not when he slipped the elastic of my pyjama bottoms over my hipbones, tugging them down my legs and off my body.

It was an effort – an enormous strain – to stay still and silent as, with a final flick at my belly-button, his tongue burnt a path to the heated pulsing centre of me. Kneeling before me, his hands raising my limp legs and spreading them more, he watched me as he lowered his mouth and, in one long languid motion, licked and tasted the very core of me.

I shuddered.

It was so intense.

And so was the next long, slow slide of his tongue.

My hands were trembling beside me, my fingers curled. *So-o g-o-o-o-d!*

I groaned again.

Rising above me, he pushed me up the bed, my head almost at the pillows. Easing back to kneel between my thighs, he raised my calves and rested them on his shoulders. And then, a wicked glint in his eyes as they held mine, he lowered his head again. His mouth open, he breathed on me. I'd never felt anything so erotic in my life. His tongue slithered along my throbbing cleft; his unshaved cheek sensitising the tender flesh of my inner thighs.

He slid his hands along the quilt and captured mine, holding them down next to my shoulders. I writhed as he kissed, and licked, and sucked me, his tongue and lips tasting and devouring me, until I tensed – my spine arching – my belly taut, and I cried out as I came, in a kaleidoscope of vivid sensation.

I was still catching my breath, my eyelids without enough strength to remain open, when I heard the sound of ripping foil, followed by the warmth of his body as he settled it over me, most of his weight braced on his forearms. I gave him a dopey smile. I felt totally ruined, and half-closed eyes and a relaxed smile was the most I could manage.

He grinned lazily, his eyes half-lidded, his head gently nodding in satisfaction. He scrutinised my face, gazing at my chaotic hair, my glazed eyes, my softly-parted lips. He leaned down and kissed me, his mouth gentle on mine. It wasn't a hungry kiss, but there was a quiet passion to it.

'You are so beautiful, Daphne,' he said. And, in that moment, I believed him. I would have believed anything. He was so gorgeous! And male. And powerful. And, yes, he was dominant.

'Are you ready?' he whispered, his breath brushing my ear.

I nodded – a tiny movement, but enough for him. As I raised my legs, rolling my hips upwards, I felt the warmth of him, seeking my opening and – gently at first, but with steadily increasing pressure – he entered me. All the way. I felt the stretch, as he filled me. And the entire time, his eyes were focused on my face, watching me, studying me. Looking for …?

'I'm going to fuck you now, Snow,' he said, his words shocking, his voice like dark chocolate – rich and decadent. 'And you're going to watch me while I do so. Keep your eyes open, Snow. And then … you're going to come again. Twice,' he promised.

I swallowed. I believed him.

And he started to move, long slow slides, in and out, whilst his face hovered above mine, his breath mingling with mine, his woodsy scent surrounding me, his warmth heating me, and his eyes dark with desire.

For me…

I was right to trust him. Right to believe him. Because I did come. Twice more. And, as hard as it was to maintain my focus, I gazed into his eyes both times.

Chapter Nine

It was Dominic, lifting the covers and sliding back into the bed, that disturbed me. It was strange – waking up next to someone. The few times I'd had sex, I'd always risen and returned home – slept in my own bed. I'd felt safer, that way. I shifted, glancing over my shoulder towards him.

'Water?' he asked, holding out a bottle and snapping open the lid. I nodded, accepting the drink, and sipping appreciatively.

Sitting up and holding the sheet against my chest, I looked around for my pyjama top. I spotted it, draped over a navy wing-chair in the corner of the room near the window. Feeling self-conscious, I glanced back at Dominic, hoping that his attention was elsewhere so I could scamper over to the chair without his seeing me. No such luck! And I could tell that he knew my thoughts by the smirk on his face.

'Go on, Snow. Nothing I haven't already explored,' he teased.

'You're no gentleman!' I blurted.

His face stilled. 'Yes. I am, Snow.' There was a pause, both of us motionless. I knew I'd pushed a button, but I wasn't sure what. 'The bathroom,' he prompted, tipping his head in that direction.

'I'm sorry,' I said, when I returned and slid between the sheets.

'S'alright, Snow,' was his response, as he tugged me against him, spooning me from behind. I felt enveloped by his warm skin, my head resting on his left biceps, his right arm curved around my waist, his fingers fondling the underside of my breast. I could hear him breathing, a deep rhythmic sound, like steady waves surging and ebbing along the beach. He gently rubbed the bristles on his jaw along the delicate nape of my neck and I shivered. I felt the tip of his tongue outlining shapes on the line of my shoulder and I moaned. He shifted his hand, cupping my breast and squeezing gently, his fingers softly pinching the tip. I groaned.

'You good?' he murmured, and it took me a moment to realise what he was asking.

'I could go again,' I said.

'Coming, not going,' he chuckled, a dirty vibration in my ear. His fingers smoothed a lazy trail down my belly, and around, and back up to caress my breasts, the teasing touch causing goosebumps on my skin, arousing me, before gliding down my side – along the indentation of my waist and the rise of my hips, before feathering along my thigh and veering towards the warmth of my sex. I held my breath as his fingers slid through my slick folds, and I arched backwards, silently guiding his hand to where I needed his touch most.

I could feel him, behind me, hard and thick, pressed against my bottom. And the sudden cool air as he leant away from me, the sound of a drawer opening and foil tearing. I twisted, turning towards him, but he settled me in a slightly higher position, his arm no longer under my head; instead wrapped around my chest; his hand raising my upper leg to rest on one of his, as he guided himself towards me. I arched my back again, pushing back against him, as he eased into my body.

I sighed. So nice.

'Is this what they call "morning glory"?' I whispered.

'Hmm,' he murmured in my ear, his chin resting on the side of my face.

'I've never done this before, Dom,' I confessed. 'I mean, not like this.'

'Shhh. Don't talk, Snow. Just … *feel* it. *Enjoy* it. *So* good.' His words were accompanied by gentle thrusts – tiny rocking movements of his hips. 'You feel … *so good*. And you smell … hmmm.'

And it was. *So good. I could become addicted to this,* I thought, before I didn't think anything at all.

'We'll go to Diggies for breakfast.' Dominic placed a cup of freshly-brewed coffee in front of me, gesturing towards the milk and sugar on the table. 'That okay with you?'

'Sure,' I said, fastening the strap on my tan leather sandals. 'I've got no idea. This is your town, Dom, not mine.' He smiled and I wasn't sure why. Maybe he was just happy. I knew that I was feeling fabulous, right at that moment. I was dressed in olive walking shorts and a lemon short-sleeved button-up shirt, and I'd plaited my hair in a neat braid – my usual weekend attire. I knew, though, that I looked pretty good. When I'd peered in the mirror to apply a touch of mascara, my flushed cheeks had highlighted the green in my eyes, and I remembered Dominic commenting on them – that the green of my eyes was his favourite colour. I wondered if he'd notice them today.

'Diggies is on North Beach. It's the best place for breakfast. The food's good, but the view's great.' I watched him tidying the kitchen, his movements economical. No wasted energy. When I didn't respond, he glanced back at me.

'You okay, Snow?'

I nodded. 'Just watching you.'

He radiated self-satisfaction. Who knew that Dominic Northcott, the overbearing, *dominating* Dominic, would get such a kick out of me just watching him!

'Down, boy!' I teased, sipping the hot brew and turning towards the long windows. Dominic had drawn back the curtains, letting in natural light, and the view of the garden was stunning. There was a mini-orchard out there, with at least four citrus trees, flowering magnolias and frangipanis, a huge gum tree – its age evident from its sturdy trunk – and rose bushes interspersed with lilacs. Jasmine, climbing the fence on the far side, was a mass of white blossoms. I wondered why I hadn't noticed its fragrance the previous evening.

And then an older, dark-haired woman passed by the windows, heading towards Dominic's door.

'Nicky?' she called. 'I know you're up. The curtains are open. May I come in?'

As Dominic approached the door, he glanced back at me. 'My mother,' was all he said, but I was too busy mouthing *Nicky?* in amazement. Big, bad, domineering Dominic was called "Nicky" at home. It was almost too much!

'The lawn needs mowing, Nicky,' she said, as she entered the room. 'Will you have time to do it today?'

And then she saw me and stopped short! Her eyes rounded – a delighted combination of excitement and curiosity. 'Nicky, who is *this*?'

Get out of this one, Nicky, I thought. *Go on. Tell your mother we spent the night having wickedly hot sex.* I could feel my face split in a cheeky grin, and I wriggled my eyebrows, enjoying the moment.

But the situation didn't seem to bother him at all. Water off a duck's back.

'Mum, this is Daphne White. I work with her.' He turned his eyes to me, in that way of his where he hardly moves his head. 'My mother, Lily

Northcott.' Flicking his eyes back to her, he continued, 'Mum, would you like to go out for dinner tonight?'

'Oh, but I bought roast pork. And apple sauce. And all the veggies.' She turned towards me, her hands forming the universal gesture of "What other option is there?"

'You eat pork, Snow?' Dom asked me.

If Lily had been animated before, she was positively charged now. 'Snow?' Her voice rose in pitch, her eyes wide, a beaming grin across her face. 'Nicky, this is *Snow?*' She turned back towards me. 'I'm very pleased to meet you, dear.'

I wasn't entirely sure what was going on, but I knew my manners. 'The feeling's mutual, Mrs Northcott. And I do like roast pork. Dinner sounds wonderful. Can I help you with it?' *Yes, my mother raised me right!* When I glanced back at Dominic, he had that I'm-so-pleased-with-myself grin on his face.

'Oh, no. No. I can manage dinner. You two need to go and have fun today. Nicky, you *are* taking Daphne out, aren't you?'

'We're heading down to Diggies for breakfast and then I'll take Snow for a tour around and about. I'll do the lawn when we get back this afternoon. Do you need me to get anything while we're out?'

'No. No. I'll take care of it.' Her eyes twinkled. 'And *you* take care of Snow,' she instructed Dominic, her expression positively ecstatic.

Chapter Ten

'So, talk to me, Snow. Tell me anything you want.' Dominic leant back in his chair and sipped his green juice. After driving to Diggies, we'd placed our orders and I'd been admiring the view of the ocean – small waves washing against the sparkling golden sand.

'You're joking, aren't you?' I almost spluttered my pineapple juice. '*Don't talk, Snow. Be quiet, Snow. Shhhh, Snow.* And now? You want me to talk to you and tell you anything I like?'

His mouth curved up in one of his slow smiles. 'There's a time and a place, Snow. I'll listen to anything you have to say – more than willing to hear you talk and listen to your voice – *out of the bedroom*. But, Snow,' he paused, his gaze on mine, 'when two people are skin-to-skin, their breaths intermingling, each other's scents drowning out any other fragrance, and their blood pulsing ...' His voice was low and dark – hypnotic. '*That's* real communication – and words are superfluous. They're just a distraction. So, no, Snow. When I'm deep inside you, surrounded by you, feeling the clench of your flesh on mine ... I don't want to *talk*.' He paused, his gaze intensely holding mine, his deep voice still resonating in my head, my attention totally captured by him. I swallowed, hard. 'So, talk to me now, Snow. Tell me anything you want.'

'Your mother seems to think we're an item!' I blurted, without thinking. 'You're going to have to tell her we're not. That this is just a one-off. A weekend *thing!*'

'Hmmm. Sure, Snow.' He drank more juice. 'Whatever you say.'

It was in his tone, as though he was dismissing my comments.

'I'm serious, Dom. You need to tell her.'

He nodded, smiling. 'Sure, Snow. Tell me about your sisters.'

'What do you want to know?' I accepted his change of subject.

'I don't know. Anything.' He leant back, relaxed, his legs out in front of him, nudging up against mine.

So, I told him about Jane and Ginny, and the fight on Thursday night, and how both Charli and Ginny hated the idea of university, and then, when our breakfast arrived, I continued to tell him about Jane's work as a geography teacher, and Ginny not really having a proper job, but wanting to work in hospitality, and Charli studying animal husbandry at uni, even though she didn't want to be there.

When we were driving to Kiama to see the Blowhole and then scout the locations where they filmed the ABC drama series, *Winter,* I told him about how Ginny does the cooking and that, even though the cat supposedly belongs to Charli, it's really everyone's cat. It's just a big sook that scavenges food and attention from whomever is around.

'So, how does it work?' I asked, peering over the protective fencing to see the gap in the rocks.

'There's a big cavern, like a chamber, under the rock. Waves wash in, trapping air in the cavern and when the pressure builds up enough, the water is forced back out and upwards through the blowhole, spurting water into the air. It can go very high and, if the wind's blowing right, it drenches the tourists standing around watching it.'

'So, why isn't it doing it now?' I complained.

'Conditions aren't right. When they are, this is excellent. It's the big blowhole, so it's an impressive display. C'mon, we'll go 'round to the Little Blowhole. Not quite as impressive, but it's more reliable. You'll most likely get to see it blow.'

'Can I get some happy snaps of the sign first? And the lighthouse?'

'Sure. Give me your phone and go stand in front of the sign.' Dominic played photographer whilst I contorted myself into lots of silly poses and, just before we left, he whipped out his phone and, with his right arm extended and his left pulling me close, he took a shot of both of us, standing in front of the lighthouse.

It didn't take long to drive around to the Little Blowhole, and then we spent the next half-hour cruising around Kiama, spotting filming locations. 'Motel 617 is there,' Dom said, pointing out the iconic blue and white accommodation.

'Where to next?'

'Thought we'd go through Jamberoo and up the mountain. We can have lunch at Robertson. Best pies, anywhere. Hands down!' I laughed at his enthusiasm.

'I thought you had another sister!' Dom asked, as he directed his ute inland, away from the coast. 'Don't you have four? You've only mentioned three.'

'Louisa!'

'What about her? You didn't talk about her.'

'Well, Louisa's Louisa. She's ... um ... there's not a great deal to say.'

'Really?' Scepticism flavoured his voice.

'Okay, then. Louisa's the second youngest – she's twenty-two. She's got a degree in Australian Literature. She works in a bookstore. Yes, I know – the most over-educated shop assistant in the country. She's quiet. Doesn't talk much. You two would get along famously,' I joked.

'I bet she's observant.'

'Well, I guess she is, but what makes you say that?'

'All of you women in one house. Four big personalities. She's probably overlooked a lot of the time. But, if she's not talking non-stop, she's most likely taking it all in. My guess: she's got all your numbers. If I wanted to know something about any one of you, I'd go to Louisa.'

'How can you say that? With just what I've said? You don't even know her!' I argued.

'Snow, most of the time it's not what people say that tells you the most, it's what people *don't* say. And, until pushed, you *didn't* say a lot about Louisa. Yep, Lou's my girl.'

'*Really?*' I said, tartly, narrowing my eyes at him.

'Jealous, Snow?' He smirked at me.

I rolled my eyes. 'Don't kid yourself!'

'She's not my type, anyway. Too much like me. But ... I reckon she'd be interesting. She's likely to have secrets that none of you know. My guess is that the rest of you maybe don't know much about her, at all.'

'You make us sound horrible,' I grumbled. 'It's not like that. We don't ignore her, or exclude her, or anything. In fact,' I said, brightening, 'she's our go-to. When we need someone to talk to, Louisa's our go-to. It's because – '

' – she's always there and she listens,' Dom interrupted me, finishing my sentence.

'Well, yeah,' I frowned. 'And she gives good advice. Not that I need her advice much,' I added.

'No, of course not.' He smiled, and I knew he was mocking me.

'Dom...' I warned.

'Yes, sweetheart?' he responded and the shock of his use of the endearment effectively shut me up. That, and the way he smiled at me: as though he *liked* me and yet was indulging me. Either way, it was a devastating smile. A gorgeous smile. It reminded me of how … incredible … he'd been the night before. And this morning. I stilled, stopping to study his mouth, and the smile faded, his lips parting slightly, as though he was breathing through his mouth.

'Tell me about the house,' he ordered roughly, breaking the building tension between us. 'What's the story there?'

And, as he drove up the winding mountain road to the Southern Highlands plateau, I described the house, with its five bedrooms and three bathrooms. And the roof with the leak. And the gutters and downpipes that needed replacing. And the tiles that were coming away from the wall in the downstairs bathroom. And the tree out the back that the neighbour was complaining shed too many leaves onto her property and that I should be getting cut down, but I *liked* that tree. And the paling fence that was almost toppling over.

We pulled into the carpark at the Robertson Pie Shop and found just enough space to park Dom's ute. 'We'll take a large cherry pie home for dessert tonight. Mum loves cherry pie. Other than that, I can recommend any of them,' he said, as he led me into the store.

'What are you having?' I asked.

'Chicken, leek and camembert.'

'Hmmm. A plain steak for me,' I decided.

'There's the whole array of pies and you pick plain steak!'

'Yes. That's how you judge a pie shop, Dom. Didn't you know that? If they stuff up the plain pie, forget all the rest.' He smiled again, looking happy with himself. I'd just argued with him and he was happy! Go figure!

Chapter Eleven

On the way back to the house, Dom veered off the main road so that he could show me Port Kembla, with its Inner and Outer Harbours providing berths for ships transporting cars, grain, coal, general cargo and bulk liquids. He drove us up to the Hill 60 Lookout and we argued about whether ships were in transit or stationary, as we counted the huge vessels waiting off the coast for their turn to berth. Then we cruised past the steelworks with their huge chimneys, clouds of steam rising into the clear blue sky.

'We'll go for a swim after I mow the lawn,' Dom stated, as he pulled into the driveway. 'Did you want to rest for a bit?'

'Nah,' I grinned. 'I'm going to go talk with your mother. Get the inside info.'

'Knock yourself out!' Again, he didn't seem in the least perturbed. His smile was pure indulgence. Strange man!

'Come in, come in!' Dominic's mother invited excitedly when I tapped on the back door. 'Did you have a good day, Daphne? I can call you Daphne, can't I? And you must call me Lily.' She beamed.

'Thank you, Lily. And Daphne is fine. Yes, we did have a good day.'

'Did Nick take you up Saddleback Mountain?'

'Er… no. I don't think he mentioned that.'

'No matter. You can do it another weekend. Sit. I'll make us a cup of tea. Or would you like coffee?'

'Tea's fine.' I paused, not sure exactly how to say this. 'You know, Lily. Dom and I aren't a *thing*… This is just one weekend. I was upset about something and he very kindly brought me down here with him. But – we work together. We're not dating or anything.'

I was expecting – I don't know what! But what I got was the same indulgent smile that Dominic gave me when I'd said the same thing to him. It was starting to irritate me a little. I wasn't used to people disregarding what I said. 'I mean it, Lily.'

'I'm sure you do, Daphne.' Her tone was gentle, almost consoling. 'But I don't think you understand. Nick's been talking about "Snow" for a while, now. My boy doesn't say much, so when he does…' She shrugged, her eyes twinkling.

'Lily, Dom and I aren't all that friendly at work. Don't misinterpret my being here. He needles me non-stop and I resent a lot of what he gets away with.'

'Hmmm. Pulling on your pigtails, is he?'

'Lily, I always wear my hair in a French knot in the office. This is only for non-work time,' I gestured to, what was for me, the casual braid that kept my long brown hair neat and tidy. 'There's no 'pigtails' to pull.'

'I meant metaphorically, Daphne,' she said, soothingly. 'You know what I'm getting at.' She smiled, and then busied herself with the kettle and tea things. 'So, tell me about your family. What do your parents do?'

I took a breath. I hated these questions. Six years had not made them any easier to answer. 'My parents died – in a plane crash – a long time ago. There's just me and my four sisters.'

Again, she surprised me. The usual response from people was a gush of 'sorrys' and 'you poor dears' and awkward hugs of sympathy. Not from Lily.

As the words left my mouth, she stilled, her hands ceasing their activity. And then her head reared back – just a little – as though she was absorbing shock. This was followed by a narrowing of her eyes, a calculated look on her face and a tiny nodding of her head, as though something was making sense to her.

'I take it that you look after your sisters. That you manage the household,' she said finally – and shrewdly. 'You must have been young when you adopted that responsibility.' This was actually quite interesting, watching her process the effects of my parents' death. 'Are you the oldest?'

'Not quite. My sister, Jane, is older than I am. We're all about two years apart in age, give or take a few months.'

'That sounds … organised.' She grinned, cheekily. 'Mother or father?'

'Father,' I answered the unspoken question. 'He was an executive director in Transport. Very precise. Train logistics.'

'Oh, my husband worked for Transport! He was a train driver – thirty-five years. He wanted Nicky to drive trains, too, but … not Nick's cup of tea, I'm afraid.' Lifting her teacup, she glanced at it, before darting me a mischievous grin. 'So to speak… But, when Bill died – suddenly, it was – a heart attack. When Bill died, our boy started applying for Transport jobs and left Health. He didn't say anything, but … I think he feels closer to his father, that way.' Her head fell, her eyes on her lap, and I waited quietly, not wanting to interrupt the moment. 'I miss Bill, but he would be so proud of Nick. Where he's working and how he looks after me.'

We both paused, listening to the rhythmic sound of the mower, as it was guided, systematically, around the front lawn, in ever-decreasing squares.

'He doesn't really need to come down as often as he does, you know,' Lily said, breaking our contemplation. 'He thinks he needs to take care of me; that I'll be lonely without him. But I'm not. I have lots of friends around here. We've lived here for thirty-two years. Before Nicky was born. That's why I didn't take him up on his offer to move to Sydney. He comes down, though, every other weekend – and I make sure I've always got some task for him to do, so he feels that I need him. And,' she paused, her eyes bright and that cheeky grin returning, 'I always make sure I've got some little treat waiting for him. What he doesn't know – and don't you tell him, Daphne,' with a warning tilt of her head, 'is that I leave him my experiments.' She laughed, delightedly.

'Your experiments?'

'Yes. I've filled my time by taking courses. *Perfecting Pies* and *Pavs & Lammoes.* I really enjoyed that one. My lamingtons have always been – well, okay. Now, I get that sponge so light and fluffy, and I've mastered dipping them in the chocolate without it soaking into the cake too much, and the coconut doesn't get all clumpy anymore!' She sat back, her hands clapped together in satisfaction, a proud grin on her face. 'And my latest course is –'

'*Creating Cupcakes!*' I offered.

'Close, Daph. *Cupcake Creations!* I figured that I had to reward him for coming home so often. And he doesn't know that he's my guinea pig, so don't you tell him!'

I laughed. I really liked Lily. The love and affection she had for Dominic was equalled only by her pride in him. And … I will admit … I felt a warm softness for him, so caring and considerate of his mother. And he let her call him "Nicky". I chuckled, trying to imagine anyone at the office getting away with that! I was tempted to have a go myself!

'You're really not lonely? Have you thought about – you know – dating again? You're only young.'

'Why would I want to, dear? I loved Bill. He was a good man and a fabulous father. An excellent role-model for Dominic, in case you're wondering!' She tipped her head, her eyebrows raised suggestively, a twinkle in her eyes. 'But ... I'm *enjoying* being a single woman. It's not as bad as people make out. I get to eat whatever I want, on any day I want. The wash pile is much smaller. And – *no sport!* I don't have to listen to the football or the races or the cricket – always on in the background. The television is *all* mine. And Nicky organised Netflix and Prime and Stan. I've taken a trip down memory lane, re-watching all those wonderful Robert Redford films, and Paul Newman – and Steve McQueen. Humphrey Bogart! He's to die for!' She was almost swooning with her hands clutched to her chest and a dreamy smile on her face. I laughed. 'Nope. I don't need another man. I had the best for over thirty years. I'm good.'

'Have you told her all my secrets?' We'd been so caught up in our conversation, we hadn't heard Dominic come in.

'Not *all*, Nicky. I'm saving some for next time,' Lily teased, as she rose, retrieving a glass from the cupboard and filling it with cold water from the fridge. 'Thank you for mowing the lawn, dear. I hate lawn-mowing.' She hugged him, planting a soft kiss on his cheek.

And he blushed!

Ooohh! This was fun! He didn't get bothered by anything else that was said, done or suggested, but he blushed when his mother kissed his cheek! *Oh, Dominic!*

'You ready for a swim?' was all he said.

'Sure. Are we going to the beach?'

'A rock pool. Mum, do you want to come?'

'No, dear. I'll finish preparing dinner. Don't be long? You going to Coaldale?'

'Just at Wollongong. Do Coaldale tomorrow. Grab your stuff, Snow. Let's go.'

Chapter Twelve

Yes, I ogled him. How could I not?

He strode across the rocks to the edge of the pool, all taut, tanned skin – he didn't get *that* at work! – stretching over his back and chest. When he extended his arms up into the air, ready to dive into the crystal, clear water, the muscles rippled over his shoulder blades, tightening down the length of his spine. *Ohhh!* His thighs bunched with power as he projected himself through the air and cleanly entered the water, hardly making a splash. Nice dive!

My dive was far less elegant, and I leisurely followed him down the pool, as his formidable swimming stroke ate up the laps, his strong arms rhythmically rising above the water, his legs creating a wake behind him. I took the time to fully appreciate the male specimen in front of me. Dominic in a suit, crisp shirt and sharp tie was gorgeous; in Speedos, all his toned flesh revealed before me, he was totally devastating.

The water was amazing, and I loved the whole idea of swimming pools carved out of the coastal rock platforms. It was like swimming in the ocean, without the fear of sharks! After I'd finished ten laps – and he'd done a gazillion – he pulled himself through the water towards me, his breast strokes lazy and languid.

Dominic was not one to grin like a loon; most of the time, his features were carefully controlled, as though he didn't want to give away his thoughts or feelings too freely. But, with the beaming smile on his face, this was as blissful as I'd ever see him. His grey eyes – almost silver against the water – sparkled with pure exhilaration; his mouth was relaxed and extended into a huge smile. He radiated happiness!

And when he reached me, he kept right on coming and kissed me: a warm, open-mouthed kiss that told me, without words, that he was pleased that I was here. I felt joy bubbling from my belly, springing up within me, and exploding in my mind. I twined my arms and legs around him, his hands on my butt, as he stood in the pool, grounding us both, and our tongues tangled, our mouths devouring each other's. I could have stayed there all afternoon, my body pressed tightly against the solid warmth of his, enjoying the exquisite pleasure of kissing Dominic. But …

'Do you two *mind*?' The harshness of the female voice grated on our moment. 'My *children* are over there! This is a *public* pool!'

We broke apart, our gazes locked, our breathing heavy and synchronised. His smile was gone. In its place was an intense stare, mesmerising. Long seconds passed when neither of us moved. The moment felt significant and neither one of us wanted to break the connection between us. And then – gently, but deliberately – Dominic pushed my hips away from his, regret lacing his features. My arms loosened and slid away from his body, as my feet found purchase on the pool floor.

A wry smile on his face, Dominic said, 'I'll just swim another couple of laps. Cool my jets!'

'You do that,' I grinned. 'I'll just float here and watch you.' I'd felt, pressed up against my belly, the jet that he needed to cool and the knowledge that I had that effect on him made me feel powerful.

The pork was cooked flawlessly, and the crackling was that perfect combination of crunchy saltiness. Lily had gone all out, with roasted potatoes, pumpkin, onion and carrots, and healthy serves of broccoli and baby spinach on the side. Her gravy was delicious, and she'd made the apple sauce from scratch – chunks of fresh fruit beautifully stewed.

Lily and I chatted throughout the meal: Dominic seemed to be content to sit back and watch us. I felt his gaze on me often, the energy sizzling between us – left over from our pool interlude – and it excited me to know that, soon enough, we'd be alone again and …

'I love your garden,' I complimented Lily, when she was slicing the cherry pie that had been warming in the oven. 'Especially the roses and lilacs.'

'Do you garden, dear?'

'Well…' I ducked my head self-consciously. 'I'm the gardener at home. I love bulbs. I've got daffodils, hyacinths, lilies, jonquils, ranunculus … You

name it! When spring hits and the weather warms, the burst of colour …
My favourite flowers, though, are pansies,' I admitted.

'Pansies! Really?'

'I know. They're such a humble flower, but so resilient. Vibrant colours.
In winter, you'd think they'd die with the cold, but … no! There they are!
All happy blossoms!' I petered off, a bit embarrassed by how much I'd
gushed, rambling on and on. Dominic was watching me, in that still way
he had, his eyes narrowed in his scrutiny. 'Well, aren't you going to talk at
all?' I demanded, defensively.

'Oh, Nicky won't say much. Never does. He's like his father, that way.
The two of them could sit for hours, watching sport or working on some
project – hardly a word between them.' Lily laughed. 'I was not sure how
they communicated, but they seemed to know what each other was
thinking. It was fine with me. No one to compete with for talking time!'
She laughed again. 'Did your father garden, Daphne?'

'No. It was Mum. She looked after the house and the garden. Dad was
always busy at work, although we had great holidays. When he was home,
he liked to relax and read the paper. He said it gave his brain a rest.' I
paused. 'I didn't really get into the garden until after they died.'

'How was your swim, dear?' Lily directed the question to Dominic, and
the conversation moved on. Dessert was eaten, the dishes were done, and
the kitchen tidied. 'Why don't you two go for a walk?' Lily suggested. 'I'm
just going to watch another episode of my show.'

Dominic's left eyebrow rose in question and I shrugged.

'Will I need a jacket?'

'Nope. You'll be fine. We won't walk for long.' He winked, and I felt
myself flush all over. I threw Dom a do-you-have-to? look, tilting my head
towards his mother. He answered me with an enormous grin, his eyes
sparking with naughtiness. 'C'mon, Snow. The sooner we're gone, the
sooner we'll be back. And I have a present for you.' Again, with the wide
eyes and waggling brows.

'Have fun, you two,' called Lily from the loungeroom, voices from the
television already sounding through the house.

The sex was hot! And steamy! Scorching, really.

There was no other way to describe it. It was like Dominic had
processed everything he'd learnt about my responses the night and
morning before, and he was upping the ante. He teased and tormented, my

hands captured in his larger one, his solid body holding me still. His lips and tongue and hands and fingers … He found places on my body I didn't know were sensitive: along the side of my waist, just inside my hipbone, the inside of my elbow. The tip of his tongue explored them all, and I wriggled and writhed as he worked his slow torture. By the time he journeyed to the hot, wet territory between my thighs, I felt like I was one huge highly-strung nerve, a flick or two away from combusting. And that was all it took … his growl – deep, dark and resonant – vibrated along my nerve-endings and I exploded, a sharp cry accompanying the powerful orgasm.

Before I had a chance to recover, he slid a well-defined arm around me and flipped my limp body over, spreading my jelly legs wider and lifting my hips at the same time. I felt him behind me, his weight on one forearm, as he sought entry to my body, his free hand guiding him in. I pushed back, twisting my head to gaze at him as he filled me. His eyes were glazed, his mouth slack, his breathing heavy, as he stared back at me, before ducking his head to slide his whisker-roughened jaw along my shoulders and the nape of my neck, causing me to shiver. His soft lips caressed the newly-sensitise skin and I groaned, a tremor passing through me. He leant forward, twisting slightly, so that our mouths met and we kissed, his hands holding mine and his body pressing down on me. I met him, thrust for thrust, our hips pumping in an ever-increasing rhythm, until our groans unravelled to mere grunts, with his release right on the heels of mine.

We were both gasping for air as he rolled us onto our sides, our bodies still joined, my cheek flush against his. I rested against one of his muscled biceps, as his other arm circled my waist, his hand cupping the underside of my breast. Bringing my hands up to my chest, I hugged him to me, my forearm squeezing his arm, and he rotated the arm that was beneath my head so that I was secure in his embrace. My eyelids heavy, my breathing slowing, I fell asleep.

Chapter Thirteen

We walked the length of the Sea Cliff Bridge the next morning, before stopping for a drink at the Scarborough Hotel and admiring the incredible view of the coastal landscape. Dom had waffled on about cantilevers and girders – it all went over my head. What I knew was that the bridge was an amazing structure, jutting out as it did over the ocean, big swooping curves and fabulous views of the bushland stretching up the escarpment. It did amuse me, though, to see Dom animated like that! All over a bridge! Go figure!

We went for a swim in another rock pool and then returned to the house to share sandwiches with Lily, prior to our departure for the railway station. I watched Dom carefully house his huge Ford Ranger ute in the garage next to his mother's Mazda and wondered why he left it here. He must have read the question on my face because, as soon as the garage door was secured, he linked his arm in mine and murmured, 'Don't need a car in the city. Not where we live, Snow. Our public transport system is perfect, most of the time.'

'That's not what a lot of people have to say about it, Dom,' I argued, noticing that he grinned at me again – that contented cat-got-the-cream smile.

'People only notice when it's *not* working, Snow. Ninety-nine percent of the time, they just go about their business, not noticing that everything's going great. Human nature.' He tugged on my hand. 'I notice when it's working. Like with us.' He leaned in and kissed me.

'Dom,' I started, pulling away, 'there is no *us*. This is just one weekend.'

'Sure, Daphne. Whatever you say.' He was being too agreeable. 'Let's say goodbye to Mum.'

We walked to the side of the house, where Lily was waiting, a posy of lilacs in her hand. 'You take care, Daphne,' she said, hugging me and holding out the flowers. 'I'll see you next time.' I scowled at Dominic's smirk, visible over his mother's shoulder as he enveloped her in his arms.

'Look after yourself, Nicky,' Lily whispered, softly, only just audible to me. 'You know I worry about you.'

'Yes, Mum,' was his only reply, as he gave her an extra squeeze. 'You, too.'

This big, strong man – thirty years old – gentle with his mother. My heart warmed and I felt myself melting.

I peered out the window of the train, keen to catch one more glimpse of the Sea Cliff Bridge from a different perspective – the railway line as it snaked its way up the Illawarra, through the Royal National Park and on to Sydney. Dom had guided me to seats on the appropriate side of the train so that I could view the coast and the bridge as we returned to the city, and my hand was still in his. I'd given it a gentle tug a while before, just to see if he'd let it loose, but he'd merely tightened his clasp. I hadn't pushed it because – well, there was something *nice* about having my hand held like that. Reassuring. Grounding.

And as he'd given me a perfect weekend, it was the least I could do for him: let him hold my hand, if that's what he wanted.

'I wonder what my mother will make for me next weekend,' he murmured, his mouth brushing my hair.

'What do you mean?' I asked, curious.

'This week, it was cupcakes. The time before, lamingtons.' He paused, his thumb gently caressing the side of my hand. 'I guess I'll just have to wait and see what new cooking course she's doing.'

I sat up, startled. 'What?'

'Mum does courses. She starts a new one every other week. And she tries out her efforts on me.' He tugged on my hand, drawing me back into the seat.

'You know?' I spluttered.

'Of course, I know. I take care of the household expenses. I pay the credit card. And she's my mother,' he finished, as though that explained everything.

'Then why haven't you said anything to her? She thinks it's her secret.'

'Exactly. If she wanted me to know, she'd tell me. She thinks she has her secret and that's okay with me. Sit back, Snow. Relax,' he said, tugging on my hand again.

'Don't you think you're being patronising? Condescending?'

'No, Snow, I don't. My mother wants her independence. She doesn't want to answer to anyone, anymore. Not that my father restricted her, but she's enjoying her freedom. And I'm happy for her to have it. She does what she wants to do, and I make sure that she can. That she's safe. That she can do whatever she wants. She's my mother. Now, sit back down and relax.' His tone brooked no argument and, strangely, I did as he said.

'So, you knew from the credit card bills?' I asked softly, thinking about how I knew what each member of my family spent on household items.

'Hmm. That, and there was a pattern. I noticed the pattern,' his voice hummed in my hair again.

'Observant of you,' I jibed.

'I pay attention, Snow. That's what you do with people you care about,' he murmured.

'We're not an item,' I stated, changing tack.

'Sure, we are, Snow,' he drawled, confidently. 'We have been for a while. It's just that, this weekend, we finally connected physically.' He paused. 'You don't really think I needed to visit your section that often, do you? I have my own department to run.'

'Well, I did think that you were interfering when you didn't need to... So, what are you telling me?' I asked, cautiously.

'C'mon, Snow. You know why I was there.'

My mind was trying to catch up. Was he really saying that he only came into my section to see *me*?

'But you don't know anything about me,' I argued.

'Really?' he smirked, his left eyebrow almost at his hairline. 'Like what don't I know?' he challenged.

'Why was I upset on Friday? You don't know that!'

'If I tell you – correctly – then you have to agree that we're – to use your expression – "an *item*".'

'Agreed.'

'Okay, here goes. Firstly, you take care of your sisters financially, managing all your monies, including the university fees. Secondly, you manage the house and the yard, including the maintenance and the garden. Thirdly, you're one of the two oldest, so responsibility for the younger three falls on you.' I stared at him, stunned. I'm not sure if my mouth was hanging open. 'So, immediately prior to Friday, you were worried about Charli's university fees, the expense of fixing the leaky roof, the problems with the neighbour and how much it was going to cost to get an arborist for the tree, and ... should I go on?' I nodded, still in shock. 'But what tipped you over the edge on Friday, what made cool, self-contained Daphne lose control, was both the fight amongst your sisters and the escalating incidence of the tension in the house, *and* the fact that Ginny hadn't come home and let you know she was safe. That had kept you up all night long, depriving you of sleep, and causing you to become more emotional than you normally are.' He sat back, so confident I wanted to slap him one. 'Am I right?'

I said nothing.

'So, Snow. I take it you agree now that we're "an item"?'

I turned and stared unseeingly out the train window. I felt like I was going to cry. I felt broken, sort of. Exposed. I hadn't realised how – *obvious* – I was. Did everyone at work see me like this? Was I so transparent?

I'd always prided myself on my self-control. That's what I did. I controlled myself and everything around me. Sure, Jane thought that she was the one in control, but she just made decisions. I was the one who carried them out. I kept them all afloat. Ginny went to the supermarket and didn't give one thought to how much she spent on groceries. Lou bought books as though she was starting her own library, without a care as to their cost. Charli entered any sporting event she wanted – swimming comps, half-marathons, tennis tournaments – and never *once* asked me if we could afford it. Yes, there'd only been a small amount still to be paid on the mortgage when our parents died, and the insurance covered it, as it did our living and university expenses for the first few years. And yes, all of us, except Charli, paid for our own personal items. But everything else fell to me to sort out. And I made it happen! And I juggled all the balls, keeping them in the air. I controlled it all.

Until Friday...

When I lost control.

And that's when it occurred to me that Dominic had exerted control over me – all weekend!

I wanted to cry. I cringed into the train seat, feeling little and defenceless. Weakened. Strong, independent Daphne – vulnerable!

I pulled my hand from his, wrapping my arms around myself, holding me together. *You must not cry in front of him!*

'Snow?' I saw, in the reflection of the window, Dominic shift in his seat, turning towards me. 'Daphne, are you alright?' His voice was soft, gentle, laced with concern. 'Daphne?'

Pull yourself together, Daphne! Now is not the time to fall apart. Fake it until you can get home!

I straightened my spine, pushing my back into the seat, pulling my shoulders back. I inhaled, long and deep, and then, with a smile on my face, I turned towards Dominic, whose face was etched with worry.

'I'm fine, Dominic,' I stated calmly, looking him squarely in the eyes. 'Yes, I agree that we've been an item.'

He nodded, but his eyes were wary, his expression guarded.

'But when we get off the train, we'll be done,' I finished firmly, holding myself together, my posture stiff.

He reached for me, his hand extended, but when I flinched, he withdrew it. He studied me, his face thoughtful, whilst I stared back at him, desperately trying to keep my expression blank.

After a long moment, he drew a deep breath and reclined in his seat. I could see he was trying to appear relaxed, but the tightness around his mouth betrayed him. When he made no other comment and no further moves towards me, I eased back against the cushioned support of my seat and gripped the armrests to keep my hands from trembling. As quietly as I could, I also took a deep breath ... and spent the next thirty minutes focused on my breathing, concentrating on keeping calm – and not crying.

'You know, Snow,' Dominic's voice – deep and soft – surprised me, interrupting the silence between us and my meditation, 'you're the one calling the shots, here. You've always been the one calling the shots.' He paused, and I snuck a quick glance at him. He was staring straight ahead and didn't return my look. 'I know I've upset you and I'm sorry.'

I didn't say anything. I wasn't sure what to say.

'I didn't mean to take away from you any say in this relationship,' he continued, his voice low. 'I know it's important to you that you feel in control. My guess is that, when your parents died, it was the way you coped. Managing things. Taking care of the details. While everyone else was probably falling apart, you were reading insurance policies, or bank statements, or telephone bills.' He paused again, inhaling deeply. 'I know, Snow, because that's what I did when Dad died. I took care of things. I still do.' He sighed. 'And I don't want to take that away from you. I know it made me feel better – to think that my father would be proud of how I'd stepped up. And I'm sure that your father would be proud of you, too. Of how you take care of your family.'

My eyes were burning and my vision blurring as tears welled. I could taste their saltiness as I swallowed, repeatedly, to stop them from falling.

'But I want you to know this, Daphne.' He turned to face me. 'You don't have to be in control with me. When we're together, you can let down your guard. I'll take care of you. Of us. You can let me do that, and you'll be safe. With me. I'll look after you.'

He shifted his body to face forward, taking his gaze away from me.

'I like to be in control, Snow, but it's not about dominating you. Not really. It's like a gift … your trust… I know you're strong and capable – an independent, intelligent woman. I know that. So, when you give up control, it's special. It's a gift. But it's your choice. And, if you wanted, you *can* choose differently. And, Daphne,' he said, turning his head to capture my attention, 'I'll still want you, no matter. Whether we're together physically or not, we *are* an item, you and me. There's still that connection between us.'

I sat there, silent – except for the snuffly sound of my sniffles as my eyes continued to fill. Dominic didn't say anything else for the remainder of our journey into Central Station and I kept my attention on the passing scenery.

When the train pulled into the station, Dominic reached down and lifted both his duffle and my overnight bag onto his shoulder, his hand coming down to steady me as I stood.

'We'll get an Uber,' he said, as we stepped onto the platform.

'It's okay. I can get a train,' I responded, looking down at the ground.

'No, Snow. We'll get an Uber and I'll see you home. You're upset and I want to make sure you get home safely.'

Well, that was settled. At least from Dominic's perspective. And … I didn't mind. I was tired, both from the weekend's activities and my rising emotions. I wasn't up to navigating the trains and the long walk home from Wollstonecraft Station.

Chapter Fourteen

'Are you going to be alright, Snow?' Dominic asked, as he opened the car door and handed me my bag.

'I'll be fine, Dominic,' I said, a little testily. I just wanted a bath now. I was worn out and feeling a bit bereft. It had been a long couple of days. I hoped I wouldn't bump into anyone before I could get to my room.

'Daph,' he started, pausing as if searching for the right words, 'I'm not going anywhere. I won't bother you at the office anymore, but … I'm not going anywhere. If you change your mind, I'm here for you.' He leant forward and I knew he was going to kiss me. I could have moved away – it wasn't as though he was holding me. But I didn't. I wanted his kiss. I wanted one last kiss … to savour … to remember him by.

It was soft. And gentle. A tender kiss. A goodbye kiss, although there was a tinge of hope embedded in it. I returned it, my tongue just dipping into his mouth to taste him – one last time.

And then I pulled away – before it became too hard to leave him. And the last thing I wanted was for any of my sisters to be peering through the blinds and seeing what was, for me, a very personal moment.

'Take care, Snow,' Dom said, as he slid back into the Uber. 'You know where to find me.'

He glanced at me through the window, his eyes sad, his expression downcast. *Really? Did I have that much power over him? Was I that important to him?*

As the car pulled away, I turned towards the house and there, standing in the doorway, was Louisa. Quiet and observant. What had Dom said about her? That she knew more about us than we did about her? I wondered if she did have the secrets Dom had been so sure she had.

Louisa said nothing as she moved aside, giving me room to enter the house.

'I'll be in my room if anyone wants me,' was all I said in greeting. Louisa nodded.

But my bath was not to be ... At least, not yet.

I could hear Ginny's voice in the hallway, just outside my room.

'Where have you been? You give *me* grief over being irresponsible, but where the hell have you been all weekend?' Was she talking to me? 'And who is *that?*' No, obviously not.

'Ginny, language, please.' Jane's voice, quietly chiding.

'Is Jane home?' I called, exiting my bedroom. 'So, you *are* still alive,' I chastised her, irritation in my voice. It felt good to redirect my emotional torment onto someone else.

'C'mon, Daph! I sent you texts.'

And then I noticed the man standing behind Jane. His attention was on Charli, as she charged into the hallway.

'Well, this is crowded. Can we please go into the living room? We don't all need to be in the hall like this,' Jane said, gesturing towards all of us, Louisa included as she sidled into the hallway. We filed, one by one, into the dining room, and I noticed that Ginny was entranced by the man with Jane. I just stood back, the last to follow.

'You look familiar,' Ginny probed. 'Who are you?' Yes, Ginny could be quite direct, even rude, sometimes.

'He's Jackson McGee,' I said.

'Who?' Charli asked, her face scrunched in confusion.

'Jackson McGee,' Louisa repeated. 'From *Earth Today* magazine.'

Jane looked stunned, as did Jackson. What! Did she think that in the – what was it? – *twelve years* she'd been idolising him, that I hadn't – once – seen his photo in all those magazines she hoarded?

And, just as Dom had said, Louisa knew, too. He'd been right – *again*. How irritating!

'Like ... are you famous? Or something?' I could tell that Charli was still trying to catch up.

'Handsome catch, I will say that for you!' declared Ginny, deliberately eyeing him off and making sure that Jane noticed her doing it. 'What are you doing with our Jane?' she asked, provocatively.

Yep, Ginny was still mad at Jane. She hadn't cooled down over the weekend.

I watched Jack narrow his eyes at Ginny, his face tilting slightly to the side.

'Not really your business, Ginny – is it?' he drawled, his hand reaching for Jane's.

Well, this was certainly interesting! I go away for one measly weekend and … this!

I saw Louisa's eyes follow Jackson's gesture, slide to Jane's overstuffed beach bag – still in Jackson's other hand – and then to the gaudy T-shirt Jane was wearing. A subtle smile flitted across her face before it disappeared again.

Yes, Dom, you're right! Again! Lou doesn't miss a thing.

'So, who is he, again? Is he a star or something?' Charli brought attention back to her.

'He's a photojournalist for *Earth Today*. The geography magazine that Jane reads,' I said. 'He travels the world, taking pictures and writing stories about different places. And people.'

'So-o-o,' Ginny drew the word out, 'how did you two get together? Has Jane been sending you fan mail?' She was being a bitch.

'Ginny!' Jane snapped, her face red with embarrassment.

I saw Jackson squeeze her hand and gently tugged her towards him. 'I'm going to go, Janey.'

'Ooooh, *Janey!*' Ginny mimicked.

'See me out,' Jackson said quietly, his voice calm.

'So, should we be asking for his autograph? Or will he take our picture?' Charli interrupted the moment.

'No, Charli. Let's go into the kitchen,' I said, and Jane flashed me a quick look of gratitude. 'Ginny, you come, too. Louisa?' I glanced around, but Louisa had already returned to her room.

'C'mon,' Jane said to Jackson. 'Let's go on the porch.'

Jane went straight to her bedroom when she came in from outside. I knew she was crying in there. I argued with myself about whether to disturb her or allow her some privacy. Finally, I decided that, as the next eldest, I should make sure she was okay. I knocked gently on the door and, when I nudged it open, I saw that I'd startled her.

'Are you alright, Jane?'

'I don't know.'

'Is he going away?' I probed.

'He asked me to go with him,' Jane confessed, her shoulders hunched, her voice small.

'Where?' I asked gently, trying not to be too pushy.

'He's heading up to Queensland.'

'So, you could go.' This was Louisa. I hadn't heard her enter the room. She was standing near the door; her usual place. 'You could try it out. It's only Queensland,' she persisted. 'If you don't like it – if you're not happy – you can come home.'

'But what about all of you?' Jane asked, looking at us. 'I'm needed here.'

'No, you're not,' Ginny said, pushing through the doorway. 'You *were* needed here, Jane, when we were all young, but you're not anymore.'

'Virginia!' I roared, turning on her. 'Stop it!'

'I'm not being a bitch, Daph. I'm not!' Ginny yelled back. 'Don't you see? Don't any of you see?' She swung around, glaring at all of us in turn, and I saw that Charli was just inside the room, hovering near the doorway. 'Jane did what she had to do when Mum and Dad died. She did. She dropped everything! She didn't want to be a *teacher!*' Ginny sneered. 'She was studying geography and geology, sure! But the only time she even *mentioned* a Diploma in Education was *after* Mum and Dad died. She's only in a school because she felt *responsible* for all of us.' She paused, gulping in air after her outburst.

'She's right,' Louisa murmured from her place near the wall. 'Ginny's right about Jane becoming a teacher so she could support us. And she's right about it being time for Jane to go do her own thing. We're all adults now.'

'Is she?' I asked Jane. 'Did you never really want to teach?'

'Daph, it's not that simple.'

'Why isn't it?' Charli demanded. 'Why can't you do what you want? Why can't all of us?'

'Because we have to be careful,' Jane yelled, shocking us.

'Why?' Charli screamed back at me.

'Because Mum and Dad died,' Louisa said, softly. 'Because Jane's afraid. Aren't you, Jane? You're afraid of what can happen.'

'Is that it?' I queried. 'Are you scared for us?'

'Of course, she is,' answered Ginny. 'That's why she's been so damned *controlling* all of these years. She's had all of us wrapped in cotton wool. Well, not cotton wool, exactly. *University degrees.*' The derision was apparent. 'Her way of keeping us all safe.'

'It wasn't just that,' Jane argued. 'I knew that Mum especially, but Dad, as well, would want all of us to be educated and financially independent. *That's* why I've been pushing you and Charli to get degrees.'

And then, right in front of our eyes, she deflated. Like all her strength just dissolved. It was sad to see.

'I want to be alone. Leave me alone.'

'Jane,' Charli began, but I stopped her.

'Let's go. Ginny, did you make dinner?' I asked, before turning back to Jane. 'I'll bring you a plate, Jane.'

'Don't. I'm not hungry.'

Finally. My bath. The soothing warmth of the rose-scented water swirled around me as my body floated, swaying from side to side. I eased my head back, my hair drifting on the surface, the liquid just lapping at the edge of my closed eyes. I was relieved that sounds were muffled by the water, so I didn't need to hear Jane crying in the next room, or the chatter from Ginny and Charli.

I thought about what Dom would say – my neglecting to consider Louisa again.

I wondered what Dom was doing. Was he sipping on a Jack Daniels Special Select? Chatting to his mother on the phone, both of them hiding their secrets? Was he naked in the bathroom, like me? And if he was, was he thinking about me? Was he remembering how it felt when our sated bodies slid against each other, slippery with sweat?

Was he thinking about how often he held my hand? Strange, but that was the most poignant memory of the weekend. So intimate, holding someone else's hand in yours. Palm to palm. Fingers intertwined. Little pulse-points beating in rhythm.

A slamming door brought me out of my reverie.

Was Jane really going to let Jackson ride off – well, *sail* off – into the wide blue yonder without her? I didn't know what had occurred over the weekend, but there'd been some potent energy there! And she had been ogling him forever. Since she was sixteen years old.

He'd asked her to go with him. And she'd said no.

Because of us – and some sense of responsibility to us. But we were all grown women now, not the children and young adults of six years ago. She shouldn't be sacrificing her happiness in some misguided idea that we still needed her the way we had, back then. That was crazy! Insanity!

And she'd always regret it. I knew that. I'd always known that there was a strong call to adventure for Jane. She was like Mum that way. When we'd all been little, Jane was the one playing the pirate, or the astronaut, or the explorer. And I knew that she'd stifled that when Mum and Dad died. Snuffed it out of her, as though it were forbidden.

Was I doing the same thing? I didn't have to sail away to Queensland to be with Dominic... All I had to do was say "yes". And it would be good to have someone to share my burdens with; someone I trusted. And I did trust Dom. I knew he was one of the good guys. I only had to look at how he treated and respected his mother to know that.

The water was getting cold, chilling me. I could have topped it up with more hot water, but ...

I towelled off and unpacked my bag, the white pyjamas – not worn after the first night – on top of my other clothes and toiletries. I raised the top and sniffed it, just a hint of Dom's aftershave scenting the fabric. I inhaled again, my eyes closed, my mind floating ... until there was a soft knock at the door.

Louisa's head curved around the door, her hand extended, a teacup balancing on a saucer.

'Who is he?' she asked, not wasting words. *Like someone else I know?*

'Dominic,' I said, taking her peace offering. Or was the tea a bribe?

'Northcott?' she responded. *Oh, yes, Dominic. She does know everything!*

'How do you know that?' I asked.

'You mention him a lot. Usually with "damned" in front of his name.' She smiled. 'Are you going to continue seeing him? I mean, aside from work?'

'I told him no. That it was just this weekend.' I wondered where she'd go with this.

'Hmmm,' was her only response, other than crossing the room to sit on the end of my bed. 'Do you think that Jane should go with Jackson?' she asked, changing the subject. Or so I thought...

'Yes.'

'Why?' Louisa was fidgeting with her dress, pleating the material and making a fan from the coloured fabric.

'Because it's time,' I said, shortly. 'It's time for her to get on with her life – the one she wanted – and for us to get on with ours. I'm tired of the constant squabbles around here – damned tired. I'm sick of hearing Charli complain about going to university and Ginny complain about what Jane wants her to do. It's high time that we all did what we wanted!' I finished, not realising how loud and angry I'd become.

'Hmmm,' Louisa continued playing with her dress. 'So, I take it that this Dominic is a lousy lay?'

My mouth gaped open in shock! Oh. My. God! *Dominic, you are so right!* Who knew that Louisa could come out with *that!*

'Louisa! Not that it's any of your business, but no! He's not a *lousy lay*, as you so delicately put it.'

'Then he's a prick!' she persisted. Was there no end to her surprises?

'No, not a *prick*, either!'

'Halitosis?' she continued, slyly.

'His oral hygiene is fine,' I huffed.

'So, Daphne, when you think that Jane should follow her dreams, why are you denying yours?' Louisa was no longer playing games. Who knew she could be so direct!

'Who said that Dominic had anything to do with my dreams?' I countered.

'Because he's the only person from the office that you ever mention. And,' she paused, studying her fingernails – who knew she was so dramatic! 'Because you say his name almost every night. *Damned Dominic this* and *Damned Dominic that!* He's had your attention for the last six months. And, Daphne, you haven't even so much as mentioned any other man's name. So, yes. I think he has something to do with your dreams. Now, the question is: are you going to fish or cut bait?'

The very words I'd said to myself when I'd been debating having sex with him!

'Well, by the expression on your face, I think my work here is done!' With one final flick of her fingernails, she left the room.

It was seven-thirty. I knew he'd be here: he was always early. As I walked through his section, I could smell the strong aroma of expensive coffee. Yes, he was here.

I'd moved quietly, stealthily, not wanting to attract the attention of anyone else on the floor, but obviously not silently enough. Either that, or he'd felt the electricity that we generated whenever we got close to each other.

He looked up, his head slowing as it rose, his gaze directed to me. In true Dominic-style, his face was still, his expression scarcely changing. But there was a softening around his eyes, the grey heating to a molten steel.

''Morning, Snow,' he greeted me.

''Morning, Dom,' I replied, as a slow smile spread across his face.

WHITE REBEL

SISTERS WHITE SERIES: Book Three

SUNNY MACKENZIE

2020

Chapter One

I loved this time of year.

Everything growing. Green, everywhere you looked. Well, with the exception of the rainbow of coloured flowers that Daphne had planted. Honestly, you'd think she'd never heard of a "kitchen garden". What I wouldn't give for her to cave in and set aside at least one measly section of the yard for herbs and vegetables, especially salad greens and tomatoes. And blueberries. Fresh blueberries. Wouldn't that be fabulous!

But no... Daphne liked her flowers. And I didn't *hate* them necessarily. Some that she had growing there – the pansies and violas, in particular – I sometimes included in summer salads. And I suppose I could do something with the hibiscus and those beautiful rich-red dahlias. But the majority – they were just there because Mum loved them, and Daphne kept them. A bit sentimental of her, considering that most of the time, she's so ... officious! All business-like, even those clothes she wears. Did she have anything that didn't look like she could wear it to work? So buttoned-down. Even her hair was always tied back, in a bun or a braid. And that askance look whenever I bought anything new for the kitchen! As though I wasted money! I loved Daphne, but – talk about a control-freak!

I plucked basil and oregano leaves from the potted plants on the wrought-iron table under the pergola. My only bit of the yard. Not much in the way of a herb garden, but better than nothing. Their fresh flavour would enhance the Mediterranean chicken and vegetables I'd planned for dinner. I washed them in the kitchen, before wandering back out to the patio, sipping on the homemade lemonade I'd fixed that morning, icy-cold now after it had been chilling in the fridge.

I enjoyed this time of day. Everyone was out: Jane, not yet home from the school where she taught Geography; Daphne, still hours off returning from her city office job; Louisa, at the bookstore, even though she'd knocked off long ago; and Charli, hanging out with her university friends, and most likely avoiding study as much as she could. The house was quiet and peaceful. The yeasty aroma of baking bread was familiar and comforting. It reminded me of when Mum was alive. We'd arrive home from school and there'd be buttered freshly baked bread on the table, waiting for our choice of Vegemite, honey or jam. I leant down and stroked Clancy's white fur as he wound himself between the chair's legs and mine, purring his contentment before stretching out on the sun-warmed pavers. I had to get moving soon and get dinner on, but it was so pleasant, just sitting and savouring the silence. We-l-l, if you ignored the hum of the cicadas.

'No! And I'm sick of talking about this, Jane. No more!' I slammed the skillet down onto the table with force. 'You do what you want! I'll do what I want! Stop interfering in my life!'

So much for my peaceful afternoon!

Jane was at me again. Her favourite topic: when was I going to get formal qualifications?

I watched the chicken and vegetables slip across the skillet, almost sliding off one side. Greek-style cooking was her favourite. Honestly! Did she not appreciate *anything* I did? Every night of the week, there was a meal on the table. Every morning, they all raided the fridge, gathering leftovers for their lunches, not taking *any* time whatsoever to consider that all that food was there because of *me*. I was the one who did the shopping. I was the one who stored and prepared and cooked the food for breakfasts, lunches and dinners, safely securing leftovers for them to forage through when they fixed something for themselves.

And yet, all I heard, day after day, was "When are you going to do something meaningful with your life?" Or "When are you going to get educated?" Or "You need to get university qualifications, Virginia!"

'Be reasonable, Ginny,' Jane continued, in that placating way that she had that drove me crazy! 'You need to be responsible –'

I went from zero to one hundred in a flash and my temper exploded!

'Responsible! That's your middle name!' My voice rose with the anger raging through me. 'You're so busy being responsible, you've turned into the most boring person on Earth!'

I couldn't look at her anymore. I needed to burn off some of my fury.

Turning away, I grabbed the chef's knife and the bunch of fresh oregano that I'd left beside the wooden cutting board. 'Stop trying to control everyone else's life,' I muttered, attacking the poor herb with furious chops.

'She's right, Jane.' That was Charli. I didn't kid myself that she was coming to my defence: it was just that we had a common cause.

'Charli, don't...' Jane implored, and I almost felt sorry for her in that moment. But she'd started it! Served her right that she now had to fight on two fronts. 'This is between Ginny and me,' she almost groaned.

'Except it's not! I didn't want to go to university, either. But no... You were on my back until I caved in.' I heard the contempt in her voice. 'So, here I am... Off to uni every day, doing a course I'm not really interested in because Saint Jane, the boss of us all, decreed it.'

'Stop being so dramatic,' Jane countered, and I would have laughed if I hadn't been so angry. 'Someone's got to manage things.'

Oh, Jane! Are you really going there? I thought. Those were words guaranteed to spread the warfare. It was almost time to get the popcorn and watch the show!

'Well, actually... Seeing as you've raised it... *I'm* the one who manages everything, not you, Jane.' And so, with Daph's comment, it was almost a whole-family fight. Lou hadn't said anything; she hardly ever said anything. She just stood there, watching. She was like Switzerland. Neutral territory.

'Daph, I know you take care of the house and finances, but this is different. And you *must* agree with me that Virginia *should* get some formal education. She can't just loll around the house all day until all the restaurants and bars open again – if we *ever* get over COVID. I don't care if it's *hospitality*, but she could at least get some TAFE qualification, other than the mandatory service requirements. But instead – nothing. *Nothing.*'

I saw red! Everything in me was trying – desperately hard – to hang onto the temper that everyone said came with my fiery red hair. I could hardly *breathe*, so much effort was going into *not* exploding. I could feel the trembling in my hands – and arms. My jaw was clenched tight and I thought my teeth would crack.

Such *disdain* in her voice! And she called me *"Virginia"*, as though I were some naughty little girl! I *hated* being called "Virginia". *Who's afraid of Virginia Woolf?* was the taunting refrain from school, the horrid torment from the snippy little bullies in primary school. I *hated* the name "Virginia". And Jane knew it. She was being all I'm-the-responsible-adult-in-this-scenario on me. As though I were a child! And just because I didn't want to do what *she* wanted.

Whilst I was grappling with my emotions, Charli butted in: 'I'm sick of uni. I want to be a jillaroo! And you can't make me stay!'

It was just enough to tip me over the edge: 'And I'm *not* going to do what you want, just because you're the eldest,' I yelled at Jane. 'If I want to be a barmaid, that's what I'll be. If I don't want qualifications, then I don't have to get them. Plenty of places employed me before the pandemic. I'll get work again once all the restrictions are lifted.' I was so worked up, I was tempted to poke my tongue out at her. If she wanted to *treat* me like a child, I could bloody-well *act* like one! But – to my credit, considering how riled I was – I restrained myself.

'You know, not *everyone* gets to do what they want!' Jane shouted back 'I don't especially like dealing with teenagers every day!'

'Then bloody-well don't!' Charli shrieked, 'but don't keep holding it over our heads.'

Jane then tried to get Daphne to change sides. 'Daph,' she said, 'can you talk sense into them?' You could see Jane attempting telepathy, her look imploring Daphne to come to her aid.

'No, I don't think I will,' Daphne responded, and I almost fist-bumped the air. 'I think it's time that you stopped trying to control us all. I think you need to let Ginny and Charli make up their own minds about what they want to do.'

Jane looked stunned, turning to stare at each of us, one at a time. And we all stared right back at her. Well, except for Lou, who slinked off, most probably going to her room.

I could feel the animosity radiating from me – my fury still hot – as I glowered at Jane. I'd really had enough!

So, evidently, had Jane.

'I'm out of here!' she yelled. 'You can all take care of yourselves!'

She stormed out of the room and I stood, silent, staring at the skillet on the table. I wasn't sure what to do or think. But the heat of the fight went out of me and I felt my shoulders drop in defeat. I glanced around to see Charli, near the sink, gumming her rolled fist in her mouth like a toddler, her eyes wide, a scared look on her face. She looked confused, as though she didn't really understand what had just happened.

I looked toward Daphne, but I didn't want her to see the hurt that was bubbling up in me. I picked up the skillet, looked at it in a daze, and then put it down again. I felt wobbly on my feet, unbalanced, the adrenalin still surging in my body making me unstable. And restlessness vibrated through me.

'I'm outta here,' I growled, and strode out of the kitchen to grab my bag from my room, swearing as I went. I slammed my bedroom door – forcefully! The bang was so satisfying, I slammed the front door, too, as I stormed off towards the train station. There was no way I'd be driving home tonight!

How fast could I get to my favourite pub in The Rocks!

Chapter Two

''Nother one,' I called out, as the cute bartender approached where I'd set up camp – hours before – at the glossy timbered bar of my favourite hotel. I grinned happily when he placed a highball glass, its surface dewy with condensation, in front of me. There were three paper-thin slices of lime floating in the clear liquid, competing with chunky ice cubes for prime glass-top real estate. I giggled, pleased with my descriptive imagery. *I'm hardly drunk at all!* I decided. *Just a wee bit inebriated.* I chuckled to myself.

'Wha's this, Sean?' I asked.

'Steven,' he corrected me, winking. 'And it's from the gentleman at the end.' He tilted his head, gesturing towards the hot, hot! *ho-o-t!* man that I'd been ogling most of the night. My happy grin returned as I lifted the tall glass, saluting him, before sipping from its edge.

I spluttered…

What the…!

'What. is. this. Shane?' I spoke very clearly and precisely. *See! Not drunk! Yet.* 'Tas'es slike water.'

'It *is* water, Ginny,' he said.

'Knew I wassen drunk!' I proclaimed, punching the air. And then I frowned, confused. 'Why'd he buy me water?'

'Maybe he thought you needed it,' was the dry reply, before he moved to serve another customer.

'I'll get you a drink, darlin'.' I twisted my head – and my whole body wobbled with it – to see who'd said this. It was the sleazy, salesman-type from the table in the corner. I'd already ignored him twice when he'd tried chatting me up a couple of times earlier. 'What do you want?' he asked.

'You buyin'?' *May as well get a decent drink out of him,* I thought. I'd been drinking beer and tequila all night – yeah, not a good combination! – but I wasn't flushed with funds, so … A girl's gotta do what a girl's gotta do.

'Sure,' he schmoozed, winking suggestively.

'I want a Wet Pussy!' I proclaimed, loudly. Suddenly, the noise in the bar dropped. Or was that my imagination? There was a disquiet in my head, as though I'd done something wrong – a feeble alarm, trying to warn me of something.

'Oh, darlin', I'll get your Wet Pussy.' Mr Sleaze's tone dripped slime – and innuendo. I instantly knew I'd made a mistake. It was as though an 'Alert' button went off in my head. *"Danger! Will Robinson!"* my brain recited from an old TV show. I struggled to free myself from Mr Sleaze's hand that was pawing at my waist, pulling me towards him. Over-balancing on the stool, I looked towards the bartender for help, but he was mixing a drink at the other end of the bar.

'*And,*' he snickered in my ear, his breathing loud and heavy, 'I'll get your pussy wet.' I tried to pull away, as his lips skidded along my cheek, his tongue touching my skin and making me blanch.

'I told you I wouldn't be long,' a male voice sounded behind me, rich and mellifluous. *Mellifluous? Maybe I wasn't so drunk after all, if I could use words like that? Or think them, at least.* 'And I told you not to drink too much,' it chastised me. Who cared? I was grateful for the interruption, as Mr Sleaze's attention slid from me to the interloper.

'Who are you?' Mr Sleaze demanded belligerently.

'I'm Michael Oldfield,' my rescuer said. I turned to see the hot man – Mr Water-Buyer – from the end of the bar. Only he wasn't at the end now. He was right here, reaching for me, tugging me towards his tall, lean body. *Safety,* I thought. 'I'm Red's fiancé,' he stated. 'And you are?' His tone was derisive. *Derisive? Yep, here I was with the words again. I should get drunk more often. I could give Lou a run for her money with fancy words. Who knew?!*

'I was just buying this young lady a drink,' Mr Sleaze responded, ignoring Mr Water-Buyer's question. 'I was keeping her company.'

'Gee, thanks. I really appreciate that. Now, as you can see, it won't be necessary.' I watched him – Mr Water-Buyer, that is – shift slightly to the right, effectively blocking Mr Sleaze. *Nice move!* 'Drink your water, Red,' he quietly instructed me, sliding the glass closer on the bar.

'I wan' a real drin',' I whined, quickly forgetting the peril I'd just been in.

'Drink the water and I'll get you one,' he promised, mesmerising me with the beauty of his blue eyes. I drunkenly realised that I was staring when I felt one of his hands curling my fingers around the cold glass that he was holding.

'A Wet Pussy?' *Was I deliberately being provocative, now that I sensed the danger had passed?* 'I like Wet Pussies!'

'I'm sure you do, sweetheart, but the cocktail is all you're getting tonight.' He paused, signalling the bartender.

'He's buyin' me a proper drin', Sam,' I said, as soon as the waiter approached. 'A Wet Pussy! Bu' only one,' I bemoaned, crestfallen, 'so you be'er make it a goo' one!' I clapped my hands, excitedly, like a kindergartner given fairy floss.

'Make it a light one, Steve,' Mr Water-Buyer murmured beside me. 'We're probably breaking the law giving her any more alcohol, at all.'

'Ooh, you're no fun! But you *are* gorgeous! Look at that *hair*! It makes me want to run my *fingers* through it. So *black*! D'you dye it? I should dye mine. Anything would be be'er than these carro's growin' outta my head,' I grumbled. I knew that I was babbling, but I didn't care. I was patting the hard chest of the sexiest guy I'd seen in a long time. One who'd rescued me from the evil clutches of Mr Sleaze! *Life was good.* I sighed, and then giggled to myself.

'Ooh, yum!' I hummed, reaching for the beautifully coloured drink that Scott placed in front of me. But, just as my fingers touched it, Mr Water-Buyer pulled it out of my reach.

'Sip it slowly, Red. This is your last drink,' he said, his face all stern as his eyes caught mine. He waited, not giving me the shot glass, until I nodded at him. *Bugger!*

'I'll get you another water, Ginny,' Stuart said, as I exaggeratedly sipped the cocktail, the pink of the cranberry juice darker than I was used to, the peachy goodness of the schnapps eliciting a sigh, as I stared, round-eyed, up at Mr Water-Buyer.

'I lo-o-o-ve Wet Pussies,' I purred, in my own little happy place.

'Doesn't everyone,' was his droll response, which made me giggle. *Well, of course a man would say that!*

'Do you want me to call her a taxi?' Sebastian asked, as he placed a glistening glass of water near my hand.

'Nah, Steve. I'll see her home.'

'No! No! I don' wan' to go home. And you can' make me!'

'Red, it's time for you to go home,' the calm voice sounded near my ear. Quiet and controlled. With a faint touch of amusement?

'I'm no' goin' home. I'll go somewhere else.' There was *no way* that I was going home! No way that I was going where I *knew* they'd all judge me. *There's Ginny again, being irresponsible. There's Ginny, drunk. No wonder she likes hospitality!* I wasn't so gone that I didn't know how drunk I was! I'd be just asking for their condemnation.

'Is there someone I can ring? To come and get you?' That same calm voice, its depth resonating in my head.

'I'm no' goin' 'ome,' I slurred. 'I'm no'.' The smooth warm wood of the bar was comforting as I rested my head on it, my cheek squished into the ring of wetness left by the condensation on my glass. *A coaster would have been good,* the thought floated in my mind.

'Mick, I'll get her a taxi,' I heard. 'She's trouble.'

'Nah. Nah, 'm no',' I protested, woozily.

And then I started to cry.

Silent tears, seeping out of my eyes, sliding down my face, pooling on my arms.

I hiccupped.

And then slippery snot dribbled down my cheek to puddle with the tears.

I closed my eyes in drunken humiliation.

Chapter Three

I was hallucinating. I knew I was hallucinating because, when I managed to crack the seal of my eyelids, crunchy with salty mascara, all I could see was The Sydney Harbour Bridge.

Thinking a "reset" was in order, I closed my eyes and – *hold for ten seconds* – opened them again.

Yep!

There was The Sydney Harbour Bridge again!

Exactly where it'd been the last time I looked!

Right in front of me. Well, not quite *right in front*. But it was there. Through the window. Or the plate glass sliding doors. Either way, it was there. In my line of vision.

I thought it had to be real because – if I squinted really tightly – I could see teeny little cars and buses going across it. So, it wasn't a picture. Or a photo. Or a mural.

Nope, it was real!

So that put me somewhere near the Sydney Opera House...

On a lounge. Nice. Soft. Smelt good. The whole room smelt good.

Optimistically, I attempted to look around.

Clang! Thud! I moaned. The slight movement was enough to cause an elephant to stomp on my head. Oh, God! I closed my eyes again, hoping that would stop the pounding.

I eased my hand out from under the quilt covering me to gently touch my face, stroking my hair back, soothingly, from where it had stuck to my cheeks.

And realised that I was naked!

Well, not totally naked. I still had my underwear on – thank God!

But ... where was I? And where were my clothes?

And Oh My God – my head hurt!

And my mouth tasted like stale vomit.

Please, God, tell me I didn't vomit!

Silence followed my plea: I guess I had my answer.

I needed water. And paracetamol. And my clothes.

Where's my bag?

There it was. On the floor, just below where my face was hanging over the edge. I rummaged through it. Yes! Wallet was there! But – no phone. Where was my phone?

Please, God, tell me I didn't lose it at the bar!

'You're awake.' No, it wasn't God, but it was a heavenly voice. Okay, I didn't *think* it was God. 'Here's some water. And a couple of Panadol. Do you think you can swallow them? I've probably got some soluble aspirin if you can't.'

I turned to the sound of the voice, the pounding in my head ramping up a notch or two.

Yep. Still hallucinating. I blinked my eyes a couple of times, just to check.

Standing in front of me, his hand holding a glass of – oh, so enticing – water, was Mr Water-Buyer, my rescuer, from last night. Clutching the quilt to cover my breasts, I pushed myself into a sitting position, while my free hand nursed my poor head, thumping out the bass beat of The Rolling Stones' "Start Me Up".

I knew I was staring. I did. But I couldn't help it...

How could he look so *fresh*? First thing in the morning? His hair, brushed back from his forehead, all soft and totally finger-running. His business shirt, all white and crisp and open at the collar, showing his totally yummy, bronzed neck; a tie loosely hanging, as though he wasn't finished dressing ... or was avoiding, until the last minute, the restriction that a necktie symbolised. His shiny black shoes perfectly matching his suit pants, the weave of the fabric suggesting excellent quality.

And his gorgeous, crooked smile, as though he *knew* how much pain I was in; as though he totally empathised with how horrible my mouth tasted and how queasy my stomach was...

But *how* did I end up here? *Oh, Ginny. You really need to know when to stop drinking!*

Or, maybe not, I thought wickedly. I mean, after all, I *was* here!

Still hanging onto the quilt and my attempt at modesty, I reached out for the water and the pills.

'Thanks,' I whispered, hoarsely, my throat burning. 'I'm Ginny,' I added.

'I know,' was his dry reply. 'Steve told me.'

'Who's Steve?' I asked.

'The bar attendant at the hotel. You were chatting with him for most of the night,' he reminded me, his eyes twinkling. 'I'm Michael. I brought you home last night as I was concerned about your wellbeing.' He grimaced. 'Ginny, drink that water more slowly. Gulping it is probably not a good idea.'

'Where're my clothes? Did you take them off me?' The water was doing its trick: speech was coming more easily for me.

'Well, yeah. As I said, gulping water when I brought you home was not such a good idea. A little accident.' He flipped his hand forward from his mouth, unmistakably confirming that I had, indeed, lost the contents of my stomach some time during the night. 'Your clothes are being laundered.'

'Laundered? Are they in the washing machine?'

'Well, no. I sent them out. They shouldn't be too long. I can lend you a T-shirt, if you'd like.' At my nod, he suggested, 'You may want to take a shower first.'

Again, I nodded. I was feeling especially vulnerable, sitting mostly-naked on a stranger's couch, in a very expensive-looking apartment. Oh, who was I kidding! I could see the Sydney Harbour Bridge! This place would be worth millions of dollars! This was beyond "expensive".

For my own peace of mind, I needed to get clothed. I wasn't sure about the shower bit, but I did feel particularly grotty, so ... I'd risk being naked in the shower. Let's face it – I was on the couch. He obviously hadn't taken advantage of my drunken state. Or maybe that was the reason he hadn't taken advantage of me: nothing more horrible than a passed-out partner with vomit mouth!

And then it occurred to me – I hadn't texted home! Jane and Daphne would probably have the police out after me! I'd broken one of the rules of the house: always let someone know where you were or when you were getting home. Bugger!

And where was my phone?

Frantically, I looked around, scrabbling at the quilt in case it was hidden in its folds.

'My phone?' I blurted, darting a glance at Michael, who was leaning against the wall, watching me.

'On the coffee table,' he answered. 'Is there a problem?'

'I didn't text home! They'll be worried about me. I should have called home.' It was reassuring to hold my phone in my hands and I just clutched it for a moment or two, taking a breath to calm myself down.

'It's alright. Someone named Daphne texted you and I replied, saying that you were fine and that you'd see her today.'

'You did *what*?' Yes, my voice rose in pitch, almost a squeak.

'Red, you weren't in a state to respond, so I did it for you. It's no big deal. You can check the conversation.'

'Don't call me Red,' I muttered, as I went into the text messages. Sure enough, Daphne had sent: *Where are you? When will you be home?* and this Michael-person had replied *I'm fine. Staying with a friend. I'll see you in the morning.* And, because he hadn't known what was supposed to be included, Daph had worried, sending another text: *Ginny, are you okay?* Yep, she'd noticed.

So, Michael's: *Sure. Had too much to drink, but I'm fine. I'll see you in the morning* wouldn't have eased her fear at all, even though he'd added a smiley face to the end of the text.

Daphne would be freaking out! I thought, wondering if she really *had* contacted the police. My fingers fumbling – I really wasn't with the program as yet – I added to the conversation: *Woolf.* And then sat back, trying to control my breathing. I looked up to see that Michael was standing, motionless, his eyes narrow as he studied me.

'Is there a problem, Red?' he asked, quietly. 'Did I do something wrong?'

'No. It'll be alright,' I said, weakly. 'And don't call me Red. My name's Ginny White.' My father had called me Red and, right then, feeling as vulnerable as I did, it brought up all sorts of emotions I didn't think I could handle.

He laughed. 'You're joking, aren't you? Really? Well, in that case, I might have to start calling you Blue.' He chuckled, his eyes alive with merriment. The tension that had invaded the apartment dissipated with his obvious enjoyment at his own joke. 'Has anyone ever given you Snow as a nickname?' he asked playfully.

'No,' I said, coldly. 'None of us have ever been called Snow, although some kids have given us other names to bully and tease us.'

'Us? How many of you are there?'

'Five. I have four sisters.' And I had no intention of telling him anything about any of them, because I was still too annoyed at them. Especially Jane. Talk about not appreciating me!

'I've got two brothers,' was all he said. 'You want that shower now? I'll get you a towel. And find you a t-shirt.' He walked from the room and I took the opportunity to stand and arrange the quilt around my mostly-naked body. Michael hadn't touched me, or even come very close to me, so I was feeling relatively safe. The paracetamol had kicked in and the throbbing in my head had eased, although my mouth tasted vile and I still felt queasy.

It was a beautiful room: light-coloured walls, expensive dark furniture – except for the lounge, which was covered in a light caramel butter-soft leather. I assumed it was real leather. The décor was very minimalist – almost like a hotel room that no-one really lived in. But, most definitely, the focus of the room was the incredible view of the Harbour Bridge through the sliding doors and the spacious balcony. It was like there was some sort of assumption that no-one would be looking anywhere else.

'I can't offer you any women's panties, but these boxers are new,' Michael said, holding out an unopened packet of men's underwear as he returned to the room, a fluffy white towel and navy T-shirt in his other hand. 'I'll show you to the bathroom. Use whatever you need. I've put a new toothbrush on the vanity.'

He led me through the main bedroom and I paused to admire the huge bed that dominated the room. *Must be what they call a king-sized bed,* I mused. The navy-and-beige doona was evenly spread across the bed, the overhang on the sides equal in length, and the pillows were perfectly fluffed and placed appropriately. *Someone knew how to make his bed in the morning!* I grinned to myself, but the thought was quickly followed by *Unless he's had a cleaning woman in here already?* I felt ill at that idea, that someone else had seen me conked out on the lounge, dishevelled and only partially clad.

'Make yourself at home.' Michael invited after he'd dropped the towel, underwear and t-shirt on the vanity. 'Yell if you need anything.'

The bathroom was bigger than my whole bedroom. The shower was *huge*, with two double-head shower fittings and a central showerhead. Count them! *Five* shower heads! You could have a party in the shower! It would be like standing under a waterfall where the stream was coming between the crevices in six rocks. If I still didn't feel quite so seedy from the previous night's partying, I could have danced in pure excitement!

But I contained myself. I didn't turn on all the taps; just one. After sniffing the bottles of body wash, shampoo and conditioner on the ledge inset in the grey marble-tiled wall, I indulged in a luxurious shower, scrubbing the remnants of alcohol and vomit odour from my skin, and massaging a rich lather into my hair and scalp, the masculine scent of his shampoo rather enticing. I stayed under the jet spray until I felt a little woozy from the steam and my empty stomach.

With my teeth freshly scrubbed, my hair wrapped in the thick fluffy towel, and dressed in my rescuer's long t-shirt and too-big boxers, I exited the bedroom to see Michael sitting at the dining table, spreading Vegemite on toasted bread with a mug of what looked like tea near his plate.

Tea and Vegemite toast – with the Harbour Bridge as a backdrop!

It was so bizarre, I laughed.

Chapter Four

'Why am I here?' I asked, as I gingerly bit into toast, not confident that my stomach was ready for food. I swallowed, and then sipped on the sweet tea that Michael had placed before me. Unusual taste. I'd been expecting Earl Grey or something ritzy, but this just tasted like normal tea, only better. 'What's the tea?'

'Daintree Tea. You were not at your best, Red, but you were very clear that you didn't want to go home, wherever that is. You said there was no-one to come and collect you. I could hardly leave you there. You were too vulnerable.'

'Do you do this often? Bring intoxicated strangers home?' *Was he some kind of weirdo?* He didn't seem to be, but …

'No.' He paused, lowering his head and closing his eyes. He inhaled, before exhaling slowly. Then he looked me directly in the eyes. 'But then again, Red, I don't often see young women, alone in a bar, deliberately getting wasted. You needed somewhere safe to be so that you could sleep it off and deal with whatever you have to deal with.'

I stared at him. Talk about blunt! And brutally honest. I had been very purposefully getting mindlessly drunk. And there had been that moment, with Mr Sleaze, before Michael had rescued me, when I knew that I was not safe. That I was engaging in very risky behaviour that could have serious repercussions. And he was right – I hadn't been in the company of girlfriends, who could at least have protected me when I'd been intoxicated. In fact, as I thought about it now, in the cold light of day, I was very, *very* lucky that Michael had taken responsibility for me. And so far, he had been nothing but chivalrous. He hadn't touched me, invaded my space, or made me feel uncomfortable in any way. He hadn't even ogled my breasts, their bralessness evident beneath the soft fabric of the borrowed shirt.

He'd only shown me respect and consideration. It occurred to me that I should be concerned that this was shocking to me. *What sort of low-lifes was I becoming accustomed to being around?* I thought, wryly.

'It's nice tea,' I said, lamely.

'Yes. Try and eat some more toast. It'll make you feel better.' I sat watching, as he cleaned up his place at the table, rinsing his plate and putting it in the dishwasher. 'I've got work to do here this morning,' he said, as he clicked the kettle on to boil again. 'I'll use this table, so feel free to rest again on the lounge or, if you'd prefer, you can sleep in the bedroom.' He looked back at me, questioningly. 'The balcony's a bit cool at this time of day. Better in the afternoon.'

'You don't mind if I stay longer?' I asked. *Was he for real?*

'Nope. Stay until you're ready to go. Only thing I ask is that you're reasonably quiet and keep out of sight when I've got a Zoom meeting in about an hour. I really don't want to have to answer questions about a woman in the apartment. My father would have a field day.' He grimaced.

'I can go,' I protested, feeling like I was imposing and hating the sensation.

'It's alright, Red. Just make yourself at home and relax.' He smiled at me – the first real smile he'd given me – and I froze. My God! This man was gorgeous! Rich and stylish and gorgeous! For a moment, I knew *exactly* how Vivienne had felt in *Pretty Woman*. Dazzled! And, like her, I tried not to show it. *A girl had to keep her dignity*, I thought wryly.

'May I make another cup of tea?' At his nod, I added, 'Would you like another?'

'Sure. Tea's in the caddy.'

I watched him settle himself at the dining room table, his laptop open, papers strewn around. He shrugged his shoulders a few times, following this up with a couple of neck rolls, and then a scrunch of his face. He gave the appearance of a teenage boy about to sit a test for which he hadn't studied. I smiled to myself, just thinking this. And then, as though he was bracing himself, he sat up straight and started tapping away at the computer keys.

'It's loose-leaf!' I squawked, breaking the quiet of the room.

Startled, he looked up. 'Of course, it is. It's better that way. Tea's meant to be gently brewed, not jiggled like you're washing clothes.'

'But it takes longer,' I protested.

Michael smiled. 'Chill, Red. You've got all day.' He paused, frowning. 'Or do you? Is there somewhere you're meant to be? Do you have a job?'

Talk about spoil the mood!

'Nope. Not gainfully employed,' I said, bitterly. 'Nope. No career for Ginny.' I looked away, embarrassed at how sulky I sounded. *Loser*, I thought.

I jolted as I felt the pressure of his hands on my shoulders. It was the first time he'd touched me – or, maybe not, as he had managed to get me into his apartment and out of my clothes. But it was the first time I was *conscious* of his touch. It was gentle. And warm. And reassuring.

'Make the tea, Red. Take your time. Tea is a drink to enjoy. I read somewhere that coffee-people *need* to drink coffee, but tea-drinkers *want* to drink tea. So, make the tea and plop yourself down on the lounge and relax.' He gently guided me to the kettle. 'I'll get back to work.'

I watched him as he returned to his quasi-office, there in the spacious living area and settled back to his laptop. The tap-tap of keys commenced again, and I busied myself boiling water, warming the tea pot, and patiently performing the gentle art of tea-making. The ritual itself was soothing. When I placed the bone-china mug of tea, laced only with a sprinkle of raw sugar, next to his elbow, he grunted his thanks before continuing with his work.

I curled up against the arm of the lounge and leisurely sipped my tea.

Maybe it was the after-effects of the fight with my sisters, whom I really did love; or maybe it was the alcohol still swishing through my system; or maybe it was the repetitive clicking of the computer keys. The last thing I remembered was the hushing murmur of Michael's voice as he slipped the cup from my fingers and the gentle pressure of his hands as he smoothed the soft quilt over me.

Chapter Five

I blinked, not sure what disturbed me. A door closing? Footsteps along the polished parquetry floor? The crunkle of paper? At least the vision of the Harbour Bridge didn't make me question my mental capacity this time.

'You awake?'

I twisted my head in acknowledgement, my eyes still only half-open.

'I brought lunch. You must be hungry by now.' He carried two sandwich bags and two bottles of juice over to the coffee table near me, and I drew my body up to make room for him on the lounge.

'There's ham and salad, or chicken and salad. Orange or apple. Your choice.'

Shaking my head to clear the fuzziness, I reached for the chicken sandwich and the apple juice, thinking it would sit more comfortably in my stomach. 'Thanks,' I muttered, my voice hoarse with sleep.

Undoing the paper bag, I asked, 'Um, did you get much work done?' in an attempt to cover the awkwardness and be sociable.

'Hmmm,' he murmured, his mouth full of sandwich. 'A lot, but never enough to satisfy the old man.'

'Your father?' I prodded. 'You work for him?' I glanced up, before taking an enormous bite of bread and goodness. I really *was* hungry.

'Yes, all three of us have roles in Dad's company. My brothers, though, are much more corporate-minded. I'm the black sheep in the family.' His sandwich was gone. How quickly had he devoured that!

'So 'm I,' I mumbled. 'I'm the rebel. Only one not gone to university.' I chewed in dejected silence for a moment. 'What're your brothers' names?'

'Gabriel and James. Gabe's not that bad. You can talk to him. James can be painful.'

'In what way?'

'Oh, I don't know. Dad has expectations of all of us. Gabe, being the eldest, is expected to take over from Dad one day – be the chairman of the board, the chief executive officer of the company. James slotted right into finance. He's the most penny-pinching, the-profit-is-the-bottom-line excuse for a person. Money is his king. Irritates the hell out of me. He's impossible to relate to. To have a decent conversation with.' He nodded towards the half a sandwich left on my plate. 'You going to eat that?'

'Well, I *could*,' I teased, watching the disappointment flash across his face, 'but I think I'd be overdoing it. I'll respect my poor belly a little more before I fill it too much,' I finished, extending the sandwich to him.

'Thanks,' he grinned.

'So … what do you do? You know, Gabe's the CEO, James' the money guy…'

'Manage the bars and restaurants.' He grimaced. 'Well, some of the restaurants.' Another pause. 'Well … I get to talk with the restaurant managers.'

'I'm not getting it. What does your family do?'

'Hotels, Red. We've got hotels in every city in Australia. And three in Sydney. That's what the family does.'

I was stunned. That explained the lavish apartment right beside the Opera House!

'So… do you own this unit?'

'The family does. I just stay here. Or, more precisely, the *company* owns the unit.'

'And you manage … what? *All* the bars? In *all* the hotels? *And* the restaurants?'

My mind was officially blown. Here I was, little ol' Ginny White – couldn't get a job in a bar throughout COVID – and I'd just spent the night with a guy who managed hundreds – well, not exactly hundreds – but *heaps* of bars, nightclubs and restaurants!

My face must have expressed my incredulity.

'You don't have to be so amazed! I am an intelligent guy. I *can* do this job.' He looked hurt and I realised that he'd misread my stunned look.

'No. No. It's not that. I just …' I didn't know how to continue without – well, basically asking for a job. 'It's not that. I'm sure you're great at what you do. I mean, you've been doing it all morning and –'

'I put you to sleep!' He laughed. 'It's okay. Finish your juice.' He returned our plates to the kitchen. 'By the way, your clothes came back. I put them in my room, if you want to change into them.'

'Oh! I should get going,' I said, that awkward sensation that I'd overstayed my welcome washing over me.

'There's no rush. I've got to meet with a couple of guys in Hyde Park later, if you want to tag along. You'll want to be dressed for that, though,' he grinned. His manner was off-hand, but I got the feeling that he *wanted* me to stay.

'Sure,' I said, 'I'll just hang out here on the balcony for a while and watch the poor people pass by. Not much of a view, though,' I finished, cheekily.

I may have dozed again. I'd watched people for a while, as they ambled along the boardwalk that led to the Opera House: singles, chatting on their phone; couples, hand-in-hand, stopping to take selfies with the Bridge as background; business pairs, so engrossed in their conversation they didn't even notice their surroundings; oldies, shuffling along and loudly criticising "The Toaster", as they disparagingly called the Bennelong Apartments, where I was hidden on one of the balconies. I'd read a novel on my phone for a while and then … I may have dozed.

Interestingly, when I opened my eyes again, the sight of the Harbour Bridge just seemed normal. *How quickly we adapt,* I thought. Who knew, yesterday evening, that today I would be here? *Life was strange,* I mused.

And then I startled to attention! I blinked – hard. Was I still drunk? For a moment, I was sure that I'd seen Jane strolling along the concourse, hand-in-hand with a blonde-haired guy. But that couldn't be. I knew that Miss Responsibility would be at work, at least for another hour or two. *No way* she would be wandering around the harbourside on a school-day. Unless, of course, she was surrounded by teenagers on some school excursion! But – it sure had *looked* like her. Maybe she had a double. *Oh, the world definitely didn't need that!* And then I cringed at my meanness. Jane didn't deserve that. I knew, in her heart of hearts, she was trying to look after us all. But sometimes …

Michael must have noticed that I was awake as he instantly appeared in the doorway.

'You getting dressed?' He was wearing faded jeans, running shoes, and a blue button-down shirt. Was it the exact same colour as his eyes? Aviator sunglasses were hanging from where he hadn't done up the top three buttons and he was casually rolling his shirt sleeves towards his elbow. *Was this the same expensively stylish man from before?* Except for the sunnies, no-one would look twice at him. Well, maybe they would. He was still a gorgeous man. At least I wouldn't feel quite so out of place next to him, dressed only in my mossy-green sundress and sandals from yesterday.

'Give me a minute,' I breathed, hoping the sheer appreciation I had for his looks wasn't all over my face.

When I reappeared, my hair in a messy braid – the best that I could do – and my face freshly scrubbed, he was tidying up the table. He glanced up, paused, and frowned. 'You may get cold.' He left, returning with a shirt, the colour of rich clotted cream, and held it out. Swirling the fingers of one hand, he said, 'See if you can turn that into a jacket-y thing.'

Okay, I had that silly smooshy smile on my face, evidence that I couldn't decide if I wanted to laugh at his "bloke" description of a tied shirt, compliment him on selecting the exact right colour to go with my carroty hair and green dress, or hug him because he was just so damned *considerate*. So, I stood there with a goofy grin!

It took me no time to finish dressing and – yeah, it felt good when I walked out and he nodded at me, warmth in his eyes and his mouth curved up in a sultry smile. I felt the heat of a blush flood my face, which, as someone whose skin was the stereotypical white to go with that hair, was not what I wanted.

'Where are we going, exactly?' I asked to cover my embarrassment, as he held the door to the apartment open and handed me my bag. I glanced around and quickly fetched my phone, before sliding through the door next to him.

'Hyde Park. A couple of guys and I are trying to resolve a housing issue. And then we're going to collect food packages for delivery. You okay to walk in those shoes?'

'Sure.' I tried to stifle my curiosity, but … 'So, the food? Is that from your restaurants?'

'Nope. It's from OBK in Bondi.'

'OBK?' I'd never heard of it. A new restaurant? A café?

'Our Big Kitchen. It's a charity. They prepare meals – hundreds each day – that get distributed through welfare agencies and charities to those in need. St. Vinnies can't run their Night Patrol Van because of COVID, but the homeless and other people doing it tough still need food, so we've been doing little runs in other vehicles.'

I stared at him. My brain was trying to compute. Maybe I was still a bit inebriated. Mr Rich Guy, living in an amazing harbour-side apartment – the bathroom of which was bigger than my bedroom – was going to drive around for – what! the next couple of hours? – and hand out meals to people? My mind was blown.

And that's what we did. I'd thought he was hot! I'd thought he was sexy! But it was *nothing* to how hot and sexy he was as he chatted with men, women and – for God's sake! – *children*, who gratefully accepted the packages he offered. He was warm and friendly and open and kind. He treated everyone, no matter how down-and-out they appeared, with respect and compassion.

Who *was* this guy? He caught me gazing at him sometimes, and I knew that my face must have reflected my awe, because he'd blush and duck his head, as though I'd embarrassed him. Me! Ginny White! Had caused *him* discomfort!

He handed me a stack of food parcels, colourful images on the recycled-cardboard packaging, and nodded towards approaching women, inviting me to be a part of this good work. It was easy, I found. The people were so appreciative and friendly, more than willing to chat, as though they were starved for human companionship, as well as the food. And, if there was one thing I was good at, it was having a chat! Their sense of humour was quite black at times, which initially shocked me, but soon I was laughing along with them.

A few people thought that Michael and I were a couple, but I ruefully shook my head. 'We've only just met,' I responded each time, with a smile.

'That's not how he looks at you,' one older woman chortled and the grey-haired woman with her nodded in agreement.

'He's got his eye on you.'

I glanced over and they were right. He was watching me, a soft smile on his face, warmth in his eyes. Now I was the one ducking my head in discomfort.

When we ran out of supplies, we said our goodbyes to the people still milling around and returned the van.

'You ready for dinner?' Michael asked.

'Sure,' I said, not sure of anything at all. Where was this heading? I'd drunk myself to unconsciousness the night before and – here I was – helping the homeless, hanging out with a hot handsome guy and wearing borrowed clothes, my face free of makeup as we entered a corner hotel for pub food.

Nope, "sureness" didn't come with any of this. I was just going with the flow …

Chapter Six

'I'm having the salmon. With veggies. I've had my salad for today. What are you having?' Michael asked, as we both studied the menu board on the bistro wall.

I wanted the salmon, but I also knew that I'd spent all my cash on alcohol the previous night and the credit card I had wasn't meant for my personal use. It was "family expenses". *This is an emergency*, I rationalised to myself. *I'll pay it back later*, I promised myself.

'Looks good. I'll have the same,' I said, fumbling in my bag for my wallet.

'No. No, it's my shout.' Michael reached out and placed his hand on my arm, his touch freezing my movements.

'But you bought lunch,' I protested. 'I can buy my own dinner.'

'I'm sure you can, Red, but this time you don't have to. I'll get it. Why don't you go to the bar and get drinks?'

'Oh, okay,' I acquiesced. I could afford that. 'What'll you have?'

'Iced water, with a twist of lemon.'

'I can buy you a real drink, Michael. What would you really like?'

'Iced water, Red. I don't drink alcohol and I try to limit sugary drinks. Gotta watch my school-boy figure,' he said, winking.

And my mouth was hanging open again! Who *was* this guy?

'You *really* don't drink alcohol?'

'Nope. Not for the last two years.'

'But *why?*' *What made a person not drink alcohol?* I thought.

'Long story, Red. I'll tell you about it later. Right now, you go get drinks and I'll order. We need to find a table.' He softened his words with one of those dazzling smiles of his. Dazedly, I nodded at him. *He is so gorgeous!* I thought, as I headed to the bar.

When I turned back, carrying his iced water and my lemon-lime-and-bitters, I saw that he'd snavelled us a table and was arranging cutlery and serviettes, precisely. It made me smile. He was such an interesting combination of wealthy class and down-to-earth simplicity. He must have felt my gaze, because he looked up, directly at me, and returned my smile.

Yep, so gorgeous! A truly beautiful man!

I want him. The thought flashed through my mind and I jolted with reaction. He was sizzling hot and I wanted to experience that. To burn with him!

I stood still, the two glasses wet from condensation in my hands, and watched as his eyes darkened, the electricity zapping between us reflected in the heated expression on his face. *He wants me, too,* I realised suddenly, swallowing with nervous excitement.

'Do you mind moving?' The harsh voice broke through my trance and I glanced back at the man who had spoken, his features stamped with irritation.

'Sorry,' I said, and headed towards Michael, whose eyes followed my progress as I navigated between tables. When I reached him, he'd already pulled my chair out and, as he assisted me to sit, I was sure I'd felt the lightest touch – just a soft caress – across the nape of my neck.

Oohhh! I shivered.

'So,' he said, sipping his water, 'where do you live, Ginny White?'

'Greenwich.'

'Hmm. Pricey neighbourhood. You're not so poor, yourself!' he teased. 'I take it you live with your parents?'

'No. They're dead.' I watched the shock blanch his face, and then his mouth fall open, his eyes widening in dawning horror.

'Is that … Was that why you were – you know – drinking so much last night? Are you in mourning?'

'No. No, that's not it. My parents died six years ago. I mean – yes, sometimes I still feel like I'm grieving, but – no, last night wasn't about that.'

'Oh.' Silence. 'So, you live in Greenwich with …?' His eyebrows were raised in question.

'My sisters. The five of us live in our house. My parents' house. We inherited it.'

'Free and clear? It's still a pricey place to live. The council rates must be huge.' Was it a question or a statement? I wasn't sure.

'I don't know,' I admitted. 'I've never really thought about it. Daphne takes care of all of that. And Jane. The two of them talk about money. And they do carry on about the bills, now that you mention it. The water bill.

The electricity bill.' I paused. It hadn't occurred to me to worry too much about the money. It wasn't my responsibility. Oh, there was that horrible R-word again. The one that Jane was always on about. Was I that irresponsible?

'They're the oldest?'

'Yeah. Jane's twenty-eight, and then there's Daph, followed by me, and Louisa, and then Charli, who's twenty. Jane's the "responsible one",' I said, air-quoting the words. 'Daphne "manages" things – don't ask me what, exactly.'

'So, what do you do?' he asked, sitting back, quietly studying me.

'I cook,' I said, proudly. 'I feed them all. Like you,' I added. 'Feeding the homeless. It's just that I feed all of them. Except, unlike those people before, my sisters don't appreciate what I do. They don't even notice all the effort I make.' *Stop it, Ginny. You're sounding pathetic.* And slightly ridiculous, I acknowledged, thinking about how selfish I was being considering the disadvantage suffered by those we'd helped that afternoon.

'What do you like to cook?' he asked, redirecting my thoughts.

'Bread. I love the smell of baking bread. And Jane loves Greek food – Mediterranean-style cooking. I swear she must have been Greek in a past lifetime. Daphne will eat anything, so she's pretty easy to cook for. But she's very precise about her lunchbox. She takes her lunch every day to work – she works in an office near Central, but she doesn't ever buy her lunch – so I make sure there's lots of stuff in the fridge for her to put her lunchbox together.' It occurred to me, then, that maybe Daphne brown-bagged it because money was tight and I just didn't know it. I wondered.

'What about the other two?' Michael prompted, breaking into my musings.

'Louisa doesn't complain. She's got a sweet tooth; she'll devour chocolate cake. And she likes Asian food; Thai is her favourite, but if we go out, she prefers Japanese. And Charli … Well, Charli likes plain food and lots of it. Rissoles, mashed potatoes, carrots and greens, with gravy. She could eat that every meal. Or any variation on that. When I do a roast dinner, which I do most Sunday evenings, Charli's as happy as!'

'It sounds like they do like your cooking,' he murmured.

'Yeah, I guess so. It's just that – I don't know – it's like they just take it all for granted.' I shrugged, looking at him for understanding. 'They don't think about how long it takes to do the grocery shopping. I mean, I don't *hate* it, but it can be boring sometimes. And they forage – that's what I call it when they go scavenging in the fridge or the cupboards – for food, but don't let me know when we run out of things, so it's a guessing game on my part. I have to basically do a stocktake before I go shopping.' I sipped my soft drink. 'Sometimes it takes a while for me to figure out what to make, because I don't want to get into too much of a routine that dinner's predictable. And then they don't come home, for some reason. I've prepared dinner and, at the last minute, I get a text saying that Charli's going to Macca's with friends, or Louisa's going to some Book Club function that she didn't tell me about. And I end up with more leftovers than I thought. Or – and this can be frustrating – they'll bring someone home with them without telling me first and I'm left to supplement the meal with something else, just to make it go around.' I shrugged again, feeling despondent.

'Yeah,' Michael nodded, sympathetically, 'I can see how you'd feel taken for granted. Unappreciated.'

'But maybe I've been doing the same thing.'

'How so?'

'Well, until you mentioned it, I hadn't even thought about the bills. I mean, I've got this credit card that Daphne gave me, and I use it whenever I buy anything for the house. Food, cleaning products, stuff. You know, I bought a new kettle last week. The old one was still working but … it just looked a bit grotty, so I bought a new one. I didn't really think about the money. Just tapped the credit card. I use my own money for personal stuff, but – yeah, I don't ask anyone if I can spend money on the house. I just do it.' I paused, resting my chin on my upturned hand, my elbow on the table. 'Maybe I've been taking Daph for granted.'

'Maybe,' was all he said.

Our meals arrived, breaking the pensive moment, and we busied ourselves with cracked pepper and squeezing lemon juice onto our fish.

'It must be difficult – all of you living together in the same house?' Again, was this a statement or a question?

'I guess so. This salmon's good. I wonder what they've seasoned it with.' I forked another mouthful up. 'Do your brothers have units in the Bennelong Apartments, too?' I asked, before I ate the fish.

'Nah. Gabe's got a place at the Wharf. You know,' he prompted, at my puzzled expression, 'the Finger Wharf. In Woolloomooloo. Where Russell Crowe lives when he's in Sydney. He's got a three-bedder there. And James has a two-bedroom place in Darling Point.'

'So you really are incredibly rich,' I whispered, overwhelmed by the extent of their wealth.

'Red, you've got to remember. I don't own that place. I just live there. I've got a bit of money, but I work hard for it. And my job pays well. But I'm not *that* rich.'

'Compared to whom?' I said, my tone arid.

'I'll admit that I'm well-off.' He did that head-ducking thing again. It was a bit cute, a bit sheepish. 'So, do you have to let your sisters know where you are?'

'Oh, God, yes! They'll be freaking. Especially when there's no dinner!' I reached around for my bag, hanging on my chair, so I could get my phone.

'You know, if you wanted ... You could tell them you won't be home until tomorrow... If you want?' That questioning statement, again. Stilling, I looked up at him. He didn't move, only one eyebrow rising in query. 'If you wanted... I mean, it might be good for you all to have a break from each other.' Even I could hear how lame that last bit was.

I smiled.

'Well, if I wasn't overstaying my welcome ...' I faded off.

'I can always kick you out in the morning if you bother me,' he teased, obviously inferring that I wasn't *totally* against the idea. 'I will tell you, though, that I have to be out reasonably early. I've got a shift with Orange Sky.'

'What's that?'

'Like a mobile laundry and shower service for homeless people. There are two types of vans: one for showers and the other with washing machines and dryers. I volunteer on Saturday mornings at Green Park.' He did that head-ducking thing again – his giveaway that he was uncomfortable. 'And I have to do the rounds tonight of the bars and nightclubs. Shouldn't take too long – unless there's a problem.'

'Does that happen often?'

'Nah. We've got excellent managers in place. They hire good staff and treat them well, which guarantees that they work above and beyond. Everyone pulls together and there's usually very little that goes wrong. Just the odd intoxicated female,' he teased, winking at me.

'I can't go with you,' I protested. 'I'm not dressed for Fridays in a nightclub,' I gestured towards my dress and his borrowed shirt. 'And I'm wearing sandals.'

'You're with me. You'll be fine,' he said, dismissively. 'I will, however, have to stop and change first.' He gestured towards my phone. 'Send your text, Red, and we can get out of here. And,' his eyes twinkled at me, 'don't forget to put the code word in.'

'I don't know what you're talking about,' I replied, my head down as I quickly typed: *At a friend's. Will be home by the usual time.*

'There was some word that I didn't write last night and the fact that I didn't, got you into a tizzy this morning. It only took you a minute and, Red, you should have seen the relief on your face!'

I held up my phone, turned so that he could see it. 'See? No code word.'

'Hmmm. It must be embedded in "the usual time",' he air-quoted. 'Anyway, it's neither here nor there. What *is* important, though, is that you're staying with me.' A more self-satisfied look I hadn't seen in a long time. Who knew that my presence would please him so much!

'Don't get too cocky!' I glanced down as my phone beeped an incoming text. *Ditto!* was all Jane had written. I frowned. That was not like her.

'Everything okay?' It was easy to forget how perceptive Michael was.

'Sure. Just that Jane's out as well. That's unusual.'

'What! A late-twenties woman stays out all night? That's unusual?' Scepticism laced his voice.

'No. She stays at Sarah's sometimes, but not all weekend.'

'Well, maybe she just wanted to get away, too. Just like you, Red. C'mon, let's get going.'

I paused as another text came in, this time from Louisa. *You okay? You didn't come home last night.*

I realised then that I'd been a bit selfish – that Louisa, even though she didn't say much, would have been aware of just how upset I'd been last night, and the fact that I hadn't returned would have worried her.

I'm good, Lou. Out with a friend. Will tell you about it later. Woolf.

'Red?' I looked up to see Michael, standing a few feet away, waiting for me.

'I'm coming. Patience, much!'

Chapter Seven

'I'm really not dressed for this,' I repeated, not quite for the thousandth time, but it wasn't the first. We were walking into an upscale nightclub and, as soon as I saw all the other women, lined up outside, dressed in their slinky little dresses, faces perfectly made up and their hair sleeked into sultry sexiness, I baulked, feeling distinctly under-dressed, scrub-faced and with my long red hair untamed and wild – except for the plait which was coming loose. 'I can't go in, Michael. I'll wait outside.'

He responded by tugging on my hand and pulling me into a recess near the door. 'Stop it, Red! You look fine. Better than fine.' His hands cupped my chin, lifting my face so that I could meet his eyes. 'You are stunningly beautiful. It boggles my mind that you don't know that. In a simple sundress and no makeup, you look gorgeous. These girls, trying so hard to look sophisticated, with their faces caked in God knows what! and their hair so stiff, it hardly moves when they do … they don't hold a candle to you. Every man in this place is going to be envious of me, walking in there with you.'

I stared at him. Did he *really* think that? About me? Ginny White? With the shocking red hair and the white freckled skin and the fiery temper? I felt my eyes well up. *God, no! Don't cry! You'll look like an idiot!*

'Plus, those men don't even know that you're wearing my shirt!' He winked, making me laugh and regain my composure.

As we entered the nightclub and he led me through the crowd, pulsating with the music, I ran his words over and over through my head. Was I truly beautiful? Really? I'd dated men before and plenty had complimented me – you know, the usual "you're hot" or "I like your eyes". I'd always thought that they were just trying to get into my pants. Michael, though, had been quite intense, what with staring into my eyes like that. Maybe, to him, I wasn't so horrid to look at.

'Would you like a drink?' he said, interrupting my thoughts as he drew out at stool for me, right at the end of the long bar.

'I'll have a Coke,' I said, and he frowned.

'Ginny, you can have anything you want. You don't have to avoid alcohol just because I don't drink.'

'Nah. It's okay. I think I had enough last night to last me a while.'

I gazed around the club, sipping my drink and enjoying the colourful strobe lights, pulsing in time to the music. I watched the women, dressed to seduce, posing, primping and dancing suggestively, whilst the men stood back, nursing their drinks and surveying the dance floor. The bar itself took up one long wall of the club, its mirrored wall reflecting the glittering bottles of coloured fluids, all lined up to entice its patrons to experiment with more expensive spirits and liqueurs. Sitting contentedly, I could hear Michael talking with a tall blonde guy, whom I assumed was the manager. COVID was mentioned a few times, as was the number of patrons in the nightclub and the clientele registering with the QR App. *Nothing like a pandemic to change the way we operate,* I thought wryly. Their stances were relaxed and their chat was interspersed with laughter, so it appeared they had a good working relationship. Maybe they were friends, as well. Michael didn't introduce me, but I hadn't really expected that.

'Ready, Red?'

'I haven't finished my Coke,' I protested, holding up the glass. He smiled indulgently.

'It's Coke, Ginny. You can get another one at the next stop.'

And that set the pattern for the next couple of hours. Entering a bar, ahead of the queue; my sipping on a drink and observing the clientele and décor, whilst Michael chatted with the manager, ensuring COVID compliance; and then we left. At one place, Michael left me when he, the manager and a security guy disappeared through an unobtrusive door hidden in the wall for fifteen minutes or so, but before he did, he gestured to the bar attendant and instructed, 'Look after her.'

When he returned, he took my hand in his and tugged me off the stool. 'C'mon, Red. Let's go home.'

He'd been doing that all night until it almost felt normal. When he'd first reached for my hand and folded it into his, back when we'd finished dinner, I'd been stunned. Deliciously stunned, but surprised, nonetheless. Up until that point, he hadn't touched me – well, if you discounted taking care of me when I'd been "indisposed" – so when he'd finally held my hand, I'd been overcome with the *rightness* of it. The solid warmth of his fingers as they curled around my palm; every so often, a gentle squeeze, just to let me know he was aware of me. By the time we were going "home", as he'd so blithely put it, I was so used to holding his hand that I was the one who gently squeezed his fingers.

I knew I was going to sleep with him. Well, not exactly sleep. I was pretty sure that he felt the same way, but ...

Was this for real? Was this hot, sexy guy, floating in money and style, in command of lots of Sydney's nightclubs, *really* into me?

I quashed my doubts. For tonight, I didn't care. If this was only a one-night-stand, I was in! Oh, I was *so* in. He'd been nothing but a gentleman to me, taking care of me when I was at my most disgusting worst, and then spending the afternoon feeding the homeless. He was like an angel! And, if it was only for one time, I was going to be touched by an angel. Corny, but I was full of sentimental feels.

As our Uber neared Circular Quay, Michael turned to me, gently touching my cheek. 'I can ask the driver to take you home, if you'd like.' Another one of those statements that sounded like a question.

Not taking my eyes from his, I shook my head. 'No,' I whispered, suddenly very sure, 'I'm staying with you.' And I lifted my face, slowly – so he had time to back away if he wanted – and pressed my lips to his. Softly. Gently.

He didn't take the kiss any further, but before I pulled away, I felt his lips curve into a smile.

Oh, yes!

Chapter Eight

I wasn't sure what I expected …

He'd been so cool, calm and controlled the entire day and all the way into the evening …

But as soon as the door closed …

Whoa!

Still holding my hand, he spun me back against the timber, grasped my other hand and raised them both above my head. He surged against me, his thighs pressing into my hips, as he stared down into my face, his expression intense. His eyes darkened and then a slow, satisfied smile slid across his face, as he tipped his head forward and his lips hovered above mine.

'You are so beautiful, Red,' he breathed, before he kissed me. A soft kiss. A gentle kiss. Only our lips touching, brushing against each other's. And then I felt the tip of his tongue, delicately tracing along the soft flesh of my lips. The sensation was so exquisite, so torturous, I couldn't move. I was held captive, with just the merest touch.

And then he pulled back. 'Breathe, Red,' he whispered. The moment was so special, so *pure*, I didn't want to spoil it with something as mundane as breathing. I stared, wordlessly, into his eyes. So clear. So blue. So beautiful.

I lifted my face in silent invitation and he didn't hesitate. The grip on my hands tightened as his mouth captured mine, no longer soft and gentle, but hungry and demanding. Desperate to touch him, to connect my body to his, I pushed my breasts against his chest, while tugging at the hold he had on my hands.

'No,' he moaned against my mouth, 'if you touch me, I'll lose it.' He shifted slightly, both of my wrists now in one of his hands, as he trailed the other down the side of my face and along my neck. I shivered. I really, *really* needed to touch him. I wriggled my leg free and lifted it, wrapping it around his, and pushed against his hard length. He jerked, as if I'd electrocuted him, and then he groaned, grinding himself against me and devouring my mouth with his.

Ohhhh, yes!

'I want you, Michael. I don't want to wait. I don't want slow.' I was pleading, but I didn't care.

He groaned as he slid his hand down the outside of my thigh, fisting the hem of my dress in his fingers. He reached around and cupped my arse-cheeks, pulling me closer. I moaned as his long fingers slid between my legs, pressing on the satiny fabric of my panties. I knew they were warm and damp with my desire and he groaned as he stroked me.

'Not against the door,' he mumbled, pulling away.

'Just hurry!' I implored, feeling bereft as soon as I felt cool air where his body had been. 'Please, Michael.'

He grunted as he lifted me, his arms around my legs and back, and I held on to him, kissing the underside of his jaw as he carried me to his room and plopped me onto the bed, his body following mine onto the covering. I turned, scrambling to pull the quilt off the bed, but was distracted when I felt him flip the hem of my sundress up my back and tug my panties down. I stilled as his tongue licked a path across the fleshy cheeks of my bottom. I tried to withstand the deliciousness of it, breathing deeply so I didn't move and stop him. The magic of his tongue, the brush of his lips, and I was rocking – back and forth – against his mouth. I could feel my core heating, becoming drenched in my arousal.

'Oh, God!' I croaked, my throat tight with want. 'Oh, please, Michael!'

And then he *licked* me. A long, slow swipe of his flattened tongue along my cleft and I almost came, right then and there. He pointed his tongue and poked at my clit and I cried out. 'Michael, stop messing around. Fuck me! *Now!*' I wailed.

I didn't move. I could hear a drawer opening and closing, and the rip of foil, and the soft clicking as he tackled his zipper.

And then, with no more wasting time, he entered me. After everything, this was when he slowed down, sliding into me in little thrusts, giving me time to accommodate his girth. And then his length! I pressed back against him, matching his rhythm, silently letting him know that all was good.

Just as he bottomed out, I moaned and heard his echoing response. He stilled, but I was having none of that. I'd never felt so *needy* in my life. Squeezing the muscles of my abdomen, I pulled off him, before thrusting back – hard! And that was all it took: Michael more than joined the party. One hand stayed on my hip, holding me steady, whilst the other reached around to cup my breast, still clad in my sundress. He gently squeezed, his fingers pinching my nipple, as he raised my upper body to align with his. His dark groan vibrated in my ear, sending shivers down my spine, as he pumped into my body, his strokes long and deep. The hand on my hip slid around to my belly, adding pressure to our grinding thrusts.

And *ohhhh!* I was a bundle of sparking nerve-endings: the heat of his body surrounding me, the resonating sounds of his groans, the rhythmic clenching of my inner muscles as he fucked me, the sharp scent of our arousal enveloping us.

And then it was all too, *too* much! Too intense!

'Michael! *Michael!'*

'Yes! Red!' He followed me over the edge. 'Yes,' he mumbled, against my ear, as we both collapsed onto the bed, his body draped over mine, before he rolled us both onto our sides.

We lay there, just breathing, neither of us moving, his arms wrapped around me and my hands gripping his forearms. I was trying to get my head – still fuzzy from post-orgasm bliss – around how quickly that had all happened. It did occur to me, though, that it had been building all day. His attention to me, his kindness to others, and his sheer sexiness had been a lengthy and lethal type of foreplay, and I'd been hungry for him. Hungry for sex with him.

And – *had it been worth it!*

'Hmm, well that lacked class,' he mumbled in my ear, the tips of his fingers gently caressing the tender skin of my inner arms.

'I'm not complaining,' I murmured, rubbing my chin along his biceps. 'Felt pretty good to me.'

'Hmmm. Wanted to do better than that. Wasn't how I planned it.'

I twisted my head. 'You planned it?'

'Been thinking about it all day,' he mumbled. 'Could hardly concentrate on anything else.'

I smiled. No, I *beamed!* Who knew?!

'Shower. It's time I got you naked.'

'You already did,' I reminded him, mortified at how I'd embarrassed myself the previous night.

'Not quite. And it's not the same. This time, we'll enjoy it more,' he said, with an accompanying squeeze of his arms. 'C'mon, Red. Let's get wet!'

Where he got the energy to bounce off the bed, I don't know, but his exuberance made me laugh! 'I still don't have any clothes.'

'You won't need them. But I will get you the t-shirt from this morning, if you want.'

We blasted all five showerheads, water coming from all directions, like a car wash for bodies. He kissed me – long, wet, sexy kisses, whilst we stood under the waterfall in the centre of the cubicle. Suds, scented by his shower gel, slid down the walls and covered the floor after we wrestled with the nylon wash ball, both determined to scrub the other clean.

And we laughed! It was fun! I'd never had a shower like it.

Nor had I ever experienced the exquisite pleasure as Michael pushed me against the wall, slid down my body, lifted my leg and rested it on his shoulder, before – his eyes on mine – he leant forward and licked me, his mouth warm against my flesh. *Oohhh!* The toes of my foot still on the ground curled, seeking purchase, so I didn't slip down the wall or slide across the floor, still slippery with suds. I could feel my eyelids droop, my focus hazy, as I held myself still against his onslaught.

'Michael,' I groaned, my hands grabbing his hair. 'Michael, I'm going to come.'

His response was to slide a finger into me – and I gasped. When he added another finger and pressed against my inner walls, the full sensation was almost too much to bear, especially as his mouth didn't stop plundering me. My muscles clenched around his fingers and he groaned, which sent vibrations along my sensitised skin and added to the spiral of deliciousness swirling through me. His tongue pressed against my clit and – it was too much!

'Michael!' I cried, my hips thrusting forward. 'Oh, God!'

Michael rose, his arms wrapping around me, as I slumped forward, a goofy grin on my face.

'That was *soooo* gooood,' I crooned. 'Sooo *gooood.*'

'And my new favourite sound is your calling my name when you come,' he teased. 'C'mon, let's get out of here. I need to put condoms on the soap dish for next time,' he added.

We towelled off in record time and scampered back to bed, this time pulling back the quilt so we could slide onto the cotton sheets. I sniffed the pillow and Michael's look was priceless.

'What are you doing?' he asked.

'They smell good,' I said. 'They smell of you.'

He grinned, obviously delighted at my words. 'Well, they'll smell of you by morning,' he promised.

I slid my hand down his body, twirling my fingers around his navel a couple of times, before reaching down to fondle his length.

'No.' He clasped my hand, pulling it back up to his mouth and pressing his lips to my palm. 'I won't last. You can play next time, if you want, but now … I just want to bury myself in you and watch you come again.'

I think I purred. It was a cross between a long, deep exhale and a moan, but it may have been a purr. And I kept on purring whilst he slowly, deliberately, joined us together again and surged against me, the undulating rhythm both sensual and tantalising. And, gazing at each other, our eyes dark with desire, we came – the intensity of our orgasm shattering us.

He growled. No other word for it. It was a growl.

We sounded like a couple of animals mating.

But it didn't *feel* like that. It didn't just feel like mating. It felt *more*. Like a *connection*.

Which was silly, really, as we'd practically only just met. It was far too early to think in terms of "connections".

But …

That was my last thought as I drifted off to sleep, curled up against him: my non-alcohol-drinking, super-sexy, amazingly-kind rescuer.

Chapter Nine

We woke late. I knew we did because Michael cursed as soon as he checked the time.

'Ginny, we need to get moving.' His tone was urgent. 'We're due at Green Park in thirty minutes and I'm guessing you'll want to stop at a shop and buy a dress before we get there.' In the midst of dressing, he turned to me, his eyebrow raised in question.

I made short work of the bathroom, using my borrowed toothbrush, and quickly dressed, scowling a little at yesterday's undies.

'Where can we stop?'

'I'm thinking Pitt Street Mall,' he said, referencing a huge shopping centre in the centre of town. 'And while you find something to wear, I'll get our coffees. And danishes, I'm thinking.' He winked. 'Gotta keep our energy levels up.'

And I wanted to swoon all over again.

'So, what will we being doing, exactly, at Orange Sky?' I was curious. Did we have to wash the clothes? Or hand out towels?

'It takes about an hour for a load of washing to finish,' he said, ushering us out the front door and down the corridor, 'and we'll sit on the orange chairs and chat with the people who come through. It's easy, but it … It'll make you feel good, Ginny. You'll meet some interesting people and they're so appreciative of everything. It's like you've given them something extra special, when really all you've done is talk with them.' He trailed off, and that tell-tale hint of pink coloured his cheeks. 'Most people don't even stop and smile at homeless people, Ginny. They don't even acknowledge them. As though they don't exist, or something.' He trailed off, obviously uncomfortable.

'I'm looking forward to it,' I reassured him. 'But only *after* I've got some clean clothes to put on.'

'And that's the point,' Michael stopped and turned to me. 'Clean clothes. A shower. Simple things that we take for granted, but as soon as we don't have it, we feel grotty. Same thing with these people. Orange Sky allows for the homeless or disadvantaged to feel like *us*, with clean skin and clothes.'

'And a shampoo,' I guessed.

'*Exactly.*' We grinned at each other, enjoying our moment of mutual understanding.

I couldn't help it. I just had to twirl the skirt of my new dress as I walked. It felt all soft and slinky against my legs and the deep blue colour didn't clash badly with my hair.

As soon as I'd entered the mall, I headed straight to Cotton On, knowing that they'd have pretty cotton dresses *and* the all-important underwear, for a reasonable price and that, too, was important as I was using the household credit card. I'd already paid and was almost to the door in my new clothes, my dirty ones in a reusable bag, when I paused and went back, gathering up another dress – pale blue this time – and an oatmeal lightweight cardigan that would go with anything. *Just in case*, I thought, hopefully. Fortunately, there was no-one else at the counter, so it didn't take too long. Michael had been waiting at the entry to the mall, two coffees in a cardboard tray and a paper bag that held the danishes.

Volunteering was fun, I decided. And Michael was right: there were interesting people to meet. One lady – I wasn't game to hazard a guess at her age – was a minefield of information about the city of Sydney. By the time she left, her clean laundry all packed neatly in plastic bags in her shopping trolley, I knew more than ever about a city that I'd lived in my entire life. I supposed that was pretty common: that people went about their business, passing buildings as they hurried about, without ever really knowing the buildings' histories, or what they housed, or the people who'd lived there.

When I mentioned this to Michael as we headed back to the Quay, he agreed. 'I had no idea about the city and the people in it for years. It's only been the last two when I've started to learn. And people like Janet – they're becoming more common. The fastest growing group of homeless people is older women. They've often been married and weren't well-represented in their divorce, not gaining a fair share of assets. Most times, they've got little or no superannuation. When things start to get tight, they end up on the streets, or taken in by their children. But they have no real home of their own.'

'I didn't know,' I admitted, feeling guilty that I'd taken the huge house my sisters and I lived in for granted. *That could have been us*, I thought. When our parents died. If it hadn't been for Jane and Daphne... Or, more to the point, *Daphne*, as she was the one who looked after our finances. *I need to be nicer to her*, I thought. Maybe I should be more careful with the money I spent. *Yes, Ginny. After you've just bought two dresses when you've got plenty at home.*

Oh, well...

'What do you want to do this afternoon?' Michael asked.

I didn't say anything. I just looked up at him and tried to look innocent. Obviously, it didn't work.

'Yeah,' his voice was gruff, the one-syllable word drawn into a long growl, his mouth curled suggestively, 'we can do *that*!' His eyes twinkled and one lid lowered in a sexy wink. I was totally on board!

We made it all the way into the apartment this time ...

All the way to the couch...

Michael sat down, still holding my hand, and pulled me onto his lap. He may have wanted to take things slowly – that had been his intention last night, but it hadn't happened – and it didn't happen this time, either. It was like we set each other alight, without trying. He held my head and kissed me gently. I wasn't having a bar of it! I lifted myself and settled back, straddling him, my hands in his hair, my mouth on his, and my knees gripping his thighs. He didn't seem to mind; his immediate response was to cup my butt-cheeks in his hands and drag me closer to meet the forward movement of his hips. I rubbed myself against him, like a desperate cat, the zipper of his jeans adding extra pressure. My panties were damp again – a constant predicament around Michael.

'How many pairs of these did you buy?' he asked, slipping his hands under my dress and sliding them across the satiny fabric.

'Only two, so don't wreck them.'

'Then we need to get them off you,' he prompted, lifting me up so I could stand and slip my underwear down my legs. And I watched, my eyes half-closed, my breathing deepening, as he twisted and pulled a condom from his pocket, before his hands went to his belt.

'No, let me,' I whispered, as I knelt between his legs. 'I can do this,' I purred, my eyes meeting his. It was his turn to watch me, as I unfastened his belt and slid his zipper, slowly, teasingly down over the hard ridge of his arousal. Gliding my hand into the opening, I caressed him through his boxers and felt him twitch in response. He eased himself lower onto the couch, his legs widening to accommodate me, his hand stroking my hair back from my face, as I pulled back the fabric, baring him to my heated gaze. God, he was beautiful. I looked up at him and smiled.

'You don't have to do this,' he murmured.

I smiled again. 'Oh, yes, I do. I really, really do,' I said, as, still holding his gaze, I lowered my head and gently licked him – from the base to the tip – my tongue swirling around the head, before slinking back down again. The only sounds in the room were his indrawn breath and his groan – a long, deep tortured sound – so I did it all over again.

'Ginny,' he whimpered, 'no more. No more. C'm'ere.' His hands pulled at my shoulders, his fingers digging under my arms. 'Lift up, Ginny.'

And when I straddled him that second time, I sank down, impaling myself on his hot flesh. Our moans mingled as he kissed me, devouring my mouth, his tongue tangling with mine, his hands fisting in my hair.

And, as before, our bodies synchronised into a rapturous rhythm and, even though we tried to slow it down, we erupted. Together.

And my body melted onto his, my face falling into the crook of his neck, as his arms encircled me, hauling me closer, as though he were trying to absorb me.

I shuddered, in a physical acknowledgement that something significant – momentous – had occurred. This wasn't just scratching an itch.

And with that thought, I felt a tremor of fear. *This man could hurt me!* Not physically, but emotionally.

And then I waved it away. I knew there was no way this – whatever it was – could last. It was for the weekend! This was a super-rich guy in a multi-million-dollar apartment. He was so effortlessly sexy, I'd watched women falter as we'd walked down the street, pausing to check him out. There was no way this was anything other than what it was – a fantasy weekend that I'd secretly savour for years to come. So, I brushed aside my misgivings and my fear. *Live for the moment, Ginny! Make it worth remembering!*

Chapter Ten

We were flirting. There was no other word for it. Had to be flirting!

We were sitting, almost face-to-face, the balcony table between us, with my feet resting on his lap, his hands massaging the soles and tickling the insteps. I made a big show of sipping my juice, pursing my lips ... just so ... and tried not to squirm when he wriggled his fingers between my toes. I was back wearing his t-shirt and we both knew that I was panty-less. His fingers snuck up the inside of my calf, to the sensitive spot behind my knee, before slithering back down to the back of my ankle. It tickled when he did it, and then left a trail of warmth behind him. And it wasn't the first time he'd mounted such a subtle attack. When I was least expecting it, when I thought I was all calm and settled again, his determined digits would set out again, on a tantalising voyage of discovery, along my legs, which were becoming more boneless with each pass.

I returned the favour by catching his eyes and then, very slowly, very deliberately, running my tongue around my lips, taking a moment to flick it against the middle of my top lip. Not too much like a porn queen, but enough to see him still, his eyes darkening and his hands stopping their teasing.

We were languid: lazily lounging after our steamy hot session on the couch. He was shirtless, his jeans zipped, but not buttoned. I alternated between salivating over his ripped chest – his pecs shifting as he reached for his water or slid his hand along my leg – and watching the ferries coming and going at Circular Quay.

'My sister likes the ferries,' I said.

'Which one?'

'Jane. Whenever she gets upset or stressed – especially around exam time at school when she's got heaps of marking – she rides the ferries. I don't even think she cares where they're going. She just uses her Opal card and off she goes. Can be gone for hours.' I paused. 'I bet that's where she went on Thursday night.'

'Why the ferries?'

'Hmm. Not really sure. Jane was always adventurous, though. When we were little, I remember her playing pirates and explorers and stuff. She'd climb to the top of the swing set and thrust her arm into the air, as though she was claiming our backyard for her own nation.' I smiled, thinking about it. 'I always imagined her off in some far-off land, doing something dangerous.'

'Like what?'

'Oh, I don't know. Saving the mountain gorilla? Or the black rhinoceros? Or Indian elephants. Something. I never imagined her teaching geography in a high school. It seems so *tame* for her.'

'Then why does she? What happened?' He seemed genuinely interested.

'The accident, I suppose. That's what happened.' I felt a wave of sadness wash over me. It was six years ago, but sometimes it felt like yesterday. 'It was my mother's birthday and Dad organised a surprise for her. I guess the surprise was on us,' I said, ruefully.

'What was the surprise?' he asked gently.

'Mum wanted to go up in an aeroplane, so Dad bought two tickets. She was so excited – and Dad had that indulgent smile on his face.' I turned to Michael, seeking his eyes. 'He always looked at her like that: like he thought she was amazing and he'd do anything she wanted, no matter how … whatever,' I finished, lamely. 'Anyway, there was a crash. And that was that. I don't know all the details. I was too scared to ask. I know that Jane and Daph spent a lot of time with our relatives, and with the Department of Community Services. And Jane kept telling us – Louisa, Charli and me – that we had to be good or they'd separate us. That we'd have to go live with the relatives, or worse – strangers! And then Jane didn't go off and have adventures. She stayed home with us.' I paused, again. 'I bet she'd like those sail boats, though,' I said, flicking my hand towards the small yachts dotting the harbour.

'Wow. That's some sister you've got there.'

We sat in silence, both of us in our own thoughts.

'I wish my brothers were like your sisters.'

'She can be very bossy! Jane, that is. And Daphne's no walk in the park! She gives me a hard time about money. All the time!' But I had realised, the last couple of days, that maybe I needed to give more thought to how I spent the family money. I mean, I had no idea how we financed the things we did. Who paid for what? Where did the money come from?

I know that I had money from when I worked, but it wasn't much. It paid for my stuff, but I didn't contribute to the rest of the house. I felt a bit guilty. Maybe I *did* need to be more responsible.

'What do you want for dinner?' Michael asked, changing the subject and lifting the pensive mood.

'Don't know. I'm easy. If I were at home, I'd cook, but I don't know what you've got in the fridge.'

'Chicken parmi? There's a good pub in the Rocks that makes excellent parmigiana. Not too far a walk. I do, though, have to do the rounds again this evening. Takes longer on a Saturday night. You up for that? Or do you want to come back here?'

'I'll go where you go!' I proclaimed, theatrically, my arms waving through the air. 'Let me get dressed. I might have a shower first.'

'I could join you,' he said, wraggling his eyebrows suggestively.

'Have we time for that?' I teased.

'Always time for that, Red.'

Chapter Eleven

'Tell me something no-one else knows,' Michael murmured, his whiskers scratching the skin of my shoulder, his body warming my back as his arms encircled me. We were pleasantly drowsy, our bellies filled, Michael's responsibilities addressed, and our desire sated – for the moment.

'Like what?'

'Anything.' The tips of his fingers lightly caressed the sensitive hollows of my palms.

'I don't have a job,' I said, my face heating in shame.

'Not good enough, Ginny. Your sisters know that. C'mon, something that no-one else knows.'

'I don't know,' I squirmed, feeling decidedly uncomfortable.

'Alright. I'll go first,' he sighed behind me. 'You know that I don't drink?' I nodded. 'Well, it wasn't always like that. I used to drink a lot. Too much. *Waaayy* too much.'

'Why?' Curiosity made me interrupt him.

'My family. My brothers. Expectations. I was a spoilt brat! Take your pick!'

'Go on.'

'I'm privileged. I know that, Ginny. I had the best of everything. I still do, in fact. And I was an entitled little snob. But I hated it. I hated the expectations that were on me. Like, it was *expected* that I'd do well at school and anything less than brilliant was … just not good enough. And it was *expected* that I'd join the family firm and it didn't matter what I wanted to do.'

'What did you want to do?'

'It doesn't really matter now.'

'Of course, it does,' I protested.

'Hear me out, Ginny. Anyway, I rebelled. I did everything that I *wasn't* supposed to do. And I took a lot of pleasure doing it. That's one of the reasons why James is such a pig to me now, I guess. Anyway, I drank. A lot. Every night. And my family owns hotels, so there was always plenty of alcohol for me to drink.' He paused, and I felt his arms squeeze me, his hands clasping mine, as though he wanted to keep me close. As though he worried that I might leave.

'Anyway, one night I got wasted. Absolutely, totally, rotten drunk. So drunk, I fell down in the street, in the gutter. I don't remember that bit. What I do remember is waking up, this old guy leaning over me, asking me if I was alright. He'd been sleeping in a shop doorway, near where I'd fallen, and dragged me out of the gutter and into the safety of his shopfront. This homeless guy – who had nothing. Well, nothing more than what he could carry around. He was sleeping on cardboard and had newspapers stuffed down the front of his jacket to keep him warm. And a little bottle of water that he offered to me. Because I'd sicked all over myself. It was all he *had* and he was offering it to me! He took care of me, when he had *nothing*, Ginny. Made sure that I was safe. My wallet was still in my pocket; my watch was still on my wrist; I still had my keys.

'And that was the last time I drank alcohol. It really put things into perspective.' He rubbed his chin against the side of my neck. I was hardly breathing. I hadn't expected a story like that. It made perfect sense, though. All of it made sense. His sobriety. His need to help the homeless. His down-to-earth *decency*, even though he was loaded.

'So, now you rebel in a different way?' I surmised.

'Yeah, I suppose. I realised that I'd been a self-important, entitled little prat and I changed my attitude. I work for the family company. It pays my bills. It satisfies my father. And it enables me to do what I want to do, which is to give back to people who haven't had my advantages. Who aren't as privileged. And, Ginny?' He paused. 'Some of the people I help – they're much better people than I am. A lot of them are. You know?' I nodded.

'But you're a pretty decent guy. You know that, don't you, Michael? You're really special.' I twisted, so that I could see his face. 'You *know* that, Michael?' I repeated, seeking to reassure him. 'You are a good person!'

'I'm trying to be, Ginny. I try.'

We both fell quiet, sighing deeply in unison. He cuddled me close and I crossed my arms over his, hugging him to me.

After a while – when I thought maybe he was asleep – I said, 'I failed my HSC.'

I heard him inhale, a sharp draw of air.

'When my parents died. I failed my HSC. I was so screwed up. I couldn't concentrate. There was all of this stuff going on around me ... And Jane thought we were going to be split up ... And she kept saying that we had to be good or bad things would happen. And I was trying so hard, but I couldn't focus. And I was struggling.' I paused, trying to catch my breath. 'The teachers tried. I know they did. Some were more sympathetic than others. I think some didn't know. And I was so tired. And Charli was crying all the time. She didn't understand. She just wanted Dad back. And Louisa just went quiet.' I turned, twisting so I could see Michael. 'She was always quiet. Always the reader. But when Mum died, it was as though she lost her voice or something. Michael, it was so horrible!

'And I didn't finish my exams. I went in – Jane expected me to. I sat there and I looked at the papers. But I couldn't remember anything.' I paused, tears rolling down my cheeks.

I knew I'd stunned Michael with my revelations. His face was a combination of shock, sympathy and concern, and I felt his gentle squeeze of support.

'There was one exam – I just started crying in the middle of it. I felt like such a fool. Everyone was staring at me. The examiner-lady took me outside.' I took a breath. 'She told me to go home, but I couldn't. Not then. Not until the exam was due to finish. I didn't want Jane or Daphne to know what I'd done. They were being so good. And so strong. And I had *cried* in an *exam!*'

'Shhh,' Michael murmured, his fingers lightly brushing the tears from my face. 'It's okay, Ginny. It's okay.'

'But it wasn't, Michael. It wasn't. The school put in an appeal for me, but it wasn't enough. I got shit marks. And Jane keeps on about university, but my HSC wasn't good enough for me to do what I wanted. And I was so *ashamed!*' I wailed, sobbing.

'It's okay, Ginny. I've got you,' he crooned in my ear. 'It's okay.'

'And now I've made such a deal about my not wanting to go to university. I mean, I could, now. It's possible that I could get in as a mature-aged student, but I've gone on and on about not wanting to go. And they just see it all as rebellion. Because they wanted me to go. And my parents would have wanted me to go. So, now I'm just this immature brat who rebels all the time. And they don't understand.'

'Shh. It's okay, Ginny. Just take a breath. It's okay.' He stroked my hair back from my face, and wiped my tears with his fingers, all the while murmuring soothing sounds and gently rocking me. When I finally quieted, he asked, 'Is that still what you'd like, Ginny? To go to university? Or have you changed your mind about that?'

'What do you mean?' I was confused.

'Well, it seems to me – and I've only known you for two days – that you like taking care of people. That you *enjoy* cooking for your sisters; preparing their food and ensuring that they've got breakfast and lunch. And you were a natural today, talking with Janet and the others. It just seems to me that maybe what you want has changed, over time. Maybe you'd like to be a chef, instead. Or work with a charitable organisation. They always need people who can cook. Maybe there are other options for you.'

'But –'

'Don't think about it now. Just know that you're *not* a failure. And you've got no reason to be ashamed. My God, Ginny! You were eighteen and trying to cope with the death of both your parents. I'm amazed you did as well as you did! Don't you dare think that you failed at all! I'm sure your parents would be so proud of you. *I'm* proud of you. I want you to think on that. What a survivor you are!' He turned my face away from his, spooning me from behind again, his arms encircled me, safe and secure. 'Now, go to sleep. I've got your back. Everything'll be alright, Ginny.'

Was he right? Was I a survivor? Would Mum and Dad be proud of me?

With these thoughts, and wrapped in the warmth from Michael's body and praise, I fell asleep.

Chapter Twelve

'Do you want to go home and get a change of clothes, Red? We can go this afternoon, if you want, and you can come back here.'

I was making toast whilst he brewed the tea. We'd slept late – again – but after the emotional night we'd had, neither one of us was complaining. And it was nice, just puttering around the kitchen, him in his boxers and me in his t-shirt. There was a familiarity and, after our disclosures in the dark of the night, an intimacy that felt special.

'I can't tonight. I have to be home for dinner.'

'Why? Are you cooking it?'

'I haven't thought that far. I do have to be home, though. We all have to be home for Sunday night's dinner.'

'Aahh! "The usual time." That's what you meant in your text message the other night.' How did he *do* that? Make his statements sound like questions?

'Yes. Jane made the rule, years ago, when we all started being out and about at night. It didn't matter where we were any other night of the week, but we'd all gather for dinner on Sunday night.'

'I can see the advantages,' he said, stroking his chin thoughtfully. 'There's one night when you're all together, so you all get the same messages or trade the same info. Start the week off together. Bit like a board meeting, I suppose. And it's not a normal date-night or, for you, work night. A quieter night in the hospitality trade; not like Friday or Saturday nights.'

'Yeah. We make an effort for birthdays and stuff like that, but usually, Sunday night is the only time we're all together. Well, other than last Thursday night, and you can tell how well that panned out,' I finished, wryly.

'So, what time do you have to be home by? I'll take you.'

'It's alright, Michael. I can go on the train. You don't have to come.' Although, there was a huge part of me that wanted him to come with me; that wanted to show him off to my sisters and show them that I wasn't such a loser, at all. That a gorgeous, stylish guy wanted *me*!

I also knew, though, that this "thing" we had couldn't last and I didn't want my sisters to know about it. I wanted to keep this weekend to myself: something awesome that was my secret; a moment in time; a romantic fantasy.

'I'll take you, Ginny. You've been gone all weekend. They're likely to wonder where you were. It's better if I go with you.' I looked up at him and thought again about what a decent man he was: kind, considerate, respectful. He was beautiful, inside and out. I chose not to argue with him, as I didn't want to spoil the rest of our time together.

'Do you want more than two slices?' I asked him, changing the topic.

'Are there any eggs in the fridge?'

'Didn't see any, but I'll look.'

The easy camaraderie returned whilst we ate scrambled eggs and cold toast, playing footsies under the table like a couple of teenagers. I rinsed our plates and boiled the kettle for a second pot of tea, and Michael stacked our few plates in the dishwasher.

'If you had your swimmers, we could go around to the Andrew Boy Charlton pool,' Michael said, as we settled ourselves on the balcony. 'Next time, bring your swimsuit, Red.'

I smiled at his obvious attempt to create a future for us. 'Sure, Michael. And I'll remember to bring my makeup.'

'You do that,' he murmured, looking pleased with himself. 'We could wander over to The Rocks Market, if you like. Get fresh fruit and veggies. There's plenty of wares.'

'Hmmm. After we finish our tea,' I agreed, enjoying the warmth of the sun, high in the sky.

'Or we could snuggle on the lounge.'

'Michael, I think you just want to get into my pants,' I teased.

His look was pure filth. 'I didn't think you were wearing any.'

I could feel the zing of the energy zapping between us, its heat warming me. At that moment, he was the sexiest man I'd ever met. His blue eyes were intense, his mouth curved in a sinful smile.

'I guess, considering how disturbed our night was, that it wouldn't *hurt* if we partook of a late morning nap,' I pronounced, dropping my head to where his t-shirt was slipping from my shoulder. 'In fact, it would probably be the *wise* thing to do.'

I sent him a saucy wink and then we both laughed. Life was good! Very, very good!

Michael was stretched out on the soft leather of the lounge, my body draped over him like a beached jellyfish, sprawling without water to give it shape. We interspersed tender little kisses, more soft pecks at each other's lips, with cuddly snuggles, my cheek pressing into his chest. I felt safe and secure in the warmth of his arms, cushioned as I was on his lean body. We were at peace. We didn't feel the need to talk, or move, or even ramp up our desire. Just lying together, enjoying the sensation of our skin touching, our breathing in sync. I'd considered turning on Spotify, but listening to the faint sounds floating through the sliding doors – the murmur of people conversing; the hum of ferry motors; the soft churn from the wash of the ferries – I was pleased I hadn't. This was bliss! My eyes had drifted closed and I was being gently lulled to sleep, the thudding beat of Michael's heart a baseline to the quiet surroundings.

Until the scrape of a key in the front door lock jolted me awake!

'What the -?' I scrambled to get my hands down, so that I could raise myself up.

'Michael, what's with the not-answering-the-phone ...' The man's voice trailed off. 'Oh, so *this* is what you've been up to?'

I could hear the sneer in his voice, the tone nasty and derisive. I was very conscious of the fact that I was only wearing Michael's t-shirt and my bare bum was most likely visible to the intruder.

'James, do you mind?' I'd never heard Michael use that tone of voice before. 'Haven't you ever heard of knocking?'

I was standing by then, tugging at the hem of the t-shirt to cover myself, with what I knew had to be a horrified expression on my face. I edged away, towards the bedroom door, as Michael rose from the lounge. I glanced at the intruder – James. He looked at me with such *disdain* that I felt for a moment that I must have crawled out from under some rock.

'E-ex-cuse me,' I stammered, darting to the bedroom and closing the door. How quickly could I get dressed!

'So, this is what you've been doing whilst you've been slacking off at work? What is it, Michael? *Three* nights now? Do you think I don't know? Really? You honestly think that you can be a slack-arse and I don't know?'

Michael was right. His brother *was* a prick. Who did he think he was? I wanted to charge back out there and give him a piece of my mind. But, just as the urge became so strong, I thought I would march out the door, I deflated. Michael was in trouble because of me? He'd not fulfilled his family responsibilities because he'd taken care of *me?*

I needed to leave. I needed to get out of here.

One thing was certain: I couldn't get in the middle of a fight between two brothers. Between two wealthy men. I was *waaaayyy* out of my league.

I could hear them talking out there, James' voice much louder than Michael's, as I hunted around for my things. *Where are my sandals?* I found them sticking out from under the bed. I left Michael's cream shirt on the chair in the corner and exited the room.

'I'll be going now,' I directed my words to Michael, even though I had my eyes on James, who turned and looked me up and down. His lip curled in distaste, evidently not liking what he saw, and I wrapped my arms across my chest, defensively, feeling like some sort of cheap whore.

'No, Ginny. Stay. I'll take you home.'

'It's best if I go. You need to talk with your brother.' Was that my voice? I sounded small and pathetic. My sisters would be shocked. Where was fiery Ginny now? 'Umm. I had a good time,' I offered, slinking down the hallway. 'Umm, thanks for everything.'

'No, Ginny.' He came towards me. 'I'll take you home,' he repeated, imploringly.

'Let her go, Michael,' I heard James' harsh voice. 'We've got things to talk about. Don't waste any more time with her.'

'Ummm. Bye, Michael. Umm... I've got to go,' I said, turning away.

And then I walked out the door ... making sure it clicked shut behind me.

Chapter Thirteen

I held it together.

I didn't cry as I walked, with my head down, to Circular Quay Station.

And I didn't cry when I boarded the train, eventually getting off at St. Leonard's Station, welcoming the long walk home down the hill. I was cold, though. There was a chill in the air – unusual for so late in the year – and I wished that I had Michael's cream shirt to keep me warm.

And I didn't cry when I entered the house, unusually quiet for a Sunday afternoon. It didn't seem as though anyone was home. Well, except for the cat, who immediately appeared, weaving himself through my legs as I stood, indecisively, in the hallway.

In the kitchen, I boiled the kettle for tea and poured cat biscuits into Clancy's bowl. He probably didn't need them, but knowing Clancy, he'd eat them anyway. Greedy cat!

But then, when I was adding the teabag to my favourite mug, I suddenly couldn't bear the thought of tea. And I started to cry, great fat drops of salty tears sliding down my face, as I sobbed. Loud, ugly sobs.

The cat meowed.

I leant against the grey kitchen cupboard and covered my face, sloppy wet snot dribbling into my cupped hands.

C'mon, Red, pull it together! I urged myself, and then started howling when I realised that I'd used Michael's nickname for me.

Abandoning any thought of making tea, I stumbled to my room and, pulling the covers back, I curled myself on the bed, buried beneath the protection of my doona.

And I cried … until I fell asleep.

I heard Louisa come home, her footsteps quiet as she moved along the hall. She was always so quiet, our Louisa. Not sneaky-quiet, but I-don't-want-to-disturb-anyone-quiet. And the sound of the shower running.

I thought about having a shower myself, but – I knew it was silly – I didn't want to wash Michael's smell off me. I could still just detect it, if I closed my eyes and inhaled the inside of my arm, where I'd rested it against his body, just a few hours ago.

And then I heard the front door again and the sound of Charli stomping through the house. Nothing delicate or quiet about Charli. The sound of the fridge door opening and closing told me she was hungry. She was always hungry, our Charli. And her talking to the cat. Crooning to it. Her voice sounded different, though. There was just an edge of excitement evident in her tone. As though she was trying to keep in a secret. Charli was horrible with secrets. Blabbed all over the place. If there was anything you didn't want the world to know, don't tell Charli. I wouldn't be telling her about Michael.

I heard the back door open and close again. Good. Charli was outside. She'd probably spend the next hour or two out there. She was always happier if she wasn't shut in: not that our house was cramped, but she did like her space.

It was time I got up and made dinner. I didn't feel like it. I really wanted to just lie here, cocooned in my bed, and be pathetic. But I was *Ginny*!

After washing my face in the bathroom, taking care not to wash away Michael's scent from my body, I ventured into the kitchen. There was minced beef in the fridge; tomato paste and pasta in the cupboard. Spaghetti Bolognese, it was then! It calmed me: crushing the garlic, chopping the onions, browning the mince, stirring in the tomato paste, a large splash of red wine and mixed herbs.

Whilst that was simmering away, I put a huge pot of water on to boil for the pasta and pulled salad vegetables from the fridge. There was leftover garlic bread in the freezer, so I warmed the oven in readiness.

And as the pasta water started to boil, so did my thoughts. I reflected on Thursday's fight. For all that Jane might think I was irresponsible, I wasn't. I hadn't been for six years. Jane might have sacrificed to take care of us, but I, too, had helped in taking care of the family. Jane might not realise that, but I did. And it was the one thing that I took pride in.

Although Michael said I could be proud of surviving…

I wondered how the afternoon had gone for Michael.   Did James continue to harangue him? What a prick he was! No wonder Michael kept his distance from him. I could understand how Michael had been a drinker.

And then I heard the front door …

It had to be Jane, because I'd heard Daphne come home and go straight to her room when I'd been chopping the onions. I couldn't resist…

'Where have you been?' I demanded, as soon as I saw her in the hallway. 'You give *me* grief over being irresponsible, but where the hell have you been all weekend?' Then I noticed the gorgeous guy behind her, easing through the door. 'And who is *that?*'

And Jane, being Jane, had to chastise me, like I was still a child. Even in front of this new guy. 'Ginny, language, please.'

'Is Jane home?' It was Daphne coming down the hallway. 'So, you *are* still alive.'

'C'mon, Daph! I sent you texts.' You could hear the defensiveness in Jane's voice. *That* was unusual.

And while Daphne was busy studying the stranger, Charli and Louisa entered. Well, Charli barrelled in, in her trademark exuberant way, whilst Louisa just sidled along the wall. I watched Jane's man checking out my sisters.

'Well, this is crowded. Can we please go into the living room? We don't all need to be in the hall like this,' Jane said, and Daph, Charli and Louisa moved. But I didn't. This guy … I didn't know who he was, but …

'You look familiar,' I probed. 'Who are you?'

'He's Jackson McGee,' Daphne was the one to answer.

'Who?' Charli asked, her face scrunched in confusion.

'Jackson McGee,' Louisa repeated. 'From *Earth Today* magazine.'

I almost laughed. I wasn't sure who this Jackson McGee person was, but I could tell that Jane wasn't expecting anyone to know who he was, either. Whoever he was, she thought that he was *her* secret. And Jack didn't think anyone would know who he was, either. Hmmm.

'Like … are you famous? Or something?' That was Charli, trying to stay with the program.

It was time to stir things up …

'Handsome catch, I will say that for you!' I declared, making a great show of eyeing him off so that even Jane would see. 'What are you doing with our Jane?' I asked, provocatively.

He narrowed his eyes at me, tilting his head. 'Not really your business, Ginny. Is it?' he drawled, reaching for Jane's hand. Hmmm. Protective of her. Our Jane, needing protection!

'So, who is he, again? Is he a star or something?' Charli brought attention back to her.

'He's a photojournalist for *Earth Today*. The geography magazine that Jane reads,' answered Daphne. 'He travels the world, taking pictures and writing stories about different places. And people.'

'So-o-o,' I said, drawing out the word, 'how did you two get together? Has Jane been sending you fan mail?' I knew I was being a bitch, but … Here Jane was, with this gorgeous guy, and my beautiful, hot, sexy man was – *not* here. He was in Bennelong Apartments – without *me*. I was feeling bitchy, and Jane was the one to cop it!

'Ginny!' she snapped right back at me, her cheeks flushed with embarrassment.

I almost felt guilty when Jane's man tugged her to him and softly said, 'I'm going to go, Janey.'

But not guilty enough…

'Ooooh, *Janey!*' I mimicked him.

To his credit, he ignored me. 'See me out,' he said quietly to Jane, his voice soothing. I could see Jane exhale, calming herself.

'So, should we be asking for his autograph? Or will he take our picture?' Charli interrupted the moment.

God, I loved Charli!

'No, Charli. Let's go into the kitchen,' Daphne said. 'Ginny, you come, too. Louisa?' Daph glanced around, but Louisa had already returned to her room.

'C'mon,' Jane said to Jackson. 'Let's go on the porch.'

I heard her come back in a short while later and retreat to her room. Daphne stood and quietly left the lounge room and I knew where she was going. When I approached the hall, I could hear them talking. I thought about joining them, but I didn't think Jane would want me there. I watched as Louisa approached and quietly slid around the door.

And then I heard Louisa's voice, more audible as she was standing near the door. 'So, you could go. You could try it out. It's only Queensland,' she persisted. 'If you don't like it – if you're not happy – you can come home.'

And then Jane's response, her voice louder in her distress. 'But what about all of you? I'm needed here.'

Okay, it was time I intervened. This was ridiculous. If there was one thing that my weekend had taught me – other than that I was *highly* susceptible to sexy, dark-haired, blue-eyed men – it was that Jane and

Daphne had given up a lot for us and – maybe – it was time they got to do what *they* wanted.

'No, you're not,' I said, pushing through the doorway. 'You *were* needed here, Jane, when we were all young, but you're not anymore.'

'Virginia!' Daphne roared at me. 'Stop it!'

'I'm not being a bitch, Daph. I'm not!' I yelled back, defending myself. 'Don't you see? Don't any of you see?' I swung around, glaring at all of them in turn, and I saw that Charli was just inside the room, hovering near the doorway. 'Jane did what she had to do when Mum and Dad died. She did. She dropped everything! She didn't want to be a *teacher!*' I sneered, lacing my voice with derision. 'She was studying geography and geology, sure! But the only time she even *mentioned* a Diploma in Education was *after* Mum and Dad died. She's only in a school because she felt *responsible* for all of us.' I paused, gulping in air.

'She's right,' Louisa murmured from her place near the wall. 'Ginny's right about Jane becoming a teacher so she could support us. And she's right about it being time for Jane to go do her own thing. We're all adults now.'

'Is she?' Daphne looked at Jane. 'Did you never really want to teach?'

'Daph, it's not that simple.' Jane sounded tired and worn out.

'Why isn't it?' Charli demanded. 'Why can't you do what you want? Why can't all of us?'

'Because we have to be careful,' Jane almost screamed, shocking us all. Jane was losing it!

'Why?' Charli screamed back.

'Because Mum and Dad died,' Louisa said, softly. 'Because Jane's afraid. Aren't you, Jane? You're afraid of what can happen.'

'Is that it?' Daphne queried. 'Are you scared for us?'

'Of course, she is,' I answered instead. 'That's why she's been so damned *controlling* all of these years. She's had all of us wrapped in cotton wool. Well, not cotton wool, exactly. *University degrees.*' I couldn't keep the disgust from my voice. 'Her way of keeping us all safe.'

'It wasn't just that,' Jane argued. 'I knew that Mum, especially, but Dad, as well, would want all of us to be educated and financially independent. *That's* why I've been pushing you and Charli to get degrees.'

And then, like a balloon with a hole pierced in it, she deflated. Right before our eyes. Like all the strength in her just dissolved.

'I want to be alone. Leave me alone.' She sounded like she was going to cry.

'Jane,' Charli began, but was stopped by Daphne.

'Let's go. Ginny, did you make dinner?' We allowed Daphne to usher us from the room. 'I'll bring you a plate, Jane.'

'Don't. I'm not hungry.' Yep, she was going to cry.

In that moment, with my own hurt so raw, I wanted to flop down, myself, and join her on the bed and sob, all over again.

Chapter Fourteen

'Do you want your eggs scrambled or poached this morning?' I asked Charli, who'd finally decided to join the Land of the Living. I had no idea how she'd spent the weekend, but from the lateness of the hour, she'd been tired.

'Boiled,' she grinned at me. 'With toast fingers.' She vibrated with excitement, her whole demeanour one of I've-got-a-secret-and-I'm-dying-to-tell-you.

'So,' I paused, as I half-filled a milk saucepan with water, 'what's new? And one egg or two?'

'Two,' she said, slicing bread for the toaster. 'And nothing much.' She grinned again, buzzing with energy.

'Hmmm.'

'I *may* have met an interesting guy on Friday,' she offered.

'Oh, yes,' I took the bait. '*How* interesting?'

'*Very* interesting.' She straightened her back, sitting higher in the chair, a cat-that-swallowed-the-cream expression on her face. 'And … I *may* have spent the weekend with him.' Her head fell to her shoulder as she shrugged, her cheeks fat with smug self-satisfaction. 'And … I *may* be going to his farm at the end of the week.'

Okay, *that* got my attention!

'What do you mean?'

'Well,' she wriggled contentedly on her chair, 'he wants me to go to his farm and his father said "yes".' She said that last bit as though it was decided; as though this mystery-man's *father* saying yes was all that mattered.

'Charli, back up.' My attention was no longer on eggs or toast or anything else in the kitchen other than my little sister. 'Start at the beginning. Who is this person? Where is he from?'

'I met him on Friday. At the uni. He was waiting for his father to finish getting tests. At the hospital. Ginny, are you watching my eggs? I hate it when they're all cracked and the whites have oozed out of them,' she whined.

'I'll make you new ones. Get back to the story. So, what's his name? How old is he? And where's he from?' Jeez, I was starting to sound like Jane!

'His name's Sam. He's from a farm outside of Condobolin. And he's twenty-three.'

'Condobolin? Where's Condobolin?'

'I didn't know, either,' she admitted, happily. 'It's in the centre of New South Wales. If you take the map of New South Wales and fold it into four,' her hands were making the appropriate gestures, 'and then you pinch the folded corner,' her fingers were busy pinching her imaginary map, 'then you've removed Condobolin.' She sat back, satisfied, having taught me something that she'd learnt.

'Okay, so he came to town with his father who is sick?' I confirmed.

'Yep. And there I was, minding my own business, sitting on a seat in the grounds of the uni, thinking about whether I really wanted to go to my tutorial or not,' she was drawing this out, her voice in a sing-song rhythm, 'and this *cute* guy comes up and sits down next to me! Are you going to start the new eggs, Ginny, 'cause I'm really hungry?'

'Okay, Charli. I'll do you a deal: I'll make the eggs; you keep talking.'

'Sure,' she agreed, almost gloating. 'After all, *you* don't get to meet cute guys who want you to move to *their* farm. I guess you want to live vivaciously through me,' she smirked.

'Vicariously,' I said, setting the timer for four minutes.

'What?' she asked, confused.

'It's vicariously; not vivaciously. Go on.'

'Anyway, we got talking and, you know, we had *so* much in common – he lives on a farm; I *want* to live on a farm. So, we spent the day together, until he had to collect his father from the hospital. And then he took his father back to the hotel – Oh, Ginny! They were staying at the Veriu in Camperdown. It was *so* posh! Really expensive looking. And they had food *delivered* from the café next door!' She paused, waiting for me to look impressed, I guessed. 'Not like pizza deliveries, Ginny. *Real*, proper-cooked food!'

'Well, you get real, proper-cooked food here, Charli.' My tone was arid-dry.

'No,' she shook her head, 'it's not the same. You cooking – nah! It's not the same, Ginny. *Real* chefs cook cafe meals.'

Did Charli ever listen to herself? I wondered. I spooned her eggs into chrome cups, slicing her toast and placing it alongside. 'Butter, Charli?' I offered.

'And we went to Roar and Snore!' she almost shrieked in her excitement.

What? What's Roar and Snore? But before I could ask the question, we were interrupted.

'Oh, are there eggs?' Louisa appeared at the door, crossing the kitchen to reheat the kettle. 'Can I get scrambled?'

'Sure. Charli's just telling us about a man she met on Friday.'

And while Charli rattled on, oohing and aahing over the amenities at the apartment and the zoo, and gushing over her new beau, I prepared Louisa's eggs, intermittently feeling the prickles of Louisa's piercing gaze.

'What I want to know about,' Lou started, as soon as Charli paused for breath, 'is *your* new man, Ginny.'

I startled, jerking my attention around to her. 'What do you mean, Lou?' I queried, innocently.

'Tell us about your man, Ginny. You left on Thursday night and didn't return at all until yesterday afternoon. And when you did come back, you were wearing a new dress. And in the wash this morning, there was *another* dress that I haven't seen before. You've also got a bit of whisker rash just under your chin. And you'd been crying when we first saw you last night and – if my ears didn't deceive me – you were crying again when you went to bed. And,' she sighed, as though all of her evidence had been enough, 'you're not normally so bitchy towards Jane. Yeah, you can be irritated by her and you can make snarky comments, but … last night … So, tell us about the man *you* met, Ginny?'

Charli's whole body turned towards me, her eyes huge and round in her face, questions and amazement vying for expression.

'Did you *meet* someone, Ginny?' she breathed. 'Someone who *likes* you?' *Again, did she ever listen to herself?*

'Yes, Charli. Someone who *liked* me. Isn't that amazing?'

Lou frowned. 'Don't be like that, Ginny. She means well.' She stirred her coffee. 'So, tell us about him,' she prompted.

'Not much to tell, really. I met a gorgeous guy, we spent some time together, there's no future in it, and that's that.' I brushed my hands together, effectively showing that there was nothing further to add.

'Why?' Charli asked.

'Why what?' I replied, picking up their used plates and putting them on the sink.

'Why is there no future to it? Why won't it work out? I mean, if there's someone who *likes* you, Ginny, why won't it work?' *There she goes again*, I thought.

'Because we're worlds apart, Charli. He's incredibly handsome, super sexy and fabulously wealthy! We've really got nothing in common. And – look at me! Do I really look like the partner of a hot, gorgeous guy from old, old, *old* money?'

'Why not?' queried Lou softly. 'Why wouldn't you fit in fine? You're intelligent. And strikingly beautiful. And he must have seen *something* in you. For you to catch his eye, I mean,' she amended.

'Well, with all that red hair, you're not *exactly* beautiful, but you're not ugly, Ginny,' Charli hastened to say.

Lou and I exchanged looks and then we both burst out laughing. Well, that sorted out that moment of self-pity!

'What was he like?' Lou asked gently. 'Other than being rich and sexy and smart?'

I paused, thinking. Lou deserved a proper response; not just some flippant throw-away comment. She cared about me: I knew that. And she wouldn't criticise me or ridicule me. Me and my silly dreams.

'He was kind. And thoughtful. He helps people, Lou. Lots of people. Strangers. He gives up time on his weekends to volunteer for charities. And he was good to me. He looked after me when I was so damned drunk that I wasn't being safe.' It was hard not to cry: I could feel the tears welling up. 'And I *liked* him, Lou. But,' I drew a deep fortifying breath, 'it wouldn't work. His brother came – oh, his brother is a piece of work! And he berated Michael – in front of me! And I could tell that Michael was embarrassed. Not just for himself, but for me.'

'Why? Why was he embarrassed for you?'

'Because his brother was a pig to me. The look he gave me. Like I was shit! Some cheap tramp!' I inhaled, my breath wobbling through me. 'And I felt like it, Lou. There I was in my simple cotton dress, in this incredible apartment. I was so out of my league.'

'Was it as good as the Veriu in Camperdown?' Charli butted in.

'Charli, I was staying at the Bennelong Apartments. Do you know where they are?'

'Ginny –' Lou's voice was low in warning.

'Right at Circular Quay, Charli. I woke up to a view of the Sydney Harbour Bridge!'

Her eyes were like saucers again, dominating her face.

'*Really?*' she breathed.

'Really.'

'And this guy *liked* you?' She was still puzzled.

'I think we've established that fact,' Lou said, coming to my aid. 'So,' she started, her expression thoughtful, 'he told you that it was a one-off thing? A weekend fling?' She slanted her face in question.

'Well, no.'

'And he didn't go out in public with you? Introduce you to anyone?'

'No, Lou. We went out lots. We went to where he volunteers and he introduced me to the people there, and we went to the venues he supervises, although I didn't get chummy with anyone. He did let the bar staff know to look after me. What's your point?'

'And before you left, he had lots of time to shut his brother down,' she nodded to herself.

'Well, no, Lou. His brother was just ranting. He couldn't get a word in. Neither could I, really. But what's your point?'

'I don't know,' she shrugged. 'It doesn't sound like he was embarrassed by you at all. It sounds like he was seeing how you fitted into his world. The world, I'm guessing, that doesn't include his brother, the dick!'

Sometimes Lou shocked me! Not just how intuitive she was, but also the language that – every so often – snuck out of her mouth. And she wasn't finished shocking me...

'You know, Ginny, you mope around here as though you're some sort of burden. Shopping for us all, cooking and preparing our food, waiting on us, cleaning the kitchen up after us. Like you need to work hard for our approval. Or your right to be a part of this family. I get the feeling, sometimes, that you're ashamed of yourself, but I've never been able to figure out why.'

Okay, this was making me feel intensely uncomfortable.

'And now this man – who by your own accounts sounds like a pretty decent human being who's not an arrogant turd – wants to spend time with you and you're – what! Baulking at it? Saying no? I don't get it. Why are you so down on yourself?'

I glanced at Charli, still round-eyed and resting her chin on her upturned hands, her gaze swinging back and forth between Lou and me. I could almost hear the gears grinding through her mind. And all of a sudden, a spurt of anger raged through me.

'Look at me, Lou! Really look at me! What do I have to offer anyone? Honestly! I'm not like you and Jane and Daph. Not even like Charli. I didn't get good enough marks to get into uni. I'm not smart. I fucked up. And now I don't even have a job!'

'I don't have a job!' chimed in Charli.

I sighed. 'That's irrelevant, Charli. You're still in school.'

'You're wrong, Ginny.' Lou's voice was gentle, soothing. 'You have lots to offer. And I bet your man – what was his name?'

'Michael,' I grunted.

'I bet he'd say the same thing. You, too, are kind. And considerate. And you help people, all the time. You take care of us. And he probably knows that. Your *goodness*, Ginny, shines out of you. Some days, you *glow* with it. And when you're out in the garden, soaking up the sun, touching the leaves of your potted herbs, you are the embodiment of natural beauty. You just don't get it. But it's true. I wouldn't lie about this to you. You know that.'

'Has he got your phone number?' Charli broke into the pensive silence. 'I made sure that Sam had mine. And I've got his. And,' a dramatic pause, 'we're Facebook friends.'

Lou and I exchanged wry smiles again, shaking our heads imperceptibly.

'Does he have your number?' Lou asked softly.

'No. We didn't need to exchange numbers. We spent the entire time together.'

Lou nodded, staying quiet.

'You think I should go and see him, don't you, Lou?' I asked, after a while.

'Yeah, Gin, I think you should.'

'Oh, yeah. If this guy likes you, you've gotta go see him,' said Charli, enthusiastically. 'I mean, when's the next time someone's gonna like you?'

Lou and I just laughed!

Charli's eyes swung back and forth, her expression revealing her lack of understanding about why we were laughing. In her mind, she hadn't said anything funny.

'At least see where it goes,' Lou urged, when she caught her breath again.

'Okay. Thanks, Lou. I … Thanks,' I said, as I reached over and hugged her.

'It'll be alright,' she whispered, and it reminded me of Michael's words when we'd been wrapped around each other in bed, as close as we could get, sharing our secrets.

Maybe they were right.

WHITE DREAMS

SISTERS WHITE SERIES: Book Four

SUNNY MACKENZIE

2021

Clancy, of the Overflow

I had written him a letter which I had, for want of better
Knowledge, sent to where I met him down the Lachlan, years ago,
He was shearing when I knew him, so I sent the letter to him,
Just on spec, addressed as follows, "Clancy, of The Overflow".

And an answer came directed in a writing unexpected,
(And I think the same was written with a thumb-nail dipped in tar)
'Twas his shearing mate who wrote it, and *verbatim* I will quote it:
"Clancy's gone to Queensland droving, and we don't know where he are."

In my wild erratic fancy visions come to me of Clancy
Gone a-droving "down the Cooper" where the Western drovers go;
As the stock are slowly stringing, Clancy rides behind them singing,
For the drover's life has pleasures that the townsfolk never know.

And the bush hath friends to meet him, and their kindly voices greet him
In the murmur of the breezes and the river on its bars,
And he sees the vision splendid of the sunlit plains extended,
And at night the wond'rous glory of the everlasting stars.

I am sitting in my dingy little office, where a stingy
Ray of sunlight struggles feebly down between the houses tall,
And the foetid air and gritty of the dusty, dirty city
Through the open window floating, spreads its foulness over all.

And in place of lowing cattle, I can hear the fiendish rattle
Of the tramways and the buses making hurry down the street,
And the language uninviting of the gutter children fighting,
Comes fitfully and faintly through the ceaseless tramp of feet.

And the hurrying people daunt me, and their pallid faces haunt me
As they shoulder one another in their rush and nervous haste,
With their eager eyes and greedy, and their stunted forms and weedy,
For townsfolk have no time to grow, they have no time to waste.

And I somehow rather fancy that I'd like to change with Clancy,
Like to take a turn at droving where the seasons come and go,
While he faced the round eternal of the cash-book and the journal —
But I doubt he'd suit the office, Clancy, of The Overflow.

A.B. (The Banjo) Paterson

Chapter One

Just run, I told myself, enjoying the stamp of my feet on the ground with each footfall. The bitumen was hard, and I could feel the jolt in my heels and knees. *Keep running.*

I thudded along the road and then up the footpath, connecting with the trail that cut through the bush and parkland. I'd slept badly and woken early, my muscles tense and aching from their having pretended, for hours on end, that they were anatomical armour protecting my back. It had been one of those nights … when the demons of my mind had romped around in my psyche, scaring up terrors.

So I ran. And, if I ran long enough or hard enough, I could connect – spiritually? psychologically? I didn't know how to refer to it – with my dead father. No, I wasn't crazy. It's just that, as the endorphins kicked in and the feel-goods washed through my body, I was calm enough, peaceful enough, to have comforting conversations in my mind with my dad. I missed him, especially when things were topsy-turvy at home.

My sisters and I were all fighting. And it scared me. It was happening way too much lately, and I was frightened of how it might end. Ever since my parents' deaths, six years ago, my sisters were all I had. That we were screaming at each other, night after night – or so it felt – was alarming.

Just keep running, I chanted, channelling Dory from *Finding Nemo.*

Yesterday had been okay. Only a laboratory practical and a couple of tutorials at university. Soccer practice had been cancelled, so I was home reasonably early. Time enough to chill on the porch swing in the garden for a while, before the delicious aroma of dinner cooking dragged me inside. Ginny, two sisters up and four years older at twenty-four, had chicken breasts in the skillet, smothered in Greek spices, and I could see the pan of vegetables, glistening with olive oil, pine nuts and herbs, roasting in the oven. Yum! Jane, the eldest at twenty-eight, was going to love that! Mediterranean food was her favourite. I preferred plain cooking, without all the herbs and spices, but I'd eat anything that Ginny dished up.

And then Jane had arrived home in a foul mood. This was getting to be the norm, as well. She was so big on all of us getting an education and a career, but a fat lot of good that was doing her. She was irritable and cranky most days. Teaching Geography definitely wasn't making *her* happy!

Jane either ignored the tantalising smells of the Greek-style chicken and vegetables, or she was just so caught up in her own head that she didn't even notice them. And she raised that dreaded E-word again. Enrolment. In courses. Jane wanted Ginny to enrol in university or TAFE courses and – BOOM! Ginny arced.

It was the same-old, same-old. It had been regularly occurring over the last six years: sometimes more often than at other times. Ginny was the only one of us without formal qualifications – or in the process of getting them, like I was. Daphne was twenty-six and had a degree in business; Louisa, the next up from me, had a degree in Australian Literature; and Jane, of course, had her degree in Science, majoring in Geography and Geology. Ginny, though, hadn't wanted to attend university and it bothered Jane. It was as though Jane saw it as a personal failure or something. I didn't know why Ginny was so set against it, but still … she should be able to make up her own mind.

Just keep running…

I probably should have stayed out of it – shouldn't have said anything – but I was so sick of Jane telling us all what we had to do, as though she had some special right. I didn't want to go to uni, either. I wanted to be a jillaroo. But no! Jane said "university" and that was that.

Shockingly, Daphne sided with Ginny and me. It stunned Jane, as well. She'd obviously thought Daphne would take her side.

And we were all yelling at each other. And then Jane stormed out the front door – and she didn't come home all night.

And Ginny slammed out the front door, too. And she didn't come home, either.

And Daphne stayed in her room.

And Louisa went out and didn't come back until really, really late.

And … it was confusing. And scary.

What was happening to all of us? It was almost as though we didn't *like* each other anymore.

Run, Charli. Just keep running.

I missed my Dad. Some days, more than others. Some days, like today, missing him was a sharp pain, more intense than the dull ache of yearning. He used to run with me. The two of us would sneak out while it was still dark. Through the kitchen and out the back door. He used to keep the hinges oiled so it wouldn't squeak and let anyone know what we were doing. I still oil it. First day of every month, just like he did. And I still sneak out the kitchen door, jog around the house and out the side fence, before doing my stretches on the front lawn. I still heard my Dad's voice in my head: *Isotonic stretches, Charli. If you're running, make sure you stretch your adductors or you'll risk groin injury. Don't start running until you stretch your calves and quadriceps. Warm up before you go hard.* We'd set off, down the road and through the bush, the two of us, our feet falling in a steady rhythm. It was peaceful in the mornings, before the rest of the world woke up. It was our thing: Dad's and mine. My sisters weren't the athletic type.

But Dad wasn't here. And neither was Mum. And my sisters were at each other's throats.

Just keep running, Charli!

I could feel the press of the whistle against my pecs. It was another one of Jane's rules. She thought she was the boss of us all – and I suppose she was. She'd been the one to run things since we'd lost our parents. Rule Number One: We all had to let each other know where we were. It was to keep us all safe. Rule Number Two: We all had to be home for Sunday night's dinner, no matter what else we had on at the weekend. Some weeks, it was the only time we were all together. Rule Number Three: Well, this one only really applied to me. When I went running in the early morning, or in the twilight, I had to take a whistle. Jane had it in her head that, if someone were attacking or chasing me, I'd have time to stop and blow on my whistle and the attacker would magically disappear. I thought this was stupid! I could run faster than most people and stopping to blow a whistle would give them an advantage. Another one of Jane's *safety* measures. But … it didn't cost me anything to tuck the damned thing into my sports bra and … it kept Jane happy. And – I wouldn't admit this to anyone else – it did make me feel a little less alone. As though I could call up my dad to protect me, if I ever really needed it.

I was in the zone. Where running was effortless. Where I was blissing on the euphoria of endorphins. Where I felt like my dad was right there next to me. That I could almost hear his footfalls. Nothing worried me when I was like this. *Maybe Jane should take up running. Hmmm, that might chill her out.*

I felt more like *me* when I hit the zone. Like I spent most of my waking hours trying to be someone else, but – when I ran for long enough and was high on feel-goods – I tapped into *me!*

And *me* didn't want to be at university. And *me* didn't want to be here, in the city, seeking solace in well-worn tracks through the harbourside bush. *Me* wanted to live in the country, working with animals on a farm. *Me* wanted to run in wide, open spaces: "sunlit plains extended, and at night … the everlasting stars". Just like in the poem that we'd learnt in English. Probably the only thing I got from all those lessons, Science and Maths being more my thing. But I liked that poem: Paterson's "Clancy, of the Overflow". That's why I'd named my cat "Clancy". Jane got it for me, just after Mum and Dad died. A white kitten, strange looking, with one blue eye and one green eye. But I loved him – instantly! And I named him "Clancy". Of the Overflow, but I never told anyone that. They'd think I was more stupid than they already thought me. Well, not exactly stupid: I did know my science, but they always treated me as the baby of the family.

As I ran, I pretended I was in the bush. The *real* bush. That I wasn't stuck in the city.

Dad had understood. I'd told him, when I was little, that I was going to live on a farm with the animals. And he'd smiled at me, that smile that I'd loved, that filled me with warmth, because I knew that my dad loved me and that smile was his way of saying it. It was the words *I love you, Charli* in a visual form.

And, as I ran, I heard *Take it easy, Charli. It'll be alright.* Maybe it was just the euphoria of the endorphins talking, or maybe it was my dad's spirit. It didn't matter. I felt better. Happy. Hopeful.

I headed back home.

Chapter Two

There was no breakfast.

Well, there was – but because Ginny wasn't home, there was none prepared for me. Usually, she'd make me a hot breakfast before I left for uni, especially if I'd been for an early morning run. Today, nothing. No-one was in the kitchen. Daphne had left for work already, most likely; her door was open.

Jane still wasn't home. I didn't know whether Daphne was worried, with both Ginny and Jane out all night. I guessed that, if there'd been cause for worry, she would have said something. But then again, she was hardly likely to ask me for advice. They must have contacted Daph, though. We all knew the rules.

And Louisa's door was closed. She was probably still asleep.

I felt a little bereft, being the only one at home, and up. It was a little lonely, fixing breakfast for myself. And I had to hunt around in the fridge for something to take for lunch. I hadn't realised how accustomed I was to Ginny preparing my meals. Usually, whilst I ate breakfast, she'd put my lunchbox together. Some of the students at uni laughed at me, taking a lunchbox as though I were still in school, but I didn't care. Ginny knew what I liked to eat and it saved me lots of money. I only had my Austudy allowance, which wasn't much, but as long as I didn't go crazy, it was enough for me to buy stuff I liked. If there was something else I needed, I told Jane, and Daphne gave me the money. So, the less I spent on lunch, the happier I was.

I wasn't in the mood for uni today, but Jane would freak if I didn't go. It was only a lecture and a tutorial, I reminded myself. It wasn't a jam-packed day. And then I could go practise soccer for a while.

The walk to the Metro station and, later, to the university was satisfying. I loved sunshiny days, when the sky was cloudless or just dotted with little white cotton balls, or wispy with strands of cirrus. Being outside was so much better than being closed in. I found it weird that Daphne was so happy to be shut up in her city office, day in and day out. She spent more time at work than she did at home. Why? was anyone's guess.

I was strolling across the university grounds – taking my time to get to the lecture – when I saw him.

He was sitting, alone, on a park bench seat. His head was down, his face resting on his hands; his elbows were supported by his knees, as he was hunched over. It may have been his hair that I noticed first: that soft, finger-running mess of sandy brown, not very long, but not short. The morning sun was catching the ends, lighting them up like tiny flames on miniature candles. Or it could have been his shirt, a check of white, pale and dark blues. But most likely, it was the combination of his shirt, moleskins and dirty leather boots.

Farm Boy!

The lights, bells and alarms of my Farm Boy radar were all flashing, pealing and buzzing. I was within coo-ee of a real, live farm boy!

Slowing my pace, I wrestled with some reasonable excuse to stop and talk with him. How could I attract his attention? Should I cough? Or sing? Nah, that was a dumb idea. I stomped my feet a couple of times which should have caught his attention, but … no. Still not looking up. Bugger!

I did the only thing I could.

I strode right up and sat down on the other end of the bench seat.

Then, he looked up.

'Hi,' I said, flashing him a friendly smile. At least, I hoped it looked friendly, and not like some random lunatic, too many teeth showing and crazy eyes.

'Hi,' he responded. Not exactly forthcoming. He looked … dejected. Maybe a little sad. This was when I wished I had better people skills. Daphne was always telling me I needed to "develop" them. How I was supposed to do that I had no idea! Most people liked me well enough. Some laughed at me, but I usually steered clear of them. If they were being mean to me, they weren't my sort of people. I knew I made Ginny and Lou laugh a lot, but they were my sisters. They were supposed to tease me. It was in some handbook somewhere.

'Are you alright?' I asked, adopting what I hoped was a concerned look.

'Yeah. No. Yeah. I suppose.'

If he wasn't so darned cute …

But he was. His face, now that he was looking at me, was cute as! He was probably about my age, or maybe more. He was tanned and, now that I was closer, I could see teeny, little lines around his eyes, as though he squinted a lot. His arms were tanned, too; his shirt sleeves rolled up to just below his elbows. He had beautiful eyes: they looked sad, at that moment, but they were a beautiful golden colour. Like warm amber.

'What's wrong? Can I help you?' I asked, with more of that concerned face. It was working, after all.

'Nah. Thanks for asking, though. Nah. Just gotta get through today.' He rubbed his hands together and then clasped them, his elbows still on his knees. 'You a student?' he asked, changing the subject.

'Yeah.'

'What're you studying?'

'Science. With agriculture.'

'You must be smart,' he smiled.

Keep him talking, Charli!

'At some things. Most people think I'm dumb.'

'Why?' He'd shifted on the seat so that he was facing me now, his hands resting on his thighs. And what beautiful thighs they were, too. The delineation of his long muscles was clearly visible through the fabric of his pants. No fat on Farm Boy!

''Cause I say dumb stuff, sometimes. I don't mean to. Sometimes things just come out wrongly. And people laugh at me.' *Stop this, Charli! Don't tell him all your faults, you idiot!* Talk about saying "dumb stuff"!

'You can't be stupid, though, or you wouldn't be studying Science. I hardly made it through high school.' He waved his hand toward the massive sandstone buildings of the university, visible across the field. 'And you're at Sydney Uni?'

'Yeah. I study here.'

'Then you must be smart,' he stated, as though this were a foregone conclusion.

'Well, yeah. Kinda.' And then I responded to his raised eyebrows, his expressive face asking the question. 'I got a scholarship. I did alright at school, like in Maths and Science, but I got a scholarship. I don't know that I'd be here without it.'

'What sort of scholarship?'

'A sport one. They wanted me for their Soccer Club. To play on their soccer team.'

'You good at soccer?' Farm Boy didn't use more words than he needed, that was for sure.

'Oh, I'm not too bad,' I said, airily. 'I know how to kick a ball.' I grinned.

'If you got a scholarship for kicking that ball, you must be good at it,' he commented, dryly.

'Well, I *did* play on the state team for two years, in the schools' competition.' I laughed at his stunned look, his eyes wide with surprise. 'Yeah, I'm not bad at it.' I shrugged, pretending to be modest.

'What's your name?' he asked.

'Charli.'

'I'm Sam. You from around here, then?'

'Sort of. I live on the other side of the harbour. In Greenwich. You?'

'Nah. I come from Condobolin. I live on a farm near there.'

'Con – what?'

'Condobolin. It's in the centre of New South Wales. Some say it *is* the centre, although it's really a little bit north of there, at Mt Tilga. Got a wheat/sheep farm out there.'

'So, what are you doing here? How come you're in Sydney?'

'My dad. He's having tests. At the Royal Prince Alfred, just across the road.' He gestured towards the tall building visible through the trees. The hospital was usually referred to as "The RPA", but maybe country boys didn't know that.

'What's wrong with him?' I asked, trying to be subtle and not blunt, as my sisters would accuse me of being.

'Dunno. Hopefully, nothin'. The visiting specialist – at Dubbo Hospital – wanted Dad to get tests done. He's over there now.' He faced away from me for a moment and I knew that he was worried about his dad.

'How long will it take?' I asked.

'Who knows. Dad said he'd ring me when I needed to pick him up. I drove him down yesterday, so he'd be rested okay for today. I figured I'd just sit here and wait.'

'I'll wait with you,' I promptly said.

'Don't you have to go to class? Or lectures? Or whatever they call them.' And then it occurred to me that, maybe, he didn't want me to wait with him. I felt my face heat up and I knew that I was blushing. I ducked my head in embarrassment. Here I was, inviting myself into this guy's space and problem, when he most probably just wanted to be left alone – to worry – by himself.

'Oh, sure. I'll just leave you alone. I'm sorry. I didn't think.' The words stumbled out of me and I picked up my backpack, which I'd dropped to the ground, and stood.

'No. No, don't go. I didn't mean for you to go. I just thought that you had to be somewhere.' He stood, too, and reached out a hand. To stop me? Maybe. Didn't matter. I sat back down, letting my backpack fall to the ground between my feet.

'So, how long are you here for?' *That's it, Charli. Keep the conversation going.*

'Dunno. The specialist said we'd get the test results back by Monday, so we booked into a hotel until then. If we need to stay longer …' His voice petered out.

'So,' I started again, 'do you own the farm? Or just work on it?'

'We own it. Or Dad does. Been in the family for generations.' He fell silent, studying the ground again.

C'mon, Charli.

'You got any brothers or sisters?' I asked.

'Got a brother. Daniel. He's a couple of years older than me. He stayed home to manage things.'

'I've got four sisters,' I volunteered. That got his attention!

'*Four* sisters?'

'Yep,' I said, proudly, as though I'd created them myself.

'No boys?' Sam queried, incredulous.

'Nope. Well, Dad used to say that *I* was his boy. You know, in a tomboy sort of way.'

Sam looked me up and down, as if he were only just noticing me. I felt self-conscious. I knew that I wasn't exactly ugly; it suited my face to have my dirty-blonde hair drawn back in a long plait down my back, highlighting my wide brow and cheekbones. I wasn't dainty and pretty as other girls were, but people had said nice things about my smile and I really liked that my eyes were a deep chocolate. None of my sisters had that colour: it was all mine.

Under his scrutiny, though, I wished I had a more shapely body, instead of the stocky athletic frame. *Get over it, Charli. Nothing you can do about it. Hold your head up and pull your shoulders back. Own it!*

'Nah, your dad was wrong. You're not a boy.' He smiled, lifting his right cheek in a little half-wink. 'Four sisters! That must be interesting.'

'That's one word for it! Sometimes, it's just painful. They can be very bossy.'

'Where do you come?'

'I'm the youngest. Jane's the eldest, and then Daphne, Ginny and Lou.'

'Do you all live at home?'

'Yeah.'

'What? None of you married? How old's – what was her name? – Jane?'

'Yeah. Twenty-eight.'

'Seven of you in the one house?'

'No. Only us five.'

'What about your parents?'

'Um.' I fidgeted with my hair, twirling the end of the plait between my fingers. I hated saying this. People didn't know how to react most of the time, either wincing and offering condolences, or finding some excuse to leave, as though normal conversation is all too hard. 'My parents passed away.'

'What? They *died*?' He leant forward, in disbelief. Then, as though he realised what he'd said and how bluntly he'd said it, caught himself. 'I'm sorry. That was rude of me.' He paused, studying my face. 'Did you want to talk about it?'

'Not particularly. It happened a long time ago.' At least he hadn't said, "I'm sorry for your loss." I hated that. 'D'you want to go for a walk? I could give you a tour of the uni, if you like?'

'Sure. That'd be good. I'm not used to sitting around.' He stood and held out his hand. I wasn't sure why, until he grasped the strap of my backpack. 'Here, I'll carry it.'

'You don't have to. I'm used to it.'

'Oh, my dad would have kittens if he knew I'd let a girl carry her own stuff when I didn't have anything in my hands. He's old-fashioned that way.' He shrugged.

'Alright.' I let go of the straps.

'Geez, what have you got in here? Bricks?' His eyes widened in surprise.

'Not much. Just a couple of textbooks.' I was used to the weight: I didn't even think about it, anymore. 'I can take it back, if you want.'

'Nah, I'll survive. So, where are you taking me first?'

I took a methodical approach, leading him around the perimeter of the grounds, before threading our way between the buildings, systematically covering the entire university. We shared my water bottle as we walked and later sat under a tree, splitting the sandwich, apple, and cheese and crackers I'd packed for my lunch. It wasn't much – and I was still hungry when we'd finished – but it felt special, the two of us sharing simple food like that. It felt significant, in some way.

We finally arrived back at our park bench, having spent hours chatting about inconsequential things – the university buildings, the people who worked and studied there, the different sporting and cultural clubs that students supported, and how hot the day was. We avoided the topic of his father and the tests he was taking; and talking about my family. It was easier that way, although every so often, Sam would turn his head towards the hospital and pause for a moment. He was obviously worried about his dad.

'You want coffee?' he asked. 'Or tea?'

'Yeah, that'd be good.' I stepped up next to him as he shouldered my backpack once more. It was then I felt the rough touch of his fingers, as his hand reached back to mine and, hand-in-hand, we strolled across the grass to a nearby cafe.

Chapter Three

I had no difficulty spotting Sam's father as he left the hospital: the two of them were like before-and-after photos of the same man, separated by about thirty years. They had the same sandy brown hair, just brushing their collars; the same sun-roughened skin, although Sam's dad's was more weathered, but less tanned than Sam's; the same warm amber eyes. In that instance, I knew what Sam's dad had looked like as a young man, and how handsome – in an RM-Williams-sort-of-way – Sam would become. And they had the same walk. An I'm-not-in-a-rush kind of amble. It made me smile. I knew that I was going to like his dad.

'Dad, this is Charli,' Sam said, flicking his hand towards me. 'Charli, this is my dad.'

'Nice to meet you, Mr …' I faltered.

'It's Walker, Charli. Dan Walker,' he said, smiling a little tiredly. He extended his hand and I was reassured by his firm clasp as he shook my hand, his skin warm against mine. *Maybe he's not really sick at all,* I hoped. The tension around his eyes, though, suggested that he was worried. He turned to Sam. 'Didn't take you long to find a new friend,' he teased.

'Do you need to sit, Dad? What do you want? Have you eaten yet?'

'Let's head back to the hotel, Sam. I've been poked and prodded. A rest on the lounge will be good. I can get something to eat once we're there.'

They both started walking – to their car, I guessed. I didn't quite know what to do. Did I say goodbye and go? Was my time with Sam over, now that his father had returned? Or should I just tag along? Accompany them to their car? Sam still had my backpack on his shoulder. I hesitated, slowing my pace, and Sam must have noticed because he stopped and turned.

'Are you coming, Charli?'

'Um… Will I be in the way? I mean, did you and your father want to be alone?'

'She may have somewhere she needs to be, Son,' his father prompted.

'Nah,' Sam said, smiling. 'Charli's been bad today, Dad. She's played hookey. Wagging her uni classes.' He winked at me and I returned his smile, enjoying his flirting.

'You're more than welcome to join us, Charli,' Mr Walker said, graciously. 'I'm not much company for Sam. Do you need to let someone know where you're going?'

'Nope. Not at this time of day.' I caught up to where they waited patiently, and Sam reached for my hand as I neared them. I squirmed a little self-consciously at the amused smile that stretched across his father's face. He glanced up at Sam, his eyebrows raised in speculation.

The drive to the hotel took only minutes, most of the time spent getting in and out of parking spaces. I realised that they'd only driven the short distance because Mr Walker was unwell. It was quite endearing to see how considerate and gentle Sam was with his father. I wondered if Sam was always like this with his dad or if it was only new behaviour, because of his dad's ill-health. I knew that my sisters would think I was silly, but I was a little envious of Sam: his being able to care for his dad like that. I'd like to think that I'd treat my dad as carefully and gently, but that could never happen now.

I'd never stayed in a hotel before, especially not one in the city. When we'd travelled for soccer games, we were usually billeted with home team players, or Jane and Daphne organised a motel room. But, wow!

It was not exactly a hotel: more like a little village of apartments, all connected to a courtyard, filled with garden beds. Everything looked very new and stylish. And the room… It wasn't a room; it was like a proper apartment. It had two bedrooms, a kitchen, lounge and a balcony. When I plonked myself down on the end of Sam's bed, the softness of the mattress and doona … It was like the bed was made of pillows! And the views! When I asked if I could see the bathroom, Sam's dad gave me that same indulgent smile I would have expected from my father. He nodded, saying, 'Knock yourself out, Charli. Feel free to explore. But there's two bathrooms; not one.'

'*Two?* Really?' It was all so *interesting*.

'What do you want to eat, Dad?' Sam was reading from a cafe menu. 'Steak sanger?'

'That'll do. Have you two eaten?'

'Yeah, but I could go a steak sanger, too. Charli?'

'Umm. I – um – don't have any money with me.' I did have some, but I didn't know how much a place like this would charge for food delivered to the room.

Sam's dad just laughed. 'Don't worry about that, Charli. They'll just charge the credit card. Have whatever you want.'

'Thank you, Mr Walker. A steak sandwich sounds good.' I wasn't sure about "charging the card", but if they weren't worried about it, then I wouldn't either.

After Sam ordered, we pulled two chairs over to lounge where Sam's dad was resting and waited for our food, which didn't take long at all.

'So, you're at university, Charli?'

'Yes, Mr Walker. Sydney Uni.'

'What're you studying?'

'Well, it's a double degree. A bit of a mouthful. If you asked my sisters, they'd tell you I was doing Animal Husbandry.'

'What are you doing, then?'

'It's a Bachelor of Science with a Bachelor of Advanced Studies in Agriculture. You see, Mr Walker, what I *really* want to do is work on a farm and be a jillaroo. But my sisters – well, mostly Jane, but Daphne as well – won't let me.'

'Your sisters?' He frowned, confusion on his face. 'What do your parents say?'

'Umm. Well,' again with this … revelation. 'My parents are dead,' I said, in a rush, getting it over with. 'It's just my sisters and me. There are five of us.'

He stilled and I saw him glance at Sam, who nodded slightly. 'Back up a bit, Charli.' I stayed silent, matching his stillness, and watched him take a deep breath. 'When did your parents pass?' he asked, gently.

'It was ages ago. Six years. I was fourteen.'

'Was it a car accident?' he probed.

'Nope.' I shook my head. 'There was a plane crash. It was on my mum's birthday. Dad and her went up for a joy flight for her birthday present. And they crashed. And I didn't see them again.'

'So, did you go to stay with relatives?'

'No. No. Although Jane said at the time that I had to be good – well, Ginny, Lou and me had to be good – or we would be taken away. To live with rellies or strangers. Jane and Daphne took care of it so we could all stay together. In our house. And we've all been there ever since.'

'How old are Jane and Daphne?' he asked, thoughtfully.

'Jane's twenty-eight and Daph's twenty-six. Then there's Ginny, Lou and then me.'

'So, your sisters – Jane and Daphne – were managing a family of five at – what? Twenty and twenty-two?'

'Yeah. I guess.'

'You've got a couple of special sisters, there, Charli.' There was admiration, both in the tone of his voice and the sharp, angled nod of his head.

'I suppose,' I conceded, 'but it's not always good. There's been lots of fights lately. And Jane thinks she knows everything and she wants to control everything that everyone does. Like, I don't want to be at university. I want to be a jillaroo, but she doesn't care. "Go to university and do animal husbandry," she said. There isn't even a course by that name, but she still calls it "animal husbandry" if anyone asks.' I knew I sounded petulant, like a spoilt child, but it irked me that I had so little say in what I was doing. I knew that it infuriated Ginny, as well, especially when Jane started up about Ginny going to uni, too.

'I can see your frustration, Charli,' Mr Walker said quietly, 'but it's not necessarily a bad thing, your going to university to study. Farm work, these days, relies more and more on scientific knowledge, rather than just the practical experience handed down from generations. What you're learning now will help when you finally get to be the jillaroo you want to be.'

'Maybe,' I agreed, unenthusiastically, 'but last night there was a huge fight with everyone – well, except for Louisa – and then Jane and Ginny didn't come home. If Jane keeps going, bossing everyone around all the time, I don't know what will happen.' I could hear the tremor in my voice and I didn't want Mr Walker to think I was a cry-baby. 'We all have to stick together and Jane is making it hard.'

'Hmm, it sounds like five young women living together can get a little tense. Maybe a circuit breaker is in order.'

I frowned. A circuit breaker? What did electricity have to do with anything?

After we'd eaten, Sam's dad rested on his bed, whilst Sam and I sat out on the balcony, amusing ourselves by trying to work out, using Google Maps on our phones, what the buildings we could see in the distance were.

'Sam,' his father called and Sam rose, venturing into his father's room.

'I'm not going to be up for that Roaring Snore thing tonight.'

'Roar and Snore, Dad. It's okay. We can cancel.'

'I'm sorry, Son. You were looking forward to it.'

'Yeah, but Dad, we both knew that it might be too much.'

'What's Roaring Snore?' I asked, having followed Sam to stand in the bedroom doorway and trying to follow the conversation.

'Roar and Snore. It's on at Taronga Zoo. I've been wanting to do it for ages. Dad and I thought we'd take advantage of coming to town to do it, but … It doesn't matter. Another time.'

'So, what is it again?' I asked. I'd never heard of it.

'You know,' Sam's dad started, his eyes half-closed in speculation, 'you could still go, Sam. Charli could, perhaps, go in my place.'

I watched the hope flash across Sam's face, followed quickly by disappointment.

'Dad, they require ID. There's no way that Charli could pass for you.' He smiled at that last bit.

'Why don't you two go down and explore the vegetable garden, and I'll just make a phone call or two.' He nodded his head towards the door. 'Give me ten minutes, Sam, and I'll see what I can do.'

'Do you think he'll be able to organise it?' I asked Sam as we walked down the stairs.

'Maybe. Dad can be pretty persuasive when he wants to be. I've seen him in action. But Charli, would you want to come?'

'I don't even know what it is. How do I know if I want to go?'

'It's the Roar and Snore at Taronga Zoo –'

'Yeah, you said that already. But what's a Roar and Snore?' I interrupted, impatiently.

'I've never been, but it sounds so exciting! You camp out at the zoo, in tents, after you do a night safari through the zoo with guides and stuff. They give you dinner and drinks, and there's sessions where they tell you about stuff. And then you get a whole day at the zoo!'

'Wow!' I breathed. Camping and animals. Two things I loved most. Well, I didn't know if I'd like camping: I'd never done it, but it *sounded* like something I'd love. I wanted to go. But ...

'Sam, I don't know how much it costs.'

'Don't worry about it, Charli. Dad most probably won't. He already paid for it.' Sam shrugged my concerns away, but ... I didn't really know these people. Would Sam's dad really shout me for what sounded like a very expensive treat? And what would Jane say? She'd be bound to say no.

'A friend of mine back home did it,' Sam continued. 'Said he had a blast! You could hear the animals outside all night. Like in their cages,' he added, as though he were reassuring me that I'd be safe. Little did he know that the *idea* of animals going for a stroll around the zoo at night was ... *thrilling!* Like in that movie, *Night at the Museum*.

'Hey, check out this garden!' Sam interrupted my musings. 'We should come down for a sunbake later.'

I laughed. 'Sam, if you're going to Roar and Snore, you won't have time for lolling around on banana lounges later.' I nudged him with my elbow. 'You're like a kid who wants all the lollies in the shop.'

'Well, yeah. Why wouldn't you?' He looked puzzled, which made me laugh all over again. 'Let's go back up and see if Dad's been lucky.'

I knew, as soon as we entered the unit, that he'd been successful by the beaming smile on his face. He was still resting on his bed in his room, lying against the bedhead with two pillows supporting his back and his arm resting on another pillow.

'Ring Jane and ask her if you can go,' he instructed, whilst Sam and I were high-fiving each other.

I arced. 'I don't need to ask her permission. I'm not a child,' I complained, sounding exactly like a child. 'The rule is that we let someone know where we are.' I nibbled on the side of my thumb nail for a moment. 'I'll text Lou.'

'Which one's Lou?' Sam asked.

'Next one up,' I smiled at him, understanding how difficult some people found it to keep track of all my sisters. 'She'll give me the least grief.'

Mr Walker stayed silent, although he watched me whilst I texted Louisa. *Won't be home tonight. I'm going to Roar and Snore at Taronga Zoo with a friend. Bronte.*

Almost immediately, Lou's response flashed back at me. *Roar and Snore? Which friend?*

You don't know him. He's new. I met him today.

I felt a bit awkward, sitting there on Sam's father's bed, holding my phone, whilst I waited for her reply. Sam's dad still didn't say anything and Sam was vibrating with impatience. And then it came.

Zoo thing sounds exciting. Can see why you want to go. Who is this person? Give him my number and get him to text me on his phone.

'What!' I must have said it out loud, because Sam's dad held his hand out, nodding towards the phone. When he read the string of text messages, he nodded and smiled.

'Sam, send a text to this number,' he rattled off Lou's phone number from my screen, 'and include your name, and then my name, the name of this hotel and my phone number.' He turned towards me. 'I like your sister. She's smart.' Glancing back at Sam, he said, 'And write that I'm your father.'

'I could have sent a text with all of that info,' I grumbled.

'Yes, but we could have given you false numbers. Lou knows Sam's number is genuine, now.' He tipped his head. 'She's a smart lady.'

'I'm smart, too,' I mumbled beneath my breath, hoping no-one heard me. I was wrong, though: Sam was busy with his phone, but I saw Sam's dad narrow his eyes, sharply looking up from his lowered eyebrows.

'I'm very sure you are, Charli. But my guess is you're smart in other ways.' He gave me a gentle smile and, just in that moment, he reminded me of my dad. A pang of loss zapped through me and I caught my breath. Sometimes. Just like that. A zap!

My phone beeped. *Do you need money?*

When I relayed the message, his father shook his head. 'No, Charli. This is already paid for and Sam has money, if you need anything.'

'I can pay for things,' I protested.

'I'm sure you can, Charli, but you're doing me a favour. You're doing both of us a favour, isn't she, Sam?' At Sam's nod, his dad continued, 'Sam wouldn't be able to go without you going, too. I'm not up to it. So, don't you worry about money.' He turned back to Sam. 'You'll need to get moving, Son. Get yourself packed. Remember, warm clothes and rain gear, just in case. Sunscreen. Walking boots. You need to be there by five thirty, but I told them you might be a little late. You still need to get over to Charli's place. Where do you live, Charli? Is it far from here?' We all walked into Sam's room.

'Not really, but the traffic might be a problem. I normally catch the Metro, so I'm not on the road.'

'You'll need walking shoes, Charli. Toiletries. Wet weather gear. Change of clothes. Sam will have sunscreen. A hat. Your swimmers, if you'd like. And Sam,' he said, watching Sam putting socks, underwear and shirts on the bed, 'throw in a couple of towels. Should be spare ones around here.' He paused, closing his eyes and taking a long breath.

'What about you, Dad? Will you be alright?'

'Sam, I won't be going anywhere. I'll just stay here and watch the Idiot Box. Might get another one of those steak sandwiches. You can ring me later if you want to check on me.' He smiled. 'I won't be having any wild parties.'

And while Sam packed, methodically laying out items and then securing them in a duffle bag, I stood, bristling with excitement. I pinched my arm a couple of times, just to prove this was real. This morning, I'd been so out-of-sorts, rattled about how much our family had been fighting, and missing my father.

And now…

Now I was going on an adventure! With a real live Farm Boy. To a zoo. With animals. And camping.

Who knew life could be this … incredible!

Chapter Four

We were late.

It'd taken us a while navigating the afternoon traffic across the harbour and, even though I'd moved as quickly as I could when we got home – I'd planned what I'd take whilst we were in transit – it still used up time. On the drive, I kept sneaking peaks at Sam: he really was super cute! Every so often, he'd look over at me and smile, that sexy little grin. And I couldn't decide what was sexier – his hair or his arms. His hair was – it was all soft … and fluffy …. and all I wanted to do was run my fingers through it. Finger-running hair, my sister Ginny would call it. But his arms … he had his sleeves rolled up to just below his elbows, showing off the dusting of fine golden hairs on his tanned skin. And when he moved – adjusting the steering wheel, changing gears, turning the indicator on to change lanes – the muscles below that tanned skin rippled. And it was *so* sexy! It made me all warm and liquid inside. The "inside" where it counted!

We were going to share a tent all night. At the zoo! With animals outside! The whole idea was so *stipulating! That's not the right word,* I could hear Lou's voice in my head. *Stimulating.* That was it!

I wondered if he felt the same way that I did. If he looked at me and thought, *"yes!"*

At that exact moment, he moved his head, just slightly to the left, and glanced at me out of the side of his eyes. And then he smiled. I felt myself redden, heat blossoming on my face. I was positive that he *knew* what I was thinking.

And then, deep inside where no-one else could see, I danced a jig! He *knew* what I was thinking and he didn't look horrified. *Oh, yes, Charli. Life is looking up!*

No-one else was home, so I made sure that I fed Clancy before I left. And … I was going to spend the night with Farm Boy! It may have been a little presumptuous of me but … I grabbed a couple of condoms from my secret stash in the bottom drawer of my dresser.

'Nice digs. Big house,' Sam had said. 'Do you all own this?'

'It was Mum and Dad's. We inherited it. All of us. I suppose I own one-fifth of it.' I'd never thought of that before. Jane and Daph were always the bosses, so I hadn't considered that I had a share in the house. Who knew!

The drive to Taronga Park Zoo was easy – we were going against the traffic – but we were still late. It didn't seem to matter, though, and we could thank Sam's dad for that. We were shown where to leave our belongings and then there was a welcoming orientation with drinks and nibbles.

'Do you want wine, Charli?'

'Nah. I don't like wine. Have they got beer?'

'A girl after my own heart.' He plucked two beers from the nearby table and we clinked the bottle necks together. 'Cheers!' we both said, smiling at each other.

'I'm so excited, Sam. I can't believe we're doing this. When I woke up this morning, I had no idea what today would bring!'

'That's what's good about life, Charli. You never know what's coming at you. Just like in that movie, *Castaway*, when the guy says about not knowing what the morning tide will bring in.'

'Oooh, you liked that movie, too? I *hated* it when Wilson left. I cried and cried.'

'Yeah, but Wilson had sort of – you know – served his *purpose*.'

'I guess. I still hated it that he went. I hate it when you lose things that are important to you.'

I could feel Sam's eyes on my face, studying me, as we both fell quiet. *You're such a downer, Charli! Way to kill the mood!*

'And then you get new things,' Sam said. 'New experiences. Like this.' He waved his right arm, with the beer in his hand, at our surroundings. I could see the Sydney Harbour Bridge from here. And the Opera House.

'Pretty amazing view,' I agreed. 'Well, except for those funny-looking buildings near the Opera House.'

'Yeah, they don't really fit, do they?'

'People call it The Toaster. It'd be strange living there, I reckon. I mean, you wouldn't have any privacy. That's one thing about our house: there's lots of privacy in the back yard because of the trees along the fence line and the bushes and stuff. But if you lived there … I mean, if you were on your balcony, everyone walking past would be able to see you. Nah. Wouldn't want to live there.'

'Good view of the bridge, though. And it's right on the harbour. You could watch all the boats coming and going.'

'I s'pose. I reckon there's good and bad in everything.'

'Yeah. I love where we live. The land's flat and the skies are huge. I love the colours: the red of the dirt, the blue of the sky – and, Charli, the sunsets are amazing! But it does have its downside. We're a long way from a lot of things. For instance, it's a long drive to the RPA Hospital. It's not like it's just down the road. And we don't have a zoo like this. The Dubbo Zoo's pretty great, but it's not the Taronga Park Zoo.'

'Hmm. I'd love to see your place. I've always wanted to live in the bush.'

'It's not exactly *bush*, Charli. Open plains. The road from Parkes to Condo is straight. For miles and miles. The worst time of day to drive west is in the late afternoon. The sun's in your eyes the entire way. And in the morning, you don't want to be heading east. We usually time things so we're not travelling right on sunrise or sunset. And,' he smiled, 'the added advantage is that we stay off the road when the 'roos are jumping about. They're more active at sunrise and sunset.'

'I've never seen a wild kangaroo before. You're so lucky, growing up there. I wish I had,' I sighed.

Dinner was incredible. I ate so much, I didn't think I'd be able to move, let alone do the evening safari walk. It was so special, being in the zoo at night; there weren't many of us as COVID restrictions limited the number of people who could attend. It was magical, wandering around the exhibits, seeing the animals in the late twilight. The guides gave us heaps of excellent information, telling us about each of the animals as we passed their enclosures: their eating, mating and sleeping habits. Some were nocturnal and slept all day, whilst others were looking weary already from their day's activities. When we'd met some animals, taken lots of selfies and photos of the harbour at night, especially the Sydney Harbour Bridge, all lit up, it was time for coffee and dessert. It was all like a fairy-tale: the pretty lights, the exotic fauna, the amazing food, the excellent service from waiters and guides, and – through it all – Farm Boy!

He was so easy to like! He made me laugh, mimicking some of the animals as we passed, and his impression of the chimpanzees was hilarious.

Even other guests stopped to laugh with us. And he was considerate of me, helping me to the front and ensuring that I had a good view of the exhibits or the sights we were being shown. And he had excellent table manners, even making me feel a little crass at times. He was polite and respectful to older guests, especially the women, and he remembered all of his "pleases" and "thankyous", prompting me to remember mine.

'I can see how your boyfriend charmed you,' oozed one smartly dressed woman, ageless in her facial perfection, her blonde hair stylishly casual. 'I could find *lots* to do with him.'

I decided I didn't like her much, although I didn't disagree with her sentiments. My imagination had joined the zoo, running wild with plenty of activities we could do together myself, mostly to do with mating habits, as we'd satisfied our hunger for food earlier. Half the time, I didn't know whether to be looking at our native animals – mostly nocturnal so they could escape the heat of the Australian climate – or looking at the native man. And I, Charli White, was with him! *Back off, Society Women!*

When we returned to our allocated tent and we'd finished with the facilities, I thought we'd be straight to bed. The guides had warned us that we'd be up with the sun the next morning – which meant "early" – and Sam had had a huge day, what with worrying about his father and all. I'd spent a fair bit of time overthinking the sleeping arrangements. Or, more to the point, the bit *before* the sleeping happened. Was I being slutty, wanting to get it on with Sam the very first day I met him? Or was I "living in the moment" and milking life for what it was giving me? I knew I was overthinking – I did that sometimes. My sisters said I didn't think enough, but how did they know what went on in my head?

All I knew for sure was that Sam had been dropped in my lap, like a gift from the gods – just when I needed *something* to ground me. And my father's words from this morning kept circling around my mind: *Take it easy, Charli. It'll be alright.* Dad used to say something like that often to me when I was a kid. *Take it easy, Charli, but take it.* It was usually when something went wrong: I missed a goal; the weather was crappy for an important game; I got a question wrong in a Maths test. *Take it easy, but take it.* His attitude was always *You can't control what happens and you have to deal with it, but you don't have to get all tied up in a knot.*

How did Dad's words apply to this? Stop stressing and just let it unfold? Probably.

'Let's sit out for a while,' Sam said, quietly, just as I was about to enter the tent.

'Oh, I thought we had to be up early.' *Shut up, Charli!*

'Yeah, we do. But let's just sit out here, in the cool, and enjoy the night for a minute or two.' He walked over to a tree just off to one side of our tent and plonked himself down, leaning back against the broad trunk. He gestured towards the space between his spread legs and said, 'C'm'ere, Charli. Take the weight off.'

I smiled. This was looking promising!

'Sure,' I chirped, happily, as I eased myself down onto the ground, taking care not to touch him. But Sam was having none of that. Sliding his hands along the length of my upper arms, he tugged me towards him, aligning my back with his front. His hands continued down to my wrists and he drew both of our arms across my chest. He inhaled deeply when I twisted my hands and clasped his forearms, releasing his breath as we both sunk into each other.

'This is what I like,' Sam whispered in my ear. 'When the night goes quiet and other people are in their beds and the heat of the day escapes from a cloudless sky. You can see the stars – well, not here. Too many lights in the city. But back home, the sky is filled with stars. You'd love it, Charli. It's like those paintings you do in kindergarten. You know, when you paint all over the paper in one colour and then, when it's dry, you load up a paintbrush with another colour and *flick* it all over, from above. Lots of little stars in a dark background.'

His voice was a murmur behind my ear, his hands slowly sliding up and down my forearms, his fingers gently caressing my skin along the backs of my hands. His touch was soft, but not smooth, a slight hitch caused by his work-roughened skin. I could feel the muscles along my spine relaxing into him, my body melting into his.

'At home, I come out at night and chill, before I go to bed. Unwind from the day. Even if it rains. I like the sound of the rain at night.'

'Maybe you're nocturnal,' I whispered, teasing him.

'Maybe I am,' he chuckled. 'I do sleep better if I've spent some time in the dark, just chilling.'

'Hmm.' The sound of his voice and rhythmic stroke of his fingers was making me drowsy, lulled into a boneless mass.

'Are you going to sleep?' His voice was low, his mouth brushing the curls of my ear. I could feel his breath on my cheek and the faint scent of the orange chocolate dessert filled my nostrils. But it was the touch of his fingers, just grazing the skin near my bellybutton, exposed by the gap in my shirt buttons, that jolted me awake!

'Ahh, n-no,' I croaked, my throat suddenly dry.

'You know,' he crooned in my ear, his chin nuzzling my neck, nudging aside my plaited hair, 'my father told me that I was to treat you like a gentleman.' I tried to stifle my gasp as his fingers explored the skin across the top of my shorts. It was such a soft touch – not really a tickle – but it felt like he had a wand, electrically charging my skin. 'And I want to be that gentleman, Charli. I really do.' His jaw rolled along my shoulder, whilst his arms tightened around me, a tiny cuddle. I think I stopped breathing. 'But what I *really* want, what I *truly* want, is to kiss you.' His hand rose to my chin and, clasping it tenderly, he tilted my face back towards him and stared into my eyes, my wide-open eyes. 'Is that what you want, Charli?' His voice was a drug and I could only offer a teeny nod, barely perceptible. But he saw it. I could tell by the darkening of his amber eyes. They heated to a treacle colour.

Oh, Farm Boy!

It was the only thought I had as he lowered his mouth to mine.

Chapter Five

He was so gentle, this farm boy with the workman's hands. Delicate little nibbles, tiny brushes of his mouth against mine, tender flicks of his tongue on the outer edges of my lips, and then a smooth swipe across the seam of my mouth, encouraging me to open. My breath left me in a long exhalation and I think I forgot to inhale again.

He lifted his head. 'Breathe, Charli. Take a breath.' His mouth curved upwards, quiet humour in his eyes, satisfaction in his smile. I lifted my mouth up towards his in silent invitation, which he accepted, his mouth covering mine in a long, lazy kiss.

Sam was kissing me slowly, reverently, and it was too much. I twisted in his grasp, kneeling on the ground in front of him, and he straightened his body away from the tree, lifting his face to meet mine. I slid my fingers along his jaw, digging them into the softness of his hair, and gave him a full, open-mouthed kiss. His hands came up to my face, holding me gently, but firmly, in an attempt to slow me down but … it was too intense, his way of kissing. It was scary intense. I could handle kissing him; indeed, I was impatient to have sex with him, but this slow passionate stuff… It terrified me.

'Charli,' Sam murmured against my mouth, 'we've got all night. We don't need to rush.' He nuzzled his cheek against my lips, the slight rasp of his whiskers making me quiver.

'We can do it your way later, Sam,' I groaned. 'But right now … I just want you. I want to climb on you and I want to ride you. Hard.' I was almost panting, the words coming out of my mouth in gasps. 'I don't want slow, Sam. I want *hard*. And I want it right *now*.' I kissed him, my tongue in his mouth, daring his to tangle with me, whilst I pushed myself against him, my breasts rubbing against his chest. Frustration at the fabric separating us clawed at me.

'Okay,' Sam said, pulling away from me and placing his hands on either side of my waist. 'Take it easy, Charli.' The words stopped me cold. I sat back on my heels, hunched over in embarrassment. Maybe I was too sluttish. What was the word? Wanton.

'Hey,' Sam soothed, his fingers beneath my chin, lifting it so that he could see my eyes, which I directed downward in my humiliation. 'Hey, Charli. Look at me.' When I looked up, peering from beneath my lashes, he smiled. 'Let's go into the tent. We don't have to worry about prying nocturnal eyes,' he joked, glancing at the tents and the bush surrounding us, before he returned his gaze to me. 'And then we can do anything you want,' he whispered, a promise in the directness of his eyes.

He steadied me as he helped me rise, before standing himself. And then, with a sexy wink, he smiled and led me back to the tent. He carefully closed the flap, ensuring the locking mechanism was secured, before walking us both to one of the camp beds. Sitting down, he tugged me forward, his hands at my waist as I lowered myself to straddle him, my knees on the bed and my backside comfortable on his strong thighs. And then he leant back, locking his elbows and resting his weight on his hands behind him.

'I'm all yours, Charli. Do with me what you want.'

I jerked in surprise. *Really?* My astonishment must have been all over my face because he smiled and dipped his head in assent.

'Sure, Cowgirl. You go for it!' he encouraged.

My immediate reaction – I'm a little embarrassed to admit – was to clap my hands on my cheeks, covering the enormous grin that I knew broke out on my face. Sam laughed, no doubt at the excitement in my wide eyes and the thrill rippling through me.

'Has no-one ever let you take the lead before, Cowgirl?' he crooned.

I shook my head. 'No. Not ever.'

'Then this is for you.' He shrugged and smiled, a deliciously sexy smile.

Bracing my hands on his shoulders, I leant forward and touched my lips to his. A soft shy kiss. So much for my fast-paced passion from before. I felt like I was exploring new territory – which I was, I suppose. Sam kissed me back, opening his mouth to accept the tentative sweep of my tongue, but he didn't take control of the kiss. He left it to me. I sucked gently on his lower lip, drawing it into my mouth, and I felt him tremble, hearing his sharp intake of breath. And I licked his lips, outlining his mouth with the tip of my tongue, before I pulled away from him, leaning back on his thighs.

He was watching me, his eyelids at half-mast, a faint smile on his parted lips. And I was watching him, feeling all sultry and powerful. I reached forward and eased the buttons through the holes on his shirt, one by one, feeling like a seductress. The rise and fall of his chest as he breathed was his only movement, except when I separated the front of his shirt and slid my hands over his skin, lightly covered with fair hair. He quivered then – a barely perceptible rippling of skin over muscle.

So much for avoiding intense sensation. I was heating, from the inside out. My core clenched in appreciation of the visual feast that was his chest and abs, and then clenched again, warming and melting in anticipation of what was in store for me, for both of us.

I reached up and slowly unbuttoned my shirt front, watching him watch me as each button was released and more of my skin was revealed. He glanced up at me, his amber eyes molten beneath heavy eyelids, when I shrugged my shirt off my shoulders and down my arms. His breathing deepened and I realised that my breaths – in and out – were synchronised with his. I thought that he'd move, then; that he would take over, but he didn't – and I wasn't sure what my next move should be. Did I stand and take off my jeans? Should I remove my bra?

The answer came from following his gaze, so hot and charged that my nipples had hardened into two solid beads. Bra, it was, then. I squirmed on his lap, as I reached behind me to unfasten my bra and slid the straps down my arms, one arm across my chest holding the cups in place. His eyes, which had been focused on my breasts, lifted and he stared for a long moment into my eyes. He nodded, then, a slight movement, but enough for me. My thighs tightening around his, my insides clenching in need, I let the bra fall. He groaned. A long, low, dark sound. I wondered, just for a moment, whether the nocturnal natives roaming in their zoo enclosures, heard the sound.

I had nice breasts, I thought. They weren't huge, but there was enough. More than a handful. Well, one of my hands. Most of the time, they were confined within well-fitted sports bras. They had to be, especially when I was running or playing soccer. Last thing I wanted was my boobs flapping in the breeze. Mortification for elite sportswomen. But the way Sam was looking at them … The heat in his gaze … The *admiration*, as though I'd had a role in designing them myself… It was something else. I'd never felt beautiful before. I knew that I was reasonably *attractive*, in a wholesome sporty kind of way, but not *beautiful*.

Under Sam's appreciative gaze … Well, maybe I'd undervalued myself.

And still, he didn't move. His breathing had changed: it was slower, deeper and more audible, but he didn't move a muscle. Except for the odd quiver that accompanied a shuddering breath.

Leaning back with my left hand on Sam's knee, I lifted my right and, all the time watching Sam's face, I ran a finger down from just below my ear, along the column of my neck, past my collar bone and just over the tip of my breast, the nipple hardening even further. I could feel his thigh muscles spasm beneath my butt as he groaned. So, I did it all over again, but this time, I slipped my index finger into my mouth first, wetting it, before trailing it over the same path. Both of us shuddered as it topped my nipple and, in response, I continued to map a line under my breast, down one side of my abdomen and along the top of my jeans.

I squirmed, my thighs taut over his trembling muscles, liquid warmth squeezed from my centre.

And still, he did nothing.

'Umm, are you – er – going to – um...?'

'This is your party, Charli.' His voice was hoarse, gruff with tightly-controlled lust. 'You tell me what you want.'

'Then sit up, Sam. I want you to touch my breasts,' I whispered and was gratified by his response, a shaky nod and a long swallow. He unlocked his shoulders, stiff from his leaning on his arms for so long, and tentatively, gently, cupped my breasts, warming them with the heat from his hands. His thumbs swiped across the taut tips and my moan was echoed by his groan.

'You're so beautiful, Charli,' he whispered. 'Do you know that?'

'Ummm. Maybe...'

'There's no "maybe" about it. Your body is exquisite. Like a thoroughbred horse.'

'A horse?' I stuttered. 'You're likening me to a horse?'

'Yeah,' he grinned. 'A thoroughbred one.' As though that made it better. 'C'mon, Charli, you know how perfect animals are. I saw you all night, in wonder at some of those animals. And you ... you're perfect.'

I ducked my head, partially so that he couldn't see the sheer pleasure his words gave me and partially in embarrassment. No-one had ever spoken to me like that. No-one had ever suggested that my body was something special. Sure, the coach and soccer trainers valued my football skills, but ... not like Sam appreciated me.

The only thing I knew that would stop Sam's words was to kiss him, so I did. I rose, his hands caught between his chest and my breasts, and kissed him on the mouth. A long kiss. A really, really, good kiss. A kiss like in the movies.

And when we stopped, and I sat back, and we stared at each other, neither of us saying a word. And then, in a low, rough voice, Sam drawled, 'Well, that was a long, slow, deep, –'

'Soft, wet kiss,' I joined him in saying, before continuing, 'that should have lasted three days.' We both laughed, joyously, our eyes never looking away from each other. 'Crash Davis!' I blurted.

'*Bull Durham!*' he returned.

And we hugged each other. Tight. And rocked back and forward a couple of times. A moment of blissful compatibility!

Chapter Six

'So, are you going to ride this bull or not, Cowgirl?' Sam taunted me, as he pushed me off his lap, toed off his boots, lifted his hips and proceeded to remove his jeans, taking his underwear with them.

'Yep, you can count on it, Farm Boy!' I kicked off my own shoes, tugging my jeans down my legs. 'Are you ready?'

He turned and grinned at me; his hands spread. 'Does it *look* like I'm ready for you, Cowgirl?'

I felt my eyes widen. And my mouth fall open. And my heart beat faster. 'Oh, *Farm Boy!*' I breathed. 'I'll try. I mean, *that's* a lot of Farm Boy.' I lifted my gaze back to his face and had to laugh at the expression on his face. Talk about male pride! I shook my head, smiling back at him. 'Get over here, why don't you!'

'Hang on,' he paused, fumbling in his duffle bag. 'I – umm – when we stopped at the servo, I – umm – I didn't mean to be presumptuous …'

'You bought us condoms when we stopped at the service station? Good Farm Boy!' I praised. 'Now, where were we up to? Oh, yeah. Over here, Farm Boy. I want to meet the challenge you've set.'

Our playfulness had dispelled some of the earlier tension and the awkwardness of being naked with each other and, when Sam sat on the camp bed once more, it was easy to climb aboard and straddle him, my knees braced on either side of his thighs.

'You're back in charge again, Cowgirl. You're riding in this rodeo,' he teased.

And in response, I kissed him, rubbing my breasts against the soft hair of his chest, and gently grinding myself against his manhood. I could feel my slippery wetness coating us both as I pressed my clit harder against him and a shudder went through me.

'You want to come like that first? Or do you want to do the honours?'

'Umm,' I hummed, not wanting to upset the rhythm of my undulating body, 'whatever you think.'

'Nah, Charli. This one's yours. You decide.'

'Then give me the damned condom,' I almost growled.

Whilst I ripped the packet with my teeth and carefully removed its contents, Sam lifted his hands to my breasts, gently kneading them and randomly plucking at my nipples. It distracted me, destroying my concentration and making rolling the condom onto him another challenge.

'You ready?' Sam asked, his hand sliding down between my legs, his fingers slipping through my folds.

'Yeah,' I grunted, balancing with one hand on his shoulder, the other holding him in place as I gently lowered myself, little by little, his hands on my hips supporting me. I controlled my breathing, purposefully relaxing my muscles to accommodate his girth, as I gradually sunk down the length of him. I could feel my eyes widen as he stretched me, and he watched me the entire time, his eyes never leaving mine. When I was seated, I gave a couple of wriggles and squirmed a bit, adjusting to the fullness of him.

'You okay?' The words were strangled out of him.

'Hmmm.' I nodded, grinning. And then I moved. I started out slow, sliding and rocking and grinding and slip-sliding again. Up. Down. Forward. Back. And all the time, I squeezed and released, clenched and relaxed. And it felt so *good*!

'*Sooo* goood.' The words were a cruisy croon.

'Hmmm.' His were a deep hum, a cross between a groan and a growl.

My hands were clasped behind his neck, my forearms resting on his shoulder, his hands on my hips, while we writhed together, undulating and rocking and swivelling and rising and falling. His face was tipped up when we kissed, his jaw rasped my cheek when I nuzzled into the side of his neck.

'Sooo *gooood*,' Sam moaned.

'Hmmmm,' I answered him.

And then it was like a spark caught fire! A wire tripped, changing our sensual motion into urgent thrusts and hard grinds, from the smooth seduction of a horse galloping to the fast jerks of a bull bucking.

And I panted. And gasped.

'Oh! Oh! *Ohhhh!*' was all that escaped from my mouth, whilst Sam stared at me, his face set in concentration, as he nodded.

'*Ohhhhhh! Oh, Sam!*' I panted, before collapsing on him, my head dropping to his shoulder, my arms limply falling down his biceps, the weight of my body pushing him back.

'Was that good, Cowgirl?' he whispered into my hair, and I nodded against his shoulder.

'Hmmm.'

'You ready for more?'

'I don't know … if I can,' I stuttered.

'Sure, you can, Cowgirl. Hang onto me.' His arms tightened around me and he flipped me, laying me gently back onto the camp bed and drawing my legs up, his elbows supporting the back of my legs. His strokes were gentle, long and slow and languid. I opened my eyes to watch him, as he moved above me, and he smiled a soft smile. 'You still good?'

'Hmmm. Nice.' It was as though the amber in his eyes warmed in response.

'Get ready, Cowgirl.' When I nodded at him, my smile drugged with contentment, he increased the speed and intensity of his thrusts. 'Hang on,' he growled, as he ignited, seeking his own orgasm. 'Come for me again, Charli. When I tell you,' he puffed. 'Come for me again,' he almost wailed. He didn't let up and I could feel pleasure swelling within me again, the intense thrusts hitting me *right* where I needed it.

And I came! Again! An explosive orgasm that left me gasping for air.

'*Yes! Yes!*' chanted Sam, as his eyes widened, losing focus, and his mouth inhaled huge gulps of air. The tension fell from his face, like a wave of relaxation, and then he smiled. A slow, satisfied smile. 'That was … That was …'

Yep, I think he liked it!

Chapter Seven

They woke us early.

Well, not really. It was just that we hadn't had a lot of sleep. Sam had bought a three-pack of condoms the previous evening and we'd put them all to good use, having woken a couple of times throughout the night. It wasn't entirely our fault, of course: how were two people supposed to be comfortable sleeping on those single cots? Every time one of us moved, the other woke. And ... well ... one thing led to another. I certainly wasn't complaining. I'd had sex before, but it hadn't been anything like what I had with Sam.

My Farm Boy! I sighed, just thinking about him.

We had to get up and moving. Being the last to queue for the amenities didn't help, but there was nothing that could happen that day that would take the smile from my face. It was a permanent fixture.

I loved the little Behind-the-Scenes sessions. There were two and they didn't last long, but we got to feed giraffes and get to know things about animal feeding and practices, and other stuff about the zoo that most people never got to know.

And I loved being with Sam in the Behind-the-Scenes sessions. It sounds sappy, but I just felt so ... *warm* ... every time he glanced in my direction and his lips curved up in a tiny smile, meant just for me! We were pretending to be oh-so-good, but he'd sneak little touches every so often. A barely-there brush of his fingers on my arm; a quick flick of his hand on my butt as he walked past; a glancing touch of his hand across the small of my back when no-one was looking. It didn't matter. We didn't know these other people at all; they were strangers, and they didn't know us. But it was the *deliciousness* of the secret contacts that made it so much more fun.

The subtlety of his touches; the flirtiness of his quick winks; the absolute *sexiness* of his smile.

After breakfast, a continental buffet, the Roar and Snore program was finished, but Sam and I got to spend the entire day at the zoo. We went everywhere. And we had a blast!

It was no surprise that Sam liked the Sumatran Tigers, the lions and the giraffes. Typical male! He was also impressed with the Andean Condor, which I thought had to be the ugliest bird ever created. Sam laughed at me when I suggested that I could take home one of the red pandas to keep Clancy company. Or the cotton-top tamarin.

'You're crazy, Charli. The tamarins didn't stop squawking the entire time. It would drive you mad. Your cat would probably do away with it in no time at all. And the pandas need bamboo. You'd have to plant a heap of bamboo in the back yard.' Then, taking the sting out of his words, he nudged up against me before slipping his arm around my shoulders, tipping his head down to tap mine.

We were exhausted by the time we got back to the ute. Happy, but exhausted.

'You brought your swimmers, didn't you?' Sam asked, as he navigated his way out of the parking area.

'Yeah.'

'Good, because after walking around all day, I can't wait to dive into the pool I saw before down the road.'

'The North Sydney Pool?'

'Yeah. Whatever it's called. Near the harbour bridge.'

I nodded happily. It meant that our time together wasn't over yet and that thought thrilled me.

The pool water was bracing when we first dived in. There weren't many people there, which was surprising for a late Saturday afternoon. I thought the pool would be packed, but then … COVID restrictions. There was a young family ensconced at one end, the mother sitting under an umbrella whilst the father played in the shallow water with two young children, both wearing floaties and hanging onto pool noodles. They packed up after we'd been there for ten minutes or so, and then there was only a bunch of teenagers, paired up with girls on the shoulders of the boys, wrestling and dunking each other; and some serious swimmers doing lap after lap, charging through the water like a cross between tiny boats and mini torpedoes. And us. The cool water, after the day's activities in the spring sunshine, was exhilarating and we scampered about like a couple of dolphins. Sam swam well, so we raced each other, length after length, until we were both breathless. And then we floated together, our limbs entangling, whilst we snuck surreptitious little kisses and tender touches beneath the surface of the water.

'Can you stay tonight?' Sam whispered against my neck. His body was pressed against mine, as I clung to his shoulders, letting my hair float on the water behind me.

'Do you really want me to?' *Way to go, Charli. Sound all insecure and needy!* 'Yeah, I'll stay.' Lifting my head, I looked straight into his eyes. 'I like being with you, Sam. And you're only here for the weekend, I guess. I want to spend as much time with you as I can. What do you think your father will say?'

'Dunno,' he said, before he kissed me. A soft kiss. A brush of our mouths. It was almost reverent. And, unlike before, I didn't pull away or change it up. I just let it happen, enjoying the moment.

That's not to say, though, that my mind didn't spin a few moments later, trying to figure out when we could be alone again, in a more private setting…

We made good time back to our Veriu apartment; Saturday afternoon traffic was minimal.

'You look heaps better, Dad,' Sam said, by way of greeting, when we entered.

'Much better, Mr Walker,' I agreed. 'The day resting has agreed with you.'

'Either that, Charli, or just getting yesterday over with. I hadn't realised how stressful it was going to be. So, how was the zoo?'

'Amazing, Mr Walker. I had the best time!' I gushed, trying hard to look anywhere but at Sam. 'The food was great and we had this orange and chocolate mousse for dessert which was to die for. I'm going to have to tell Ginny about it.'

Sam's dad gave me an amused look. 'You went to the *zoo* and I'm hearing about the *food*?'

'I'm going for a shower,' Sam said, taking his duffle bag into his bedroom.

'Oh, well, it was wonderful, seeing the animals at night. The nocturnal ones. And the guides were great. I asked lots and lots of questions and they didn't seem to mind. Most people get irritated when I ask too many questions. We fed the giraffes and went behind some of the enclosures and saw how they cared for different types of animals.'

Sam was returning to the living room when his father said, 'I suppose those nocturnal ones kept you awake most of the night? They'd make a fair bit of noise, I'm guessing.'

I felt my cheeks redden and looked down at the floor, sneaking a quick glance at Sam – which was a *huge* mistake. He was standing there in his board shorts, bare feet and bare chest, a cheeky grin on his face, and I was mesmerised, all over again. Farm Boy had such gorgeous pecs and abs. He could be an athlete. I felt all swoony just looking at him.

And then I realised how quiet it was. Both Sam and his father were silent, and both were watching me, watching Sam's body. At least the interest was returned, as Sam's eyes had heated to that dark amber colour again. Mr Walker's eyes, though, were twinkling with amusement, his mouth lifting in a half-smile. He glanced back at Sam and, noticing his son's preoccupation, his smile deepened.

'You go first in the shower, Charli,' Sam suggested, tossing a towel towards me.

'We'll head out for dinner at 6.30.' Sam's father said, as I started to the door. 'Charli, do you have clean clothes?'

'I'll lend her a shirt, Dad. Don't worry about it.'

'Do you need to let anyone know where you are, Charli?'

'I'll text Lou after my shower.'

'If you want to, you could let her know that you can stay here tonight. We can go to Bondi Beach tomorrow, if you two want to.' I nodded, glancing quickly at Sam, who was grinning. I tried to hide my excitement!

As I hurried to the bathroom, I overheard the start of their conversation. 'You treated her right, didn't you, Son?' but I didn't catch Sam's response.

Chapter Eight

We went to the Alfred Hotel, a venue renowned for its pub steaks, apparently. We walked there from our apartment, the distance enough to give Mr Walker a little exercise without his overdoing it. He seemed pleased to be out in the fresh air. And I was pleased that Sam held my hand the entire way. It was strange, having spent the last six years in a family of only girls, to be walking down the road with a tall man on either side of me. I'm not a short person and I'm physically strong, but walking between these men, I felt almost *dainty* and feminine. I wondered if this was how Louisa felt, most of the time. She has the smallest build and was the least athletic of my sisters. *I'd have to ask her*, I mused.

We all ordered steaks: I was happy with the rump, with salad and chips, but Sam and his father went with the rib eye and vegetables. We all drank beer and we experimented with some of the different craft beers on tap. Sam and I tasted each other's, whilst his father relaxed and watched us with the same amused look that he'd given us before. When the food arrived, I eyed Sam's mushrooms – they smelt divine – and he winked at me as he held his fork aloft, offering me one to try. The steaks, thick and juicy, were cooked to perfection, and I had to protect my chips from Sam's sneaky fingers. Every time I swiped at him with my knife, his father laughed.

'She's got your number, Sam.'

'This is nice, Mr Walker.'

'Hmm?'

'Eating in a restaurant. Not with my sisters or girlfriends. This is nice.' I blushed, realising how silly that sounded.

'Tell me about your father, Charli. What did he do for a living?'

'He was a public servant. In Transport. He worked with the trains.'

'A train driver?'

'No, he worked in an office in town. He took me there once, when I was little. A huge building near Central Station. Most of the desks were all out in the open, but Dad had an office. It was pretty big, too. And he had an assistant. She was nice. She gave me lollies, I remember.'

'And your mother?'

'She stayed at home, looking after all of us. She read books. There are lots of them in our house. Lou reads them. Her – no, it's "she", I corrected myself, thinking that Lou would be proud. 'She and Mum used to spend hours talking about their books.'

'What does Lou do now?' he asked.

'Oh, Louisa works in a bookstore. She got her degree in Australian Literature, which makes sense considering how much she reads. She's got a *huge* vocabulary and she's always correcting me when I use the wrong word, which I do sometimes ...' I admitted, petering off.

'And Jane?'

'She's a Geography teacher. I think she hates it.'

'Really? Why do you say that?'

'She's always cranky when she gets home from school. And she spends a *lot* of time reading her magazines. *National Geographic*, *Australian Geographic*, *Earth Today*. She has a stack of them in her room and she's always got her nose in one or another. When I was little, she'd pretend that her bed was a magic carpet, like in *Aladdin*, and we'd go to places all over the world. She'd tell me about continents and countries and – you know, all sorts of landscapes. Her degree's in Geography and Geology.' I shook my head. 'Not my sort of Science. I much prefer Biology and Ag.'

'And your other sisters?' he prompted.

'Daphne works in the same building as Dad did. She's got a degree in business.'

'So, she's with the trains, as well?'

'Sort of. I think she's working on the Metro. You know – getting it all built.'

'And she's happy in her job?'

'Oh, God yes! Daph loves it. I sometimes think that she feels close to Dad by working there. I do that. Get close to Dad, I mean.' I ducked my head, feeling self-conscious. 'When I run in the mornings... That's when I feel close to my dad.' I didn't like how maudlin I was sounding. 'Anyway, yeah, she loves working in an office. I couldn't imagine anything *worse!*' They both laughed with me. 'There's a new guy, though. Daph hates him. She's always complaining about him. *Dominic this* and *Dominic that*. I'm not sure if he's really as bad as she makes out or if she secretly likes him. I know she thinks he's competing with her, so she'd hate that. I might compete on the playing fields, but Daph ... she doesn't like anyone to take anything away from her. "Hold your space" is what she says to me all the time. "Don't let people take your space."'

'Hmmm,' Mr Walker nodded thoughtfully. 'And is it – Ginny?'

'Ginny's in the middle. Her real name's Virginia, but she hates it. I hate being called Charlotte, too, but Dad always just called me Charli. Said I was his tomboy. Anyway, Ginny's the one the fight was about the other night. Jane wants Ginny to get "a proper education" and Ginny doesn't want to.'

'So, what does Ginny do?'

Sam had remained quiet throughout the conversation, sitting back, content to listen to his dad and me. He sipped his beer and toyed with a cardboard coaster.

'Well, before COVID hit, she had a couple of part-time hospitality jobs. You know, waitressing and bar work. She seemed to like it. I know she liked the odd hours.'

'Why? What else did she do?'

'Well, she likes being home in the daytime. She cooks me breakfast, although she didn't come home on Thursday night, so I had to get my own breakfast. And she cooks dinner every night. Well, any night when she's not working, but then she leaves dinner in the fridge or the oven.' I pondered for a moment, trying to think of what Ginny actually did. 'Oh, and she does the shopping. If I want anything, I tell Ginny and she usually buys it for me.'

'So why doesn't Ginny want to go to university?'

'Oh, I don't know. Let's face it: it hasn't exactly made Jane happy, going to university and getting a "career",' I made air-quotes with my fingers. 'And Daphne's happy enough, but Lou? It's not like she's using an expensive education for anything much. She works in a *book store*. Anyone can do that!'

'Well, when you think about it, if a bookstore is still open and operating, she's probably very good at what she does.'

'What?' I was confused. 'I mean, it's just putting books on shelves, looking them up when a customer asks, and putting them in bags after you ring up the register. It's not rocket science!' I protested.

'Hmm,' Sam's dad's mouth was twisted, his eyes narrowed in speculation. 'I'm sure it's more than that. So many people buy books online these days, and then there're the big stores. To be able to keep a small store open… She must be doing something right.' He paused, studying me, and I will admit it made me feel a little uncomfortable.

'And you want to work on a farm, Charli?' At my enthusiastic nod, he continued, 'Have you ever *been* on a farm? A working farm? With early morning starts, and downpours so that you're soaked through, and hot, dry winds where you can't seem to drink enough water to stop your thirst? Do you really know what it's like, this farm life to which you aspire?' There was a questioning – almost, disbelieving – tilt to his head, and a shrewdness in his expression. 'Are you so sure that's what you want?'

'Well, of course I know what it's like. I mean, I haven't *exactly* been on a farm, but … You know, we *studied* "Clancy, of the Overflow" at school. I know what the bush is like.' I frowned when Mr Walker burst out laughing and, when I looked at Sam, he was trying to cover a smile. 'What did I say?' I asked, defensively.

'Oh, Charli, m'girl, it's not like the poem at all. Although,' he paused, rubbing his chin, 'you do realise that The Overflow Station, mentioned in that poem, was not too far from where our property is?'

I could feel my eyes, round like saucers. Those tiny muscles had never worked so hard. 'Are you for real? The Overflow is a *real* property? And it's right near you? *Ohhhh!*' I bounced in my seat. It was all too much! 'I thought the Overflow referred to a river or a creek or something. You know, a flood plain. I didn't think it was a real *station.* Oh, you are *so* lucky to live near there!'

That was too much for Sam. He lost the control he'd obviously been exerting on his laughter and it burst out from him. His father chuckled, enjoying my excitement.

'Maybe we ought to get you out there, Charli,' he said, 'so you can experience a *real* station. And, more practically, you can see what it is you're signing up for *before* you finish a four-year degree in agriculture.'

'*Really?* Do you *mean* it? Can I really go out to your farm?' I turned to Sam. 'Oh, Farm Boy!'

Mr Walker jolted, a startled look on his face. 'She calls you "Farm Boy"?' he asked Sam, with a grin.

'Well, yeah, Dad.' His face reddened with embarrassment. 'Don't make anything out of it.'

His father smiled. 'As you wish.'

My saucer eyes were back. 'You said that! You said, "As you wish"! You know the movie!' I was almost shrieking, the pitch of my voice was so high.

They both laughed at me and then Sam flicked me a quick wink. 'Of course, we do, Charli.'

'But how? I mean, not everyone knows *The Princess Bride*.'

'Charli, we don't always have good television reception and the internet can't be relied upon. We've got quite the DVD collection,' Sam's father explained. 'And Sam, here ... Well, he did like the Dread Pirate Roberts.' He chuckled.

'My name is Inigo Montoya,' I started.

'You killed my father,' Sam intoned.

'Prepare to die!' finished his father.

And we all laughed.

'That's why you know all the quotes,' I said, delighted in our shared interests.

'That's why I know all your quotes, Cowgirl,' he drawled, all gruff and sexy.

Chapter Nine

'We won't be long, Dad,' Sam said, as we were leaving the hotel room. We'd walked back – well, I had hardly *walked*. More like *floated* back from the Alfred to "our" apartment. It was almost too much for my mind to handle! Mr Walker had invited me – *me!* – out to their property, in the *country*! And I was going to be right near where Banjo Paterson had written "Clancy, of the Overflow", my favourite poem of all time. Well, the only poem I'd ever really liked: all the others were pretty boring. And I was going to be on a real, live farm. With my real, live Farm Boy! *Ooooooohh!* I almost skipped along the pavement.

And I was so happy, so ecstatic, I didn't care that Sam and his father kept exchanging amused looks and randomly chuckling. Who cared! My life was *sooo* goooood!

Oh, Dad, you were right! It is going to be alright!

In that moment, I felt like he was *there*, walking down the street with us. Sharing in my excitement.

When we arrived back at the room, Sam's dad excused himself to visit the bathroom and Sam tugged my hand, pulling me close to him, our bodies aligned. He dipped his head and nuzzled the side of my neck, and I tipped my head to the side to give him better access.

'Wanna go for a drive?' he murmured against my skin, and the rasp of his unshaven jaw sent shivers through me.

'Sure,' I whimpered.

At the sound of the bedroom door opening, he pulled away from me and, while I straightened the collar of my borrowed shirt, Sam left the room. I watched Mr Walker move to the television and turn it on.

'Anything you want to watch?' he asked, glancing at both Sam and me.

'Err, no, Dad. Charli and I – we're going for a bit of a drive.' It amused me that Sam's cheeks warmed.

'Oh, a *drive*? Yes, I guess there is a lot of sightseeing at this time of night.' There was a pause and Mr Walker pierced Sam with his eyes. 'Drive carefully, Sam. And be mindful of Charli. You take care of her.' There was an edge to his voice, like a warning. *As if Sam wouldn't take care of me,* I thought. *And I was a big girl. I could take care of myself!*

We didn't drive far. Sam found a secluded spot near the harbour foreshore where we parked. He immediately got out of his side, came around and opened my door for me, and we barrelled into the back seat of the ute. And then we were all mouths, lips and tongues; arms, hands and fingers; legs spread. How quickly we kicked off our boots, unbuttoned our shirts and unzipped our jeans – while we didn't stop kissing. We were greedy for each other. It had been a long time since this morning – hours, at least. And the little kisses we'd shared in the pool really hadn't taken the edge off our hunger. It seemed to take forever before Sam, having sheathed himself – thank God he'd retrieved the condoms from his duffle – and joined us, entering me in one long slide. *Talk about "driving home",* I thought, with a giggle.

We didn't want slow; at least, not this time. It was as though we now knew just how good we were together and we wanted to get there fast. I could see the focus on Sam's face as he desperately tried to stave off his climax until I came, and it thrilled me. Staring into his eyes, I clenched my inner muscles, enjoying the intense pleasure that flashed across his face, before he regained his concentration.

'You need to come, Charli. I don't know if I can last much longer,' he groaned.

'I'm almost there, Farm Boy. Just like that, only harder,' I gasped.

'*Charleeeee!*'

'*Yes! Yes.* Yes. Oh, Sam. So good,' I panted.

He flopped onto me, taking most of his weight on his forearms. His breathing against my neck slowed down, and I felt his lips nibbling along the curve of my shoulder. My eyes fluttered open enough to see the window, all fogged up, above us.

'We steamed up the window,' I said, inanely.

'Hmmm. It did get hot in here.'

'Well, your Dad did tell you to take care of me.'

'That's not what he meant.'

'Do you think he knows what we're doing?' I asked, a little intimidated by the thought of Sam's father's disapproval.

'I'm sure he knows. But he won't say anything directly.'

'Why not?'

'He knows I like you. A lot.'

'*Really?*' I almost squealed again.

'Yeah. So he knows I'll look after you.' His voice was soft and low. A bit rough. As though he wasn't used to sharing intimacies.

'Sam?'

'Yeah.'

'I like you, too. A lot.' My arms encircled him, squeezing into a tight hug.

He lifted his head away from my shoulder and smiled at me, before lowering his face and kissing me. Softly. Gently. A long, slow, deep, wet kiss. I wanted it to last for three days.

Chapter Ten

'You having eggs?' Sam's father asked me, that same amused expression on his face, as we sat at the outdoor table at a Bondi café.

He'd been giving Sam and me that look all morning. I was sure that he knew: that after his light had gone off in his bedroom, Sam had left the makeshift bed on the lounge and snuck into my room, where his father had instructed that I was to sleep. We'd been as quiet as we could, Sam's hand covering my mouth when I'd climaxed – twice – during the night. No athletic, hanging-off-the-chandelier sex when his father was only a room away. And then, this morning, just as daylight was creeping through the slats in the blinds, Sam kissed me gently – seemingly not minding my morning breath – and snuck back out to the lounge.

'Sure,' I said, ordering bacon, eggs, mushrooms, tomatoes, toast, and tomato relish. I could get used to this. I didn't even feel self-conscious about eating. Some of the other girls – not those in the soccer team, who had appetites like mine – but the ones at uni … Most of them were on some sort of diet: counting calories to lose weight; or gluten-free; or dairy-free; or vegan. They wrinkled their faces in distaste when I was eating my lunch. But I didn't have to worry about that with Sam and his dad.

Mr Walker positioned himself in the shade, away from the sand of the beach, and rested there, whilst Sam and I cavorted in the surf. The water was beautiful – cool and clear – and the waves weren't too rough. By the time we left the water, the skin on our fingers and toes was all crinkly and soft. We'd worked up quite an appetite and the three of us shared fish and chips, straight from the paper wrapping, for lunch, before Sam returned his father to the apartment and brought me home.

'I'll text you when I get back to the unit,' Sam promised, the time we'd be apart seeming far too long.

'Okay,' I whispered. I'd had the most amazing weekend and now it seemed it was over. I had to believe that it was just the start of something, but ... I was scared that – maybe – it was all too good to be true.

'We'll come and see you – see you and your sisters – tomorrow afternoon, Charli. After we get the results back from Dad's tests.'

'But what if they're not good, Sam? You won't want to come then, will you?'

'They're going to be fine, Charli. I have to believe that. These tests – they're just to make sure. To rule things out. Dad'll be fine, Charli.'

When I stayed silent, thinking about my Dad, Sam pulled me to him. 'Hey, Cowgirl. Chin up. Everything's going to work out. You'll see.'

And then he kissed me. One of our *Bull Durham* kisses.

'I'll see you tomorrow, Charli. Dad and I will come.' He smiled, before turning to the ute.

'Farm Boy,' I called.

He looked back at me.

'As you wish!'

And his face broke into one of his slow, sexy smiles.

'As you wish, Cowgirl!'

Chapter Eleven

There didn't seem to be anyone at home, although you never knew. Louisa was always so quiet, reading – mostly in her room. I checked out the contents of the fridge, more from habit than from hunger: the fish and chips had filled me up. And I fed Clancy, whilst I talked to him, hoping that someone had fed him in my absence. I was sure that Lou would have. She was good that way. Quiet. Just going about her business. But she noticed things. And filled in the spaces. Funny, but I hadn't realised that before.

I could barely contain my excitement. I was just so thrilled with the weekend and the world of possibilities that had opened up for me. I'd go for a run later, I decided, and tell my Dad all about it – although in my heart, I thought he already knew. I couldn't stay inside. It was too stifling with all the energy rippling through me.

I could smell garlic and onions. Ginny was cooking dinner. Good! She was home. I'd been worried when she hadn't returned on Thursday night.

And the next thing I knew, Ginny was yelling.

'Where have you been?' I could hear it all the way out the back. 'You give *me* grief over being irresponsible, but where the hell have you been all weekend?' There was a pause. 'And who is *that?*'

Then Jane's voice. 'Ginny, language, please.'

I was moving to the hall when I heard Daphne. 'Is Jane home? So, you *are* still alive.' Ooh, Daphne was being sarcastic. This should be good.

'C'mon, Daph! I sent you texts.' You could hear the defensiveness in Jane's voice. *That* was unusual.

I barrelled in, curious as to what was going on. I hated being left out of anything, especially if there was drama that involved the *others* and not me.

And there was a strange man. With Jane.

'Well, this is crowded. Can we please go into the living room? We don't all need to be in the hall like this,' Jane said, looking decidedly uncomfortable.

'You look familiar,' Ginny probed. 'Who are you?'

'He's Jackson McGee,' Daphne was the one to answer.

'Who?' I asked, confused. *Who was Jackson McGee and how did Daphne and Jane know him?*

'Jackson McGee,' Louisa repeated. 'From *Earth Today* magazine.'

Louisa knew him as well.

'Like ... are you famous? Or something?' I asked.

'Handsome catch, I will say that for you!' Ginny declared, making a great show of eyeing him off so that even Jane would see. 'What are you doing with our Jane?' Ginny asked, provocatively.

Geez, Ginny was being game. It was a wonder that Jane didn't take her head off!

He narrowed his eyes at Ginny. 'Not really your business, Ginny. Is it?' he drawled, reaching for Jane's hand.

Whooaaa! Whoever he was, he liked our Jane and was prepared to enter into a fight at our house!

'So, who is he, again? Is he a star or something?' I asked, again.

'He's a photojournalist for *Earth Today*. The geography magazine that Jane reads,' answered Daphne. 'He travels the world, taking pictures and writing stories about different places. And people.'

'So-o-o,' Ginny said, drawing out the word, 'how did you two get together? Has Jane been sending you fan mail?' Ginny was being a bitch. Even *I* knew that.

But where did Jane get this gorgeous guy from?

'Ginny!' Jane snapped. Yep, I'd thought she'd take Ginny's head off.

Jane's man tugged her to him and softly said, 'I'm going to go, Janey.'

'Ooooh, *Janey!*' Ginny mimicked him.

'See me out,' this Jackson person said quietly to Jane, his voice soothing. I could see Jane exhale, calming herself.

'So, should we be asking for his autograph? Or will he take our picture?' I asked, interrupting their moment.

'No, Charli. Let's go into the kitchen,' Daphne said. 'Ginny, you come, too. Louisa?' Daph glanced around, but Louisa had already returned to her room.

'C'mon,' Jane said to Jackson. 'Let's go on the porch.'

Everything was quiet and then I heard Louisa's voice. She was standing near the door to Jane's room. 'So, you could go. You could try it out. It's only Queensland,' Lou was saying. 'If you don't like it – if you're not happy – you can come home.'

And then Jane's response, her voice louder in her distress. 'But what about all of you? I'm needed here.'

'No, you're not,' Ginny said, pushing through the doorway. 'You *were* needed here, Jane, when we were all young, but you're not anymore.'

'Virginia!' Daphne roared at Ginny. 'Stop it!'

'I'm not being a bitch, Daph. I'm not!' Ginny yelled. 'Don't you see? Don't any of you see?' She swung around, glaring at all of us.

What were we supposed to see?

'Jane did what she had to do when Mum and Dad died. She did. She dropped everything! She didn't want to be a *teacher*! She was studying geography and geology, sure! But the only time she even *mentioned* a Diploma in Education was *after* Mum and Dad died. She's only in a school because she felt *responsible* for all of us.'

'She's right,' Louisa murmured from her place near the wall. 'Ginny's right about Jane becoming a teacher so she could support us. And she's right about it being time for Jane to go do her own thing. We're all adults now.'

This is interesting, I thought. *If Jane gets to do her own thing, do I get to do mine?*

'Is she?' Daphne looked at Jane. 'Did you never really want to teach?'

'Daph, it's not that simple.' Jane sounded tired and worn out.

'Why isn't it?' I demanded. 'Why can't you do what you want? Why can't all of us?'

'Because we have to be careful,' Jane almost screamed, shocking us all. Jane was losing it!

'Why?' I screamed back.

'Because Mum and Dad died,' Louisa said, softly. 'Because Jane's afraid. Aren't you, Jane? You're afraid of what can happen.'

'Is that it?' Daphne queried. 'Are you scared for us?'

'Of course, she is,' Ginny answered instead. 'That's why she's been so damned *controlling* all of these years. She's had all of us wrapped in cotton wool. Well, not cotton wool, exactly. *University degrees.'* There was disgust in her voice. 'Her way of keeping us all safe.'

'It wasn't just that,' Jane argued. 'I knew that Mum, especially, but Dad, as well, would want all of us to be educated and financially independent. *That's* why I've been pushing you and Charli to get degrees.'

And then, like a balloon with a hole pierced in it, she deflated. Right before our eyes. Like all the strength in her just dissolved.

'I want to be alone. Leave me alone.' She sounded like she was going to cry.

'Jane,' I began, but was stopped by Daphne.

'Let's go. Ginny, did you make dinner?' We allowed Daphne to usher us from the room. 'I'll bring you a plate, Jane.'

'Don't. I'm not hungry.' Yep, she was going to cry.

I was confused. What was happening? It was like Friday morning all over again.

I felt better, though, when my phone beeped an incoming text message. *I miss you. I can smell you on my pillow.*

How quickly did I return his text! *Miss you too. How's your dad?*

His reply came straight back. *He's fine. In bed already. Can't wait for tomorrow afternoon.*

Neither can I. I can't wait to kiss you again.

As you wish.

'Night, Farm Boy.

'Night, Cowgirl.

Chapter Twelve

I slept late on Monday morning. Like on Friday, I hadn't had a good night's sleep. Only this time, it was because of excitement – as well as worry.

The anticipation of Monday night, when Sam and his father were going to come and speak to my sisters, was overwhelming. That, and the sheer excitement of my dreams, finally coming true. I was going to go to a farm – maybe, *live* on it – and not just any farm. No, *this* farm was near The Overflow! I was going to be a *jillaroo!* At last!

And I kept disturbing, thinking that I could still feel Sam's hands on me, his body connected to mine, the thick slide of him in me. I knew that was silly. I mean, we hadn't had sex in more than twelve hours, but still … It was like he was *imprinted* on me; a part of him embedded in me, a part of my soul. Alright, maybe I was making too much out of one weekend's encounter, but …

And I was tense. Here we were, three days after the Big Fight Night, and we were still at each other's throats. Still yelling at each other. And Jane had been crying in her room. And she hadn't eaten dinner.

And after dinner, Daphne and Ginny were both quiet. And they'd *both* looked like they'd been crying. I mean, *crying*, for God's sake. Daphne *never* cried. I don't think I'd ever *seen* her cry, but … it sure had sounded like she was crying. And Ginny … What was with her?

None of it made sense. It was all so confusing.

The only person that didn't seem all out of sorts was Louisa. But then, Lou didn't get upset at much.

I ventured to the kitchen and – thank God! – Ginny was there, as though everything was normal, preparing breakfast and fixing my lunch.

'Do you want your eggs scrambled or poached this morning?' she asked me, as I yawned.

'Boiled,' I said, just to be contrary, and grinned at her. 'With toast fingers.'

It was such a *normal* exchange, I was reassured. *Everything would be alright*, I told myself. *I can get back to being excited about the absolutely thrilling secret I have.*

'So,' she paused, filling a milk saucepan with water and turning to me, 'what's new? And one egg or two?'

'Two,' I said, slicing bread for the toaster. 'And nothing much.' But I spoilt my nonchalant response by grinning again, and I buzzed with energy.

'Hmmm.'

'I *may* have met an interesting guy on Friday,' I offered, teasing her with bite-sized bits of information.

'Oh, yes,' she took the bait. Ginny always did. '*How* interesting?'

'*Very* interesting.' I sat up straight, and I could feel my beaming smile stretch across my face. 'And ... I *may* have spent the weekend with him.' I shrugged, dropping my head to my shoulder in a cutesy kind of way, feeling all smug. 'And ... I *may* be going to his farm at the end of the week,' I added, as though it were an afterthought. *Was I being dramatic, much?*

That got her attention!

'What do you mean?'

'Well,' I said, wriggling contentedly, 'he wants me to go to his farm and his father said "yes".'

'Charli, back up.' Ginny's attention was no longer on eggs or toast or anything else in the kitchen other than me, and she spoke in that voice that Jane usually used: all authority and bossiness. 'Start at the beginning. Who is this person? Where is he from?'

'I met him on Friday. At the uni. He was waiting for his father to finish getting tests. At the hospital. Ginny, are you watching my eggs? I hate it when they're all cracked and the whites have oozed out of them,' I said, although it did sound a little whiny.

'I'll make you new ones. Get back to the story. So, what's his name? How old is he? And where's he from?' Jeez, Ginny was really starting to sound like Jane! And I didn't like it!

'His name's Sam. He's from a farm outside of Condobolin. And he's twenty-three.'

'Condobolin? Where's Condobolin?'

'I didn't know, either,' I admitted, happy that I knew something that Ginny didn't. 'It's in the centre of New South Wales. If you take the map of New South Wales and fold it into four,' I showed her with my hands, 'and then you pinch the folded corner,' my fingers pinched my imaginary map, 'then you've removed Condobolin.' I sat back, satisfied, having taught her something new.

'Okay, so he came to town with his father who is sick?' she asked.

'Yep. And there I was, minding my own business, sitting on a seat in the grounds of the uni, thinking about whether I really wanted to go to my tutorial or not,' I was drawing this out, my voice in a sing-song rhythm, 'and this *cute* guy comes up and sits down next to me! Are you going to start the new eggs, Ginny, 'cause I'm really hungry?'

'Okay, Charli. I'll do you a deal: I'll make the eggs; you keep talking.'

'Sure,' I agreed, almost gloating. 'After all, *you* don't get to meet cute guys who want you to move to *their* farm. I guess you want to live vivaciously through me,' I smirked.

'Vicariously,' she said, setting the timer.

'What?' I was confused.

'It's vicariously; not vivaciously. Go on.'

'Anyway, we got talking and, you know, we had *so* much in common – he lives on a farm; I *want* to live on a farm. So, we spent the day together, until he had to collect his father from the hospital. And then he took his father back to the hotel – Oh, Ginny! They were staying at the Veriu in Camperdown. It was *so* posh! Really expensive looking. And they had food *delivered* from the café next door!' I paused, letting that sink in. 'Not like pizza deliveries, Ginny. *Real*, proper-cooked food!'

'Well, you get real, proper-cooked food here, Charli.' Her tone was arid-dry.

'No,' I shook my head, 'it's not the same. You cooking – nah! It's not the same, Ginny. *Real* chefs cook café meals.'

I watched Ginny spoon my eggs into chrome cups, slicing my toast and placing it alongside. 'Butter, Charli?' she asked.

'And we went to Roar and Snore!' I shrieked with the thrill of it.

I could see the question on her face, but before she could ask it, we were interrupted.

'Oh, are there eggs?' Louisa appeared at the door, crossing the kitchen to reheat the kettle. 'Can I get scrambled?'

'Sure. Charli's just telling us about a man she met on Friday.'

And while I told them about the apartment, and the zoo, and – I will admit it – I gushed over my Farm Boy, Ginny prepared Louisa's eggs, and Louisa gazed at Ginny.

'What I want to know about,' Lou started, as soon as I paused for breath, 'is *your* new man, Ginny.'

Ginny jerked, obviously startled. 'What do you mean, Lou?' she queried, in that fake-innocent tone she used sometimes.

'Tell us about your man, Ginny. You left on Thursday night and didn't return at all until yesterday afternoon. And when you did come back, you were wearing a new dress. And in the wash this morning, there was *another* dress that I haven't seen before. You've also got a bit of whisker rash just under your chin. And you'd been crying when we first saw you last night and – if my ears didn't deceive me – you were crying again when you went to bed. And,' she sighed, as though all of her evidence had been enough, 'you're not normally so bitchy towards Jane. Yeah, you can be irritated by her and you can make snarky comments, but ... last night ... So, tell us about the man *you* met, Ginny?'

I swung my face to Ginny, and I knew my eyes had to be huge, because I could feel the pull of my muscles. *What the ...? Ginny? With a man?*

'Did you *meet* someone, Ginny?' I whispered, in awe. 'Someone who *likes* you?'

'Yes, Charli. Someone who *liked* me. Isn't that amazing?'

Lou frowned. 'Don't be like that, Ginny. She means well.' She stirred her coffee. 'So, tell us about him,' she prompted.

'Not much to tell, really. I met a gorgeous guy, we spent some time together, there's no future in it, and that's that.' Ginny brushed her hands together, effectively showing that there was nothing further to add.

I wasn't buying it. 'Why?' I asked.

'Why what?' she replied, picking up the used plates and putting them on the sink.

'Why is there no future to it? Why won't it work out? I mean, if there's someone who *likes* you, Ginny, why won't it work?' *Why was Ginny being so negative?* I thought. But then ... she didn't know that Dad had told me that everything would be okay. That it would be alright.

'Because we're worlds apart, Charli. He's incredibly handsome, super sexy and fabulously wealthy. We've really got nothing in common. And – look at me! Do I really look like the partner of a hot, gorgeous guy from old, old, *old* money?'

'Why not?' queried Lou softly. 'Why wouldn't you fit in fine? You're intelligent. And strikingly beautiful. And he must have seen *something* in you. For you to catch his eye, I mean,' she amended.

'Well, with all that red hair, you're not *exactly* beautiful, but you're not ugly, Ginny,' I hastened to say. *Who knew that Ginny had such a poor self-image. I'll have to be nicer to her.*

Lou and Ginny burst out laughing. I didn't know why. It wasn't like I'd said anything funny.

'What was he like?' Lou asked gently. 'Other than being rich and sexy and smart?'

Ginny went quiet for a bit, and then she said, 'He was kind. And thoughtful. He helps people, Lou. Lots of people. Strangers. He gives up time on his weekends to volunteer for charities. And he was good to me. He looked after me when I was so damned drunk that I wasn't being safe.'

She looked like she was going to cry and her voice sounded wet and pathetic. Like she had to swallow tears. 'And I *liked* him, Lou. But,' she paused, taking a depth breath, 'it wouldn't work. His brother came – oh, his brother is a piece of work! And he berated Michael – in front of me! And I could tell that Michael was embarrassed. Not just for himself, but for me.'

What? What's this with the brother?

'Why? Why was he embarrassed for you?' Lou pried.

'Because his brother was a pig to me. The look he gave me. Like I was shit! Some cheap tramp!' Ginny inhaled, and her breath was all wobbly. I'd never seen Ginny quite so ... broken. 'And I felt like it, Lou,' she continued. 'There I was in my simple cotton dress, in this incredible apartment. I was so out of my league.'

'Was it as good as Veniu?' I asked. I mean, I knew about "incredible apartments" now.

'Charli, I was staying at the Bennelong Apartments. Do you know where they are?'

'Ginny –' Lou's voice was low in warning.

'Right at Circular Quay, Charli. I woke up to a view of the Sydney Harbour Bridge!'

I was stunned. The Sydney Harbour Bridge? She was near me, at Taronga Park Zoo.

'*Really?*' I breathed.

'Really.'

'And this guy *liked* you?' This was the puzzling bit.

'I think we've established that fact,' Lou said dryly. 'So,' she started, her expression thoughtful, 'he told you that it was a one-off thing? A weekend fling?' She slanted her face in question.

'Well, no.' Ginny admitted.

'And he didn't go out in public with you? Introduce you to anyone?' *What was Lou trying to get at?*

'No, Lou. We went out lots. We went to where he volunteers and he introduced me to the people there, and we went to the venues he supervises, although I didn't get chummy with anyone. He did let the bar staff know to look after me. What's your point?'

That's what I wanted to know!

'And before you left, he had lots of time to shut his brother down,' Lou nodded to herself.

'Well, no, Lou. His brother was just ranting. He couldn't get a word in. Neither could I, really. But what's your point?'

'I don't know,' Lou shrugged. 'It doesn't sound like he was embarrassed by you at all. It sounds like he was seeing how you fitted into his world. The world, I'm guessing, that doesn't include his brother, the dick!'

That was Lou! She knew things and she worked things out. Without someone having to tell her everything. What was the word? Intutored? *Intuitive.* That was it. And she sometimes said shocking things. Like calling people a "dick". Not that this guy didn't sound like one. I was tempted, myself, to go and hit him, on Ginny's behalf. I mean, *I'm* the athletic one, the strong one. I could punch him and it would bloody hurt him.

Lou hadn't finished, though. 'You know, Ginny, you mope around here as though you're some sort of burden. Shopping for us all, cooking and preparing our food, waiting on us, cleaning the kitchen up after us. Like you need to work hard for our approval. Or your right to be a part of this family. I get the feeling, sometimes, that you're ashamed of yourself, but I've never been able to figure out why.'

Wow! I hadn't expected her to say *that!* I liked it that Ginny cooked my food for me. I liked it that she did shopping for me. *Lou, what are you doing?*

'And now this man – who by your own accounts sounds like a pretty decent human being who's not an arrogant turd – wants to spend time with you and you're – what! Baulking at it? Saying no? I don't get it. Why are you so down on yourself?'

Ginny looked at me and then she got really angry. *I* hadn't said anything! It was Louisa!

'Look at me, Lou! Really look at me!' Ginny yelled. 'What do I have to offer anyone? Honestly! I'm not like you and Jane and Daph. Not even

263

like Charli. I didn't get good enough marks to get into uni. I'm not smart. I fucked up! And now I don't even have a job!'

'I don't have a job,' I said, hoping to make her feel better, and stop her from yelling.

Ginny sighed. 'That's irrelevant, Charli. You're still in school.'

'You're wrong, Ginny.' Lou's voice was gentle, soothing. 'You have lots to offer. And I bet your man – what was his name?'

'Michael,' she grunted.

'I bet he'd say the same thing. You, too, are kind. And considerate. And you help people, all the time. You take care of us. And he probably knows that. Your *goodness*, Ginny, shines out of you. Some days, you *glow* with it. And when you're out in the garden, soaking up the sun, touching the leaves of your potted herbs, you are the embodiment of natural beauty. You just don't get it. But it's true. I wouldn't lie about this to you. You know that.'

'Has he got your phone number?' I asked, trying to be practical. 'I made sure that Sam had mine. And I've got his. And,' I added, dramatically, because – really – I had good news, too. 'We're Facebook friends!'

'Does he have your number?' Lou asked softly.

'No. We didn't need to exchange numbers. We spent the entire time together.'

Lou nodded, staying quiet.

'You think I should go and see him, don't you, Lou?' Ginny asked, after a while, and I thought it was pretty obvious what she needed to do. *Who knew that I was smarter than Ginny!*

'Yeah, Gin, I think you should.' Louisa obviously agreed with me.

'Oh, yeah. If this guy likes you, you've gotta go see him,' I said, enthusiastically. 'I mean, when's the next time someone's gonna like you?'

And they laughed again. At me! This was what I found so confusing!

'At least see where it goes,' Lou urged, when she caught her breath again.

'Okay. Thanks, Lou. I … Thanks,' Ginny said, hugging Louisa.

'It'll be alright,' Lou whispered, and I nodded.

I knew it would, because Dad had said so, and Mr Walker was going to make my dreams come true.

Being a jillaroo! On a farm! With my Farm Boy, Sam!

WHITE SECRETS

SISTERS WHITE SERIES: Book Five

SUNNY MACKENZIE

2021

Prologue

Lulu98:   *Loved it! Loved it! LOVED IT! Iris, you've done it again.*
                 Your books get better every time. And you included my idea
                 about him grieving for her when she's returned to her mother's
                 place! That's such a thrill for me! Thank you.

IrisG: *Glad you liked it! Of course I included your idea. You should*
                 know by now that I value your opinions. I'm expecting your
                 full critique later. I know you've got more comments.

Lulu98:   *I'll try and get something together today. Busy day at work.*
                 Thursdays always are.

IrisG: *Take your time. Busy day myself. Got a book signing gig*
                 tonight.

Lulu98:   *It's the one in Sydney, right?*

Chapter One

I was late.

It wasn't my fault. Just another volatile night at the White residence.

I understood. Truly, I did. I got it!

Five women under one roof: all with their own agendas. All with their own desires – or, more to the point – their own thwarted desires.

But, right now, I was more worried about *my* desires.

Tonight, I was going to meet my favourite author of all time. Not just my favourite author, but the author of *all* my favourite books. Novels. Romance novels. Well, *erotic* romance novels.

Iris Grayson.

I discovered her when I was eighteen – by accident. And, Oh My God! – her books! I went looking for her backlist and *devoured* her previous novels. Thank God for Kindle Unlimited. My sister, Daphne, paid the subscription because … well, I was the reader in the family and I told her I needed access to literature. She had no idea what I downloaded on my Kindle.

And Iris just got better, book after book!

And she was going to be here, in Sydney, tonight!

Signing her books.

And I was going to finally – *finally* – meet her.

She and I had been writing to each other for years. Three years, to be exact. We were *friends*, or so I liked to pretend. I mean, how much did she really know me, Louisa White? Probably, not much. But she *wrote* to me. This world-famous author – wrote to *me*. And occasionally, after I'd critiqued something she'd written, she'd thank me and – unbelievably – *incorporate* it into her next work. She respected me and my ideas.

Iris Grayson – consistently in the top 10 in her Amazon book category – listened to *me*!

And I was late.

What was the fastest way to get there? Public transport? But I'd have to walk to the station. How often would the trains go into the city at this time?

Car? But where would I park when I got there? And how much would the parking station cost? And – and this was a big "and" – I was so *nervous*. I'd probably have an accident, just getting there.

Uber? Probably my best bet. At this hour on a Thursday night, though, and into the city, I'd have to pay a premium rate. Oh, who cared!

There was a part of my brain that was registering how uncharacteristic it was for me to be this … rattled. I was Louisa. The quiet one. The stable one. The sister who didn't get rattled nor flustered. I was the calm in the middle of my sisters' storms.

But not tonight.

Iris Grayson! I couldn't wait! The anticipation of this had been vibrating through me all week. I'd almost let it slip in my last email with her, but I caught myself. Hadn't had a response from that email, but I knew that she was a busy woman.

I was going to meet her tonight. I planned it as a surprise.

If only I could figure out the fastest way to get there. I'd just have to spend the money and order an Uber.

There was a queue. I should have known there'd be a queue.

And some people – let's face it, they were all women – had brought multiple books for autographs. I'd thought about doing the same, but it seemed a little – *desperate*, maybe – to bring a stack of books to a signing, and I had *all* of her books. In the early days, I may have punished my Kindle account buying e-books, but since Iris and I had communicated over the last three years, I had systematically bought the paperback versions of all her backlist. I had a shelf inside my wardrobe where I had them stashed.

So, I'd deliberated for a while: take all her books for signing; some of her books for signing; or only one? And if only one, which one? After a *lot* of consideration – during my breaks at work at the bookstore; whilst I travelled to and from work on public transport; when I was plopped on my bed, my feet up on the wall behind the bedhead in my ponder-the-meaning-of-life favourite pose – I decided that I'd take her latest story,

Satan's Obsession. It was by far her best writing and it made sense to take her most recent release. I didn't want to appear a bit obsessed, myself. The irony of this made me smile: I'd spent hours obsessing just on what book to take.

You're losing it, I said to myself. If just thinking about meeting Iris was affecting me like this, what would actually *meeting* her do to me? *Now, there's a worry!*

And there she was.

I caught glimpses of her as the queue moved, women shuffling forward, some chatting with each other; others awkwardly avoiding eye contact with anyone else. All of us self-consciously gripping our treasures to our chests, each aware of the nature of our reading material. *Yes, we like erotica! We are women!* Except, I kind of wasn't.

She wasn't how I imagined her. In my mind, I'd pictured a dark-haired woman, older than my twenty-two years by a decade, or maybe more. I thought she'd be tall and stylish, with a commanding presence. Her voice, in her books, was powerful, intelligent, authoritative. Yes, the female characters were not always like that, but there was an edge to her writing, a strength.

She didn't look like that. She was very stylish, but in that high-maintenance kind of way. The impression I'd formed of her was much more down-to-earth, although looks could be deceiving. *Maybe this blonde-haired, slender woman was very down-to-earth,* I thought. *Maybe she'd been to a stylist and hairdresser, and had her make-up professionally applied, just for this book-signing.* If I were a best-selling author and I had an event, I'd probably do the same. But she appeared to be only a year or two older than I was.

I swallowed a lump of disappointment, all the while telling myself that I was being ridiculous: that it was the same as when you listened to your favourite DJ on the radio and, when their photograph was splashed, in a three-metre-high billboard, above the escalators at your shopping centre, they weren't as you imagined them. Or you spoke to someone on the phone and didn't recognise them when you met them in person. *It's still Iris,* I reminded myself. *Be thrilled that you're finally meeting her.*

I shifted my weight from one foot to the other, wishing that I'd been sensible and worn my flats, instead of the nude peep-toe court shoes that were currently strangling my feet. They weren't suited to standing for very long, but I'd dressed up. Well, for me, I was dressed up. I'd traded my "casual literary bookstore worker" look for something smarter and timelessly classy: an emerald green sheath-dress that just glanced at my knees and which complemented my blonde curls and brown eyes. But the shoes were killing me and I felt totally outclassed by the stunning specimen of womanhood casually gifting her autograph to her waiting fans.

Buck up, Louisa. It'll still be alright. Don't be grumpy.

My excitement, though, was waning and I started to feel out of place. Restlessly, I glanced around the room, noting the other "author stations", with women in small lines awaiting their special moment with their preferred writers. Refreshments were available at a long, white-clothed table at the far end of the venue, and groups of animated women were chatting enthusiastically. Despondently, I looked away.

And that was when I saw him…

Talk about "out of place"!

There were very few men in the room: those that were there were wait staff, or carrying boxes of books, or providing security.

But there he was. Tall. Well over six feet. Dark hair and beard. Not really a beard. Trimmed. Perfectly designed three-day stubble. *He spends a lot of time at the barber's* was my immediate coherent thought, after *Yum!* He was casually leaning against the wall, not far from me: his shoulders resting against the dark surface, his hands in the pockets of his expensive black pants, his legs braced with his feet slightly apart. He was the epitome of a relaxed, confident male who owned the world – or at least the part that he inhabited. His focus was on Iris and it immediately made sense to me that a woman as beautiful as she was, as perfectly put-together, would have captured a man as self-assured, as eye-catching, as downright *heart-stopping*, as him.

I swallowed. And remembered to breathe.

No wonder Iris wrote such hot *erotica! It was amazing that she found time to write at all, when she had him to keep her occupied!*

Get your mind out of the gutter, Louisa, I remonstrated with myself.

And then, without even turning his head, just a movement of his eyes, he looked directly at me. And I wanted to turn away. I wanted *not* for him to catch me studying him. But it was as though a magnet kept my eyes focused on his. I had somehow captured his attention and he wasn't releasing mine.

And then, without turning his head, just a movement of his eyes, his gaze dropped to my feet and I felt heat as his focus slowly followed the length of my body, returning to my face, which I was sure was bright red with the blush that I so despised.

He stared and, like a deer caught in the headlights, I stared right back at him. His face didn't change. There was no smile – thank God! There was

... nothing. Just the intensity of his gaze and – did I imagine that? – a softening around his eyes which, at the same time, appeared to darken?

It could have been the light in the room... Or it could have been a mirage, caused by the effects of his sheer presence... Either way, the air felt charged and it was only when I gasped that I remembered that I needed to breathe.

'Excuse me... Miss? Are you next?' The voice startled me, breaking the connection I felt with this man. I felt my face heat again as I realised that it was Iris, waiting for me to step up in line. How much time had passed while I'd been enraptured?

His eyes flicked toward Iris, his head only barely nodding, before returning to me: he, too, was prompting me to take my place at the signing table.

Mortified, I glanced around at the people staring at me and stumbled up to Iris, who was smiling curiously at me.

'You were in the queue, weren't you?' she asked.

'Umm... yes ...' I quickly peeked behind me to see if he was still watching.

He was gone.

Chapter Two

What had I expected? A hug? An expression of undying friendship? A handshake? Well, perhaps not in these COVID-infested times. But … *nothing!* I hadn't expected that.

It was beyond disappointment. It was like being told that Santa Claus didn't exist, and neither did the Easter Bunny, the Tooth Fairy, nor the Glinda the Good Witch!

Grow up, Louisa! This was becoming a refrain. *The woman must talk with millions of readers every day,* I exaggerated to myself. *Did you* really *expect her to remember you?*

The thing was, I had. I thought she and I had been writing to each other for so long – three years *is* a long time – that she would have remembered me. Or at least, *pretended* to remember me.

But … nothing!

She asked: *Who do I make this out to?* And I wasn't going to correct her and say that it was "to whom do I make this out?".

I said: *Louisa.*

And she said: *Louisa, that's a nice name.* And she smiled at me, a fairly vacuous smile. Probably her professional, book-signing smile.

And I said: *Iris, it's me. Lulu.*

And she looked at me blankly and said: *Oh, is that what you'd like to me write? Lulu?*

And I said: *Iris. I'm Lulu.* I put emphasis on the name, hoping to jog her out of her book-signing coma.

And she said: *Sure. I'll write it to Lulu.* And she gave me that vacuous smile again.

And that was that. She wrote in my book: *Lulu. Thanks for your support. Happy reading. Iris G.* This last bit was in a girly swirl – not at all like I'd imagined Iris would write.

And she said: *Thanks for taking the time to come tonight.*

And then she looked behind me to the next person and I was … dismissed.

Just like that.

I turned and moved out of the way, faltering just as I passed some chairs situated towards the back of the room. I plonked down on one, trying to absorb the wave of disappointment that swamped me. Was that really *it*? I'd looked forward to meeting Iris for weeks, ever since I'd been able to obtain a ticket to this event. I'd kept it a secret, every time she and I had written. I'd been thrilled that, finally, we'd meet and, in my little heart of hearts, I'd thought she might suggest that we get a cup of tea, or a drink, or *something*! That she'd want to talk with me as much as I wanted to talk with *her*.

Sure, there'd been a practical, realistic side of me that had thought that – maybe – she'd be too busy. Or that she had another commitment after the signing. Or that she had to leave immediately to travel to the airport and go … somewhere. Or that she really didn't like to socialise with her fans.

But I'd dismissed that.

No, Iris and I had been sharing for *years*.

I opened the front page of my book, staring at the autograph. So impersonal. She must have written exactly the same thing – save the name – to everyone who'd come this evening. It made me wonder what she'd written on each book when people rocked up with a stack of them.

After the fight my sisters had had at home, my fear of being late and the scramble to get here on time, I felt deflated. There was nothing about my evening that had turned out as I'd expected, as I'd spent the day anticipating.

And it was all over …

Time to go home, Louisa.

'Are you alright?'

The deep, phone-sex voice interrupted my self-absorption. I looked up and … it was *him*. Iris' handsome, I'm-so-hot-but-I'm-used-to-it man. Standing in front of me, his beautiful body angled toward me, his face etched with concern. Genuine concern, by all appearances.

'Umm... Yes. No. Um. Yes, I'm fine,' I stammered, flustered by both my disillusionment and his proximity.

'You don't sound fine.' The concern was now laced with amusement.

'I'm fine,' I repeated, hoping to sound a little more decisive.

'Is there something wrong with the autograph?' he asked, nodding to the open book in my hands.

'Oh, no. Yes. No, it's fine.' *Geez, Louise. You sound like an imbecile! Get with the program!* 'It's fine,' I said again, and gave a smile. Most probably a weak smile, but I was making the effort, at least.

'Did everything go alright over there?' he asked, tipping his head towards where Iris was sitting, still scribbling her signature on readers' precious souvenirs.

'Oh ... umm ... sure.' *C'mon, Lou! This isn't you!*

'You don't seem happy with your book?' Was that a question or a statement?

'It's okay. Really,' I added, when he didn't seem convinced. I wanted to get away from this man and his observant eyes. Did he actually think that I was going to complain about his girlfriend when she was sitting, just over there? 'It just wasn't as I expected.' His eyes were trained on me, his focus intense.

'In what way?' There was a deceptive calm to his voice; an edge, as though he wasn't to be messed with.

'Oh, it's nothing.' I waved my hand dismissively. 'I was just being silly.'

'Silly, how?' he persisted.

I don't know whether it was the day and its accumulative effects, or just how tired and despondent I felt, but I did an unusual thing for me. I opened up and discussed my inner thoughts with a stranger.

'I've been reading Iris Grayson's books for years and ... I was excited to finally meet her. I had expectations, I suppose,' I trailed off, suddenly on the verge of tears.

He dropped down on his haunches in front of me and he gently asked, 'What type of expectations? What did Iris,' he tipped his head towards her, 'do or not do that disappointed you?'

'It's nothing. I just ...' His gaze was steady on me, and he was still. Waiting. Patiently. 'I told her it was me and ... nothing! It was like she didn't know me.' His forehead dropped and his right eye half-closed as he looked at me. 'I said, "It's Lulu," and she just ... Nothing! And look!' I held my book out to him. 'She just wrote "Lulu" in my book, and gave me what's probably her standard autograph, as though she'd never heard of me before.'

Pull yourself together, Louisa! This man will think you're an idiot!

'I've got to go,' I said, rising as I closed the book and slid it into my bag. 'Thanks for your concern. Iris was fine. Perfectly professional. She's very busy. Lots of people to see. It was unrealistic of me to think that she'd remember every person who ever corresponded with her on the internet. It was stupid of me.'

He stood, too, and I felt very small next to him. He was huge. Not in an I-spend-my-life-in-a-gym-and-I've-got-the-shoulders-to-carry-an-enormous-log-around way. It was more a sturdy, I'm-a-man-and-you-can-depend-on-me stance.

I made to move around him when his hand reached out, halting me. He didn't say anything for a long while; he just stood there, still as a statue, studying me, his eyes narrowed in contemplation. I was frozen in his focus, incapable of moving, as he regarded me. And then he drew a long, slow breath and nodded, such a small movement that I thought that it was more like he was nodding to himself.

And then he smiled. At me. A slow smile, seductive in its execution.

'Have a drink with me.' It wasn't quite a command, yet not just an invitation.

I startled. Did I just hear what I thought I heard?

'Excuse me?' I squeaked.

'I'm inviting you to have a drink with me,' he drawled, that sinful smile matching the warm, low tone of his voice.

'Umm... but ... aren't you here with Iris?' I stuttered, flustered all over again.

'Well, yes. In a way,' he conceded. 'But that doesn't negate my invitation. You've had a disappointment,' he spread his hands, palms up in the universal I-don't-mean-you-any-harm gesture. 'And this event is almost over. Come for a drink with me, Lulu,' he coaxed.

'It's not Lulu,' I said. 'My name's Louisa. Louisa White.'

He startled. He did a double-take – his jaw tilted up on one side, his eyes narrowed and a huge smile bloomed across his face – before he burst out laughing!

'Ohhh! It just gets better!' he chortled. No other word for it: it was a "chortle". I knew the word – had read it in a hundred books – but I'd never actually seen and heard a chortle. Until then.

I was confused. What had I said? I had no idea what had caused him to react in such an explosive way and it embarrassed me. I felt the heat of a blush suffuse my face, and I ducked my head to avoid his scrutiny. His hand slid into my line of vision.

'Patrick,' he said, his voice soft and gentle, as though he were taming a wild thing. Passing through my mind was the fleeting thought that the "wild thing" was *me*. 'Patrick Black.'

And I knew then why he laughed.

Chapter Three

'What would you like to drink?' Patrick asked, as he gestured towards the two-seater leather lounge in the intimate hotel bar. It was all dark woods and lantern lighting, reminiscent of an old Irish pub, only more expensive.

'A white wine. Sauvignon blanc, if they've got one.' Even before he smiled, I realised how ridiculous that was: of course, a hotel of this size and a bar this luxurious would carry a full complement of award-winning wines and liqueurs. I shook my head at my social ineptitude.

'I'm sure they will,' Patrick looked amused, his eyes twinkling, before turning and signalling a wine waiter. After he placed our order – he requested a bottle of Penfolds Bin 389, and a fruit and cheese platter, as well as my wine – he lowered himself to the coffee table in front of the lounge where I was sitting and said, 'I've just got to go and take care of a few things. Make yourself comfortable. The wine and cheese should be here in a moment. I'll be right back.'

And then he smiled.

And I melted into the soft leather. Just a little.

Because that smile should be bottled. If it were, couriers, world-wide, wouldn't be able to keep up with deliveries of it to demanding women.

I watched him as he strode away. It was definitely a "stride", not a saunter. A masterful, confident stride; without the cockiness of a saunter, although I predicted that he could be very cocky, in the right circumstances. He had that I-rule-the-world aura about him.

I amused myself by surveying the room: the backlit bar, with carefully-arranged coloured bottles of liqueurs; the quietly efficient waitstaff, their voices hushed as they addressed the sophisticated clientele; the polished timber tables and fixtures; the comfortable armchairs and lounges. Women were expensively dressed in designer clothing; the men in either suits or elegant casual wear. Music, so soft it was only just audible, was floating on the airwaves from discreetly hidden speakers. There was no yeasty beer nor tart liquor aromas evident: the bar was redolent of a woodsy leather scent.

Sitting alone, I started – once again – to feel out of place. I'd never been in such luxury and, whilst I considered my self-esteem to be quite healthy, this bar was intimidating to me. Totally out of my realm. *What am I doing here? Who is Patrick Black? And why am I having a drink with a complete stranger?*

I was just rising, preparing to leave, when the wine waiter approached, bearing my glass of wine on a small tray.

'Ma'am, your 2019 Cloudy Bay Sauvignon Blanc,' he intoned, as he precisely laid a napkin on the coffee table, then placed a wine glass, its clear contents sparkling in the lantern light, on top of it.

'Thank you,' I said, channelling Maggie Smith from *Downton Abbey* and I deliberately left the wine where it was until he left. Then I reached forward and carefully lifted the delicate glass, taking a moment to inhale the beautiful fruity scents before tasting it.

I loved wine. I didn't know that much about it and hadn't yet developed a palate that could discern excellent wine from the merely great, but I could tell when it was bad wine. For all of that, I loved the whole *idea* of wine: the effort – year after year – that went into making each batch, from the tilling of the soil, which had to be *just* right; the cultivation of the vines, protecting them from pests and disease and drought and flood; the picking and processing of the grapes, so they weren't damaged and the wine tainted; the fermentation and blending of the wine; the scents and notes introduced by the oak barrels when they're stored. It is *huge* – the effort invested in creating the perfect glass of wine to accompany a family celebration, an exquisite meal, or a special occasion.

And I was calling this a special occasion. Yes, nerves much! But I'd never been invited for a drink in a – what level of luxury did this bar epitomise? – *opulent* bar in an expensive hotel by a totally gorgeous, sophisticated man before! He oozed self-assurance and a confidence in his capabilities that I envied. Yes, this was definitely a "special occasion". I relaxed back into the plush leather and decided that I wasn't going to run – my usual reaction to being out of my comfort zone – I was going to savour every precious moment. I could relive this, over and over, when I was alone in my room, reading Iris Grayson's steamy stories.

Placing the glass against my lower lip, I tipped another dribble of wine into my mouth, swirling it around with my tongue, savouring the flavours and scents I could detect. It was a game to me: teasing the nectar in my mouth so I could experience every … last … note.

I must have closed my eyes. I became aware of a strange energy, a current in the air and, when I opened my eyes, he was there. A couple of metres away. Standing and watching me. His face was still, expressionless, but his eyes were focused on me. And I felt the warmth of blood flowing into my face, and neck, and chest. Well, really my decolletage, but now wasn't the time to fuss over vocabulary.

And, for a wordsmith like myself, I struggled to find words for how I was feeling, right at that moment.

Terrified? Well, not in the he's-going-to-kill-me sense, but this electricity, this *connection*, was outside anything I'd ever experienced. It was scary!

Exhilarated? I was definitely feeling that. It was like I was *alive* for the first time in … forever!

Aroused? Such a tame word for the overwhelming lust that was churning through me, a heavy swirl of hot desire.

Wanting? *Oh, yes!* Anxious. Excited. Downright *hungry*!

And all caused from just a level look. A solid stare.

Oh, you're in over your head, Lou! I thought, relishing the power of our attraction. Or, at least, I hoped he was feeling what I was feeling.

Oh, my, God! What if he wasn't, and it was just innocent little me, caught up in my own erotic imagination!

The heat in my cheeks rose and my hands shook, making me fumble the glass, a trickle of wine washing over the lip and onto the back of my hand. When I glanced back up at him, still standing there watching me, the expression on his face had morphed into something a little … predatory? There was definitely satisfaction there, but … what was the other? Interest? Could I call it "desire"?

Oh, please God, make him as enthralled with me as I am with him! Don't let this be all one-sided!

Not sure if it was a direct answer, but we were interrupted by the arrival of a waiter, who placed the fruit and cheese platter, two small, fine-bone china plates and linen serviettes on the coffee table before me. This small event assumed greater significance than it merited, as it shattered the magnetic connection oscillating between Patrick and me. I turned my attention to the waiter and the platter, whilst Patrick shifted, walking over and sitting on the lounge across from me. He, too, glanced at the waiter, nodding in acknowledgement of the service.

Almost immediately, the steward returned, a pristine white cloth encircling the neck of a wine bottle; a red-wine glass in his other hand. I ducked my head, peeking through the light fringe of my hair as they completed the ritual of tasting, accepting and pouring the wine. There was a part of me that thought the process slightly ridiculous – I mean, if you're paying a king's ransom for wine, surely you know it's going to be good – but then again, if you're paying a king's ransom for wine, I guess you'd want to make sure it's good.

There was something very sexy about the whole thing, though. The wordlessness throughout as the bottle was proffered so that Patrick could check the label, the carefully cultivated actions of the waiter as he undid the screw top (I almost laughed, again, at the ridiculousness of this), the elegant pour of a teensy amount of ruby liquid into the glass, the tasting and nod of acceptance of the wine, with the final pour and placement of the bottle on the table with an embellished aplomb.

And Patrick had upped the ante on the sexiness scale, sending the metaphoric needle spinning off into orbit.

Up until the waiter had decanted the tasting sample, Patrick's attention had been focused on the wine and its dispenser. But when he lifted the glass to his lips, he slowly turned his head, and his undiluted focus, towards me. He held my gaze as he sipped the wine, the tip of his tongue peeking out at the last moment to delicately lick at the rim of the glass. I swallowed, hard, as my breath caught in my throat. *Oh, My!*

And, just as I'd swirled my white wine in my mouth, I watched the tiny muscles around his mouth subtly tense and I *knew* that his tongue was mimicking mine, in decadent appreciation of the wine.

And neither of us broke the invisible cord connecting our eyes, even as he nodded acceptance to the waiter, his glass filled and the bottle placed.

Suddenly, I couldn't stand the tension anymore! It was too much!

'Isn't Iris your girlfriend?' I blurted, feeling the heat of blood flooding my face again.

He frowned, glancing off to the side – a quick flick of his eyes, before they returned to meet mine.

'What makes you say that?' he asked, his voice low.

'Well,' I began, flustered all over again, 'you're obviously with her. I mean, you were staring at her back there, in the room, when she was signing the books. And – you know – she's stunning. Stunningly beautiful, and you're – you know – not exactly ugly, yourself.' He grinned at that – a cat-that-swallowed-the-canary grin – and his eyes widened with surprised merriment. 'And you said it yourself, that you were with her.'

'I said "in a way",' he interrupted me, amusement lacing his words. I tried not to notice the twinkling of his eyes, as it was too damned distracting.

'And I'm guessing that when you were gone, just then, that you went to see her,' I tipped my head in the general direction of the function room where the signing was probably still underway.

'I did, but she's not my girlfriend.'

'Then why did you go? Are you her manager or something?'

'Let's just say that I'm connected to Iris and there were things I needed to do.' He sipped his wine, eyeing me over the top of his glass. 'Tell me about you, Louisa. You were upset before. Was it just about not being remembered?'

He studied my face, waiting for my reaction. I wasn't sure how to respond. If I said it was *just* about Iris not acknowledging me, it would make me seem a bit – I don't know – childish? Immature? But did I really want to tell him about the situation at home? A complete stranger?

Maybe a complete stranger was the perfect person to talk to about the escalating tensions in my family, I thought. *Maybe getting a male perspective would be a good thing.*

'I have four sisters,' I started, before grinning at the surprise splashed across his face. 'You weren't expecting that, were you?' I teased.

'Go on. This sounds like a story,' he said, rolling his shoulders and shifting into a more comfortable position, his legs out in front of him, crossed at the ankles. He draped one arm on the armrest, whilst the hand holding his glass casually rested on his thigh. He was the picture of alpha male at rest, relaxed, yet self-assured. 'Are they older or younger than you?' he prompted, as in my silent regard of him, I'd lost track of my thoughts.

'One is younger – that's Charli, and the others are older.' He nodded, encouragingly. 'Tonight, before I came, there was a huge fight. Every so often we have them – we're sisters, after all. But tonight ...' I petered off, and grimaced.

'What was different about it? What was it about?' He reached for the cheese platter, slicing a piece of cheddar and pairing it with a cracker, offering it to me. I shook my head, selecting a small cluster of grapes and a sliver of apple, instead.

I shrugged as I ate the fruit and then replied, 'The difference is the intensity and how often they're happening now. I mean, we've always had squabbles and disagreements. They're usually over nothing much at all.

We're all so different from each other, so it's inevitable. But lately ...' I leant over, knifing a chunk of Brie and topping it with quince paste. 'It's like we're living in a pressure cooker, with these unfulfilled desires ramping up heat and, every so often, a little explosion happens. What worries me is what will happen if the heat isn't turned off and the pressure builds up so much that there's such an explosion that it will tear our family apart.'

Patrick was silent. Still and silent. He wasn't sipping his wine. He wasn't sampling from the platter. He just sat, silently observing me.

I felt intensely uncomfortable then. Awkward. I'd revealed so much and said things I hadn't said to another living soul. Things that just whirled around in my head. I grimaced in embarrassment.

'Look, it's nothing. I'm just being dramatic,' I said, waving my hand in front of my face as though that was going to be effective in diffusing the reddening of my cheeks that I was sure was there. 'Forget I said anything. Tell me about you,' I finished, clumsily.

He slowly lifted his glass to his mouth and took a deep mouthful of his wine.

'No,' he said, a slight shake of his head, 'I think you need to talk about this. Tell me what's happening, Louisa. What do your parents say about it?'

I dropped my head, looking at my lap. I'd said these words so many times in the past, but this time ... I felt moved to tears, which was so unlike me. I inhaled deeply, the air filling my lungs and imbuing me with the strength to look up and meet his gaze.

'Our parents are deceased, Patrick. They died six years ago.' Again, I watched the shock wash over his face. He really did have the most expressive face. Especially for a man. It was like he didn't need to check his responses: whatever they were was fine with him. That level of self-assurance and confidence he had. Oh, I did envy him!

'O-kaaay,' he said, drawing the word out to a length I didn't think possible. 'Go on. What was the fight about?'

'Do you really want to know this, Patrick? *Really?*' I heard the scepticism in my voice, the pitch rising at the end.

'Yeah, Louisa, I do.' Nods accompanied his words. 'Tell me the story of the White sisters,' he smiled. 'I like a good story, well told, and I'm sure you can tell a story well.'

I felt myself glow. The blood infusing my face this time wasn't from embarrassment or discomfort. It was from the sheer pleasure I felt at his words. No-one had ever said anything like that to me before. Well, not since my mother was alive. She used to tell me that I could write novels, that I was a born storyteller. We shared that, she and I – a love of stories, well-told. They didn't have to be from the classic canon: any good story would do. Yarns, my mother called them. Long narratives, with twists and turns, and well-defined characters, and the full gamut of emotions – love, hate, vengeance, pride, rage, kindnesses. Action-packed yarns. She loved them.

At that moment, sitting there with Patrick, in that darkened lounge bar, with the conversational hum of the other clientele providing a soothing backdrop, I felt the sharp pang of missing my mother. An acute twang of a heartstring. I swallowed the lump in my throat.

Yes, the professors at university had awarded me high marks for my writing, but that didn't count.

The only person – other than my mother – who had ever acknowledged my skill as a wordsmith and valued the ideas that I suggested, had just ignored me. Or, more to the point, forgotten me. As though I were inconsequential.

It stung. Cut me to the quick that, after what I thought was a mutually respectful relationship, Iris Grayson had rejected me. Or so it seemed to my bruised feelings at that moment.

But here, Patrick Black, a total stranger, believed in me.

I felt validated. And fulfilled. And powerful.

Chapter Four

'So, there are five of you,' Patrick brought me back to his tell-me-a-story demand.

'Yes, there are five of us,' I agreed, getting comfortable in the cushiness of the lounge and taking a sip of my wine. 'Jane is the oldest. She's twenty-eight and a Geography teacher. Daphne works in the public sector and is twenty-six. Ginny – Virginia – works in hospitality when she has a job and she's twenty-four.'

'I'm seeing a pattern here,' he joked. 'Someone was in to planning.'

'It was most probably Dad's influence. He worked in Transport, scheduling trains. My guess is that it carried over a bit.'

'A bit?' Patrick's smile was incredulous. 'Sounds like a lot, to me. Let me guess,' he held his hand up, preventing me from continuing, 'Charli's twenty, making you twenty-two.' At my nod, he threw his head back and laughed.

'It's not that funny!' I protested.

'Yeah, it is,' he chuckled.

'Anyway, our parents died six years ago. In a plane accident.'

'No, Louisa, don't parrot facts at me. Tell me a story.'

He was right. I was just relating information. I was selling him short. Selling both of us short, really. I started again.

'Once upon a time, the Greek god, Apollo, god of the Sun, bringer of civic organisation, and giver of laws, also known as Andrew, met a muse, knower of origins and ancient myths, inspiration to writers and poets and artists – let's call her Mary – and they joined their legendary forces and brought forth five goddesses, named Jane, Daphne, Virginia, Louisa and Charlotte.'

I paused and plucked some grapes from the diminishing platter. Patrick took advantage of the break by cutting cheese from the variety on offer, and creating bite-sized, cracker-based combinations which he lined up around the rim of the platter. As I sipped my wine, he sat back, admiring his endeavour and looking quite pleased with himself.

'These goddesses were quite dissimilar, each with their own strengths and – some have said – weaknesses.' He smiled, obviously enjoying the theatre of the story. 'All were happy, until the day that Apollo granted his muse her dearest wish: to fly through the skies, free as a bird, and see the world from the Heavens. This occurred on her Feast Day, a celebration of her birth, that was marred by also being, forever more, the anniversary of her death.'

For all that I was absorbed in this re-telling of my family history, I couldn't help the slight hitch to my voice when I said those last four words. Fortunately, the gods rescued me, in the form of the wine steward, returning, to refill Patrick's glass. The waiter's raised eyebrow at my empty glass resulted in a flick of Patrick's wrist, requesting a refill.

'Go on,' Patrick urged gently.

'And so,' I intoned, 'the world of the goddesses was forever changed. Artemis, the eldest, goddess of the natural world, embodied by Jane, The Responsible, gave up her dream of travelling the globe, exploring exotic landscapes and communicating with indigenous and foreign peoples, and adopted the mantle of Protector of Girls. Together with Daphne, the Daughter of Apollo, keeper of civil organisation and domestic finances, Jane ensured that the family stayed together, not divided amongst familial gods and goddesses, avid in their greed, eager to adopt the younger orphaned goddesses, together with their inheritances; not removed by cold-hearted public servants, keen to remove them from their professional caseloads.'

'Hang on,' interrupted Patrick, snapping his fingers. 'Jane, Daphne, Virginia, Charlotte and … Louisa.' He was silent momentarily, whilst his face gradually split into a beaming smile. 'Was it your father or your mother that named you all after female writers? No!' he interjected, 'don't tell me! It was your mother, wasn't it?' He dipped his head, his face a picture of self-satisfaction, and then slapped his thigh with glee. 'It was your mother!'

I laughed. I had to. He looked so damned pleased with himself. And, to his credit, he could be. 'You know, there are very few people who have ever picked up on that,' I conceded, praising him. 'I guess that not many people still read the classics and, with Ginny refusing to be called Virginia and Dad always calling Charlotte "Charli", it wasn't such an easy puzzle for people to solve.'

'I'm not just a pretty face, you know,' he joked, although I detected an underlying hint of an insecurity. *Hmmm, interesting.*

We both drank from our refreshed glasses and I watched as Patrick loaded three of his little makeshift hors d'oeuvres on top of each other and opened his mouth. When he noticed me looking, he winked, just as his mouth closed and the mini-meal disappeared from sight. Patrick exuded a sense of contentment and happiness, which was contagious. Here I was, relating my family tragedy, and the disappointments and thwarted dreams of my sisters, and I had never experienced such a feeling of pleasure and well-being. *Go figure!*

'So, Jane and Daphne took on the responsibility for the younger sisters – how old were you at the time? Six years ago? You were – what? Sixteen?' At my nod, his eyes widened, a mixture of astonishment and compassion. 'And Charli was … fourteen?' I nodded and smiled as he continued his calculations. 'So, Jane was twenty-two and Daphne, twenty, and they looked after three teenagers? Oh my god! That's incredible!'

'Yeah, I know, right? Jane is really like Artemis – a goddess. And so is Daphne. But they don't see themselves that way. Jane is dying inside.' I paused, waiting until I had his full attention. 'Patrick, I'm serious. It's like watching her *die*, she's so unhappy. She hates teaching. *Hates* it. She loves geology and geography so much, but the kids … I'm guessing there're a few that get into it, but she's throwing pearls before swine most of the time. It's a mandatory subject and teenagers don't like being told what they *have* to do.

'And Daph,' I took a breath, steadying myself, disbelieving that I'd become so emotional so quickly, 'she's got this *thing* for a guy at work, but it's like she doesn't see it. She's so caught up in *managing* everything, from the household finances, to the maintenance and scheduling our appointments and things, that she can't see anything but organise, organise, organise. She doesn't *let* herself unwind. Oh, she pretends to, Patrick. She thinks she does. She slinks into her room and sneaks shots of Scotch. Her preferred whiskey? Glenfiddich. And then she runs these huge bubble baths and slides into them, spending ages soaking her spirit in scotch and suds. Scotch and suds! What's worse is that she thinks no-one knows.' Inhaling, I paused, and then drank from my wine glass.

'Do the others know?' was Patrick's quiet question.

'I'm not sure. Sometimes I think that Ginny knows.' I accepted the pretend-hors d'oeuvre that Patrick offered.

'Tell me about the guy from work. Is he friend or foe?'

'Friend, I think, although if you asked Daph, she'd tell you foe. To her, he's competition. She's worked for Transport since she finished university – she has a degree in business – and he's a fairly recent arrival. She's been promoted quite quickly, I think, and she's been acknowledged as very good at what she does, which is solving the hardest of problems, that others can't resolve, and remedying complicated stuff-ups. Not their words, but that's what it is. He's come in on the same level – grade, they call it – as her and it's irritated her to no end.'

'So, is he a threat to her advancement?'

'I don't know. But she's obsessed with him and, from the stories she tells – most of which are complaints about him – he doesn't seem to have wronged her in any way. It's all in her perspective.'

'And so?...' he prompted.

'I think she really likes him. She's never spoken about anyone else at work as much as she refers to him. It's like he's all she sees. And – this is the kicker – it would probably do her the power of good to have an intelligent ally in her department. Strong friends can watch your back, provide you with an honest appraisal of incidents, be insightful to resolve conflicts and issues. He could be the best thing that has happened to her. But,' I finished, forlornly – even if I did say so myself – 'from her own account, she's quite dismissive of him, short and mean in her interactions.'

'What makes you think he likes her?'

'Oh, I don't know,' I mused, airily, 'instinct. Intuition. I can't quite fathom, when he's involved in so much other work, why he's in her office space so often. It makes me think he's pursuing her. And … maybe there's some pigtail-pulling going on.'

'Pigtail pulling?'

'Oh, come on, Patrick. You know what I mean. When a boy likes a girl, he'll throw spitballs at her to get her attention. Pigtail-pulling.'

He laughed and, *oh!* He was so gorgeous when he laughed. He truly was a breath-takingly handsome man. And he probably knew it, as well. Who was I kidding? He *definitely* knew it.

'Okay, pigtail-pulling. I get it.' He nodded, his mouth still tilted in amusement. And then it was like a screen was lowered over his face as the smile dropped, and the muscles relaxed. 'So, Artemis and Apollo's Daughter are each, in their own way, miserable, yet imprisoned … By their own actions? Why do they stay that way?'

'Habit, maybe. Or maybe they lost their own dreams.' At his questioning look, I elaborated. 'As a child, Jane – Artemis – always talked of travel and exploration – '

'But the death of Apollo and his muse changed all that,' Patrick finished.

'Yes.'

'And Apollo's Daughter took on her father's role.'

'Yes.'

'Sacrificial lambs in the Greek tragedy.'

'Yes,' I whispered.

We both sat in a silence singed with sadness, wordlessly communicating with our eyes, our only movement the intermittent raising and lowering of our wine glasses.

And then Patrick glanced at his watch – a gesture signalling the evening's end. The disappointment I felt at that moment must have flashed across my face – although I had tried to school my expression – because when Patrick looked back at me, there was a hint of – was it triumph? – around his eyes.

'It's getting late,' he said, superfluously. 'What are you doing tomorrow?'

'Tomorrow?' *Oh God! Was that my voice squeaking?*

'Yes, tomorrow.' He smiled, totally in control of himself, a fact that irked me.

'I'm working,' I said, flatly.

'Oh. In the bookstore. Right?'

I frowned. Had I told him that? I must have. I didn't remember, though. *Maybe, Lou, you've had more to drink than you think you have.* I glanced at my glass and tried to remember if it was my second drink or my third. It definitely wasn't the first!

'Yes. In the bookstore.'

'What time do you finish?'

'One o'clock. I'm on the morning shift. Why?'

'Have lunch with me.' He said it in the same tone that he'd said "Have a drink with me" earlier. Not a command, but not just an invitation.

'Why?' I parroted, again. *Really, Lou? You're conversational skills are fading … fast!*

'Because I haven't heard about the remaining goddesses yet,' he said, grinning before snapping a cheeky wink at me. 'Your story is only half-told, Lou.' Sweeping his hands before him, indicating the table with its ravaged cheese platter and the glasses in our hands, he continued, 'I wined you and dined you. You *owe* me the rest of the story.' And then, tempering his words, his eyes glinting in merriment, he smiled, a slow seduction softening any protest I might have offered.

He was temptation itself and he knew it. Were there male sirens in ancient Greece? Patrick would have been one, if there were.

The thing was: I didn't want the night to end. I didn't want to leave him at all. I'd never had an evening, or a companion, like this and I didn't want to go home, like Cinderella when the clock struck midnight, to my "normal" life.

He must have read my acquiescence in my face by the expression of satisfaction in his. He glanced toward the bar and indicated, through a sharp nod of his head, that he required service. As the waiter approached, Patrick turned to me.

'Where do you live?'

'Live?'

'Hmm,' he smiled, 'what suburb, Louisa?'

'Greenwich.'

Turning back to the waiter, he declared, 'I'll need a car to go to Greenwich. Could you arrange that, please?'

'Certainly, sir. I won't be a moment.'

I stared, speechless. Was that how things were done in "Rich-Land"? *You're a long way from Kansas, Louisa!*

While I was still processing that I was about to be scooped into a chauffeured car and escorted home, Patrick leant forward and retrieved his mobile phone from the coffee table where it had – magically – stayed silent all evening and, after entering a few numbers to unlock it, he handed it to me.

'Enter your digits in there.' Again, not quite a command, but definitely not a request.

I was irked enough to play with him a little.

Diligently, I created a contact in his phone and entered my mobile phone number, before handing the phone back to him. I watched as he flicked through his list of contacts, looking for my number.

'There's no "Louisa". No "Lou". Didn't you save it?' he asked, confusion and incredulity fighting each other to dominate his tone.

'Yes, I saved it,' I responded, calmly and deliberately. 'You're not looking in the right spot.'

Without moving his head, he eyed me, calculation in the slight squinting of his eyes. I watched him scroll up through his contact list and knew the exact moment when he found my entry. It was so obvious: the widening of his eyes in surprise, the dawning curve of his lips, his cheeks chunky with amusement, and the dark chuckle of delight.

'Athena,' was all he said, looking up at me, warm appreciation in his gaze. 'Warrior goddess of wisdom,' he added.

'Athena,' I confirmed.

'I should have known.'

'Yes, you should have.'

I could become addicted to the liquid heat in his eyes, I thought, reminding myself to breathe.

Chapter Five

'This is amazing!'

I couldn't believe my eyes. Who knew that, in the heart of the Sydney Botanic Gardens, there was a restaurant – *Terrace* – that prepared gourmet picnic baskets so that people – mostly couples, I'm guessing – could sit on a blanket under a tree and *chill* whilst relaxing and enjoying the sheer splendour of our beautiful trees and flora!

The morning at work had sped and dragged and sped and dragged, the terror and excitement of the approaching lunch date gripping me in alternating spurts. Patrick had collected me in the "hotel car" – read, limousine – and we'd walked down to the Gardens. I was expecting some chic little café, or maybe a pub lunch, but not this!

'I haven't had a picnic since I was a little girl!' I exclaimed, and was rewarded with Patrick's look of pleased satisfaction.

He wants to please me! I thought, suddenly. It hadn't occurred to me before that Patrick was *trying* to make me happy; that this was not just his normal behaviour – his usual seduction routine – but he was investing effort into pleasing me. Was he *wooing* me? *Courting* me? Now there were two old-fashioned words: two old-fashioned concepts.

Oh, Patrick, I thought, as I watched him spread the picnic blanket beneath a huge, old Moreton Bay Fig Tree, *you're already there! My mind is blown, my defences are down, I'm already swooning!*

'I thought you'd like something different,' he said, smugly. 'I didn't want to be average.' The wink told me that he knew he wasn't in any way average, but I laughed, anyway.

It was a beautiful day: the sun was high in a blue, cloudless sky; there was a gentle breeze – a zephyr – just tousling the ends of my curls; only a few people were ambling near us, with no-one else sitting, so it was as though we had the gardens to ourselves; and this beautiful man with the sexy winks was … well, he was either seducing me or I had an incredibly vivid imagination. In my mind, he seemed to really like me. Me! Louisa White – quiet, stable, placid Reader of Books! I found it hard to believe that I'd captured the attention of this God! Maybe I *was* Athena, after all.

'You know, "Iris" is a name from Greek mythology,' I said, as Patrick undid the picnic basket.

'Hmm,' was his only response.

'She was a goddess. Some say the female version of Hermes, the messenger.' He didn't respond as he removed little containers and paper-wrapped items from the basket. 'Goddess of rainbows,' I continued. 'She was the partner of Zephyrus, the west wind.'

He looked up. 'What made you think of that?' he asked.

'I was just thinking that this breeze is really a zephyr – a light, gentle wind. And that got me thinking about Iris. You know, she was supposed to be the link between the gods and humanity.'

'Yes, I did know that.'

'You did?'

'Louisa, you're not the only one who can read Greek mythology.' *Oooh, what was with that tone!*

'Do you think that Iris knows about her name?' I asked and was surprised at the hardening in his eyes, the setting of his jaw.

'Let's not talk about Iris, okay?' He gestured to the food that he'd laid out on the centre of the blanket. 'What, here, would you like first?'

And that was when I noticed the arrangement.

'Do you live on this stuff?' I spluttered, taking in the cheeses, olives, salami, fig chutney and grapes.

'Well, no,' he frowned, 'but this is what's in the basket. It comes like this. There's chicken wraps, as well,' he pointed, his tone defensive. 'And chocolate brownies.'

I laughed. 'Well, as long as there's chocolate brownies,' I teased, lightening the mood and the little self-conscious duck of his head warmed me. It was probably the first hint I'd seen that Patrick wasn't entirely the uber-confident man he appeared to be and, for some reason, that was reassuring to me. He opened a bottle of sparkling wine, pouring the effervescent liquid into *glass* champagne flutes. Glass, on a picnic!

'So what do you do for work, Patrick?' I asked, as I uncovered the said chicken wrap, appreciating the accompanying guacamole and salad.

'I have a degree in Communications, majoring in journalism and marketing.'

'Oh, where did you study?'

'Brisbane.'

'A long way from home,' I mumbled, around a mouthful of pulled chicken and lettuce.

'Not really. I live on the Gold Coast.'

'Oh!' Disappointment swamped me. In my little heart of hearts, I'd hoped that something … *more* … would come of this. But if he lived on the Gold Coast …

'Yep. Gold Coast boy, through and through,' he continued, while his words stabbed at me and my fledgling fantasies.

My appetite had waned, but I continued munching away at the wrap, ignoring the lump in my throat and doggedly swallowing the food. I waited, using my eating as an excuse, before I started to speak again. I didn't want my voice to sound small and pathetic.

'So, is that what you do for Iris?' I asked. 'Marketing?'

He threw a quick glance my way before turning to study two small children who were scampering on ahead of their parents, strolling behind.

'Well, I do make sure that the Iris Grayson books are out in the marketplace. And I am invested in their success,' he said, finally.

It struck me that that was a strange way of phrasing things. It didn't tell me a lot at all.

'What goddess is Virginia?' he asked, stretching out on the other side of the blanket and resting his head on his raised hand.

'Oh, she's Hestia,' I replied, happy for the change of subject.

'Hearth and home?'

'Hmm. She cooks – '

'And cleans?' he interrupted, teasingly.

'Well, yes, but only the kitchen.'

'Who does the rest of the house?' A beat. 'Oh, *you*.' Another beat. 'Hmm, Athena.' His voice was a deep growl. 'I didn't take you for the cleaner,' he teased, smirking.

'Back in your box, Patrick!' I sipped at my wine. 'You know, this is really good! What is it?' I asked, tipping my glass towards him.

'Babes' Blessing. It's a new wine; I haven't had it before, but I thought of you when I read about it, so … I thought we'd try it. It's not bad, is it?' Again, he looked pleased with himself.

Maybe that was the secret to Patrick's confidence: constantly try things and, if they work out, congratulate yourself for your achievement.

'What about "Babes' Blessing" reminded you of me?'

'The wine has been created as part of a social justice program. Proceeds from its sales go to fund initiatives in Africa to support women and mothers – to promote their empowerment and look after the health of mothers and babies. What with all your goddesses, I thought you'd like that.'

Again, he'd surprised me. Charmed me, thrilled me and captivated me.

I had to mentally shake myself so I didn't dissolve into a puddle of gooey swooniness.

And he knew!

I could tell.

It was in the way his eyes held my gaze: there was heat, and satisfaction, and male *pride!* He knew that I was melting; that I was smitten with him.

I cleared my throat. 'So, Ginny – '

'Yes, what's our Hestia's story?' he grinned, seeming to know that he was rattling me.

'She takes care of all of us.'

'I thought Artemis and Apollo's Daughter were doing that.'

'Yes, but Hestia does all the shopping, especially the food, and she does all the cooking. I doubt that Artemis or Apollo's Daughter have done *anything* in the kitchen for the past six years. It's all been Hestia.'

'She likes to cook. What does she do for a job?'

'As I said, she worked hospitality, until COVID hit. Now she gets a shift or two, but mostly she hangs around the house, cooking, or spends time out in the garden. If Jane is dying, Ginny is lost.'

'A lost goddess? I like it.'

'No, you don't. It's sad, Patrick. Ginny's not a character in a book,' I reprimanded him.

'I beg to differ, Lulu. If anything, you could *all* be characters in a book. It's got it all! Tragedy, loss, heartache, stolen dreams, unrequited love. And you haven't told me about yourself or Charli, yet.'

I didn't know what I felt about Patrick's words. This was my *family.* These were my *sisters.* Rationally, I could see his point: there *were* all the elements of a great "yarn", as my mother would say. But emotionally … Well, I didn't want to see my sisters and our lives reduced to characters in a damned *novel!*

'C'mon, Louisa. Keep going with the story. Tell me more about Hestia.'

'I don't know that I want to, Patrick. I don't know how I feel about your perspective on my family.'

'Don't sulk, Athena. It's beneath you. You're better than that.'

And there he went again. I didn't know if I wanted to kiss him – for the compliment that was embedded in that comment – or hit him, for calling out my pouting and not understanding *my* perspective.

'I'm not sulking,' I grumbled, sulking some more.

He laughed at me.

'Here,' he said, amused, 'have some brownie. The chocolate will make you feel better.' I stared for a moment at the dessert he held towards me, and then looked back at him.

'Don't patronise me, Patrick. I don't like it.'

His hand dropped, the brownie still between his fingers.

'I'm not patronising you, Louisa. Or maybe I am.' He shook his head. 'I get it. I understand. You love and care for your sisters and you want them to be happy. And you're annoyed with me for seeing them as nothing more than story-book characters. I get that. And I didn't mean to offend you.' He paused. 'Tell me – if there was a wish you could grant for each of them, what would it be?'

That surprised me. And then I frowned, all over again. Was he still reducing this to a fairy story?

'A wish? Like in *Aladdin*?' I asked suspiciously.

'A wish. Like a fairy godmother. Or Athena, the Goddess of Wisdom,' he replied, seriously.

'Oh, then I'd wish for Jane to leave her job and go travelling. Explore places where there aren't a lot of people. Jane doesn't belong in big cities. She belongs in nature. But,' I shrugged, 'that can't happen with COVID.'

'Sure it can. She's just got to limit her travel to Australia, for a while. And what about Daphne?'

'That's easy. She needs to take a time-out. Slow down for a while. Smell the roses. She's so stressed. She swears all the time, you know. "Damned this" and "damned that". It's like she's impatient and irritable at the world. So, yes. I'd like for Daph to have a break and chill. And then, maybe, she'll *see* this guy – Dominic, his name is – for something other than a threat.'

'And what about Ginny? Our Hestia?'

He'd distracted me. I realised it when I found myself licking chocolate from my fingers and then reached for my wine glass, only to realise it was empty. I glanced up at him and saw his gaze, steady and measured, focused on me.

And then he pushed up, gradually shifting his weight until he was in a sitting position, before leaning over the remnants of our picnic, a slow move – like a cat stretching after a long snooze – and reached his hand towards my face.

I could have moved. I could have averted my face.

But I didn't. I wanted to see what he would do.

And then he touched me.

It was the first time he'd touched me.

He gently wiped his finger across my bottom lip, a slow swipe on my mouth, before he withdrew his finger, his body retreating to his side of the picnic. And I sat, mesmerised, as he lifted that finger – a smear of chocolate on its tip – and slid it into his mouth, his tongue caressing it before his lips closed and his cheeks hollowed as he sucked. Once. Twice. Three times.

My lip felt like it was burning, a hot flame flicking along the line that his finger had traced.

Oooohhhhh!

I swallowed, hard, around the lump in my throat. It was difficult because it felt like my tongue had grown in size in my mouth.

Oh! My! God!

His eyelids lowered, half-mast, as his hot stare splashed liquid heat over my face. I swallowed again. And then, as though he took pity on me, his eyes released their hold on mine and he dropped his gaze to my mouth, which I belatedly realised had fallen open. I must have looked like a fish out of water, gaping, gasping for air.

This man is too much for you, Louisa. The mental voice of reason cautioned me. *You'll get burned.*

Oh, but what a way to go! I thought, calling on a force greater than Zephyrus to blow caution aside.

And then, as though a switch had been pushed, Patrick straightened and started to pack up the remains of our picnic. Flustered, I attempted to help, but my hands were useless, fumbling with the lids of containers and knocking over the champagne flutes.

I sat back, feeling embarrassed at my over-reaction to his moves. His seduction. It was probably a practiced manoeuvre that he'd used on countless women. And little innocent me had lost all perspective!

The silence that stretched between us whilst he completed the clean-up became uncomfortable, until he looked up and noticed me watching him.

'I'm going to the Blue Mountains this evening. Been meaning to go for ages. Come with me.'

'Wh-what?' I stammered.

'Come with me, Athena.' Another one of his not-a-command/not-quite-an-invitation.

'To the Blue Mountains?' I managed to say, dumbfounded.

'Hmm,' he nodded. 'Katoomba. I have a room in a Bed-'n'-Breakfast there. For two nights. Come with me.'

'Katoomba?' I parroted, staring at him.

He smiled. 'Yes, Lulu. Katoomba.'

And then he waited. Silently. Holding my gaze – whilst I was a mess of conflicting desires.

Oh, make no mistake, I wanted to go. I wanted to jump this man's bones, something fierce. But … he was so gorgeous. And self-assured. And sophisticated. And I was confident that he was used to women who were much more poised and sophisticated and *experienced* than I was.

The thought that I would disappoint him terrified me. I really *liked* this guy. I don't know which of the gods had dropped him into my lap from theirs, but I would be making offerings of fruits and floral tributes for a long, long time after this.

The question was: was I more scared of not satisfying him or of missing out on something special – something extraordinary – that might not come along again any time soon?

'The question is,' he started, as though he could hear my internal ruminations, 'how would you like to spend this weekend? What wish would you grant for yourself, Athena?'

I released the breath I hadn't known I was holding. And nodded.

Chapter Six

I'll give this to him: Patrick didn't muck around.

As soon as I'd agreed, he fished his phone from his pocket, scrolled through his contact list for a second or two, before hitting the dial icon.

'Hello.' Oh, he had a phone voice, too. 'This is Patrick Black, from Room 1203. I'm needing a rental car for the weekend. Make it until Sunday afternoon. A sedan will do, but nothing too compact.' He was silent for a moment, only the decisive nod of his head indicating the conversation underway. 'That will be fine,' he said, after a few minutes. 'Oh, and I'll be checking out. Could you finalise my account, please?' Another pause. 'Half an hour? That will do.' Another pause, but this time he looked at me and smiled. 'That's great. Thanks for that. Yes. Goodbye.'

I hadn't realised how sexy it was to watch a man do business on the phone. The owner of the bookstore where I worked was a woman and, though she had her official "phone voice", she was a lot chattier and less … bossy. And Patrick's voice was deep and commanding, a take-charge man-about-town who knew what he wanted. He stood up and bent down, extending his hand to me, helping me to rise.

'C'mon, Athena. We've got places to go, things to do!' His whole demeanour had instantly changed: he looked and sounded like a boy on an adventure, all thrilled delight and excited anticipation. 'Let's get moving!'

Once I was standing, he grabbed up the picnic blanket, flicking it a couple of times to remove blades of grass, and focaccia and brownie crumbs, before folding it, quickly and precisely, and draping it over his arm. And then, in a movement of fluid strength – almost graceful in its execution – he bent and lifted the picnic basket, and turned to me, his hand outstretched.

It was only the third time we'd touched – yes, I was counting – but it seemed natural. My hand, so small when clasped in his larger one, felt at home with his. I felt small – no, not small in a belittled sense – but delicate and dainty, *feminine*, next to his broad-shouldered height. I could feel his restrained energy and realised that, although he was keen to return to the hotel and start his adventure, he'd slowed his eager steps, tamping down his own needs, to wordlessly accommodate mine.

I *liked* this man.

It all happened so seamlessly: there was paperwork to be completed upon our arrival at the hotel, and magically there was the rental SUV parked in the porte-cochere, and Patrick's luggage, which he'd obviously packed prior to our lunch, was rolled out of the lift and into the foyer. As I excused myself to visit the Ladies Room, it did occur to me that there were quite a few bags for a man on his own, but then I reasoned that another guest's luggage may have been included on the trolley.

When I returned, we were away. Patrick entered my address into the GPS – I did tell him that I could direct him, but … boys!

It was then that it hit me that I had no idea what to pack. I'd never been away for a weekend before – well, not since hanging out with girlfriends at uni, and that definitely didn't count for this venture!

Patrick must have noticed my unnatural stillness. 'What's up?'

'Umm… I'm just thinking about what I'll need.' Was that my voice? So timid? Uncertain? Really?

'Not much. We're going to a BnB, so they'll have most toiletries and towels and things. It's the Blue Mountains, so I imagine it'll be cooler at night – maybe a jacket and jeans. Swimmers, definitely. Underwear, shorts, shirts – couple of each. We could go out tomorrow night, but what you're wearing is fine. You look good. Walking shoes, socks, hat. Sunscreen, if you need it.' He'd been glancing over to me as he drove, but at that, his look was lengthened. 'Yeah, definitely sunscreen. Your pale skin will burn easily. That should do. Oh, and any makeup you want to take, but really, Athena, you don't need any.'

How did he do that? Smash in together a couple of compliments: "you look good" and "you don't need makeup" with "your pale skin"?

And he'd rattled the packing list off just like I'd imagine a man would: shorts, shirts, jocks…

That made me smile.

'Listen,' he interrupted my ruminations, 'you don't need me to come in, do you? I've got a few phone calls to make.'

'No, I think I can pack my socks and jocks by myself,' I replied, drolly. And then I laughed, as his forehead scrunched up in confusion. 'It's nothing,' I reassured him.

It didn't take me long: Patrick's checklist was stamped in my brain and I added a few basics, like deodorant, moisturiser and bras, as well as a dress. Not the green sheath from the night before, but a simple wrap-around dress. It wasn't classy or sophisticated, but I did love the deep navy colour and the tiny pale blue forget-me-nots were whimsical. It was the sort of dress that could go most places without seeming too gauche, and Patrick would already know that I would never be the most stylish person in the room.

I took a minute to feed Clancy, the cat, as I wasn't sure what time Charli would come home – she often went out with her friends on Friday night – and I picked up the whiteboard marker to leave a note on the fridge, but … I put it back down again. Somehow, putting in words – writing – that I was planning on going off on a "dirty weekend" robbed it of some of its magic. *I'll text later*, I thought.

'I didn't plan this very well, did I?' Patrick grumbled, tipping his head towards the Friday afternoon traffic heading along the M2 motorway.

'It doesn't matter, does it? We're not in a hurry?'

'Nah,' he agreed, his eyes twinkling, as he shifted in his seat, his elbow on the door's windowsill, his body turned towards me. 'We've got plenty of time. Enough for more of your story. So, Hestia? Was she always in the kitchen? Like Cinderella?'

'Hmmm,' I pondered for a moment. 'Not when we were growing up. I mean, Ginny did like the kitchen, but not for cooking. More for eating. Ginny liked her food.' I grinned.

'She overweight?' he asked, with a minimum of words.

'No. She burnt it off. But she was Ginny…'

'What does that mean?'

'I don't know. Middle child syndrome? Jane was the eldest ... How do I describe that? It was as though our parents still looked at Jane as the miraculous treasure that they'd created together – like they'd never forgotten the awe and wonder of seeing her for the first time and they seemed to always look at her that way. Like she was a miracle.' I chuckled. 'The wonder had obviously gone by the time they had the rest of us.'

'I'm sure that's not true,' Patrick soothed.

'Oh, it's okay, Patrick. You see, Dad and Daphne – they were like two peas in the same pod. It's like she's the female version of him – only more stressed, at the moment. And Charli ... she was Dad's pseudo-son. The two of them were both sporty – athletic. Dad would tiptoe in – Charli and I shared a room in those days – and wake her up, before the sun was up, and the two of them would go running. They'd sneak out the kitchen door and around the side. I'd hear the gate creak, even though I saw my Dad oiling the hinge. That and the kitchen door. It was their thing, you know? The two of them, in the morning light, running. I think about it, now and then, when I hear Charli still getting up and sneaking out the back door ... all on her own. She must miss him terribly.'

Both of us were silent: Patrick seemed to respect my melancholy and I needed time to let it pass through me.

'And Mum and I were close,' I finally said. 'She and I shared a lot of similar interests and, when she'd boot all the others out, so she could have time to herself – "my sanity time", she called it – she didn't seem to mind that I stayed home with her. As long as I was quiet and didn't get in her way.'

'Why did you stay home? Why not go with the others?'

I grimaced. Did I have to reveal all my weaknesses at once?

'Because Dad took us on the ferries. Dad loved the harbour. That's why he bought the place in Greenwich. So he could be near the water. There's an irony: he worked on the trains, but he loved the ferries.' I laughed. 'Anyway, he'd take us all on the ferries and – every time – I'd be sick. I *hated* those ferries. You won't catch me on one – not on your life!'

'I live on the water. My brother's got a boat.'

'Ugghhh!' A shudder rippled through me. 'I never want to be seasick again.' I shuddered again, reliving the memory of it.

'And so Ginny was on her own?'

'Kind of... She wasn't exactly a *rebel*, but she didn't seem to fit in. That sounds silly, considering how different we all were, but it was as though we all had a strong connection with our parents, but Ginny ... She muddled along, mostly. I mean, she didn't smoke or binge drink or hang out all night and not come home… But I suppose there was always something a little lost about Ginny. And then our parents died and …' I swallowed. 'I think it hit Ginny the hardest, somehow. Which sounds strange – I know – because she had the least connection to them, but their deaths …'

I felt the warmth of his hand as he enclosed mine, gently lifting it across the console and resting our joined hands on the strength of his thigh. His thumb, ever so lightly, brushed along the outer edge of my little finger, the stroke softly soothing. The quiet empathy of his actions warmed me, made me feel safe.

'She'd been so loud and opinionated, our Ginny,' I continued. 'Always knew exactly how she felt about almost everything and wasn't in the least bit hesitant about voicing those thoughts and feelings. But after Mum and Dad died … It was as though she lost her voice. Or her forthrightness.' I stopped and looked around, needing a minute, needing to break the tension. 'Where are we?'

'Just left the M2 and on the M7, according to the GPS. Still got a fair way to go.'

'She didn't do well in her HSC. Ginny, that is,' I clarified, as though I needed to.

'Year 12?' he asked, again with the minimum of words.

'Yeah. Her marks were pretty woeful. It was a nightmare – her getting through her exams. I never saw her cry, but I saw the blotched face often enough. There was one day when she came home from her exam … she looked a wreck! It broke my heart just to see it.'

The pressure of his thumb against my little finger increased incrementally, but I felt it. It was like our nervous systems had connected, a new electrical circuitry forming, and I was part of more than just me.

'But we were all trying to deal,' I continued. 'Jane and Daph – they were in overdrive. There were the authorities to deal with: the police, the coroner's office, the funeral home, the insurance and bank. And there were the relatives circling… This one wanted Charli; that one wanted me. I'm not sure that any of them picked Ginny.'

'Was she that bad?'

'Well, no. But she does have a mass of molten red hair and – sometimes – her temper can match it. And she had been quite outspoken in her views, even for a teenager. Or, especially for a teenager. Not sure which is correct, there.'

'Well, I was an outspoken teenager,' he offered.

'Why am I not surprised!' I teased, recognising his effort to lighten the mood.

'So what happened?'

'Well, it was always expected that we'd all go to university. Mum had her degree in English Lit; Dad in Commerce. I don't know what Ginny planned to do at uni. I don't think she ever expressed interest in any particular field or degree, but I'm sure she thought she'd go. But her marks … She could still have got in, I'm sure, but she just withdrew – closed in on herself. And then she became rebellious, but only about uni. Whenever anyone said anything, she'd just be angry and say she didn't want to go. I think she felt ashamed.'

'What? About her marks?' His tone was incredulous. 'She was grieving her parents. No-one would expect that she'd do brilliantly in her exams, did they?'

'No, but I still think that she's ashamed. She became like a servant in our house, as though she doesn't deserve anything better. I told you she's lost. She withdrew to the kitchen and she cooks and cleans and waits on all of us. If I went to the fridge at the moment, I'd be bound to find lots of food, ready to eat. When she brings home the shopping, she cuts up fruit and vegetables and stores them in containers so, if you're feeling peckish, it's ready for you to eat. And she always makes enough dinner so there's leftovers for lunch the next day, if you want to take it. And she bakes bread… It's heartbreaking.' I sighed – a heavy sigh, even for me.

'I don't get it. What's heartbreaking about baking bread?' His tone was quizzical.

'Mum used to bake bread.'

There was silence after my declaration.

A gentle squeeze of my fingers. A stroke of his thumb.

'And so? Your wish for Hestia?' His voice was low and gentle.

'Purpose. And somewhere to belong, where she feels valued.'

'Don't you all value her?'

'Well, yes. But I think we take her for granted, most of the time. That we don't really notice what she does. And there's this ghostliness about her now. Like her fire's gone. Every so often it flares to life, like in the fight last night. But mostly, she needs to find her *thing*, her mission. So she feels whole again. So she doesn't feel like she has to be beholden to anyone, especially us.'

'From your lips to the Gods' ears, then,' he said, lifting our hands and softly – gently – brushing his lips against the back of my hand.

Ohhhh! I felt my entire insides clench, a tightening of my throat and chest and abdomen and hidden, secret core!

Was it possible to dissolve into a puddle on a car seat?

Chapter Seven

'And Charli? Which goddess is she?'

We were on the M7. Progress was being made. Talk about bad planning, travelling on a Friday afternoon!

'Nike. But the modern version of Nike, not the traditional.'

'What d'you mean?'

'Well, the Nike of mythology was more the bestower of congratulations, than a sportsperson. She flew around, anointing the victors with laurel leaves – wreathes – after competitions. She didn't actually *compete* herself. But the modern Nike – the brand – and now the company... Did you know that Nike was originally just a brand of sports gear from Blue Ribbon Sports until the 1970's? Then they registered it as a company?'

'No. Is that relevant?'

'Well, no. But it *is* interesting.' He smiled at that, as though I'd amused him.

'Anyway,' I continued, a trifle flustered at the effect his approval had on me, 'Charli is an athlete. She played in the state soccer team – you know, the schools' competition. She was awarded a sports scholarship at Sydney University. And, between you and me, I doubt she would have made their Science program, if it hadn't been for the scholarship. She's smart – well, in Maths and Science, she is. Otherwise, she can be a bit ... hmmm... obtuse? Is "vacuous" too harsh a word?'

'I don't know her, but I'll trust your instinct,' he answered benignly. 'So-o-o, Nike?'

'Well, yes. But just running and soccer. I think, if she had her way, she'd be Demeter, the goddess of agriculture, except that Demeter's more into growing trees and plants – fruit and vegetables – and Charli wants to work on a cattle farm. She sees herself as Clancy, "gone a'drovin'". You know,'

I prompted with a quick tip of my head when he frowned in confusion, 'from the Banjo Paterson poem, "Clancy, of the Overflow". Charli's obsessed with the poem. Has been since she was about ten.'

'So that would be your wish for her? A cattle farm?'

'I suppose. She's always saying she wants to be a jillaroo. At least she should get the opportunity to try. Not sure it will work, though.'

'Why do you say that?'

'Because she's been born and bred in a city. It's all right to romanticise the bush – that was Paterson's forte, as opposed to Henry Lawson, who maybe saw it more clearly – but Charli's never been west of Strathfield. It's all her imagination and watching *The Man From Snowy River* far too many times. But, yeah… It'd be nice for her to get her wish and, at least, spend time in the bush. It would make her happy.' I smiled, thinking about it. Thinking about Charli, all rigged up in R.M Williams moleskins, shirts and boots, and an Akubra hat. She'd prance around, happy as a fly in peach nectar.'

And with that, my phone buzzed.

'Speak of the Devil,' I laughed. And then I read her text, and frowned.

'What is it?'

'Won't be home tonight. I'm going to Roar and Snore at Taronga Zoo with a friend. Bronte,' I read out to him.

'What's Roar and Snore? Is that a music festival?' Patrick asked.

'Don't know,' I said, as I texted back to her: *Roar and Snore? Which friend?*

Her reply was instantaneous: *You don't know him. He's new. I met him today.*

'It's someone she met today. A male,' I said aloud.

'Does she go off with new people often? Men? And stay the night?' Patrick asked, sounding concerned, which thrilled me a little. It was as though he cared about Charli.

'Not that I know of,' I said, uncertainly. 'I'm not sure what to say. It's not like she's asking my *permission*, exactly. But … she's only twenty. And she can be … impulsive.'

He shot me a look, raising his eyebrow, but didn't vocalise the fact that I, too, had been impulsive, taking off for the weekend with a relative stranger.

'Write back to her and tell her that she's to give this man your phone number. Tell her that he's to text you with his details.'

'Why?'

'So you know where to start if something goes wrong.'

'Don't say that, Patrick. Now I'm worried.'

'You don't need to worry. Just send the text and see what comes back. If he's on the up-and-up, he'll do as you say. If he's not? Well, then we'll deal.' It was Patrick in his I-rule-the-world mode and it simultaneously made me smile … and melt.

Zoo thing sounds exciting. Can see why you want to go. Who is this person? Give him my number and get him to text me on his phone, I wrote and pushed the "send" icon.

'What happens now?' I asked.

'Now we wait and see.'

In no time at all, my phone buzzed incoming texts. More than one.

'Sam Walker from Condo,' I read aloud to Patrick. 'The next one says that his father's name is Daniel Walker. And then Veriu Apartments, Camperdown. And another mobile phone number. Must be the father's. Well,' I breathed, relieved, 'that all sounds promising.'

'Bronte, eh? Do you finish your text messages with Alcott?' Patrick asked, far too smart for his own good.

'Maybe,' was all I said.

There was a companionable silence for a while, as I looked out the window and Patrick was alone in his own thoughts.

'It's all so pretty, isn't it?' I finally said, commenting on the view as we travelled along the Great Western Highway, ascending the mountains. 'You know, I've lived in Sydney all my life and have never ventured up here.'

'That's because your father couldn't get a ferry here,' Patrick teased, his hand playfully tightening on mine.

'Yes, but I've got a car now. Well, access to one. We only bought two cars for all of us to share. Mostly we use public transport to get around, but Jane needs one to get to work and I usually use the other one, unless Ginny's going shopping.' I was rambling, I realised.

'We'll be there soon,' was his response and I stayed silent, suddenly feeling anxious.

I must have given off some signal because Patrick turned my hand – still resting on his thigh – over, placing his palm directly onto mine.

A tremble quivered through me at the intimacy of the gesture.

Chapter Eight

'Oh, *Patrick!*' I exclaimed, overwhelmed by the incredible sight before me. 'This is *amazing!* I can't believe we're staying *here!*'

We were standing in the driveway, having just alighted from the SUV, of the Bed 'n Breakfast that Patrick had booked and … words failed me! Me! I had no words!

We were right *there!* Right near The Three Sisters at Echo Point, with a whole valley spread out before us. Forget The Grand Canyon! Was there anything more perfect, more *beautiful*, more *stunning* than the landscape of the Blue Mountains! And we were *right* there!

'Oh, *Patrick!*' I breathed again, whirling around, trying to take it all in: the natural beauty of the scenery; the gorgeous old 1920's house, carefully restored to highlight its heritage; the magnificent thoughtfulness of this *man*!

A man who looked so pleased with himself, so proud of himself, that he may as well have carved the sandstone rock formations as well, all by himself!

'You're happy?' he asked, superfluously.

'Oh, *Patrick!*' was my only response. As I said, I had no words.

'C'mon, Lulu. Wait until you see inside.' He reached out for my hand and I immediately grabbed a hold of his, squeezing it and hugging it to my side. 'I'm glad you like it.' His voice was rough – gravelly – but his smile was warm. I squished his hand some more.

But the suite, when we were shown it … !

It was overwhelming, but in a totally different sense. Instead of excited pleasure, I was overcome with nerves, flooded with anxiety.

Central to the room – dominating it, really – was a massive four-poster bed, complete with a lacy overhang dangling all the way around the frame at the top. It was a beautiful bed, the timber dark and swirly, the bottle-green cushions and quilt folded at the foot of the bed providing contrast to the crisp, snowy-white sheets and pillowcases. It was a showcase bed, from another time, another era.

And it starkly brought to my mind the night ahead … and I was filled with anxiety … trepidation.

I stilled and, in my peripheral vision, I could see Patrick falter, as though he'd expected a different reaction from me.

C'mon, Louisa, I coached. *Channel Athena. You're Athena, Warrior Goddess. Act like it!*

I turned towards Patrick and smiled, tightening my clasp on his hand to reassure him as I breathed, 'It's beautiful, Patrick.'

He grinned then, proclaiming, 'Wait until you see the bathtub!'

Yes, a boy, showing off his toys! Underneath that sophisticated man was just an excited boy! It made me smile, thinking this, and calmed my nerves.

And the bathtub was special. And ancient clawfoot, stand-alone tub with a raised back, designed for long, leisurely soaks. It was equally obvious that Patrick had plans for that bathtub!

And my nerves ratcheted up again.

'I've booked us in to a little restaurant down the road for dinner,' he enthused, 'but would you like to go for a walk before then? Stretch your legs after the drive?'

That sounded like a perfect idea to me: let me out of this room for a while longer.

I nodded and was rewarded with his happy, beaming smile once more.

It was all so beautiful. That was the only word I could use to describe the scenery, the cooling breeze of the late afternoon easing the heat of the day, the scent of roses and jasmine permeating the air, and the attentiveness of the gorgeous man at my side. He was happy to amble along, languidly take in the sights, sounds and scents of the mountain bushland.

And all the while, he held my hand, his thumb leisurely stroking the back of my hand; softly, gently, not a rubbing, but a light caress. It kept my attention on him, my focus on his skin, sliding against mine.

When we returned to our room, he offered me first use of the bathroom, a gentlemanly courtesy. And whilst he showered, I perched on the cushioned window seat which extended the length of the huge bay windows, some plain glass, others leadlight – or was it stained glass? I didn't know the difference – and calmed myself by watching the changing colours of the trees in the valley as the afternoon sun sunk below the horizon.

Dinner, which I'm sure was delicious, passed in a blur. It was a quaint little restaurant, with linen tablecloths and lacy curtains, and I ordered comfort food in the vain hope of easing my nerves. My mind, though, was having none of it, arguing with itself throughout the meal.

Settle, petal. You want this! When's the next time such a thoughtful, decent, gorgeous man is going to want to sleep with you? How often do you meet men like this! And, oh! I wanted him! Something fierce!

Alternating with, *Look at him! He's so incredible! And sophisticated. And experienced! You're not going to be enough. He'll be disappointed. He's used to women far more knowledgeable and experienced than you are, Louisa!*

It was doing my head in. So the food may as well have been sawdust, for all the attention I gave it. And Patrick? He was doing nothing to help the situation. *Nothing!*

There he sat, across from me, looking all showered and crisp and *edible*. His dark hair was all smoothed back, making me want to mess with it; his three-day growth all tantalising, images of his dragging those whiskers across my midriff; his mouth so … Oh my god! It was all too much.

And I was positive that he knew it!

Every so often, he raised his hand towards his face and – ever so slowly – dragged his index finger along his bottom lip.

And every time he did it, I had to swallow. Hard.

And every time I did that, his eyes glowed and darkened: two glittering pools of black.

I can't even remember what we talked about. Or if we spoke, at all!

When the waitress, a very efficient, smartly dressed woman in her early thirties who'd been eyeing off Patrick the entire time, cleared our plates and asked if we'd like to see the dessert menu, I broke!

'Can we go?' I croaked, my throat dry, my vocal chords seized.

His eyes didn't leave mine as he smiled, that slow smile that spread across his face, seducing me with its sexiness, satisfaction in the warmth of his gaze, and dark promises in the lowering of his eyelids.

Without taking his focus from me, he said – his voice quite normal, I thought – 'We'll be going. Could you bring the check?'

And neither of us spoke as he viewed the bill and tapped his card against the electronic reader.

Nor when he rose and pulled my chair back as I stood, clumsily, my legs wobbling underneath me. He steadied me with a hand beneath my elbow and I wondered if my forearm would be burned away. Were little puffs of smoke wafting from the heat of his clasp?

I can't remember the walk back to the BnB.

And I can't remember entering our room.

But I do remember the moment Patrick sat on the edge of that four-poster bed that dripped with decadent romance and gently pulled me to him, guiding me down to sit on the sturdy length of his thigh.

Oh, I do remember that!

And I remember the feather-soft touch of his fingertips, as he brushed them across the skin of my forehead and along my hairline, finishing in a delicate sweep below my jaw. I shivered and was slightly comforted to realise that his fingers trembled against my throat. He was as affected as I was.

And I remember that, with his other hand, he lifted one of mine, raising it to his mouth and, his gaze on mine, touched his lips to the sensitive skin of my palm. I was still trying to catch my breath when he parted his lips, just enough to flick out the tip of his tongue to lick me, and then he exhaled onto my damp skin. I quivered from the exquisiteness of the sensory overload.

'Don't you want to know about Athena?' I blurted, breaking into the intensity of the moment.

Patrick stilled, his eyes intent upon me.

'Don't you want to know about me?' I asked, my voice wavering.

'I know about you,' he answered, in that deep, gravelly voice. He straightened, but his hand was still resting on my collarbone, the back of it against my neck; the other hand, still holding mine, resting in my lap. 'I know you're smart – incredibly intelligent. I know you're perceptive and insightful and intuitive. I know that you're caring and compassionate and kind. I know that you pay attention to details, and listen to others, hearing more than the words that they say and seeing more than the things that they show you. I don't need you to tell me about Athena, Louisa.'

His words and his voice …

And then he moved the hand at my neck, sliding it along my jawbone, cupping my chin and lowered his mouth, ever so slowly, so I had time to draw away – if I'd wanted to – and he kissed me.

Such a soft kiss …

A warm kiss ...

So gentle, it was destroying any defence I could have ...

'Athena's one of the virgin goddesses,' I blurted.

He stilled. Then he drew a long breath. His withdrawal was almost imperceptible, barely a movement, just a setting of the muscles in his arms, his chest, along his spine.

I waited, not knowing what to do or say next.

'Yes,' he said, finally, 'she *is* one of the virgin goddesses.' He paused, studying me. 'But, Louisa, you read erotica... I didn't imagine that ...' He broke off, glancing away to the side, and I felt the stiffening of his arms as his retreat became more defined.

'Well, yes, but don't all women?' I asked softly, uncertainly.

That got his attention. 'C'mon, Lulu,' he said, his tone sharper now, 'where do you keep your books? On the coffee table in the lounge room? On a bookshelf in the living room? Or do you have them somewhere in your bedroom? On the bedside table? Or somewhere else?'

I felt myself redden, both from the argumentative tone of his voice – I felt under attack – and from the truth of his words. I did have them hidden. But ... bugger it! I'd just been honest with him. Bluntly, truthfully, *painfully* honest with him! I didn't deserve to be attacked, even if they were just words!

'There are things, Patrick,' I said, imbuing my voice with as much condescension as I could manage, 'that all women have, but they don't put out in public. And you're enough of a grown man to know that!' *So there!* I thought. *Take that!*

I hadn't predicted he'd smile. That was unexpected. It was as though he *liked* it that I'd fought back.

'Why are you here, Louisa?' he asked, gently. 'What are you doing here?'

'You know, Patrick. You know why I'm here.'

'Are you sure? I mean, you've had to have had offers before, surely?' His eyebrows were raised, his tone quizzical.

'Well, no. Not really,' I admitted, my voice small.

'You're joking!' He seemed to be truly astonished. 'Look at you, Athena! *Look* at you! You are ... beautiful. Enchanting,' he continued, the volume of his voice dropping, his tone almost reverent. 'You are an alluring woman, all fairy-blonde hair and enormous eyes and ... such *heart*,' he whispered.

'Well,' I said, my voice equally as hushed, 'maybe you're the only one who knows that ... who sees that. And Patrick, I choose to be here. I didn't want you to stop, before, when I told you. I just wanted you to know. I didn't want there to be secrets between us.'

He winced. Yes, that was what it was – a wince. *Why?* I wondered. *Was it because I still wanted to have sex with him and he no longer wanted to? Was it because I was so inexperienced and he wasn't interested?*

All I knew was that that wince hurt me. A sharp slice in my heart. I could feel hot tears welling up in my eyes and I was scared I was going to cry in front of him.

No! Warrior goddess! I am Athena! Warrior goddess! We do not *cry in front of our foes.*

I shifted my weight, my hands on his shoulders, as I struggled to rise. I wanted to get away, preferably to the bathroom for some privacy.

'No,' he muttered. 'No. Just stay, for a minute. Just … don't move, Louisa. Give me a moment.'

'What for?' I asked, belligerently.

'Just … give me a minute. I just need to rethink this.'

'Why?' I hadn't lost my stroppiness.

'Because … You threw me for a loop, okay?'

'And you rejected me. Call us even!'

'I'm not rejecting you. Just … give me a minute. I just need to regroup.'

'You're *not* rejecting me?' I asked, the aggression gone, a waif-like insecurity lacing my voice.

'No, Athena. I'm not man enough to reject you,' he smiled. 'Not a warrior princess like you.'

And then he hugged me. He tugged me against his body and wrapped both of his arms around me, resting his face over the crown of my head.

And I squirrelled my hands around him, around the warm hard muscles of his abdomen, around the solid strength of his back, and clasped my hands together, tightening my upper arms to hug him in return.

Chapter Nine

We stayed that way – I don't know for how long. It seemed like a long time, but then ...

I listened to his heart beating, steady and strong. And I felt safe in his arms. Warm and secure. There was a gentle rocking motion – I hardly felt it, but when I did, I couldn't unfeel it. It was soothing, in a quiet sort of way. Calming.

But then I didn't want "soothing" and "calming". I'd waited so long for this moment: fantasised about it whilst reading my romance novels; dreamt about it with my favourite celebrities taking a leading role; thought about it endlessly. And here we were, two single people in an incredibly romantic room, and we were hugging like a couple of geriatrics in a nursing home. No, that wasn't what I wanted!

I wriggled a little, just enough to create some space so I could twist my head and burrow into the hollow of his neck. I could smell him: a combination of warm male and some sort of cologne, a bit spicy, a bit woodsy. It was nice. Subtle. Sexy, without being overdone. I nosed the bare skin of his throat, breathing him in, and he responded by loosening the hold of his arms around me, just enough that I could squirrel my hand up his torso to the buttons on his shirt. I nuzzled his neck, then, and lifted my face a little higher, so I could kiss the warm skin of his throat. I felt him still, but he didn't stop me. So I did it again, an open-mouthed kiss this time. And still, he held motionless. Feeling daring, I licked a line, with the tip of my tongue, along the length of his neck. I felt his breath shudder through him. I did it again, on the other side of his throat and busied my fingers with the buttons on his shirt, opening one, and then another, as I peppered soft open-mouthed kisses along his throat, his collarbone, and the tanned skin of his chest.

He didn't say anything or do anything, other than ease his hold on me to allow me greater access to his body. So I kept going, exploring his chest muscles with my mouth, my fingers wriggling and squirming as they ventured across the muscles of his abdomen, which tightened as they passed, and around to explore the hot skin of his back, all the while loosening his shirt.

And then I turned my attention back to his throat, kissing my way up his neck and along his jaw. And that was when he moved, pulling back and capturing my gaze, whilst I stretched up to put my mouth on his – a gentle press of lips on lips – no other movement, our eyes not breaking the heated visual connection. I waited to see what he would do, but he didn't make another move. So, I retreated, turning my attention to the rough whiskers along his jaw and rubbed my cheek against them, feeling the soft scratch on my skin.

I moaned, a low-pitched purr from deep in my chest.

And that was all it took.

Patrick turned his face towards me, covering my lips with his, and invaded my mouth with his tongue. There was nothing subtle about it; nothing gentle about it. It was prime alpha-male taking control and it was what I wanted, what I needed. I moaned again, and reached my hands up to encircle his neck, looping them together behind his head, while his hands rose to my face, one on each side cupping my jaw and holding me … just so … just where he wanted me … as his mouth and tongue lapped at me.

With a well-timed twist, he rolled us both back onto the bed, his upper body moving over me as his lips held mine, still working their magic. His hand shifted from my jaw to cushion the back of my head, which he continued to tilt, this way and that, as though seeking the perfect angle.

And then he raised his head, his eyes capturing mine, his look hot and intense, and said, 'Athena, don't *ever* think that you were rejected.'

And I couldn't think anything.

I could barely breathe.

All I could do was smile back at him as intense emotion overwhelmed me.

No matter what else happened, I would *never* forget this night and this precise moment. No matter what else was said or done, this – this *here* – was real.

And he lowered his head, his eyes closing as he did so, and kissed me again. And again. And while he kept kissing me – long, drugging kisses, with lots of tongue; quick nips, barely-there flicks of his lips; gentle suckles from his open mouth – he gradually unveiled me, my clothes magically undone and removed from my aroused flesh. It was like a dance – a slow, sensual ballet – graceful sways and lifts of my body and his – as we twisted and turned, writhed and squirmed against each other, becoming hotter and hotter in our desire.

And then I became impatient!

This was all well and good – and it felt amazing – but there was something … just out of reach … and I wanted it! And my body was clenching – on *nothing*, when it wanted – oh, did it want!

'Patrick,' I whimpered, pushing myself against him, my legs spreading so I could rub against his hip.

'Shhh,' he whispered back. 'I just want to make sure that you're ready.'

'Then do it,' I begged. 'I want …' and I ground myself against him some more.

'Okay, okay,' he murmured, 'just let me …' and he slid his huge hand between my thighs, his fingers sliding easily along my sensitive flesh, the heel of his hand pressing against my clit. 'Oh, so wet, my little warrior. So wet for me.'

And I pressed harder against him as his finger eased into me – a strange, yet totally welcome sensation.

'Oh, *yes!*' I groaned. 'Oh, yes. *More* of that.'

I heard his chuckle, just before his mouth covered mine again, his kiss, long and slow and deep, swallowing my moans, as he continued to work his magical torment on my flesh.

'Oh, God!' I broke away from his mouth, feeling overcome with exquisite sensation. 'Oh, *yes!* Oh god, Patrick, don't *stop!*' I cried, as – ooohhh! – a huge wave of bliss? – was it ecstasy? – oh, who could think of words at a time like this! – surged through me.

'Good?' his deep voice rumbled over me.

'Hmmm, God yes! Give me a minute and can we do it again?' I managed to say.

'I'll make it better than that, Lulu,' he said, and I felt him roll away and heard the crackle of foil being ripped. 'But we'll take it slow, okay?' He captured my chin, waiting until I looked directly at him. 'We're doing this my way, okay, Lulu?'

And I just nodded. Anything he wanted. I was putty in his hands.

'Your way, Patrick, but – you know – anytime soon?' I teased, cheekily.

'Brat!' was all he said, as he lowered himself between my legs, shifting them to accommodate his girth. 'We're taking this slowly,' he said, as I felt the gentle nudge against my sensitised opening. 'I don't want to hurt you and,' he paused, inhaling deeply, as he pressed into me, 'I don't want you to hurt yourself,' he chuckled. His body stilled in mine, whilst he released a long breath. 'Are you good?' he asked, as he pushed further into me and my legs lifted up to grip his hips.

'Mmmm,' I responded, eloquently.

'Let me know if it hurts,' he murmured, filling me with his heat, and breathing slowly and deeply, deliberately holding himself back, I thought.

'I'm good. Don't stop, Patrick.'

'I won't, Lulu. Just don't let me hurt you.'

'I won't,' I repeated back to him. 'But don't stop.'

'I won't.' It was our chorus – until we composed a new one.

'So *good!*' I moaned, pushing myself against him.

'Hmmmm, *so* good,' he responded.

'Oh, it's *good*,' I rewrote the lyrics.

'Mmmmm,' he sounded the bass line.

'Are you ready, Lulu? Can I...?'

I wasn't sure what he was asking, but I only had one answer. 'Hmmm.'

And it was as though I'd released him from his restraint. The rhythm and length of his thrusts increased, and they finished with a little hitch, a jerk, an extra jolt, as he pushed his weight up onto his arms, locked in place, and his gaze went to where his hips were pistoning, where we were joined. I was curled, almost back onto myself, my spine curved towards him, and I watched as he slowed his movements, lifted his eyes to mine and stared deeply – as though into my soul – as his body clenched, and jerked, and thrust, and jerked. I could feel heat in my core as his body stilled in mine and I drowned in his eyes.

He grunted as he lowered himself – carefully, I thought – onto me, his elbows taking his weight, whilst my legs dropped from the side of his body.

'I wanted you to come,' he murmured against my neck.

'I did,' I whispered back.

'No, a second time.'

'Bit unrealistic, isn't it? Even *I* know that.'

'Yeah, but ... I wanted you to.'

'Who do you think you are? Zeus?' I teased, more strength in my voice now.

'Well, *yeah!*'

'Oh, *Patrick!*' I chuckled, wrapping my arms around him and squeezing.

'You okay?' He lifted his head to look at me, concern flooding his face.

'I'm *excellent!*' I said, proudly. 'More than excellent!'

'Good,' he mumbled, dropping his head and nuzzling my neck. 'I'll get up in a second.'

'No rush,' I said, savouring the feel of "man" on me: the warmth, the heaviness, the roughness of his leg hair.

And then my phone buzzed. An incoming text. Almost instantly, it buzzed again.

'Time to get up, I guess,' Patrick said, as he gently eased himself from my body, and gingerly lifted his weight from me. 'I'll get your phone,' he said, stepping away from the bed and reaching for my handbag. He tossed it to me as he walked towards the bathroom, but I was so distracted by the sight of him – his long legs, his tight butt, the line of his back – as he strode across the room, that I missed the catch and the bag fell open on the bed.

Oh! My! God!

I was still sitting, stunned, when he returned from the bathroom and I got to be enthralled all over again, only this time with the front view of his long, hair-clad thighs, his tight abs, and solid chest, his still-damp short beard and slicked-back hair – and of course – his manhood, still impressive, even without being erect.

Whoa, mama! Maybe he was Zeus!

'Who's texting?' He asked, his eyes flicking towards the phone, lying on the bed. 'And the bathroom's free. I left a warm flannel on the sink for you.'

'Umm, not sure.' I reached over to check the screen. 'Oh, it's Ginny. She's out for the night. Oh, and so is Jane.' It was hard to keep the surprise out of my voice.

'So the goddesses are out playing? Stirring up trouble, no doubt,' he teased, before adding, 'Should you have phoned or texted someone?'

'Well, yes. It's the rules. But ...'

'But what?'

'I don't suppose it matters,' I shrugged. 'If Jane and Ginny are out, and we know that Charli's out ... Daph's probably already asleep, thinking that I'm in my room... It doesn't make sense to disturb her, and she'll text me if she's worried.'

'As long as it's alright,' he agreed, yawning. 'Go use the bathroom and get back here, so we can get some sleep. Gotta big day tomorrow.'

'What are we doing?' I asked, reaching for his discarded shirt so I didn't have to walk across the room naked.

He laughed. 'Got no idea, but Louisa?'

'Yeah,' I looked back at him.

'I've seen you naked,' he grinned, flicking me a sexy wink. 'You can't get more naked. Just hurry up.'

Chapter Ten

Who would have guessed that Patrick – big, bad Patrick, sophisticated man of the world, who caused luxury hotel staff to jump at his requests – was a snuggler? But he was.

And a stroker? He was that, too.

And also a furnace.

He was so wrapped around me, his front against my back, his legs intertwined with mine, his arm encircling my waist and his head on the pillow above mine, that I felt enveloped by him. And he gave off a warmth that was all-encompassing. I think even his toes were little heat beads.

And, in that position, I felt like his cuddle-toy.

I'd disturbed at different intervals throughout the night – probably from being over-warm and I'd kicked my feet free from the covers to cool off – and felt the gentle stroke of his fingers on my arm. Just a soft brush, but in a regular rhythm. I wondered, at one stage, if he was awake and consciously stroking me, but I realised that it was an unconscious action. Was he dreaming? And if so, what of? Was he dreaming about me? Or was his stroking a self-soothing act, designed to calm his own nightmares? Who knew? But it sure felt good.

I woke in the early morning light to a coolness on my back, my furnace detached from me, but I shivered with the brush of fingertips across the nape of my neck, following the line of my shoulder and down my arm. Then back, up the arm, across the shoulder and down the length of my spine. Another shiver. And then, along the curve of my hip, following the demarcation where my leg and butt cheek met, a barely-there touch on the short curls between my thighs and up the crack of my bottom. This time, I quivered and released a tiny moan – more a low-vibration exhalation than a real sound.

'You awake?' His sleep-roughened voice had the same effect on me as the rasp of his bristles on the nape of my neck. And I quivered again.

'Hmmm.'

'Are you … how shall I put this delicately? Uncomfortable? Sore?' His whiskers scratched me some more.

'Umm, I don't think so.'

'Good.' Satisfaction seeped into his voice, and his fingers started their travels all over again, only this time, his tongue and beard-roughened jaw joined the journey, licking and scraping across the sensitive skin on my shoulders and behind my neck, his breathing vibrating in my ears, all combining for goosebumps to rise – all over my body. This time, when his fingers completed their voyage to my heated core, they lingered, sliding through the slick skin and circling my clit, swollen and sensitised.

I could feel him behind me, his cock – hard and hot – nestled against my butt cheeks, and I pushed back against him. He responded by pressing himself against my back, short little thrusts.

'Are you okay?' His voice was gruff.

'Yeah.'

'Good.' And I felt cool air as he leant away from me, his arm reaching to the bedside table, and the crinkly crackle of a condom packet being ripped and discarded followed. Then his warmth returned to me and he guided himself along the slippery valley between my legs, gliding back and forth, nudging my clit on each pass. Whilst one arm was wrapped around me, his hand fondling my breast and tweaking my tender nipple, his other hand grasped my hip, tilting me so that, on his next glide along my slick flesh, he gently eased himself inside me. I arched my back in response and moaned softly as he filled me, each time plunging a little deeper. And then we rocked, our bodies swooping and swaying against each other's, and he dragged his fingers through my body's juice and swirled them around my clit: a circle this way, a slide that way, a micro-massage all over.

And it felt … amazing. Incredible. Unbelievably good.

My breathing hitched as he increased the tempo of his movements, as he varied the rhythm, as he deepened his thrusts. And all the time, his fingers kept up their magical motions, and his breathing in my ear became the soundtrack to my pleasure, and I stretched my neck, lengthening the line of my throat, to better enjoy the scruff of his beard against my skin.

'So good,' I breathed.

'So good,' he echoed.

I gripped his arms with my hands, hugging them to me, my best effort at holding him closer.

'Let me know when,' he murmured in my ear.

'When what?' I asked in a haze of pleasure.

'You'll know.'

And then sensation surged, swamping me with deliciousness, with pleasure, with ... oh, damn! I couldn't find the word!

'Patrick!' I cried.

'That's it, Lulu. Let go,' he urged, his voice gravel-gruff.

'Oh, ohh, ohhh!' I puffed as I rode the wondrous wave that washed over me. 'Oh, *Patrick!*'

There was only the sound of his breathing, gradually slowing.

And then he chuckled. 'You know, "Oh, *Patrick*" is rapidly becoming my favourite phrase.'

I pinched his arm – hard and sharply!

'Don't mock me!' I rebuked him.

'Oh, Lulu, I'm not!' His voice was warm and mellow, like molten honey. 'I'm most definitely not.'

'C'mon, Athena! The day's a-wasting! Time to get up!' Patrick jerked the covers off me and the sudden coolness was almost as shocking as his exuberant words. I must have dozed off, which didn't surprise me. It wasn't every day I had sex! And not twice in the same night!

'Patrick, stop it!' I complained, as he flicked my bare butt with the towel in his hand. 'What the ...!'

'C'mon, my warrior goddess. We've got places to go, things to do. No time to lie around!'

How could he possibly be this energetic? What was *wrong* with the man?

'What are we doing? What plans have you made?' I asked, as I turned over, tugging the covers back over my naked body. He grinned, that cheeky I've-already-seen-you-naked wicked grin.

'Well, for starters, we need breakfast. And the dining room closes in,' he checked his watch, 'fifteen minutes, so get a wriggle.'

'Oh, God,' I groaned. 'Does it matter if I don't have breakfast?'

'Not my problem, but I am and you might want a coffee, at the very least. So, get a move on.'

Why did he have to sound so ... *awake?*

I discovered that Patrick's exuberance and enthusiasm allowed him to cram an awful lot into one day! I was exhausted – totally and utterly done in – by the setting of the sun on Saturday. We'd visited so many lookouts, I could no longer remember their names. They were all incredible, with stunning vistas along and across valleys, with quaint names like Jamison and Megalong, and beautiful cliffs and crags, coated with the eucalyptus trees that gave the landscape its blue tinge. And we visited the cascades and I soothed my walk-weary feet in the clear, cool water, before donning my walking shoes again. And we seemed to eat all day – Devonshire tea, with scones, jam and cream; chunky salad sandwiches with thick, soft wholegrain bread; cold, sweet ice-cream in wafer cones.

And all the while, Patrick held my hand. Or, when we were standing still, he'd lift a finger and stroke it down the side of my face, always finishing with a flourish just below my jaw near my ear. Who knew this was such an erogenous zone for me! Or he'd press up against my back when he was taking a selfie of us at some spectacular scenic attraction, sneaking a hand around my belly and pulling me close. Or he watched me, intently, with heat in his gaze, as I ate my ice-cream, causing me to lick the cold sweet more slowly, and deliberately, and thoroughly, my tongue flattening, and pointing, and swirling with creamy goodness.

Oh, yes, two could play at this game… and we both did. The whole day seemed like seductive foreplay for the evening ahead. Building our desire. Turning up the heat. Ramping our lust to new heights.

'We can fill that bathtub when we get back,' Patrick suggested, as we drove home from the last of the bushwalks. 'It probably needs a workout,' he leered at me.

'Hmmm, maybe,' I responded, faking disinterest.

'Or not,' he teased, obviously not falling for my ploy.

'What are we doing for dinner?'

'I'm not bothered. We can order in, if you want. I could go a pizza. We could get a salad, too, if you want?'

'I thought you wanted to go out for dinner,' I asked.

'If you want to, we can, but I thought … It's been a long day, so I'm happy to stay in. And we don't have to get dressed again if we have pizza.' He waggled his eyebrows suggestively.

'Is that *all* you think about?' I feigned offence.

'Oh, God, yes, Athena! Especially near you!'

Well, I could hardly fault that response.

The bath was chaos. Patrick squirted way too much bubble bath in the water as it was filling and the result looked like the biggest cappuccino ever, frothy suds piled high, rising to a peak, like a soapy Mt Everest. And when we climbed in – well, *I* at least tried to keep the water from flooding the bathroom, but it seemed that such a consideration was well beyond Patrick's sensibilities. The bath began with us both sitting, facing each other, but that didn't last long. Patrick was intent upon getting his hands on me and, really, I didn't mind. So, in no time at all, he was leaning on the high back of the tub, his legs spread and me sandwiched in between his thighs. Patrick amused himself by cupping handfuls of soapy froth and smoothing them over any part of me he could reach: my arms, and hands, and neck, and shoulders, and breasts. And then he lifted each leg in turn, presumably to wash them, but most probably just to get his hands on them. And then he smoothed his soapy hands down my belly, taking time to twirl his fingertip in my bellybutton, before setting out for more interesting sites, hidden between my thighs.

And I loved it! I could have stayed in that tub forever.

Except the water cooled, chilling us both, and the skin on my fingers had become all wrinkly and pruney.

I imagined that he'd lead us straight back to bed after all of that foreplay, but he surprised me. We both donned the complementary bathrobes and lounged, my body nestled in the sturdy frame of his, on the window seat, looking out at the darkness that was the Jamieson Valley, as we awaited our pizza delivery. We pulled a chair over, placing the pizza box on its wooden seat, and picnicked on the window seat, being careful not to spill food or damage the plush, bottle-green velvet cushion.

And while we sipped red wine – Patrick's selection that tasted pretty special to me – he said, 'So tell me about Louisa.'

'I thought you knew all about her,' I responded, a tart tone to my voice. 'At least, that's what you said last night.'

'Oh, I do. I know all the important things: about her intelligence, and her qualities, and her personality. But tell me the boring bits. What's with the bookshop? What do you do in your spare time? Other than read erotica,' he said, teasing me.

'I've worked in the bookstore for years,' I began, but he interrupted me.

'No, Lulu. Tell me a *story*. Don't just relate the details.'

I sipped my wine, contemplating what he was asking of me. How did I answer that?

I started again.

'Athena knew, from a very young age, that in order to gain the wisdom essential to being a great goddess, a goddess renowned for her intelligence, her wisdom and her courage, she would need to learn – and that there was no better way to learn than through reading, and books. So, she accompanied her mother, a muse of exceptional intellect and inspiration, on all of her jaunts to the great book emporiums of the known world – otherwise known as Sydney libraries and bookshops – to surround herself with tomes of knowledge and wisdom.' I sipped my wine, enjoying the rapt attention, the total focus, that Patrick bestowed on me. 'And she shared with her mother, the muse, her learning, her insights and perspectives, and the two of them discussed and debated, challenged and critiqued, the knowledge and interpretations that she had gathered.'

'Go on,' Patrick murmured, his gaze warm, before drinking from his glass.

'And they were happy, high in their tower, engaged in dialogue, and conversing, and exploring and testing ideas. The mere mortals amused themselves with trivial pursuits – boating, running and kicking balls into the air, and adding numbers in their booklets, and rabble-rousing – but the Muse and her treasured daughter, Athena, had answered a higher calling.'

'Ego, much?' Patrick teased.

'Hey! I'm telling this story! And remember, you asked for it!'

This was fun. I liked playing with Patrick.

And he *understood* things – like my mother did.

'Well, then, feel free to continue,' he invited, wafting his pizza-laden hand across the space between us.

'But the gods were jealous of the love and respect between the Muse and Athena, and they gathered together – possibly on Mount Olympus, it has been suggested,' I ad-libbed, with a flourish, and was rewarded with Patrick raising his glass in a mock-toast, his eyes twinkling, ' – and plotted, orchestrating the demise of not only the Muse, but also her partner, Apollo himself.'

'Oooohh, the plot thickens!'

'It does. Tragedy struck. The gods deemed that flying through the air and viewing the world from the heavens was only for the Gods themselves. Some gods,' I quickly added, when I could see that Patrick was going to argue Apollo's god-status, 'and definitely not muses. So, when Apollo and his muse deigned to usurp the privileges of the gods, they sent a lightning bolt through the air, when there was no storm, and *struck* their flying carriage down. Down, down, down. Until it shattered on the hard, hard surface of the earth, killing Apollo, his muse and the presumptuous, dastardly wretch who had dared take them into the air.'

Silence and stillness followed. Patrick held my gaze as I attempted to swallow the lump that had somehow found its way into my throat.

'And then what happened to Athena?'

'She was alone – yet not alone,' I whispered. 'There were four other goddesses in the temple, wailing goddesses.' I paused and cleared my throat. 'And they needed guidance. They needed someone to listen to them, to help them, to steer them through the tragedy that had befallen them all. So, drawing all that she had learnt about the human condition, and on the spirit of her mother, the Muse, Athena adopted the role of Counsellor, of the Wise Oracle. And she hid her love of storytelling, subjugating it in order to listen to and advise the other goddesses.' I took a steadying breath, preparing myself for the pain of the next words. 'Until Iris.'

'Iris?' Patrick straightened, tilting his head at an angle, suddenly alert.

'Yes, Iris,' I confirmed, sadly, breaking eye contact with Patrick and staring at my wine glass, resting in my lap. 'Athena discovered Iris' books and stories, and she liked them. And one day, Athena wrote to Iris, two goddesses who loved stories, and Iris wrote back. They engaged in conversation. Athena had found, not quite her mother, the Muse, but a soul mate. She'd offer insights into Iris' stories – the plot development, the characters, the archetypes, and themes – and Iris seemed to respect Athena's contributions. But then … she didn't remember… The gods must have smote her memory.'

I looked up, then, and saw that Patrick looked distressed. Was he ill? He'd … *blanched*. Yes, that was the word. Like he was nauseous and alarmed.

'Patrick, are you alright?' I asked, leaning forward to touch his hand. 'You look sick. Was the pizza no good? There weren't anchovies on it, were there? Are you alright?'

He recoiled from me. It was as though he were stung.

'Patrick? Are you okay?' What should I do?

He rose, jerkily, stumbling to his feet and turned away from me.

'I need to … the bathroom,' he said and strode swiftly across the room, closing the bathroom door behind him.

I didn't know what to do. Was he going to be okay? Maybe a few minutes in the bathroom and he'd be okay again.

I busied myself tidying up from our picnic: placing the pizza box near the garbage bin; brushing crumbs from the beautiful fabric-covered window-seat; putting the chair back where it belonged; positioning our wine glasses on the side table.

And then I sat on the end of the bed, my hand mindlessly stroking the damask weave of the quilt cover, and waited, and worried.

The door finally opened and Patrick moved to his side of the bed, pulling back the covers. 'It's time for bed,' he said, sounding distant and focused only on the sheets, not looking at me. 'Do you need to use the bathroom before we turn the lights out?'

Something was wrong, but I didn't know what. It was confusing. My only conclusion was that Patrick wasn't feeling well and I needed to be compassionate.

'Sure,' I said, 'I'll be right back.'

And when I returned, I wriggled my way across the bed, aligning my body to his as he lay, on his back, staring at the ceiling, his hands behind his head. I felt a bit awkward. Should I leave him alone, if he wasn't feeling well, or snuggle into him and offer comfort? I curled my body, facing him, and rested one hand on his nearest biceps – a small connection, but a connection, nonetheless.

No sex tonight was my thought, as I closed my eyes, focused on my breathing and calmed my mind for sleep.

Chapter Eleven

We didn't stay that way.

I woke at one point – overheated – and realised that I was, once again, encircled by Patrick's body: his arms curled around me, his legs intertwined with mine, his face above me, his breathing swirling tiny puffs of Patrick-scented air down my cheeks.

And, in the cool of the pre-dawn hour, I thought I dreamt of a cat swiping a roughened tongue across my shoulders... When a very human hand stroked across the cheek of my bottom, up and around the curve of my hipbone, tickling the sensitive skin just in front of it, before sliding down to the increasingly damp valley between my legs, I knew it was my very own Priapus, the god of sex and lust.

It was slow and easy, sensual and seductive. I wasn't sure if he was being considerate of my tender flesh from my recently-departed virgin status, or if he was not quite his normal energetic self, but we came together in a gentle, trance-like merging, a true "intercourse" – a communication between two people. Because it did feel like we were communicating, on a deeply intimate, deeply spiritual level. Maybe I was imagining it, but this time – it felt different. I allowed myself to dream of ... *more* ... with this man – this gorgeous human being – who made me feel significant and important and ... empowered.

And when I came – a quiet, but strong, surge rippling through me, leaving me quivering with the eddying aftershocks – I felt my heart swell, emotion overwhelming me, bringing salty tears to my eyes. And when he came – long, slow slides through my slick swollen flesh, deepening his thrusts after I'd whispered his favourite words, "Oh, *Patrick!*", against his ear – he mumbled, "Lulu", over and over again, in a gravelly incantation.

And then we slept, wrapped in each other's arms, our breaths intermingling, our bodies still joined.

He was awake before me, dressed and sitting on the chair, that he'd drawn up to the side of the bed, when I opened my eyes, blinking against the sunlight, spearing through the leadlight windows.

'Louisa, we need to talk.'

That didn't sound good. I'm sure they're the words that people, world-wide, hated to hear first thing in the morning.

'Can I get up first?' I asked, delaying whatever bad thing he was going to say.

'Sure. I'll go get coffee from the breakfast room,' he offered, as if realising how … off-putting? Unsettling? Downright frightening? … he was being.

I wasted no time in freshening up and dressing. If something bad was about to happen, I wanted to be prepared. Armoured up. Ready for battle…

Should I pack my things? I didn't know.

Breathe, Louisa. Channel Athena. You can cope with anything that comes, I reminded myself.

He brought a tray back: two mugs of coffee and a plate of muffins, and placed it on the side table before sitting on the chair that remained where he'd left it, beside the bed, near where I was sitting, waiting.

'What did you want to talk about?' I asked, refusing the passive role I'd been cast into.

'Here's your coffee,' he prevaricated, holding out the beverage. 'Did you want a muffin?'

'Patrick,' I sighed, 'it's really nice that you're playing the gracious host, but there's obviously something wrong, so could you cut to the chase?' *Yes, Louisa. Be in control of this!*

He inhaled deeply, glancing at the floor, before lifting his head and looking directly at me.

'There are two things we need to talk about,' he started, discomfort radiating from him. 'Firstly, I'd like to see you again.'

I was confused. I wanted to be gleeful, but he looked so *pained*.

'And?' I prompted, hopefully giving nothing away of my feelings.

'I'd like for you to come to the Gold Coast. Maybe next weekend. I'm sure the borders will be open by then.'

'Oh!' I still didn't get why he was looking so ... uncomfortable. Awkward. 'Well, they might be,' I offered, really having no idea what the COVID restrictions were at that very moment, bar the following week.

'Would you like to come? If I organise a plane ticket? Would you come?'

'Sure. Maybe. I don't know.' This was confusing. What was his *problem?* 'Are planes safe? I mean, you know ... the virus?'

'I'm sure they are. I mean, I flew down here.'

'Do you have to self-isolate when you go home?'

'Well, yeah, but that's not a problem. I have a few projects to take care of at home.'

I still didn't get it. He kept looking away from me, and this conversation was so *awkward*. Not at all like every other conversation we'd had. And he seemed so distant. *What was going on?*

'There's something I need to tell you. Another thing to tell you ...' His voice petered off.

'Well, whatever it is, can you get this over with? C'mon, Patrick!' A wave of impatience overtook me: so unlike me. I was normally so calm and – you know – *not* flustered. 'What can be so bad that you're pussy-footing around like this? I'm squirming in my pants over here and I've got no idea what this is about. Spit it out!'

He inhaled again, a long deep breath, and said, 'I'm Iris, Louisa. I'm Iris Grayson.'

What!

'You're *what?*'

'I'm Iris Grayson,' he repeated.

'No, you're not,' I argued, refusing to believe him. My mind started to spin. *I know Iris. I've written to her for years. Patrick* – Patrick – *is not her. She's a woman. She writes romances for* women! *Erotic romances for women! This man – this giant of a man – this man ... is not her!*

But ... Then I thought about my initial impression of Iris: how I'd *thought* she'd look and how she'd surprised me when I'd met her. What had I thought? *Older, by a decade – maybe two. Dark hair. Strong personality.* Oh My God! I was describing *Patrick!*

'I am, Lulu. I know you're Lulu98.'

And, with those two digits, he damned himself.

'Don't call me Lulu!' I spat at him.

'Louisa, I'm sorry – '

'And don't call me *Louisa!*' My voice was so loud, it was almost a scream.

332

I started to shake. I'd *slept* with him. He'd *lied* to me. I had *sex* with him. This *liar!* I felt like I was simultaneously shrivelling up inside and ready to *explode!* Was that even possible?

'Athena,' he began again, his voice steady.

'And don't call me *Athena!*' I almost shrieked. Oh, what a *fool* he'd made of me! Was it all just a game? With my eyes scrunched tight, I buried my head in my hands. If I couldn't see him, …

I wanted to cry. *Do NOT cry in front of him! Do NOT cry in front of him! Do you hear me, Louisa! Do not cry in front of him! Pull it together. You are a goddess. A warrior goddess. You are Athena! Channel Athena! What would a warrior goddess do now?*

I drew a deep breath, a deep, deep breath, inhaling air all the way down to my toes.

Then, I dropped my hands away from my face, straightened my back and released the breath. Slowly. As though I were in control.

'I want to go home,' I stated, clearly, concisely, taking care to keep my face expressionless – although I can't guarantee I managed this – and staring him in the eyes. 'I want to go home, *now*.' I reaffirmed.

'Lou, give me a chance to explain.'

I watched, calmly, coldly, as he swiped his hand through his hair. He did look frazzled. Anxious? Definitely, concerned.

Stay silent, Louisa. I instructed myself. *After all, that's what he's done. He stayed silent. When he should have spoken.*

'Look, Lou,' he started again, and I was just *loving* the "look" part of this – *not!* as though I had to *see* something. 'I don't tell anyone that I'm Iris Grayson; that I write *romance* novels.'

Ooooh, he just kept digging himself deeper. In my little heart of hearts, I didn't want to think that I was just "anyone". And what was with the disparaging tone when he said "romance"? What was wrong with romance novels? Love and commitment and passion and desire and sex and lust: these things made the world go around. These were the driving forces. Some men might pretend that it was about money, or building phallic towers, or fast cars, or football, but … it was men who wrote so many of the most beautiful love songs; who wrote the poetry; who wrote the tragedies.

Stop intellectualising, Louisa! Your life is falling apart here.

He was still talking. I'd missed what he was saying: I don't think any of his words were registering in my brain, right then. All I knew was that I had been betrayed; that he had kept a *secret* from me, when I had been so honest – painfully honest – with him! I didn't want to look at him, and I definitely didn't want to *hear* anything else he had to say.

'Take me home, Patrick. Take me home *now!*'

Oh, I'm so proud of you, Louisa. You sounded so in control just then. Keep it up, girl! Maintain your dignity! Don't let him take your dignity, I coached myself.

I stood and gathered my things. He was still sitting on the bed, his back curved, his hands turned upwards, beseechingly, resting on his spread knees.

'Lou, if you'd just take a minute to listen,' he started again, his face twisted in – was it torment? 'I started writing the romances in uni, as a joke.'

Yes, Patrick. Dig the hole deeper. You're not helping yourself.

'Patrick,' I interrupted him.

'Yes, Lou.' He looked relieved, as though the fact that I'd said his name was going to absolve him.

'Take me home. Now. And don't call me Lou!'

Irritation flickered over his face. 'Don't call me Lulu. Don't call me Louisa. Don't call me Lou. What am I supposed to call you? I'm guessing you don't want Athena.'

Oh, yes, Patrick. Attack me, why don't you! You're the one in the wrong. So turn it on me!

Channel Athena. What would Athena do with a mere mortal who has shown himself undeserving of her?

'Patrick,' I used my most imperious voice, 'you don't need to talk to me at all. All you need to do is take me home. And,' I drew a breath and lengthened my spine to my full height – which still wasn't much, but ... 'if you can't do *that* – that simple thing, Patrick – then I will order an Uber to take me to Katoomba station. I'm sure there's a train leaving sometime soon.'

He sighed. A long, deep sigh which sounded like it came from the depths of his chest.

'Okay. I'll take you home.'

'Good. Do whatever you need to do to check us out. I'll meet you at the car.'

And, with as much dignity as I could muster, as regally as my small frame could manage carrying my bags, I walked out of the room.

I felt numb.

That was good, I kept telling myself. *Stay numb.*

I knew that when I got home, I could process all of this. And there was a lot to process. I couldn't totally fault him, I knew. I was a grown woman – well, as grown as I was going to be. I had made decisions to go with him for a drink; for lunch; for a weekend away. No-one had forced me. It had been my choice.

And I'd known that he was a player; that he had much more stunningly beautiful women than I to bed; definitely much more experienced women; and that he – most likely – bedded them often. I knew that. And I knew from the start that this was just a fantasy weekend for me: I mean, I *hoped* that something might come of it – we hit it off so quickly and so well. He seemed to *know* me – well, the joke was definitely on me, wasn't it? He *did* know me!

Stop thinking about this now, Louisa. Stay numb. At least until you get home.

He'd been silent, too, as we'd loaded our bags into his rental car. When I saw the huge suitcase and canvas covered whatever-it-was still lying in the back of the SUV, I realised what they were: the stock of Iris' books, and the banner stand with her name, logo and the cover of her latest release, from the book-signing event. I stared at them: evidence of his deception, and realised that he had paused, his arm poised, holding the hatch open, and I glanced at him to see that he was watching me, studying me. What? Waiting for a reaction? I felt sick. *How about I vomit about now, Patrick?* I thought.

Stay numb, Louisa. You'll get through this. You've been through worse.

He didn't speak as he drove the SUV through the streets of Katoomba, and directed it along the mountain road, heading towards Sydney. Under other circumstances, I would have appreciated the efficiency of his movements, the inherent sex appeal of his competence, the flexing of his thigh muscles as he worked the pedals, the sexiness of his hair dusted forearms as he manipulated the steering wheel. But … these weren't other circumstances and I swallowed hard.

Stay numb, Louisa. It was my mantra.

It was once we were off the mountain, down on the plain, that he started talking again. I stared out the window, pretending not to listen to him, the deep tones of his voice washing over me and making me wish for other things.

'I told you that I went to university in Brisbane,' he said, reminding me of his prevarication when I asked him what he did for work. *"So what do you do for work, Patrick?" I'd asked when we had our picnic lunch. And his response had been "I have a degree in Communications, majoring in journalism and marketing." And I'd asked where he studied and he said "Brisbane."*

'And there were these girls – female students,' he corrected himself, 'and they were all – you know – doing creative writing, as though they were going to be able to make a living out of it. And we were there, my mates and me,' – "*mates and I*", I silently corrected – 'doing real writing – you know, journalism and investigative reporting and marketing,' – *yes, dig that hole deeper, Patrick,* – 'and there was a dare.' He paused, his gaze flicking back and forth as we merged onto the motorway. 'Anyway, as a bit of a joke, we decided that one of us would write a romance novel and we'd market it and … You know, we sort of didn't expect it to do anything. What did we know about writing a romance novel? But then, how difficult could it be? That's what we thought.'

He glanced over at me. I could feel the heat of his gaze and caught his reflection in the windscreen.

'I mean, we thought: boy meets girl, boy chases girl, boy gets girl, girl gets in a twitter, boy runs for the hills, boy comes back and they live happily ever after. How easy is that!'

Okay, I *did* give him a death-stare about then. My head swivelled towards him, my mouth hanging open. I was *appalled* at what he'd just said. He'd reduced romance readers – *me* and others like me: intelligent, busy, professional women who liked – no, *enjoyed* – escaping from the daily routines and *stresses* of their hectic lives by indulging in a few hours of reading something that wasn't facts and figures, reports and spreadsheets, fairy stories and picture books – he'd reduced us to imbeciles.

It registered with him. He realised what he'd said. I could tell from his double-take. He'd started with just a glance towards me, checking to see if I understood, I thought. But that double-take... He *knew* that I was riled; that my numbness had thawed, even if it was just for that moment. He also knew, though, that I was listening to him. Score one: Patrick.

'Look, it didn't last. You know, my …' he paused, searching for the word.

'Condescension,' I offered, with a sneer. 'Patronisation. Disrespect. Contempt. Arrogance.'

'Well, it didn't last,' he said, weakly. 'The first book – it was probably pretty rough.'

"Yes, it was,' I interjected. 'It was *very* evident that it was your first *attempt*.'

'Yeah, well, I had to start somewhere. But it sold. Not a lot, but enough to tweak my interest. And so I wrote another one. And it sold more. And then … it sort of grew from there.'

336

'There are writers who would *kill* for your success,' I ground out. 'And to you, it was all a joke.'

'It definitely started that way, Lulu, I won't deny it. But,' he hesitated and then glanced at me, 'then it was different.' I thought he was waiting for me to prompt him, but I was already annoyed with myself for how much I'd engaged, so I stayed silent. 'The customers – readers... They wrote to me, complimenting me and telling me which bits of the story they liked. And they read *lots*. I mean, lots of books. Women who read romance novels – they read *lots* of books. I discovered that most of them were professional women, with their own income. Disposable income, that they could spend on anything they wanted. And they spent it on my books. And they were *loyal*. That surprised me. I wasn't expecting that level of support and faithfulness. It stunned me. And, over the years, I grew to respect them, and their views and input on my stories. They'd tell me what characters they liked and why; what storylines worked and which ones didn't.'

I wondered where I fit in with all of this. I'd been writing to him for three years. Was I just one of many? Hundreds? *Thousands?*

'So, I decided I'd give back a bit. To my readers. That's when I started doing signings, and things. Events. But ... I couldn't, after all that time, be me – Patrick Black. So... I pay an actress. That woman – Libby – she's an actress and she does my signings. I figured she was what women would expect that Iris was like: beautiful, poised, well-groomed, a *woman*.' He grimaced. 'And most women seem happy. They come, either with the books they've already bought or willing to buy books from the table, and get a few minutes of conversation and their autographs and ... they seem happy. They chat amongst themselves and visit the tables of other authors and ... it seemed to be mutually beneficial.' He sounded uncertain, but I wasn't in the mood to reassure him. 'Women like to talk with other women about their reading, and their favourite authors, and their favourite books. It's a social event for them. And I felt like I was ... you know, giving back.'

'Until Thursday night.' I couldn't resist butting in.

'Well, yeah. Until Thursday night. You're the first person who wasn't satisfied. I should have known.' He was silent, for a long time. I didn't think he was going to talk again.

'Why, Patrick? Why should you have known?' Okay, I engaged.

'Because you and I ... When you wrote to me, it was different. It wasn't just "I love your work" and I didn't write back, "Thanks for your kind words". It was different.'

'How?'

'Oh, I don't know,' he burst out. 'It was different. You started writing a few years ago –'

'Three,' I interrupted.

'Alright, well, *three* years ago and I was a bit ... stale ... then. You made some comments about what I'd done and ... it was like a light switch was flicked on and ...' He took a breath. 'My writing got better because of you, Lulu. I sort of – it was sort of like I was *writing* for you – to see what you'd think. And you told me things – like literature things – that I didn't know. I'd put things in – techniques, you called them – without knowing I was doing it and you'd *label* them, as though they were real things. And...' he took another breath, ' it was just *different*.' He glanced out the driver's window, turning his face away from me, and I realised that he was blushing. *Blushing!*

'You could have told me,' I accused.

He turned his head to me, his expression serious. 'Louisa, I don't tell *anyone*. My mother doesn't even know what I do. Nor do my brothers. The only people who have any idea – and I'm sure most of them have forgotten by now – are my mates from uni. They were there for the first books. But,' he shook his head, 'I doubt they'd remember and I hardly see them anymore. I'm sure they're not scrolling through Amazon to see if Iris Grayson is still writing.'

We were almost home, the GPS doing its job and navigating us through the last few streets before we "reached our destination".

'Tell me, Patrick, where did the "Iris" come from? I've figured out the Grey, but how did "Iris" come about? Your grandmother's name? An aunt's?'

He winced. Yes, he ducked his head and winced. 'I had a girlfriend at the time,' he admitted, sheepishly. *Oh, of course you did!* I couldn't contain the snarkiness of my thought. 'And she was studying ancient mythologies. She likened herself to Aphrodite.' *Of course she did.* This was becoming a refrain. 'But I liked the idea of Iris, the female equivalent of Hermes, the messenger god. That Iris was the goddess of communication. And she hung out with the West Wind. There was something – *free* – about her. So, I adopted Iris Greyson as my pen-name.'

He'd pulled up out the front of my place – or my family's house – and I reached for the door latch, before glancing back at him.

'Why now, Patrick? Why bother to tell me now? You've managed to conceal this all weekend. I mean, you prevaricated when I asked if you were with Iris. You did the same when I asked if you were her marketing person. Why tell me now?'

'Because I want to keep seeing you, Lulu.'

'Oh,' the penny dropped. 'So, if you didn't want to keep seeing me, you would have just gone back to – the Gold Coast? – and what? IrisG would continue writing to Lulu98, as though nothing had happened?' My voice had risen; I was sounding a little hysterical, I thought. *Calm down, Louisa,* I berated myself. *Calm down! Don't let this man make you pathetic!*

He had the decency to flinch, his face reddening with what I hoped was shame.

'Was that it, Patrick? Lulu98 was just going to be another one of your fucks?'

He swallowed and then reached out to me.

I cringed, and felt my face distort in disgust and revulsion.

'Don't *touch* me, Patrick!' I snapped.

I stood and stepped back to open the rear door, reaching inside for my bags. Patrick had come around to my side, his hand out to take me bag from me.

I shook my head. 'You can go now, Patrick.' When he hesitated, I gathered what was left of my dignity and said, clearly and coldly, 'Just *leave!*'

He stood there, his expression puzzled, uncertainty flickering across his face and softening his stance.

'Lulu,' he beseeched, softly.

'Go, Patrick. I'm going to convince myself that I never met you.'

His face shut down, like a screen closing over his features.

'I'm sorry, Lulu. I never meant to hurt you.'

'But you did, Patrick. With your deceit. Just go.'

I turned and hurried through the front gate and up the path to the door. I *had* to get inside, before I started to cry. I could *not* cry in front of him. *Athena does not cry in front of mere mortals!*

And I escaped to my room.

Chapter Twelve

It was like when my mother died. Only not.

When Mum had died, I stayed cloistered in my room, grieving stoically, only leaving to listen to my sisters, their grief and emotional trauma expressed more visibly and vocally. I'd offered what counsel I could to Jane and Daphne, as they'd sorted through the mountainous legal and financial debris caused by the accident, and held Charli as she cried. And then I'd retreated to my room, to mourn the loss of my twin-soul, my mentor, my mother.

But today …

It wasn't like that.

For the first time, I needed my father. I craved the warmth of his solid chest when he'd cuddled me as a child; I craved the strength of his arms; and I craved the safety and security that he'd embodied, all throughout my childhood. It may have been my mother who offered conversation, counsel and mental stimulation, but – behind the scenes – in the background – there had been my father, a stable presence that could be relied upon, leant on, and depended upon.

So, I didn't stay in my room where I'd escaped after Patrick had driven off. I went to the wharf. I fed and watered the cat, taking a minute to stroke his soft fur and cuddle him – just for a moment – just because the cat probably needed the affection – and left my bedroom and the house, and walked down the road towards the harbour and the wharf.

And, for a long time, I just sat on a wooden bench-seat near the water's edge, watching the glitter of the sunlight on the water move and change as the day progressed and the sun slid across the brilliant blue sky, and absently following the path of the ferries as they criss-crossed the harbour, white wash in their wake, and I wrapped myself in memories of my father.

Did it help? I don't know.

I was determined not to cry, so the sharp pain of Patrick's betrayal was locked in my chest, slicing every so often as the events of the weekend twisted, like a knife, through my body.

I thought about his grimaces when I'd referred to Iris and my disappointment in her failure to recognise me. I thought about his wince when I told him, prior to our having sex the first time, that I wanted no secrets between us. I thought about the times when he'd glanced away from me, refusing to look me in the eye. *The sign of a liar*, I reminded myself. And I thought about how many opportunities he'd had to tell me the truth. *Slice!*

And, just to torture myself, I thought about his easy smile and his joyful laugh. I thought about how he'd complimented me "I'm sure you can tell a story well" and his focused regard, as though I was the only person in the world at that moment. And I thought about how he touched me, and kissed me, and stroked me, and pleasured me. And I thought about the feel of his skin, and the taste of his mouth, and the scent of his clean sweat as he'd risen above me, gliding and sliding and driving and thrusting, as he'd pleasured me. *Slice!*

I stayed there, by the water, trying to connect with my father's spirit, needing his strength and his wisdom, if I were to get through this, recover from this, heal from this.

I stayed there, until I was chilled to the bone. Too cold to feel anything anymore. My body as frozen as my numbed emotions.

And then I walked home and let myself into the house, down the hall and into the shower, where I could wash from me the last remnants of Patrick: the scent of his skin still on mine. I watched the sudsy water, briny with betrayal, as it eddied down the drain. And then, my body warm at least, I dressed.

I heard Charli stop in through the front door: she always had such a deliberate tread, as though it was imperative that she place her feet firmly on the earth. Then she was in the kitchen: no surprises there, and out the back. I wondered if she'd fed the cat, too. Maybe. The cat certainly wasn't fading away to nothing, its plumpness not just because of its thick fur. And Ginny was moving around. And Daphne came home, heading straight to her room. Nothing new there. She was probably going to run a bath and pour herself a whiskey.

Situation Normal in the White Household: the only difference was with me. A bruised and broken me. I refused to regret the loss of my virginity, but I did regret my foolishness with Patrick. He was too handsome, too smooth, too sophisticated. I should have known that he didn't have the honour, the integrity, that I'd imagined would be inherent in the man who was destined to be mine.

The house was quiet, then. Daph in her room; Ginny in the kitchen; Charli in the backyard. Who knew where Jane was! And I – well, I was maintaining my stoic silence, sitting on a stool by the window, gazing at the trees and flowers that my mother had planted, and soothing my soul.

'Where have you been?' That was Ginny's voice. Was Jane home?

'You give *me* grief over being irresponsible, but where the hell have you been all weekend?' Yes, it was most likely she was talking to Jane. The two of them ruffled each other's feathers so often.

'And who is *that?*' Oh, had Jane brought someone home? That Ginny didn't know?

'Ginny, language, please.' By the tone of Jane's voice, she was embarrassed and … nope, just embarrassed.

'Is Jane home?' That was Daphne. 'So, you are still alive?' Hmmm, Daph had a bone to pick with Jane, too. What had I missed out on?

'C'mon, Daph! I sent you texts.' Defensiveness in Jane's voice. Hmmm, she must have done something wrong.

I sidled out of my room and took up my usual post, against the hall wall, to observe.

'Well, this is crowded. Can we please go into the living room? We don't all need to be in the hall like this,' Jane said, in an effort to regain control over us all. It was obvious that she felt uncomfortable with her man – oh! I knew that face! If I hadn't been feeling quite so – despairing – my face would have been split in a beaming smile. *Look what Jane brought home with her!*

We shuffled along, but Ginny kept glancing back and Daph hesitated a little. Hmmm, was Daph figuring this out?

'You look familiar. Who are you?' Trust Ginny to be blunt.

'He's Jackson McGee,' Daphne answered. Yep, Score One for Daph!

'Who?' Charli blurted, her face scrunched in confusion.

'Jackson McGee,' I said. 'From *Earth Today* magazine.'

I almost smiled at the stunned expression on Jane and Jackson's faces. Really? Had Jane honestly thought that we didn't pay attention to her crushes? She'd been mooning over Jackson's picture for as long as I could remember.

'Like … are you famous? Or something?' That was Charli, still six steps behind.

'Handsome catch, I will say that for you!' Ginny taunted Jane, her tone provocative as she added, 'What are you doing with our Jane?'

And that was when I saw Jackson narrow his eyes, his face tilting and his expression challenging. Oooohh, he was going to defend Jane! This was so *interesting*. I only wished that my chest didn't hurt so much, so I could truly appreciate the drama unfolding before me.

'Not really your business, Ginny – is it?' he drawled, and I wasn't sure if he was questioning her name or her right to engage in Jane's life. That he enclosed Jane's hand in his was noteworthy! As was the overstuffed beach bag that Jackson was holding. And where had that shockingly-coloured T-shirt come from? Hmmm. The plot thickened. It made me want to smile.

'So, who is he, again? Is he a star or something?' Charli was still confused.

'He's a photojournalist for *Earth Today*,' Daph answered, adding, 'He travels the world, taking pictures and writing stories about different places. And people.'

'So-o-o,' Ginny drew the word out and this caught my attention. Something was about to go down! 'How did you two get together? Has Jane been sending you fan mail?'

Oh! Slice! Twist! That knife! I couldn't breathe! Jesus, Ginny! A bit too close to home!

But everyone's attention was elsewhere. Jane snapped at Ginny and Jackson drew her to him, in a protective move, and that was all the others noticed.

'I'm going to go, Janey,' Jackson murmured to her, but it was loud enough for us to hear.

'Ooooh, *Janey!*' Ginny mimicked. She really *was* being a bitch!

'See me out,' Jackson said quietly, and his calm voice, low-pitched and slightly gruff, reminded me of Patrick's.

'So, should we be asking for his autograph? Or will he take our picture?' I heard Charli say, but I was too swamped in *feelings* to pay close attention to her.

'No, Charli. Let's go into the kitchen.' That was Daph's voice, but I was already sliding back to my room.

I heard Jane close the front door and knew that Jackson had left. She went to her bedroom, but it wasn't long before I heard the soft murmur of voices. Daph must have gone in. She and Jane had always been close, most likely as they'd been the ones to ensure the wellbeing of the rest of us.

I ventured out of my room and was just in the hall when I heard Jane say, her voice small and wet from her tears, 'He asked me to go with him.'

'Where?' Daphne asked, gently, as though Jane might bolt or burst into tears.

'Just go. He's heading up to Queensland.'

Well, this was a turn-up for the books. Who knew this was on the cards? Jane had a love interest! And a love interest that wanted her to go away with him. Artemis had found her man.

Oh, I must tell Patrick! I thought, before the crushing weight of his betrayal overwhelmed me again. But I couldn't stay quiet. Patrick had asked me what I wished for Jane and … *this was it!*

I stepped into the room, but only near the door. I felt like I was invading her privacy, but I couldn't *not*.

'So, you could go,' I said. 'You could try it out. It's only Queensland.' *Are you listening to yourself, Louisa! Gold Coast! Queensland!* But I had to get back to Jane and her problem. 'If you don't like it – if you're not happy – you can come home.'

Jane looked torn. 'But what about all of you? I'm needed here,' she protested.

'No, you're not,' Ginny said, charging through the doorway. 'You *were* needed here, Jane, when we were all young, but you're not anymore.' My, she'd put it bluntly, but she wasn't wrong!

'Virginia!' Daphne roared, turning on her. 'Stop it!'

'I'm not being a bitch, Daph. I'm not!' Ginny yelled back. 'Don't you see? Don't any of you see?' She swung around, glaring at all of us: Jane, Daphne, me, and Charli, who was hovering near the door, looking frightened and uncertain. 'Jane did what she had to do when Mum and Dad died. She did. She dropped everything! She didn't want to be a *teacher!*' Ginny sneered. 'She was studying geography and geology, sure! But the only time she even *mentioned* a Diploma in Education was *after* Mum and Dad died. She's only in a school because she feels *responsible* for all of us.' She paused, gulping in air after her outburst.

'She's right,' I agreed. 'Ginny's right about Jane becoming a teacher so she could support us. And she's right about it being time for Jane to go do her own thing. We're all adults now.'

'Is she?' Daphne looked straight at Jane, a curious expression on her face. 'Did you never really want to teach?'

'Daph, it's not that simple,' Jane protested.

'Why isn't it?' Charli demanded, getting all riled up. 'Why can't you do what you want? Why can't all of us?'

'Because we have to be careful!' Jane shocked us all by screaming.

'Why?' Charli screamed back at her, coming further into the room.

'Because Mum and Dad died,' I said, softly. 'Because Jane's afraid. Aren't you, Jane? You're afraid of what can happen.' I tried to be gentle with her. I didn't want to hurt her any more than she was already hurting.

'Is that it?' Daphne queried. 'Are you scared for us?'

'Of course, she is,' answered Ginny. 'That's why she's been so damned *controlling* all of these years. She's had all of us wrapped in cotton wool. Well, not cotton wool, exactly. *University degrees.*' The derision was apparent. 'Her way of keeping us all safe.'

'It wasn't just that,' Jane argued, her voice stronger now. 'I knew that Mum – especially – but Dad, as well, would want all of us to be educated and financially independent. *That's* why I've been pushing you and Charli to get degrees.'

And then, like a balloon that's been poked by a sharp knife – *Boy, did I know that feeling!* – she deflated. Like all the strength in her just dissolved.

'I want to be alone. Leave me alone.' It was the whimper of a wounded animal.

'Jane –' Charli began, but was stopped by Daphne.

'Let's go. Ginny, did you make dinner?' Daphne ushered us all from the room. 'I'll bring you a plate, Jane.'

'Don't. I'm not hungry.' And with that, she flopped onto the bed.

Can I join you? I thought.

Daphne was still in her room. Her bath had taken longer than normal and her face had been splotchy when she'd been talking with Jane. Something was wrong.

Time for one of my little talks. Mum would be proud of me, doing this when all I wanted to do was curl up in a ball.

I made tea and took it to Daph's room.

'Who is he?' I asked, as soon as I entered. I'd discovered long ago that, if you surprised people, they invariably answered your question before they had a chance to think about it.

'Dominic.' Her voice was flat.

'Northcott?' I confirmed, watching the startled expression flash across her face. *Yes, Daphne, I do know things.*

'How do you know that?' she asked.

'You mention him a lot. Usually with "damned" in front of his name.' I smiled at her, even though it was an effort. 'Are you going to continue seeing him? I mean, aside from work?'

'I told him no,' she said. 'That it was just this weekend.'

'Hmmm.' *What was with we White women? Knocking back men who were interested in us?* I crossed to sit on her bed, seeing as she was receptive to a chat. And, strategically, I changed the subject. Or appeared to change the subject. 'Do you think that Jane should go with Jackson?' I asked.

'Yes,' was Daph's immediate response.

'Why?' I asked, fidgeting with my dress, seemingly not paying too much attention to Daphne.

'Because it's time,' she said, bluntly. 'It's time for her to get on with her life – the one she wanted – and for us to get on with ours.' She sipped the tea, before continuing. 'I'm tired of the constant squabbles around here – damned tired. I'm sick of hearing Charli complain about going to university and Ginny complain about what Jane wants her to do. It's high time that we all did what we wanted!' *Whoooaaa! Who knew that Daph had such a head of steam under her? But then ... I'd known that she was stressed ... and frustrated.*

'Hmmm,' I said, still not looking directly at her, my attention on my dress. 'So, I take it that this Dominic is a lousy lay?'

Oh, it was fun seeing the shock on Daphne's face. Did she think I was some innocent? *That's what happens when people don't take the time to realise that I've spent the last four years reading erotica!*

'Louisa! Not that it's any of your business, but no! He's not a *lousy lay*, as you so delicately put it.' Daph was very affronted.

'Then he's a prick!' I persisted, enjoying myself.

'No, not a *prick*, either!'

'Halitosis?' I asked, slyly.

'His oral hygiene is fine,' she huffed at me, irritation on her face.

'So, Daphne, when you think that Jane should follow her dreams, why are you denying yours?' I was no longer playing games. I was hurting, and watching Daph in pain didn't help. And the killer was: Daph didn't need to reject Dominic. He was right there, still in Sydney, hers for the taking.

'Who said that Dominic had anything to do with my dreams?' she countered, glaring at me.

'Because he's the only person from the office that you ever mention. And,' I paused, studying my fingernails. *Oh, Patrick! I can do dramatic scenes, too!* 'Because you say his name almost every night. *Damned Dominic this* and *Damned Dominic that*! He's had your attention for the last six months. And, Daphne, you haven't even so much as mentioned any other man's name. So, yes. I think he has something to do with your dreams. Now, the question is: are you going to fish or cut bait?'

She looked pole-axed and, in that moment, I would have loved to have known what was going through her mind.

'Well, by the expression on your face, I think my work here is done!' I said, with a flourish, flicking my fingernails and leaving the room.

Chapter Thirteen

I didn't sleep well. Who knew that you could become accustomed to nestling against a warm, hard body after only two nights?

Jane had left already: I'd heard her rise and fuss in the kitchen – most likely raiding the fridge for something for her morning tea and lunch. Daphne had long gone, earlier than usual. I wondered whether she would approach Dominic today. I hoped so.

This had been my wish for Daphne and … it was startling to me how well my wishes were turning out. Who knew that I had such power! Maybe I truly was Athena, warrior goddess, after all!

I could hear Ginny and Charli in the kitchen. Or, more to the point, I could hear Charli in the kitchen, her voice excited, bubbling from her with her enthusiasm for … not sure.

'Oh, are there eggs?' I said, as way of greeting before crossing the kitchen to reheat the kettle. 'Can I get scrambled?'

'Sure. Charli's just telling us about a man she met on Friday,' Ginny replied, reaching for a saucepan.

And while Charli rattled on, oohing and aahing over the amenities at the apartment and the zoo, and gushing over her new man, I watched Ginny prepare my eggs and gazed at her face, looking for signs of … I wasn't sure, but I was prepared to take a stab in the dark.

'What I want to know about,' I said, as soon as Charli paused for breath, 'is *your* new man, Ginny.'

Bingo! It was almost amusing, watching Ginny startle, jerking around to look at me. 'What do you mean, Lou?' she asked, no doubt thinking she sounded innocent.

'Tell us about your man, Ginny. You left on Thursday night and didn't return at all until yesterday afternoon.' I wasn't sure about this, but – again, a stab in the dark. 'And when you did come back, you were wearing a new dress. And in the wash this morning, there was *another* dress that I haven't seen before. You've also got a bit of whisker rash just under your chin. And you'd been crying when we first saw you last night and – if my ears didn't deceive me – you were crying again when you went to bed. And,' I sighed dramatically, as though all of her evidence had been enough, 'you're not normally so bitchy towards Jane. Yeah, you can be irritated by her and you can make snarky comments, but … last night … So, tell us about the man *you* met, Ginny?'

Charli's whole head spun around to face Ginny, like a bobble-head on a car dashboard, her eyes huge and round in her face, questions and amazement vying for expression.

'Did you *meet* someone, Ginny?' she breathed. 'Someone who *likes* you?' I tried not to smile at Charli's social clumsiness.

'Yes, Charli. Someone who *liked* me. Isn't that amazing?'

I frowned at Ginny. 'Don't be like that, Ginny. She means well.' I stirred her coffee. 'So, tell us about him,' I prompted, sitting back and sipping the hot drink.

'Not much to tell, really. I met a gorgeous guy, we spent some time together, there's no future in it, and that's that.' She brushed her hands together, effectively showing that there was nothing further to add.

'Why?' Charli asked.

'Why what?' Ginny replied, picking up our used plates and putting them on the sink.

'Why is there no future to it? Why won't it work out? I mean, if there's someone who *likes* you, Ginny, why won't it work?' I sat back, letting Charli take over the interrogation, in her own inimitable way.

'Because we're worlds apart, Charli. He's incredibly handsome, super sexy and fabulously wealthy. We've really got nothing in common. And – look at me! Do I really look like the partner of a hot, gorgeous guy from old, old, *old* money?'

'Why not?' I asked softly. 'Why wouldn't you fit in fine? You're intelligent. And strikingly beautiful. And he must have seen *something* in you. For you to catch his eye, I mean,' I amended hastily, not wanting to hurt her feelings.

'Well, with all that red hair, you're not *exactly* beautiful, but you're not ugly, Ginny,' Charli hastened to say.

Ginny and I exchanged looks and then we both burst out laughing. Well, that sorted out that moment of self-pity!

'What was he like?' I asked gently. 'Other than being rich and sexy and smart?'

She paused, thinking. 'He was kind. And thoughtful. He helps people, Lou. Lots of people. Strangers. He gives up time on his weekends to volunteer for charities. And he was good to me.' She paused, looking towards her hands, resting in her lap. And then she said, in a small voice, 'He looked after me when I was so damned drunk that I wasn't being safe.' Her face crumpled in, like she was going to cry: I could see the tears welling up. 'And I *liked* him, Lou. But,' she inhaled, deeply, as though drawing strength from the air, 'it wouldn't work. His brother came – oh, his brother is a piece of work! And he berated Michael – in front of me! And I could tell that Michael was embarrassed. Not just for himself, but for me.'

'Why? Why was he embarrassed for you?' I asked, gently.

'Because his brother was a pig to me. The look he gave me. Like I was shit! Some cheap tramp!' She inhaled a wobbly breath. 'And I felt like it, Lou. There I was, in my simple cotton dress, in this incredible apartment. I was so out of my league.'

'Was it as good as the Veriu in Camperdown?' Charli butted in.

'Charli, I was staying at the Bennelong Apartments. Do you know where they are?'

'Ginny –' I warned.

'Right at Circular Quay, Charli. I woke up to a view of the Sydney Harbour Bridge!'

Charli's eyes were like saucers again, dominating her face.

'*Really?*' she breathed.

'Really.'

'And this guy *liked* you?' She was still puzzled.

'I think we've established that fact,' I said, going to Ginny's rescue. 'So, he told you that it was a one-off thing? A weekend fling?' I tilted my face in question.

'Well, no.'

'And he didn't go out in public with you? Introduce you to anyone?' I persisted.

'No, Lou. We went out lots. We went to where he volunteers and he introduced me to the people there, and we went to the venues he supervises, although I didn't get chummy with anyone. He did let the bar staff know to look after me. What's your point?'

'And before you left, he had lots of time to shut his brother down.' I nodded, seemingly to myself, enjoying my theatrics.

'Well, no, Lou. His brother was just ranting. He couldn't get a word in. Neither could I, really. But what's your point?'

'I don't know,' I shrugged. 'It doesn't sound like he was embarrassed by you at all. It sounds like he was seeing how you fitted into his world. The world, I'm guessing, that doesn't include his brother, the dick!'

I knew I shocked people sometimes. I often thought that my sisters really didn't know me at all. In that moment, with the stunned-mullet expression on Ginny's face and Charli's eyes like saucers, I was reminded about how little they'd ever bothered to get to know me. I tried not to let that thought pierce any more holes in my already-wounded psyche.

I decided to go for broke. 'You know, Ginny, you mope around here as though you're some sort of burden. Shopping for us all, cooking and preparing our food, waiting on us, cleaning the kitchen up after us. Like you need to work hard for our approval. Or your right to be a part of this family. I get the feeling, sometimes, that you're ashamed of yourself, but I've never been able to figure out why.'

She was intensely uncomfortable with my words: I could tell. She was practically squirming in her seat.

'And now this man – who by your own accounts sounds like a pretty decent human being who's not an arrogant turd – wants to spend time with you and you're – what! Baulking at it? Saying no? I don't get it. Why are you so down on yourself?'

Ginny glanced at Charli, still round-eyed and resting her chin on her upturned hands, her gaze swinging back and forth between Ginny and me. The gears grinding through her mind were almost audible.

And then Ginny arced! I'd been expecting it. I'd done my best to make her explode.

'Look at me, Lou! Really look at me! What do I have to offer anyone? Honestly! I'm not like you and Jane and Daph. Not even like Charli. I didn't get good enough marks to get into uni. I'm not smart. I fucked up. And now I don't even have a job!'

'I don't have a job,' chimed in Charli.

Ginny sighed. 'That's irrelevant, Charli. You're still in school.'

'You're wrong, Ginny.' I said, trying to be gentle and soothing. 'You have lots to offer. And I bet your man – what was his name?'

'Michael,' she grunted the name at me.

'I bet he'd say the same thing. You, too, are kind. And considerate. And you help people, all the time. You take care of us. And he probably knows that. Your *goodness*, Ginny, shines out of you. Some days, you *glow* with it. And when you're out in the garden, soaking up the sun, touching the leaves of your potted herbs, you are the embodiment of natural beauty. You just don't get it. But it's true. I wouldn't lie about this to you. You know that.'

'Has he got your phone number?' Charli broke into the pensive silence. 'I made sure that Sam had mine. And I've got his. And,' a dramatic pause, 'we're Facebook friends.'

Ginny and I exchanged wry smiles again, shaking our heads imperceptibly.

'Does he have your number?' I asked softly.

'No. We didn't need to exchange numbers. We spent the entire time together.'

I nodded, staying quiet.

'You think I should go and see him, don't you, Lou?' Ginny asked, after a while.

'Yeah, Gin, I think you should.'

'Oh, yeah. If this guy likes you, you've gotta go see him,' said Charli, enthusiastically. 'I mean, when's the next time someone's gonna like you?'

Ginny and I just laughed!

Charli's eyes swung back and forth, her expression revealing her lack of understanding about why we were laughing. I knew that, in *her* mind, she hadn't said anything funny.

'At least see where it goes,' I urged, when we caught our breaths.

'Okay. Thanks, Lou. I … Thanks,' she said, as she reached over and hugged me.

'It'll be alright,' I whispered, hoping that it would be. That this man, Michael, would help Ginny find her purpose.

Chapter Fourteen

The house was quiet and I was left to my own thoughts.

I'd given the best advice I had to each of my sisters. It amazed me that all of us, over one weekend, had met or engaged with men that captured each of our attentions.

That, from the sounds of it, Charli had found someone that could, potentially, provide her with the dream that she'd been nursing since she was a child.

That Jane had somehow – magically – bumped into a man that lived the life she'd fantasised about since she'd swung off the monkey-bars, as a toddler.

That Daphne had – finally, I thought – *seen* Dominic, acknowledged that he was more than just a threat, or competition, at the office, but was someone who saw *her*.

And that Ginny had possibly met her kindred spirit – someone who would recognise her goodness and compassion and kindness – traits forged in her when she'd withstood the horror of failing her exams – and that he might support her in finding her life mission.

I wanted it to work out for them. With the exception of Charli, who was full-steam-ahead in her expectations of the fledgling relationship, imagining years and years of mustering and shearing sheep, of "sunlit plains extended", "murmuring breezes", and "everlasting stars" – I'd heard all of that often enough over the years – the others were hesitating: offering up resistance to – what seemed to me – fantastic opportunities. And I meant "fantastic" in its proper sense: of fantasy, out of this world.

I understood their struggle: they were trying to protect themselves. From hurt. From loss. From heart-breaking pain. We had all suffered trauma, in our own ways, with the death of our parents and, whilst I thought I knew how each of my sisters had reacted, I knew it was possible that I was wrong; that their suffering included bruises and splinters about which I had no idea.

And what about me? Was I over-reacting with Patrick because of past trauma?

I knew that I was still trying to reconcile Iris and Patrick in my head. With Patrick's betrayal – or what I thought of as his betrayal, his deceit – I'd not only lost him and my blossoming hope that I, too, had found a life partner, but I'd also lost Iris and that was a shard, piercing my heart.

Because Iris wasn't just some author whose books I enjoyed. She hadn't just been a connection on the Internet, with whom I'd exchanged emails. I'd thought of Iris as … a friend and had relished the intellectual discourse I had shared with her.

And I couldn't equate Iris-friend with Patrick-sex-god. It seemed … icky.

But then … he and I *had* enjoyed our conversations, our banter, our storytelling. He appreciated me: I knew that. He had, as "Iris" these last three years, respected my opinions and suggestions. And he'd been gentle with me, considerate of me, and playful with me. We'd had fun, the two of us, exploring the Blue Mountains and wandering through the bush, the waterfalls, the landscape, on Saturday.

And he'd treated me like a queen, or the goddess, Athena, herself, every minute of our time together. I swallowed the lump clogging my throat when I thought about his kisses, his touch, his lovemaking.

I knew – even though I didn't want to admit it – that he regretted not telling me sooner. I knew that, because I'd seen him twitch, and wince, and grimace. It hadn't sat comfortably with him. He did have some integrity.

And, if I had any doubt, I only had to remember how *ill* he'd looked, how nauseous he'd seemed, when I'd talked about my mother and Iris on Saturday night. How he'd retreated to the bathroom and kept his distance when he'd finally returned.

Yes, it had turned his stomach – his deceit. If it made me feel sick – if it was a stab in my guts – it was to his, too.

I had to be at work at eleven. Eleven to five, today. That was my shift. I really didn't feel like going, but … stoicism. My middle name.

I was fingering product into my hair, fluffing up the curls so they didn't look quite so … limp, when the sound of the doorbell pealed through the house. I was still fidgeting with my hair as I approached the door, pausing to peer through the peephole. A courier stood on the other side, a parcel in his hands. I shrugged. *Life is one long series of surprises lately,* I thought.

When I opened the door, the frazzled man, his cap pulled low on his wrinkled forehead, studied me.

'There could be a mistake,' he started. 'I've got a parcel here but the address label says "Athens". That can't be right. It's this address, though, here in Greenwich. But ...' he shook his head.

'Show me,' I said, stepping towards him and reaching for the white package. He held it out, not letting my hands touch it – as though I was going to make a grab for it – and I saw, in bold handwriting, the words "Athena White" on the address line.

'That's for me,' I said, feeling giddy with excitement.

'You're named Athens?' he asked, incredulity colouring his tone. 'Your parents named you Athens?'

'Yes. Yes, they did,' I responded, eager now to see what was in the package. 'Do I need to sign for it?'

'No, I'll do it. COVID, you know,' he said as he handed the treasure to me. 'Have a good day, Athens,' he called over his shoulder, as he hurried back up the path.

'Oh, I will,' I returned, trying to contain my excitement.

What has he sent? I wondered, shutting the front door with my hip and heading to the kitchen to find the scissors, keen to remove the wrapper.

And I slowed, as two books were uncovered. The first, a copy of his latest release, *Satan's Obsession*. I wondered why he'd bothered to send this, as he knew I had my own. The one "signed" by "Iris-the-actress".

I opened it, anyway, curious as to his reasoning and there, on the white page just inside the cover, in handwriting such that I had imagined Iris would use, he had written:

> *To Athena, Goddess of Wisdom, Courage, Justice and Strength,*
> *I couldn't have written this without you: you were my inspiration, my*
> *champion, my laurel wreath.*
> *You are the vibrant hues that enrich the colours of my rainbow.*
> *With high esteem,*
> *Iris,*
> *Messenger of the Gods.*

Ooohhh! He'd pulled out all the stops! Could I forgive him? *Should* I forgive him?

And then there was the other book. It was a plain exercise book – a 96-page ruled exercise book, like you'd have in school. It was thick – stuffed with paper.

On the cover, there was only one word: Lulu98.

I opened it, my curiosity almost excruciating. And, page by page, there were the emails we'd exchanged – Iris and I – from the very first one. Cut-and-pasted into this exercise book. With notes scribbled all over the place, in Patrick's handwriting. Sometimes in a thick black pen; and at others in a fine-point blue biro. Some in pencil. The earlier emails were ratty and the pages a bit dog-eared. He had all sorts of markings on the pages: big, excited ticks; squiggly question marks; a bold "Good Idea"; an instruction to "Look This Up!!" against a literary term I'd used; and a Happy-Face below "She Likes It" written with three exclamation marks.

In my hands was a record of every communication – prior to Thursday – we'd had with each other. And his private thoughts and responses. The only one missing was the last that I'd written to him: *It's the one in Sydney, right?*

I wondered, as I sat at the kitchen table, the two books held tightly against my chest, my eyes welling with tears, how things might have been different if he'd seen that last email, before Thursday night…

WHITE MONDAY

SISTERS WHITE SERIES: Book Six

SUNNY MACKENZIE

2021

Jane

The principal had agreed!

He'd granted me three months' Leave Without Pay!

I was really going to do this!

I almost scampered down the corridor, peeking into the glass panes on the doors to find a classroom, empty of teachers and students for the recess break. Hurriedly securing the latch behind me, I leant against the door and fumbled with my phone. The adrenalin was surging through me and I misdialled.

Damn! I tried again and still ... wrong number again!

Slow down, Jane! Take a breath. Take it easy.

This time, I carefully and methodically pressed the numbers on my phone and waited, listening as Jackson's phone rang.

He's got to be still in Sydney, I almost prayed. *Please let him still be in Sydney.*

The br-r-r sound of the phone ringing continued and I panicked. *What if he's gone already?*

It's okay, Jane, I calmed myself, *you can always meet him somewhere up the coast. It'll be alright.*

But what if he's changed his mind? I tormented myself.

And then the ringing stopped.

'Jane?' The familiar sound of his voice stopped me in my tracks and my whole body slumped as relief flooded through me.

'Have you left yet? Have you gone?' Who knew my voice could be this timorous? So breathy and weak.

'No. Are you alright?' I could hear the concern in his tone.

'Yes. Don't go without me, Jackson. Don't leave me behind.' Was that me? That desperate person?

The long pause that followed my words made me nervous. And then, when my skin started to feel itchy with anxiety, his laughter boomed down the phone.

'Oh, Janey, there's *no* way I'll go without you.' His voice was redolent with such warmth and affection.

He laughed again and I started laughing, too.

'Have you gone already?'

'Nah. I spent all weekend with this gorgeous red-head and I haven't written my Freshwater article yet. Thought I'd spend the day finishing that before I headed out.'

'Good.' Yep, that was more like me. Much stronger and more decisive.

'When will you be ready to go, Janey?'

'Tomorrow, Jack. I'm coming tomorrow.' I stopped to think. 'Can you come 'round tonight and help me get organised?'

'Sure, Janey. Whatever you want.' The warm promise in his tone, the mellow humour, washed over me and my knees buckled as I slid down the door and hugged my knees in a semi-squat-come-self-cuddle.

'It's going to work, isn't it, Jack?' I whispered into the phone, my hand cupped around its end as though I was sharing a secret.

'Janey, we're going to work. And you're going to be safe. And you and I, we're going to have a lifelong adventure. All around the world.'

I smiled.

And then I jerked! The harsh sound of the bell jarred our private moment and jolted me back into the reality of my school day and all that I had to accomplish in the next few hours.

'I gotta go, Jack! I'll be late home because I've got heaps to do. Come around at six?'

'I'll be there. And Janey?'

'Yes,' I breathed.

'I wasn't planning on leaving without you.'

As the beep indicated that he'd hung up, I sighed. *My man!*

I struggled to quickly stand as I heard the sound of a key being inserted into the door lock above me. The door opened and I tried to cover my embarrassment at the incredulous look on the teacher's face, but hey! I was about to embark on the biggest adventure of my life! I laughed out loud and watched as the incredulity flipped to surprise before morphing into puzzlement. Yep, the staffroom would be agog with gossip about my sudden departure!

I was in a flap and that wasn't like me. I was sitting at my ancient, wooden desk in the staffroom, pulling at books and papers and my Teachers' Chronicle and … I didn't know where to start. So much to do. I'd never taken off like this before, with only a day to prepare. I'd never thrown caution to the winds – literally – and sailed off into the wide blue yonder, with no planning and – wait for it! – without being weighed down with responsibility. No wonder I was in a tizzy.

Take it easy, Jane. One step at a time. Write a list.

I only had one free period today and this was it. What didn't get done right now would have to be done after school and all I wanted to do was go home and pack my bikini!

Oh! Clothes! Washing!

What was I going to pack tonight? What clothes did you need to go sailing up the coast? I grabbed my phone and sent a quick text to Ginny, knowing that she'd be home: *Can you do a load of washing? Whatever's in the laundry basket? Needs to be dry today. Thx.*

That was one thing out of the way. Now what?

Tell the Head Teacher. Organise a casual. Organise lessons for the next couple of days. Make sure your chronicle is up-to-date. Thank God my reports were finished!

I inhaled – deeply – and exhaled, a long shuddery release of the jittery feelings threatening to overwhelm me.

First things first: Tell the Head Teacher. I wished I'd had the presence of mind to have my phone handy when I told my supervisor that I was going on leave for three months because the photos I could have taken would have been hilarious additions to the staffroom noticeboard! After his initial shock, though, he straightened and reinforced his authority with a whole list of instructions.

Thank God I was out of here! I ducked my head to hide the grin that split my face, and mumbled lots of yeses and okays to his demands. Only five hours and I'd be gone!

I knew that it would be easy for a relief teacher to pick up my programs and continue especially as all the classes were commencing new units of work, and because of the detailed lessons I'd already prepared. I completed some scheduling sheets to cover the next few days and organised my course folders and teaching resources to facilitate an easy transition.

'Spring cleaning, Jane?' asked Emily, the second-year teacher at lunchtime, standing and studying my desk critically. 'I know you're obsessive-compulsive, but this is taking it to new levels,' she finished, snidely, glancing around to see what other teachers were paying attention.

'No,' I responded, plastering a sad and woeful expression to my face, my mouth turned down, my head dipped in acquiescence. 'There's a family crisis. I need to go on leave for a while. I'm just hoping I can sort it all out.' I deserved an Oscar for the pathos of the last remark and it took all of my control not to fist-bump the air as I watched the alarm on her face at her seeming faux pas and lack of empathy, as she again looked around the room to see if she'd earned disgust from our colleagues.

'Oh, I'm sorry,' she gushed. 'I didn't know. Is there anything I can do?' she asked, belatedly.

'Well, seeing as you asked,' I said, dipping my head meekly to hide my jubilation, 'could you take these photocopy requests to the print room for me?'

'Sure.'

Another job out of the way!

'What's goin' on, Miss?'

The curious voice interrupted my musings, where my thoughts were spinning and crashing into each other: *I'm going to sail on a yacht! Up the New South Wales coast! On the Pacific Ocean! Tomorrow.* I had to pinch myself to believe that this was for real; that I was truly going to do this – a massive adventure – at *last!*

'Hmm. What?' I asked, dazedly.

'What's goin' on? You look like you're planning a surprise test for us. Or there's some sort of geography documentary marathon on television tonight and you're trying to decide between popcorn or ice-cream. You're not yourself. You're all *dreamy*. Are you alright?'

'Oh ... umm ... yes. Yes, I'm fine,' I said, sitting upright and adopting my "teacher" face. 'I'm fine, Zoe. And, yes, I am contemplating a documentary... on the Great Barrier Reef, to be precise,' I fabricated, only a little inaccurately. 'Have you finished your work?'

'You don't have to be like that, Miss. I was only asking. You just didn't seem like you. You looked all *nice*.'

Well, if that wasn't a back-handed compliment. But I'd always known that students knew more than we often gave them credit for; that they picked up on changes in their worlds – even the classroom and the teachers – more precisely than adults.

'Well, thank you for your concern, Zoe, but it's time to get back to work.'

And then I turned towards the whiteboard on the front wall and smiled to myself, my shoulders rising in a little self-hug. An excited shudder rippled through me.

I'm going to sail the seas with Jackson!

And I couldn't wait!

Charli

Cowgirl: Heard anything yet?

FarmBoy: Nah. Appt not until 2.

Cowgirl: ?? Your dad??

FarmBoy: OK. Can you talk?

Cowgirl: Not atm. In lecture.

FarmBoy: When?

Cowgirl: Call you when I get out.

FarmBoy: I missed you last night.

Cowgirl: Me too.

Ginny

The dishes were done, the kitchen was clean, the house was quiet.

Charli had left for university, her backpack heavy with food she'd pilfered from the fridge for her lunch. That girl could eat her weight, some days, and today – with excitement radiating from her in almost visible incandescent waves – she'd definitely be hungry.

Louisa was most likely in her room, reading. Sometimes I felt sorry for Louisa. I'd worried for a while, especially after Mum and Dad had died, that she suffered from agoraphobia, she spent so little time out of her room. She'd always been the quiet one: the daughter who took after Mum the most, with her books and reading and their long discussions about God-knew-what! She hadn't been sporty like Charli, or adventurous like Jane, or organised like Daphne and Dad, or rebellious like – just maybe – I could be.

So, I'd worried about her. Six years ago, there wasn't such a focus on mental health and – let's face facts – Jane and Daphne were doing everything they could just to *manage* things. And teachers – they just liked quiet students, so Lou probably just slipped beneath the radar.

Not like me. They knew I existed.

I wandered out to the garden and sat on the porch swing. And rocked – to and fro – back and forth. It was a beautiful day: the morning sun had dried the overnight dew that would have earlier sparkled on the blades of grass and the leafy foliage of the bushes and trees, and a gentle breeze riffled through my hair that was still loose. It promised to be a warm day – excellent for drying washing and it occurred to me that I should get to the piles of clothes that we'd all dropped on the laundry floor in the last day or so.

In a minute, I thought, enjoying the movement of the swing. *The washing can wait.*

What was with Charli? As though Jane and Daphne would allow her to traipse off to some farm in the middle of the state without knowing anything about these men. What? A father and a son? Most likely, they were nice people – solid country folk – but this was Charli. Our littlest sister. Off with some strange people? Never gonna happen.

I wondered what Jane would do. Would she really let this opportunity slip through her fingers? After all these years of constraining herself, locking down her true nature to care for all of us and meet society's expectations of a responsible adult, would she really say "no" to the chance to sail off into whatever adventures this Jackson-guy followed?

I knew I'd recognised his face. Standing there in the hallway the previous night, he'd just looked so familiar. And as soon as Daphne had said his name and then Louisa had mentioned that magazine, it all clicked. Jane had been swooning over his picture for years, like a teenaged girl over the trending adolescent popstar. *She'd be a fool to let him get away*, I thought, one foot and then the other keeping the porch swing in motion.

Is that what you're doing, Ginny? I asked myself. Was I going to let Michael slip through my fingers? Would I be a fool to let him get away? We had so little in common: he was rich, and I wasn't; he was gorgeous and sexy and hot and sophisticated, and I wasn't. Or maybe, just maybe, I was – just a little bit. Louisa seemed to think that I had something to offer him. Lou seemed to think that I wasn't such a loser. And when I'd been with Michael – when he'd looked at me with such … *desire*, I'd felt beautiful. And *important*. And *desirable*.

My phone beeped. An incoming message.

My heart leapt into my throat!

Was it Michael? *No, Ginny. He doesn't have your number*, I reminded myself, sadly, as I reached for the phone.

Austen: Can you do a load of washing? Whatever's in the laundry basket? Needs to be dry today. Thx.

I swallowed, my throat thick. Heat prickled my eyes and I felt tears well up. *Eye sweat*, I thought, half-heartedly. Disappointment engulfed me and my head fell forward, in silent sorrow. I didn't know whether to be annoyed with Jane for her assumption that I'd be Cinderella? Or annoyed at Michael for forcing me to admit that I was a semi-slave to my family's needs? Or annoyed at myself for daring to *hope* that Michael had – somehow – managed to find my contact details.

Yes, Jane, I thought, despondently, *I will do your laundry.*

The "today" part of the request, though, gave me pause. Was Jane in a hurry? Was she going to go off, after all, with her man? Go off on an adventure? Break loose from the constraints of the last six years?

And if she was, what did that mean for *me*? Could *I* do the same thing? Could *I* explore a future with Michael?

Louisa definitely thought I could. She'd urged me to seek out Michael and give our fledgling little relationship a chance...

What do you have to lose, Ginny? If it goes pear-shaped, you've only lost a bit of dignity and ... you already lost that on Thursday night when you passed out and up-chucked all over him.

I stretched my feet, my toes pushing against the cool grass, tipping me back so the swing was in motion, again. With the gentle rocking, I allowed myself to dream – just a little. What would life be like – dating Michael? I'd need to get a job. It didn't sit comfortably with me – the idea that Michael had so much money at his disposal and I had none. I *had* to earn money of my own. It was one thing to look after my sisters and allow Daphne to manage the finances: a whole other thing when a man and sex was involved.

Which brought me back to the elephant in the room... Or the garden, so to speak. I didn't have qualifications, the whole COVID thing had obliterated most hospitality jobs (if you ignored home deliveries) and there was no way I was going to ask Michael for one.

You don't have to worry about that today, Ginny. One thing at a time. See if he even wants *to pursue a relationship.*

He had seemed like he wanted to – yesterday, before his brother had blasted into the apartment and shattered the sweet closeness we'd been sharing. Did he still?

There's only one way to find out! Get the laundry done and go find him!

I planted both feet on the ground – the swing jolting to a jarring stop – and stood, inhaling deep breaths of determination. I would do this! I would remember the "me" I was when I was young: before my mum and dad died; before I failed the exams; before I became a pathetic loser! I was going to *fight* for something and ... if I didn't succeed, at least I'll have tried.

Or that was what I told myself.

Laundry first. Then get dressed. Something empowering, that I looked good in. Check the train times. Hang the wash.

I could do this!

Charli

I snuck around the side of the building, seeking privacy and hoping no-one noticed, whilst I hit the green "call" icon on my phone. It answered. Only two rings.

'Cowgirl?'

'Farmboy,' I breathed back at him.

'Have you got long?'

'Nope. Gotta tutorial and they notice when we're missing.'

'Bugger.'

'Yeah. Bugger,' I agreed.

'I missed you last night.'

'Yeah, so did I. Miss you, I mean.' I paused, listening to his breathing and syncing mine with his. 'How's your dad?'

'Good. Resting. A bit impatient, if you ask me.'

'He worried?'

'Well, yeah, Charli. But I keep telling him it'll be alright.'

'How can you be so sure?'

'Dunno. But I am.'

'Are you staying another night?'

'Yeah.'

'You and your dad can come for dinner, if you want,' I offered and was a bit mortified that I sounded coy. "Coy" was not a word I would ever have used to describe me, but it occurred to me that Louisa would have used it, right at that moment.

'Can I let you know? After... you know.'

'Sure. Gotta go, Sam. I'm out of class in about an hour.'

'Okay. Can you come back here? Later?'

'Alright. I mean, "as you wish".'

'Yeah. As you wish, Cowgirl.'

I hung up, wrapping my arms around myself in a happy hug, and giggled.

As I wished!

Ginny

He wasn't there.

I'd pressed the "call" button on the security panel near the locked doors of the Bennelong Apartments and he hadn't answered.

I'd pushed it seven times – I think. I lost count after the first three or four.

And I'd waited. And waited.

I didn't know whether to just wait and keep pressing the button every so often. Or to sneak in behind someone else when they entered and squat on the floor outside his door until he came home. Or to just go on home.

I wanted to cry. I couldn't believe this was happening. After all my preparations…

I'd broken speed records sorting the washing, filling the machine and selecting the wash cycle, before pawing through my wardrobe for something that said, "I didn't go to any trouble looking good enough for you and your rich, successful family". The effort in trying to tame my hair! Again, I wanted the "I didn't make an effort" crossed with "don't I look sleek and fabulous!".

Second load of washing was in and I pegged the first on the line before tackling my makeup. Who knew it was such a trial getting the "Effortless Natural Look"! Peg the second load on the line and I was out the door.

And he wasn't here!

Now what? I didn't have his phone number and he could be any number of places: work, the kitchen at Bondi, St Vinnies, in Hyde Park. And "work" encompassed lots of options: which one of the nightclubs or restaurants? Was he in an office, somewhere? A meeting? Who knew!

Go home, Ginny, I thought, dispiritedly. *This was a waste of time.*

I trudged back to Circular Quay Station, my feet heavy with disappointment. I'd thought that, somehow, it was all going to work out, just like Louisa – and Michael – had said. Instead, there was just this emptiness... Not at all like when I'd been with him: helping with distributing food, watching him interact with the homeless people, waiting whilst he checked on the venues for which he was responsible...

The *venues!*

At least try, *Ginny.*

I tried to think of the one where he left me in the safe keeping of the bar attendant... How did we get back from that one? How could I find it now? I pulled out my phone and clicked on Google Maps.

And off I charged – determination and purpose driving my steps. It might not pan out, but at least I was doing *something.*

I was in luck.

Same bartender, lifting a rack of sparkling glasses into the fridge behind him, and then swiping the droplets of water from the burnished top of the bar. He looked up as I approached, his face not registering any response to what must have been a giddy grin on my face.

When I pulled myself up onto the barstool, though, he raised one eyebrow in query.

'Do you remember me?' I asked, breathless in my excitement.

'Maybe,' was his non-committal reply.

'I was in here the other night. With Michael. Saturday night.'

'So?'

He wasn't making this easy.

'Well, I need to contact Michael. Can you give me his number?'

'Nope.' He moved away, as though the conversation was finished. He hadn't even bothered to invest enough energy to shake his head: just a monosyllabic "nope" and that was that!

'Hey, wait,' I called after him. He turned. 'He'd want you to give me his number.'

'Uh-huh.' Well, at least I was up to two syllables.

'He would.' I sounded dismal, even to my own ears.

'Red, if he wanted you to have his number,' he dipped his forehead, squinting his right eye slightly, 'you'd have it.'

Okay, that riled me up a bit. What did he know? He didn't know what happened.

'*Don't* call me Red. My name's Virginia, but you can call me Ginny. Only *Michael* calls me Red.'

He smiled. He had a beautiful smile, I noticed, which must have captivated women when he used it. There was a touch of appreciation? admiration? in the one he sent me. It didn't change his answer, though.

'If you wanted a drink, the bar's not open yet.' Again, how difficult was he making this. I was starting to feel a bit embarrassed, like I was being a nuisance, chasing after Michael.

'Can you at least call him?' I asked, a bit desperately. I didn't know what to do, other than camp out at the Bennelong Apartments all day or perch on this stool all night.

'Yeah, nah,' was his only response as he started filling the drinks fridge with bottles of coke, bitter lemon and tonic water.

I slumped, leaning on the bar in front of me, my head resting in my folded arms. What next? It occurred to me that I'd reacted foolishly yesterday, leaving as I had, all drama and petulance, without giving Michael time to say anything ... do anything.

And now I was paying the price. Maybe my red hair and hot temper really were a curse.

But then, in the quiet stillness of the bar, I heard the attendant, his voice just above a male whisper.

'Sorry to interrupt you, mate.' Silence. 'Yeah, nah. It's just that there's a woman here ... the one from the other night ... red-headed.' Silence. 'Yeah, that's the one. Fiery. Persistent. Tried to get rid of her, but she's determined.' He chuckled. 'Nah, doesn't like people calling her Red. She wants your number. What d'you want me to do?' Silence. 'Okay. Will you be long?' Another chuckle. 'Bit whipped, mate?' Silence. 'See you then.'

Yes! I almost fist-bumped the air, but I contained myself. I didn't want him to know I'd heard all of that.

Michael was coming!

I watched, peering out the crook of my elbow, as the bar attendant – I really needed to ask his name – nonchalantly made his way down the bar towards me.

'So, you want a drink?' he asked.

'Thought the bar was closed,' I mumbled, through my folded arms.

'Not selling you anything. Call it a courtesy refreshment. So, what would you like?'

'An iced water would be good.' I sat up straight then and smiled at him.

He grinned, knowingly, in response. 'You know, you can have something harder if you'd like.'

'An iced water will be fine.'

'Splash of lime in that?'

'Oh. Yes. Please.' My muscles relaxed in relief that Michael was coming. I watched as the bartender made my drink, fixing a slice of fresh lime to the rim of the frosty glass.

And then my muscles tensed again, knowing that Michael was coming... What was I going to say? I hadn't prepared anything. I hadn't rehearsed anything.

'You okay?' My drink was placed on a coaster in front of me.

'Yeah... umm... just a bit ... nervous,' I stuttered, as I reached for the drink.

He paused, studying me for a moment, before his mouth softened. 'Don't be.' He moved away, then, and I called after him.

'What's your name?'

'Ned, Red. The name's Ned.' He winked and went back to work.

Daphne

'What happened on Friday?'

I looked up to see Jasmine standing in the doorway. Today was one of the days when she wasn't working from home and she'd been flitting in and out of my office all day. Strangely, it hadn't bothered me as it usually did. I'd been riding a wave of calm all day, like nothing could rattle me. I liked the feeling. It was different, but different good!

'What do you mean?' I asked, annoyed at the lack of context to her query. I hated it when she asked random shit and expected me to play forty-questions with her.

'The Hunk hasn't been around all day. That's unlike him. So, what? Did you lodge a complaint of harassment or something?'

I frowned. Really? Is that what she thought I'd do? Make a formal complaint about a colleague? She was right, though. Dominic hadn't graced us with his presence once today. Since I'd taken him coffee earlier, I hadn't seen him at all. But this didn't worry me. I felt a sense of security in the slow smile he'd given me this morning.

'They had a meeting. On Friday. *Afternoon.*' These tidbits of information were being drip-fed by Melissa, the clerical assistant who'd been hovering when Dominic and I had left on the previous business day.

'Really?' Could Jasmine's eyebrows go any higher? 'He made his move?'

'What are you talking about?' I asked, irritably.

'Well, he has been hovering … So, I take it you slapped him down.' It wasn't even a question: she said it as though it were a foregone conclusion.

'I don't know what you're talking about.' I shot Jasmine, and then Melissa, my most formidable stare. 'You both need to get back to work.'

'She shot him down,' I overheard Jasmine say as they moved away from my office door.

'Yeah, that'd be like her.' A pause. 'Well, on the bright side, at least he's still available. Now, if *only* he'd notice the rest of us.'

'Yeah. It's a bugger.'

'You can say that again.'

To anyone outside, looking into my office, all they would see was a very conscientious woman, her head down, totally focused on the paper on the desk in front of her.

What they would miss was the huge, happy grin – sappy and self-satisfied – that exploded across my face!

Ginny

Was this a big mistake?

That was what was rolling through my head as I sat there, sipping on the tart lime cordial, and waiting…

Was he mad at me? For walking out? For not giving him a chance?

Was he humiliated at his brother's disgusting behaviour towards him and the fact that I'd seen it? Did he think that he'd been belittled in front of me? And not want to see me anymore?

Was he coming here to tell me that it had only been a weekend and not to seek him out anymore?

Oh, please, please, *please*, let him be happy to see me!

I heard the heavy sound of the entry door opening and held my breath, too nervous to turn around. Was it him? Or someone else?

'Red.' Just one word. I turned and watched him approach, his face hard to read in the semi-dark of the bar.

I waited, not knowing what to do. Should I stand? What should I say? My hands shook in my lap.

He strode right up to me, pausing only when he was right there – his body resting against my knees. I stared into his eyes, trying to read him and the air rushed out of me in relief as he reached up to cup my chin – gently, delicately – in his palms. He leaned in and kissed me.

"Kiss" is such a short and simple word: quick and precise. What his mouth did to mine was nothing simple, quick or precise. It was a symphony of sensation: it started as a hard pressing of his lips against mine, with an urgency, a demand; and then softened into a sensual slide of his mouth over mine, his lips gently caressing, a silky suction sensitising my lips before his tongue dipped into my mouth, playfully teasing me with long sweeps along the tender flesh of my inner lips and tantalising flicks against my searching tongue.

It was only the hahr-umph of Ned clearing his throat that jolted us out of the kiss, although Michael snuck another quick peck at my lips before turning to shrug a guilty grin at the bartender, his hands still gripping my waist as though to hold me in place.

'Sorry, mate. Couldn't help myself,' he offered in insincere apology.

'Hmmm.'

'Give me your phone,' Michael demanded, as he turned back to me, holding his hand out.

'What?' I was slow to comprehend.

'Your phone, Red,' he said, before reaching himself for my phone on the bar. I watched as he pressed icons on the screen and then I heard the ringing of his phone in his pocket. 'Now, I've got your number and you've got mine. I'll never go through another twenty-four hours like that again.'

I smiled. He'd missed me. My absence had caused him grief. I knew I shouldn't be happy about that, but ... I had spent a good part of the previous day crying. It was good to know that my feelings were reciprocated.

'Look, Red,' he said, glancing down, 'I've got to go. Ned's call interrupted a meeting and I've got to get back to it. I'll call you later and we'll go out for dinner.' His look was pleading, as though he thought I might decline his invitation.

'No, Michael. Come to mine for dinner. I'll cook. You fed me all weekend. It's my turn to feed you. I'll text you the address.'

He nodded and smiled again before turning to Ned. 'Get her a ride home. Cabcharge. Uber. Whatever. Okay?'

'Sure, Michael. Consider it done.'

'I'll see you later,' he said, before kissing me one more time – a quick kiss, but I felt the intensity in his lips as they met mine. 'I'm glad you're here,' he added and the pleasure in his eyes warmed me.

I watched him walk to the door, his stride cocky with a jauntiness in his step and, just before he disappeared from sight behind the closing door, he glanced back, flicking me a cheeky wink.

And I melted into my seat.

Louisa

'You'll want her latest,' I said to the forty-something woman – one of my regulars – as I slid TL Swan's *The Stopover* into a paper bag. 'And there's a new one coming, if you'd like to pre-order it. I know you're a huge fan of hers,' I added, ringing up the sale.

'Do you have the next one?' my customer asked, glancing at me as she drew her wallet from her bag.

'Sure. Would you like me to get it for you?'

'Umm. Yes. So when will the third one be here?' she asked, her voice following me as I plucked the romance novel from the shelf.

'Not sure, but we're taking orders. So, if you'd like…?'

'Yeah, nah. I'll be back in again. Let me know, though, won't you, if it comes in.'

'Definitely.' I smiled at her as I finalised the sale. There I went again, turning the sale of one book into two. And it amused me that every customer expected that I'd remember every detail about them. I remembered lots, often, but they had this *expectation*. A sense of entitlement, I thought.

'Have a good day,' I called, as she exited the store.

There were no other customers. I enjoyed the moment of peace and quiet. It had been hectic since noon, with a late courier delivery of books, and the usual lunch-time swarm of readers, stocking up after a weekend of escaping into the fantasy world of novels, and into other times or other places of non-fiction texts, or looking for some light entertainment to fill their daily commutes.

I perched on the stool behind the counter and lifted, from the shelf below, my new treasure: the bedraggled exercise book, labelled Lulu98. I'd spent the remaining time at home before I'd started work captivated by the insights this book had offered me, both in the depth of Patrick's and my communications, and in the way he had processed my criticisms, suggestions and praise for his writing. I wanted to hug the contents of his journal to me, and warm myself with the care that he'd obviously taken in printing off and keeping our email exchanges. It was a record of the appreciation and respect he had to me, I realised.

My musings were interrupted by a ringing, but not from the bell above the bookstore door. It was coming from my bag, secured in the locked drawer beneath the counter. I fumbled with the key, wondering which of my sisters was contacting me in the middle of the day. *Won't it be great if one of them is pursuing their man!*

But it wasn't Jane, nor Daph, nor Ginny, nor Charli.

My screen was lit with digits forming an unsaved number, but I knew whose it was.

'Patrick,' I breathed, before even touching the green icon on the phone.

Once we were connected, there was almost silence, only the sound of our breathing and the background din of – what? an airport? Was that what I could hear?

'Louisa?'

'Patrick.'

'I called …' his voice broke off. 'I wanted to say …' I thought I heard him swallow and then he spoke again, his voice stronger, more definite. 'Louisa, I'm sorry. I didn't mean to hurt you. I just want you to know that.' A pause. 'I didn't want to leave without saying "goodbye".'

I gripped my phone with both hands, scared that I'd drop it. I heard the anguish in his last words and knew what I had to say.

'Don't go.'

'What?'

'Don't go, Patrick. Not now. Not like this.'

One heartbeat. Two heartbeats.

'Okay.'

'Okay? You won't leave?'

'No. I'm at the airport and I've checked in, but … It's okay. I can get a flight later. My brother can pick up my checked baggage and … It's okay. Where are you now?'

I sagged onto the counter in relief. He wasn't going. He was still here.

And then I straightened. I was Athena, Warrior Goddess!

'I'm at work. I don't knock off until five.'

'Text me the address and I'll pick you up. At five.'

'Okay. At five.' I repeated, feeling numb all of a sudden. Like my brain hadn't caught up with this latest twist in my life.

'Are you okay, Lulu?' His voice was pitched low, intimate and tinged with concern.

'Yeah,' I whispered, and then, 'Yes. Yes, I'm good. Patrick, I'm pleased that you rang.'

'So am I, Lou. So am I.' A heartbeat. Maybe, two. 'I'm sorry, Louisa,' he repeated.

'You said that, Patrick. It's alright. I'll see you at five.'

'We'll go somewhere for dinner.'

'No. Come home for dinner. Ginny always makes plenty. There's usually leftovers. She won't mind.'

'Okay.' Another beat. 'Thank you, Athena. For forgiving me.'

'You're welcome, Iris,' I teased, lightening the moment before disconnecting and hugging the phone to myself. My fingers fumbled as I texted him the address of the bookstore.

I stood and bounced up and down, a ditzy dance of excitement – totally unlike me, the quiet, staid Book Reader – before I noticed an elderly man, standing outside the window and peering in, a frown marring his face. Laughing out loud, I ducked my head, my hands flying to cover my embarrassed face. When I looked back up, he'd disappeared. *Probably wondering what lunatic they have working here.*

I couldn't contain the excited thrill zipping through me and I twirled around and around in glee. If my sisters were there, they wouldn't recognise their serious, sedate sister!

Calm down, Louisa, I admonished myself. *Control yourself!*

Nah! This was worth being excited about: a hot, sexy, literate man who knew his way around a woman's body and – most importantly – knew how to make a grand gesture!

And, if you counted walking away from a checked-in flight, *two* grand gestures!

Charli

They weren't home yet. It was a two o'clock appointment with a *specialist*. You'd think they'd keep good time and people wouldn't have to wait forever to get in!

But maybe this meant bad news…

If a medical consultation ran overtime, did that mean bad news? It was doing my head in, just thinking about it. Sam had said it would be alright and I really, *really* wanted to believe him. Not just because I wanted Sam's dad to be okay, and not just because I didn't want bad news for *Sam*, but – I know, it's bad to admit it – but I wanted it to be alright so *I* could go to the farm at the weekend. Selfish, much!

And … because I liked Sam's dad. Even though he said that I should finish uni, which I really don't want to do.

But it was nearly three-thirty and they weren't home yet. It wasn't as though the specialist's rooms were a long way away.

I could have used the time to review my tutorial notes, but … my excuse was that I was too distracted! I just *had* to play a LogiBrain Binary game on my phone. Plus, it was useful to have my phone handy, in case Sam needed to ring me.

I heard the sound of their footsteps before their voices, which were muted. What did that mean? Were quiet voices a sign of bad news? Or were they just being polite?

As soon as they rounded the stairwell and Sam saw me, he broke out into a huge grin.

Yep. That had to be good news.

'Cowgirl! You're here!'

'As you wished, Farm Boy. As you wished!' I bounced up from where I'd been squatting against the wall and darted towards his open arms. He squeezed me tight and, in that moment, I realised how scared he must have been, even though he'd kept up his "it'll be alright" demeanour. I tightened my arms in response, hugging him hard, so he knew that I understood. He rubbed his whisker-soft cheek against my skin before sliding his mouth around to meet mine. His kiss was quick and hard, but I felt his need. Sam had been truly frightened for his father and had put on a brave face. I pulled back and smiled at him, brushing his hair away from his forehead, before leaning in and giving him a soft kiss on his lips.

'Good to see you, Charli,' Sam's dad said, sliding the keycard along the locking device. 'Sam says you've invited us to your house for dinner.'

'Yeah, Mr Walker,' I said, hugging Sam's arm to me as we walked into the room. 'We can celebrate.' I paused for a moment, swallowing. 'It *is* good news, isn't it?' I almost whispered, scared for a moment.

'Yes, Charli, it *is* good news. We've just been worried for nothing. Although the doctor did originally say that he just wanted to check; that he was ruling things out. We really shouldn't have worried so much. Sam, here, though, wasn't worried at all. Were you, Sam?'

'Nah, Dad. Knew you were faking it!'

They both laughed but, in a moment of insight – Louisa would freak if she knew I'd had two today – I knew they'd both been lying to each other. Men!

'What time should we leave for dinner, Charli? I'd like to lie down for a little while; I'm a bit tired.'

'Oh, Ginny doesn't usually serve anything before six o'clock, Mr Walker. We've got heaps of time,' I hastened to reassure him.

'Sam, we'll need to take wine. Organise a bottle, will you?'

'Sure, Dad. Not a problem.'

'Charli, you have *asked* if it's okay, haven't you?'

'Oh, Mr Walker, you don't have to worry about that. Ginny always makes heaps of food. Usually, we have leftovers for lunch the next day. And sometimes we don't all show up, anyway. She'll have enough,' I said, confidently.

'I'd feel better if you let her know we're coming. She might want warning that there's another two mouths to feed.'

'Alright. I'll text her later. But it'll be fine, Mr Walker. Don't you worry. You go rest, and Sam and I will go get wine. Not a problem.'

I couldn't wait to get Sam alone. How fast could we find somewhere quiet and private to "celebrate"!

Daphne

My concentration was broken by a gentle tap on my door and I looked up to see Dominic, slouching against the frame. A quick glance to the outer office and I almost smirked at the surprised expression on Jasmine's face.

'You busy?' His low tone was seductive: he didn't even have to *try*.

'Always,' I answered, glad that he was there.

I watched as he entered my office, closing the door behind him and, just before it blocked the view, I could see Melissa's face, all goggle-eyed and open-mouthed. The smirk escaped, then. There was no trying to hide it.

'What are you smirking at?' There was amusement in his voice.

'Jasmine and Melissa. They've spent most of today speculating about your absence and wondering what I did to stop you from hovering. I must admit, it's a bit insulting how quickly you've lost interest.' It was only a half-teasing comment: I had been surprised that he'd stayed away all day, even though I knew that he was deliberately leaving me alone to work.

His eyes narrowed, a speculative gleam lightening them, as he studied me with a shrewd expression. 'Did you miss me, Snow?' he crooned. 'Was your day boring without my stopping by?'

'In your dreams, Dominic!' I retorted. 'I finally managed to get work done, without the constant disruption.'

'Disruption? Or distraction?'

'Both! Now, why are you here?'

'Couldn't keep away, Snow. You know that. You're the flame that beckons me.'

'Dom,' I scoffed and, instead of shutting him down, my response just made him smile.

'Invite me home, Daphne.' It was a command, spoken deep and dark.

'What?'

'Invite me to your house, to meet your sisters. And then we'll go out to dinner.' His gaze was steady, his grey eyes holding mine.

'Okay.' I swallowed.

'Tonight?'

'Okay. Only … we don't have to go out for dinner. Ginny always makes plenty. I don't know what she's cooking, but there's always lots.'

'I'll come by when I'm done here and collect you. We'll pick up wine on the way to the station.'

'You don't have to do that, Dominic. There's wine at home. And anyway, you drink bourbon.'

'I'm not going empty-handed to your house, the very first time I meet your sisters, Snow. We'll get wine. I'll be back in about thirty. Okay?'

'Sure. I'll be ready.'

'Good girl,' he said, with that satisfied signature-smile of his, before opening the door and sauntering out to the lift. I wasn't sure whether to laugh at the two women outside, following his progress across the floor, or be shocked at how much I liked hearing him praise me in that dark, sexy voice.

Ginny

The kitchen smelt divine.

When Ned had organised an Uber for me, I'd asked him if he could make it a double-trip and I stopped at the shops on the way home. Ned had grinned when I said that, shaking his head in amusement, before entering the relevant information into the app. So, a large piece of top round beef, beautifully seasoned and basted, was roasting in the oven, and I'd just slathered a pan of vegetables with oil and herbs: potatoes, pumpkin, whole beetroot, onions, carrots and sweet potatoes. Fresh greens adorned the benchtop: string beans, broccoli and baby spinach leaves, waiting for the right time to be steamed.

I hoped Michael was hungry. For the first time in a long time, I was nervous about my cooking. I wanted everything to be perfect! I had cheated, though, and bought a Sara Lee apple pie and ice-cream for dessert. I hadn't had time to prepare something sweet, as well.

And, as this was such a special occasion for me, I gently lifted my mother's good tablecloth from the sideboard and spread it out over the table. It had been so long since we'd used this: our mother had bought this for her "glory box", years before she'd even met our father. And here it was, sheer white cloth, with delicate flowers embroidered in a rainbow of silk threads, perfect shadow-stitching, lazy daisies, satin and chain stitches.

I set the table, including side plates for the soft dinner rolls I'd bought, and wine glasses, even though I knew that Jane and Charli wouldn't drink wine, and Daphne only if she'd run out of whiskey. It all looked so beautiful, though, and I wished my mother were here to see it.

The sound of the front door opening drew me into the hall and I was startled to see Jane struggling with boxes, balanced on top of each other, and two bags hanging from the crook of her arm.

'What's going on?' I asked, as she simultaneously exclaimed, 'Oh, something smells heavenly! Help me with these?'

'It's dinner. What's all of this?' I asked again, taking the boxes from her hands.

'Stuff from school. What's for dinner?' she responded, shifting the bags from her arms.

'Roast beef and veggies.' We both entered her room and unburdened ourselves of her baggage. 'Why'd you bring all of this home?'

'Because I'm doing it, Ginny. I've taken Leave,' she burst out, a huge grin on her face.

'Leave of your senses!' I couldn't help but retort. 'What are you doing?'

'Going with Jackson. Oh, and by the way, I invited him to dinner.'

'When? Tonight?'

'Yes. He's coming to help me get packed. I'm leaving tomorrow. With him.' She was almost breathless in her excitement.

'You invited Jackson to dinner? Tonight?' I repeated, trying to absorb what she was saying.

'Yes, Ginny, tonight.' She frowned at me, as though I was being obtuse and difficult. 'It's a roast. There'll be enough for one more, won't there?' she asked, as though I were being unreasonable.

'Well, Jane, I invited someone for dinner too,' I said – a little snidely, I will admit. We'd entered the dining room as I said this and – I'll admit this, too – I took extreme pleasure in the shock on her face when she saw the table setting.

'Wow! It *must* be someone special, for you to pull out all the stops like this! Who'd you invite? It can't be one of your girlfriends – you hardly even bother with cutlery when they're around.'

Yep, the astonishment on her face was worth the effort I'd made.

'You know, Jane, you're not the only person in this house who had an interesting weekend. You *do* have four sisters.' I enjoyed watching the expression changes on her face, like backdrops flapping down in the recess of a theatre stage: irritation at my tone, surprise at the idea that she was not the only one who met a man and, finally, speculation and wonder at what revelations there were in store.

'Did you meet someone? *Really?*' A pause whilst she absorbed the grin on my face. 'And did one of the others?' Her eyebrows were at her hairline when I nodded. '*Who?*'

This was too much fun.

'Guess!'

'No, Ginny, I'm not playing that game.' Oh, she'd pulled out the school-teacher voice! 'Was it Daphne?'

'Guess again,' I teased.

'Well, it wouldn't have been Louisa. She doesn't go anywhere, except the bookshop. It has to be Charli!'

When I nodded, she grinned, triumphantly, as though she'd won some sort of hard-to-achieve trophy.

'Who?'

'I don't know all the details, but he's from a farm in the middle of the state. Charli's all fired up that she's going out there this weekend and I figured you'd have something to say about that, knowing you.' A touch of snide on the last two words, but ... I knew Jane.

'I'll set another place for Jackson,' was all Jane said, before she burst out with, 'This is like when Mum and Dad were still here! Seven settings at the table!' And then, as though it had finally sunk in, 'Who did *you* invite for dinner? What's his name?'

'I wondered when you were going to ask.' I grinned at her to soften the harshness of my words. 'His name's Michael. I met him on Thursday night, although ... well, it wasn't actually a *meeting* then, but ...' I trailed off. I really didn't want Jane, of all people, to know what happened on Thursday night. I was sure that Michael wouldn't say anything, so there was no reason any of my sisters needed to know how ... *inebriated* I'd been.

'Will there be enough? I'm sorry, Ginny. I should have called you and let you know I'd invited someone.'

I almost fell over with shock. Jane was apologising. To me! Oh. My. God. This guy must be someone else. He'd looked alright when we'd had that miniscule introduction the night before, but ... Jane apologised! To me!

'It'll be okay, Jane,' I reassured, feeling generous towards her. 'I bought the dozen-pack of dinner rolls, and I got the largest roast I could get. There'll be plenty.' I gestured towards the two chairs that, so long ago, we'd put in the corners of the dining room. It had been too sad to sit at a table with so many empty chairs, but we'd kept the sixth to keep the setting even. She and I moved them to each end of the long table.

'Do you need a hand with anything? Say "no" because I really need to get into my bedroom and work out what to pack.'

'No, it's all okay,' I smiled. 'Go do what you have to.'

'Did you get the washing done?'

'Yeah, but I haven't ironed. Your folding's on your bed.'

'Yell out if you need anything,' she said, leaving the room. And then, just as I was heading back to the kitchen, she ducked her head through the door. 'What's he like, your Michael?'

'You'll get to meet him soon enough. You can make up your own mind. But Jane?' She turned fully towards me. 'I really like him, so ... Don't tell him bad stuff about me, will you?'

'Oh, Ginny!' she breathed and came all the way across the room to me, opening her hands and hugging me. 'I wouldn't do that. I'm sorry if you think that I would, but ... I just want you to be happy, Ginny. That's all I've ever wanted. I was just worried about you, all these years. You seemed so ... directionless, and I didn't know what to do to fix things. I may have been a bit ham-fisted, but I love you, Ginny. I wouldn't wreck things for you.'

And there we were, both of us crying, when we should have been blissfully happy that we'd found people who might just be The One. *Women!* I thought, as I felt a wry smile grace my face.

'Go, Jane. Go get packing. I'll finish dinner.' And I batted her away, dipping my head and swiping at the wetness on my cheeks.

Everything was coming along well. The roast had browned beautifully, pan juices begging to be turned into gravy, and the veggies were sizzling in their fragrant oil. All that still needed to happen was the steaming of the greens and then popping the bread rolls into the oven when the roast came out to rest.

Again, the sound of the front door opening caught my attention. Yes, my ears were pealed for Michael's knock, so it made sense that the door only needed to squeak on its hinges for my ears to twitch.

'Something smells fabulous!' It was Daphne. I swallowed my disappointment. Surely, Michael would be here soon.

I turned to see Daph enter the dining room, but she wasn't alone. A seriously sexy stud was behind her.

'Don't gape, Ginny,' she teased, although she wasn't as relaxed as she'd like me to think. I wouldn't be either, with such a sex-on-a-stick guy like that. He *oozed* alpha-male pheromones. Michael was hot, and sexy, and hot, and mine! But this guy – off the charts!

'This is Dominic,' she offered casually, as though she brought men home every other day. My mind was trying to compute: was this "Damned Dominic"? From work, Dominic? 'I invited him for dinner. Whatever we're having smells great!' It was then that she glanced at the table, set for seven. 'Oh, this looks good! Is someone else coming for dinner? Will there be enough?' Her voice was a higher pitch than usual. A dead giveaway: Daph was nervous, but that didn't excuse her taking me for granted, yet again.

'Ummm, hi. Dominic, is it?' I smiled weakly at his nod, before turning to Daphne. 'Daph, you could have rung. Jane invited that Jackson guy, as well.'

'Oh, sorry, Ginny. I didn't think. I mean, you always have plenty.' She looked uncomfortable and her face reddened in embarrassment. But at the last minute I realised that this wasn't what I wanted for her, especially not in front of Alpha Stud!

''S'alright, Daph. I can stretch it a bit further. It won't be a problem,' I reassured her, although I wasn't quite so sure.

Dominic still hadn't said anything: he was holding Daph's hand, which was unusual in itself – Daphne wasn't much for PDAs – but, otherwise, he was still, unmoving. Well, except for his eyes: they'd swept the room, taking in – I imagined – the carefully laid table, the number of chairs and the array of framed photos on the sideboard. It was then he moved, but only to place two bottles of wine onto the middle of the table.

'By the way,' Daphne began, just as there was a knock at the door, 'there was a strange man hovering around out the front, looking lost. Is that who you were expecting?'

But I was already in the hallway, so I didn't bother to answer. Twisting the lock and pulling on the door, I was a flurry of excited nervousness as I greeted Michael.

'Red,' he growled, reaching out to wrap his arms around me, pulling me in for an embrace that was hampered only by the wine bottles in one hand. His mouth met mine in a mind-boggling kiss – so much more intense than the one before, when he knew that Ned was there watching us.

'*Red*?' Two incredulous voices sounded in unison. I pulled back, suddenly aware that we had an audience: Jane must have come from her bedroom and Daph from the dining room.

'Is this Michael?' asked Jane, the first to recover, although both of their faces revealed their amazement. What? That I, too, could find a hot guy? And then it occurred to me that they were shocked at the nickname: they both knew that I *hated* references to my red hair.

'Michael,' I said formally, brushing my hands down my dress, 'these are two of my sisters: Jane,' I nodded towards her, 'and Daphne. And that man in the doorway down there is a friend of Daph's. His name is …' My mind went blank.

'Dominic,' Daph's man said smoothly, finally speaking, his voice a deep commanding baritone. He covered the hallway carpet in long, confident strides, his right hand extended in greeting. 'Dominic Northcott. And you are?' he questioned, as Michael juggled the wine and extended his hand.

'Michael Oldfield. Nice to meet you.' He turned towards me, but Jane and I were still staring at each other, our eyes rounded in amazement, both of us mouthing *"Damned Dominic?"*

'Something smells good, Ginny,' Michael said, prompting me to shut my mouth and adopt a "normal" expression.

'We're having roast beef, with all the trimmings,' I directed my words to him, and the warmth in my face wasn't because of the oven, I knew.

'Sounds good, Red. Do you need a hand?'

'Nah, I'm good. But you can join me in the kitchen, if you want.'

'Umm,' Jane interrupted our mushy moment, 'I'll set another place, shall I?'

'Oh, yeah,' I said, coming back down to earth. 'Umm, I might not have enough dessert. I only bought one apple pie. I'll see what's in the freezer.'

We'd hardly made it into the dining room when the front door opened again.

'That should be Charli,' I said. 'She should have been home already. Not sure what's keeping her.'

But it wasn't Charli. And it wasn't Jane's Jackson, either.

Louisa

'You can just park out the front,' I directed Patrick, who was driving the SUV he'd rented at the airport. He'd arrived earlier than my five-o'clock finish and spent the time wandering through the bookstore, pretending to be a customer and asking ridiculous questions about a myriad of books he'd picked off the shelf: *Did we stock an original edition of* The Canterbury Tales? *Was William Shakespeare still writing plays? Was there a fourth volume in* The Lord of the Rings *series? Did we have a copy of Jane Austen's* Pride and Prejudice *in Spanish? Did Lexxie Couper know that her surname should be spelt Cooper?*

The store's owner, my boss, glared at him as though he was an idiot. If only she knew! Meanwhile, I spent my time trying not to either laugh at his silliness or ogle his gorgeousness! I had to keep pinching myself to believe that he was *here.*

The expression on my boss' face when five o'clock finally arrived and we both left together was priceless. I knew I'd have an interrogation to face the next day.

'I probably should have let Ginny know I was bringing an extra for dinner,' I said, sliding out of the car and waiting for Patrick to join me. I reached out to take one of the wine bottles from him. 'You didn't need to bring anything, Patrick.'

'Yeah, no, Lou. Not coming empty-handed. My mother would have a fit,' and then he smiled at me, a cheeky-mother's-boy grin, and I couldn't help but swoon a bit. I really liked this man!

'I wonder if Jane decided to go with Jackson,' I said, as we walked up the path.

'Who's Jackson?'

'Oh, Patrick, I've got *so* much to tell you. You've missed so much!' I hugged his arm to my side. 'I really *am* a goddess.' I enthused.

'Well, Athena, we both know that.' He stopped, tugging on my arm, and pulled me to him. His fingers gripped my chin and tipped my face towards his descending mouth, and I sighed as his lips covered mine. I'd waited for this: ever since his phone call, all afternoon when I'd anticipated his arrival, throughout his wanderings in the shop, whilst he'd been asking stupid questions and making ridiculous comments. I'd waited for this: his warm mouth on mine, his tongue teasing and tantalising, his lips covering my lips – soft, sensual, arousing.

He pulled away, his eyes dark with desire, his mouth relaxed. 'C'mon, Lulu, let's get this over with.'

My eyes widened. 'It won't be that bad!' I protested.

'Four sisters! You're joking, aren't you? My guess is that they'll be mega-protective of you and I'll be facing a third degree. *Four* women! All with a vested interest in looking out for you! And I, the only male!' He clutched his chest, feigning fear.

'Yes, Patrick. Your life is in peril,' I shook my head at him, grinning. 'You'll be fine,' I said, patting his chest. 'They'll be all over you. I won't be able to get a word in, edgewise. They'll love you.'

Tugging him along beside me, I approached the front door, and paused …

There was a lot more sound coming from inside than I was expecting. After all, it was Monday night: not an evening when we White sisters were bristling with excitement at going out or squabbling tiredly at the end of the work-week.

Pushing the door open, I was surprised to see Ginny appear from the dining room, Jane fast in her tracks.

And they were obviously equally surprised to see me … or maybe it wasn't me, but Patrick, his body warm behind mine.

But still … I didn't expect their mouths to be that *agape*.

'Lou!' They cried in unison and I watched as Daphne pushed in behind them.

'What's going on?' Daph said, confused. Her eyes widened, her mouth fell open, as she stared at me, and then behind me, and then her focus returned to me. 'Well, Louisa. Aren't you full of surprises?' Her tone was amused and I watched, puzzled, as they all laughed.

And then the penny dropped!

'So, Jane, Daphne, Ginny.' I paused, drawing out the moment. 'I take it that all of you decided to *act*!' I invested emphasis in the last word and turned to Patrick. 'I told you that I have special powers. I'm betting that Artemis, Apollo's Daughter and Hestia have found their matches!' I turned back to my sisters. 'Is that right?'

I almost laughed at the bewilderment on their faces: it was comical.

'What are you talking about, Lou?' asked Ginny.

'And who is this man?' added Jane, adopting her head-of-the-household tone of voice.

'Do we know him?' chimed in Daphne who looked remarkably relaxed for pre-shot-of-whiskey Daphne.

'Patrick, these are my sisters.'

'Yes,' he said, his voice deliciously deep and amused. 'I gathered that. Lulu, are we staying here in the doorway?' His hand, holding the wine, nudged my upper arm.

'No,' I said, turning to him and gifting him with the biggest smile I had, 'we're not.' I turned back to Ginny. 'I know I didn't give you any warning, but I invited Patrick to dinner. There'll be enough, won't there?'

I had an immediate flash of guilt as I saw Ginny's stricken face.

'It's okay, Lou. We can go out for dinner.' I was relieved that Patrick read the room as quickly and accurately as he did.

'Umm, come inside,' Jane belatedly beckoned. 'We'll sort this out.'

I wasn't entirely surprised, having registered Ginny's dilemma, to see strange men in the dining room when I passed through the doorway. Both were handsome men, but in totally different ways. Before either of them could speak, or Daph or Ginny could introduce them, I said, 'Patrick, this is Dominic,' indicating with my hand, still holding one of the wine bottles, 'and this is Michael.'

'How did you know?' blurted Jane. 'I'd never heard of them until today.' She paused and then, 'Well, we've all heard of Dominic, but Michael?'

'Jane!' admonished Daphne, red with embarrassment.

'Oh, come off it, Daph! This is Damned Dominic!'

The colour on Daphne's cheeks deepened, spreading over her face and down her neck, but Dominic's response was to laugh, a deeply amused chuckle. 'Yes, that would be me,' he agreed. 'The bane of Snow's existence!'

There was silence!

No-one spoke!

I watched as the nickname sunk in, like a rounded rock in a placid pond, whilst Jane, Ginny and I shared stunned looks, our eyes wide with astonishment, our mouths broad with beaming grins. And, almost by some imperceptible command, we all mouthed, *"Snow!"*

'Ginny, you said that none of you were called "Snow",' Michael commented, his voice loud in the quiet of the room.

'Well, Michael, that's what I *thought*. Who knew that Daph here had been likened to a fairy-tale princess?'

'H-hmmm!' Dominic wasn't clearing his throat: it was obvious to all of us that he was not happy, most likely with the tone of Ginny's words. *Interesting*, I thought.

'So, Ginny,' Dominic said, having gained the attention of the room, 'I take it that you were expecting your sisters and Michael for dinner and this has,' his right hand gestured towards us, 'grown?'

'Well, yes. I haven't heard from Charli yet, so she might not be home for dinner, but ...'

'You're now having *nine* for dinner,' Dominic said, glancing at the table.

'Louisa and I can go out to dine, Dominic, is it?' Patrick suggested. 'It's not a problem. I wanted to take her out, anyway.' I squeezed his hand in mine. He looked down and winked at me as he squeezed back. *Melting much?*

'Ginny, a moment?' Michael nodded towards the kitchen. *Hmmm, interesting!* Ginny followed without a word.

'Well, the table can sit ten, in a pinch, as long as we have two on each end,' Jane said. 'I guess we can squeeze nine in.'

Before anyone could respond to Jane's proposal, the sound of the front door slamming against the wall was followed by Charli's excited voice.

'Hey, everyone! I'm home! And I brought Sam and his dad!'

Yep, that was Charli. Formal introductions, be damned.

The dining room, with all its occupants, was silent once more and, in the stillness, it was possible to hear the front door being gently latched closed.

'C'mon, Sam! Mr Walker! I'll introduce you to everyone!' Her voice was loud, as were her footsteps, as she charged down the hallway, with her usual exuberance.

And it was almost comical, watching her come to a dead stop at the doorway, her startled gaze swinging around the room to take in the number of people present.

'Who are all of you?' she blurted, in her usual Charli-fashion. 'Where's Ginny?' she continued, without waiting for a response.

'Charli,' the older man accompanying them admonished gently, 'are you going to introduce us to your family?'

'Well, yeah. But I don't know who those people are,' she complained, indicating Dominic and Patrick, who glanced at each other, silently determining who was going to respond to these new arrivals.

It was Jane.

'Charli, what's happening here?' Her voice was quiet, her tone polite, but there was that hint of school-teacher embedded in her stance.

'I invited Sam and his dad for dinner,' Charli's forehead puckered in bewilderment. 'It's allowed.' Her voice took on the child-like whine that she sometimes used when confronted. 'We have friends to dinner all the time.' She looked around, slowly reddening in embarrassment, and I felt sorry for her. How was she to know that tonight we'd all decided to extend invitations?

'It's okay, Charli,' I said, stepping forward to her and touching her shoulder in reassurance. 'I'm Louisa.' I offered my hand to the elder of the two men and smiled. 'I take it you're Sam's father.'

'Daniel Walker. Yes, Sam is my son.' He nodded to Sam, before indicating to him that he needed to step forward to shake hands. 'Your sister very kindly invited us for dinner, but we can go,' he offered.

'No,' Michael answered, firmly. I hadn't realised that he'd returned to the room: Ginny stood next to him, smiling faintly. 'I'll just make a call. Ginny's prepared a roast dinner, so I'll just add to it. We may need another table, though.'

'It's fine, Michael. Louisa and I can go elsewhere.'

'It's taken care of, Patrick,' Michael said, decisively. 'Red's made a roast beef and I'll top it up with a couple of roast chickens and extra vegetables. More bread rolls, I think, and a dozen desserts.' He glanced at the table, now with six wine bottles on it. 'I guess we have enough wine,' he noted, prompting Sam's father to proffer a bottle-shop bag.

'We brought some as well,' he said. 'Wasn't sure what we were having, so I've got white and red.'

'It should be a good evening, then,' Michael smiled. 'If someone can organise seating, I'll help Ginny in the kitchen.'

'Consider it done,' Dominic stated. 'Daph, is there another table? A card table? Outdoor furniture?'

'I'll help move this table a little further toward the wall,' Daniel Walker offered.

'No, Mr Walker,' Charli chimed in. 'You sit and rest.' She threw a quick look at us as we stood shocked at her protectiveness – so unlike our boisterous youngest sister – and explained, 'He's been sick. He needs to take it easy.'

'Charli,' Daniel chided.

'You can supervise, Daniel,' Dominic said in his authoritative voice. 'We'll provide the muscles.'

I took a moment to admire Dominic's physique. It was obvious that, beneath his shirt and suit jacket, there was a muscular body, solid without flabbiness. *Well done, Daphne*, I thought, bemusedly. And while the men were outdoing each other to demonstrate their physical abilities, I watched the wonder on the faces of my sisters, all stunned at the turn of events. I felt slightly superior, knowing that I was the only one aware of each of their adventures over the weekend, and I smiled, a smug little lifting of the corners of my mouth.

'You weren't surprised at any of this, were you, Louisa?'

I *was* surprised at the voice just behind me, as I hadn't noticed Dominic move towards me. When I turned to face him, I was mute for a moment, admiring the sexy dominance evident in his facial features: his shrewd, assessing eyes; the strength of his jaw; his full lips, relaxed in a non-smile. No wonder that he had Daphne bedazzled. He'd bedazzle me, if he were my type.

'What do you mean?' I obfuscated, looking him in the eyes.

'You knew about all of us,' he stated, as though he were sure of my answer. 'You were caught unawares that we were all here, but you knew that your sisters had all partnered up.'

'Maybe,' was all I would admit. He nodded, as though I had confirmed something that he'd surmised.

'I like you, Louisa.' I felt my face still, unsure of what he meant, but it didn't surprise me that he noticed and correctly interpreted my response. 'Not like that, Louisa, but you'd be a good person to have on side.' He nodded again, a slight smile on his face, as he moved back to Daphne.

'What was that all about?' Patrick asked, as he returned to my side.

'Oh, nothing. Dominic was just letting me know that he had my number, I think.'

'As long as that was all it was about,' he grumbled, his fingers closing around my hand and tightening.

'Oh, Patrick!' I crooned, 'who knew you were into chest-beating?'

'You're all beautiful women, Lulu, so it's no wonder that there's a roomful of half-decent-good-looking men here.' He shrugged. 'I'm not chest-beating: merely protecting what's mine.' The look he gave me was hot! And *significant*, I thought. Although he was speaking alpha-male prattle out loud, it was the unspoken communication that was important, I realised. Patrick wasn't as sure of me as he pretended: he was still apprehensive about how things had ended the previous day and it occurred to me that, as we hadn't had time to really talk, he probably needed reassurance. I'd been so worried about *me*, and then the strangers that had crowded our house, I hadn't really considered how he must be feeling.

Entwining my arm with his and hugging it to my side, I lifted my face to his, waiting until I had his total attention. 'I'm not my sisters, Patrick. And a goddess, such as myself, demands more in her consort that mere *looks*,' I slowed my speech, my eyes holding his as I emphasised my words, 'No, Patrick, a goddess such as myself commands a worthy man, one who is intelligent and lettered, sexy and sophisticated, courageous and *humble*,' I almost snorted at that, 'such as yourself. There is no male competition for my affections in this room. Now, whilst we have a moment of privacy, before everyone turns and notices, are you going to kiss me, Patrick, or not?'

It was fascinating, watching the dynamics of the group. Charli had left Daniel sitting in a chair at one end of the table – an unconscious choice? I wasn't sure – whilst she slipped away with Sam: most likely, out to the back garden. I had visions of them snuggled up on the porch swinging, canoodling. I loved that word! So onomatopoeic! A combination of close cuddling and spooning, with lots of kissing action tossed in.

Ginny and Michael were still in the kitchen, but every so often, he strode through the dining room to the front door, impatient for his delivery. Patrick had extended an arm, halting Michael on one of his circular treks, and said in a low, quiet voice, 'The food you've ordered? What's my share?'

Michael smiled, but shook his head. 'It's not a problem. It's taken care of.'

'But still…' Patrick persisted.

'Nah, but Patrick, is it? Thanks for offering.' They nudged each other's arms in that "manly" way – a gesture of embarrassed respect – and then Michael left to check the front door again.

Jane was fussing in her bedroom and I could hear her bedroom door opening and closing, as she, too, monitored any activity at the front of the house. Her nervousness was palpable and I excused myself from where I stood, observing the scene with Patrick, to calm Jane down.

'This isn't like you,' I said, as soon as I entered her bedroom and saw the chaos spread across her bed and the floor, drawers and wardrobe doors gaping open.

'I don't know what to take and … where's Jackson?' Her rising anxiety was clearly audible in the ascending pitch of her last two words.

'What time did you tell him to come?' I asked, keeping my voice calm, my words measured.

'I didn't really,' she said, twisting her fingers together. *She's losing it,* I thought, amazed at how stressed Jane was. I'd seldom seen her like this: her usual demeanour at this time of day was weary resoluteness. 'I just told him that I wouldn't be home until after five and asked him to come help me pack.'

'Then ring him, Jane. It sounds like you didn't make dinner clear. Ring him.'

'What if he's changed his mind, Lou?'

'He hasn't, Jane.'

'How can you be so sure? You don't even know him.'

'Sure, I do. I met him last night. And,' I paused, catching her eyes and holding the look for a long moment, so that my words would penetrate her panic, 'I *saw* the way he looked at you, and the way he held your hand, and carried your bag, as though you were a queen and he was your knight, grateful that he could serve you. And I *heard* the way he spoke, the intimate tone of his voice, his gentleness in talking with you. And I saw how you shone when you looked at him, as though he'd hung the moon. That's catnip for men.' I stopped talking for a moment, holding her gaze, before I started to slowly nod my head – a conscious attempt to encourage her to nod hers in agreement at my next words. 'He won't have changed his mind, Jane. He's coming.'

'You really think?'

'Yes, but ...' I glanced around the room, pointedly, 'first we need to tidy up this mess. There's no way he'd want such a slob on his yacht, which is probably all sailor-like ship-shape.' I grinned, pleased that she followed suit, before looking around the room as though she'd only just noticed it.

'God, Lou! Look what a mess I've made!'

'S'okay, Jane.' I walked to the door and called, 'Daph!'

'Yeah?' A voice sounded from her bedroom, before the sound of two pairs of footsteps entering the hall could be heard.

'We need you in here! Oh, and you can send that man of yours to keep Patrick company. He's not wanted.' Jane and I shared a grin, before dissolving into giggles, as one set of footsteps retreated.

'Oh my god!' Daph exclaimed as she entered, a glass of scotch in her hand. 'Jane, what have you done?'

'Well, I think that's obvious.' It was good to hear the dry tone in Jane's voice. Panic averted!

Daphne took over: her preferred response to any calamity. It was what she was good at. 'I take it you don't have much cabin space, so you'll need comfortable clothes that mix and match; that you can dress up and down; that will wash and wear well.' Jane and I exchanged grins, listening to the gears grinding in Daph's brain. 'Shoes: flat-heeled, canvas, a pair of low-heeled good ones to wear out. Have you got a rain jacket, Jane?'

'You know, she *can* buy whatever she doesn't have,' I said. 'She's only going to Queensland. They do have shops. It's probably better that she travels light.'

Daph ignored me. 'Toiletries, Jane. Get them organised while I put some outfits together. Lou, pick up all that stuff on the floor, fold it and put it away, will you?'

Jane and I mock-saluted, but Daph wasn't paying attention.

'What's going on?' It was Charli at the door. 'Oh, you're packing!' She entered the room and plonked herself down on the bed, her face alive with excitement and wonder. 'How many bikinis are you taking?' She glanced around. 'Where's your photographer, Jane? Isn't he coming?'

Jane's eyes widened in alarm. 'Lou, can you take Charli out to … I don't know – see if Jackson's here yet?'

'Sure,' I said, grabbing Charli by the arm. 'C'mon, Charli. Introduce me to your man again.' And, just like that, Charli's attention was diverted.

Jackson's arrival coincided with the delivery of the food that Michael had ordered and it wasn't long before we were all seated at the now-extended table, platters of sliced roast beef, carved roast chicken, baked vegetables and steamed greens lining the table's centre. Jane and Daphne shared one end of the long table, with Daniel Walker given the courtesy of being seated at the other end. Jackson and Dominic sat next to Jane and Daph, each at the end of the long sides, and Charli and Sam sat on either side of Sam's father.

It was strange: our dining room so crowded, especially with so many unfamiliar people. There'd been a moment of awkwardness when we'd all sat down, a hesitancy on what should happen first. Michael and Ginny sat opposite Patrick and me and I saw them exchange uncertain looks, as though they weren't sure, as the evening's hosts, if they should invite us all to eat.

And then Daniel solved the dilemma…

'Before we all start eating,' he began, pausing until all of us turned towards him, 'I'd like to express my gratitude for including me and my son, here, in your family dinner. It's been a difficult weekend for us both, and Charli has been a godsend to us, assisting in creating a sense of normalcy in the midst of our family crisis. It didn't occur to me that the weekend would end with our being invited to a roast dinner, so,' he paused again, lifting his wineglass, 'thank you all. Especially you, Ginny, and your friend, Michael, for putting on this magnificent feast.'

And, as one, we all turned to Ginny and Michael, raising our glasses and saying, 'Hear, hear!'

'Well, then,' said Ginny, her face flaming in embarrassment, not used to such glowing praise, 'let's eat! Michael, pass a platter.'

On cue, he picked up the nearest bowl of greens and passed it to his right, handing Ginny the accompanying tongs, and this small action broke the silence in the room. Whilst I selected slices of the beef from the serving dish offered to me by Patrick, I observed Dominic, Sam and Jackson each lift a platter and offer it to my sisters.

'This is *so* good, Ginny! I'm *starved*,' Charli exclaimed effusively, loading sweet potatoes and chunks of pumpkin onto her plate.

'You're welcome, Charli. I didn't imagine that we'd have this many to dinner. Do you want chicken?' She passed the platter on to her sister.

'So, you're heading out tomorrow?' Patrick asked, looking towards Jackson.

'Yes. I was initially leaving today, but ...' He turned to Jane and they exchanged a cutesy, contented smile. 'So, tomorrow,' he finished, looking once again at Patrick.

'On a boat!' Charli chimed in.

'It's a yacht,' Jane corrected, dryly.

'Where're you headed?' Michael asked, grinding fresh black pepper onto his vegetables.

'The Reef. There's a portion of it that was bleached white not so long ago, but there's talk that it's regenerating. Thought I'd take a look; maybe, do a story.'

'Jackson writes for *Earth Today* magazine,' Ginny said in explanation. 'Jane's been following his articles for years.'

I exchanged a smile with Daphne and neither of us said anything. The way Ginny had spoken, no-one would think that, until yesterday, she hadn't known that Jackson McGee existed. Well, she *had* recognised his face: just not known from where.

'What I want to know about, Jane,' Daphne said, 'is the look on your principal's face when you asked for the leave.'

'You know, maybe he was just busy, or he really didn't care, but it was just … I don't know… like business, as usual. There was no real response. Just "make sure your reports are done".'

'What'd you tell him?' Charli mumbled, a mouthful of food muffling her words.

'That I had a family crisis.'

'Blame us, why don't you?' Charli blurted.

'Jane, I've invited Charli to visit our farm this weekend. I was going to ask you about it tonight, but I didn't realise that you'd be going away.' Daniel's voice was quiet and respectful, obviously gathering that Jane was, ostensibly, the head of our family.

By the expression on Jane's face – the surprise, the indecision – it was clear that she'd been taken unawares. Her eyes darted, in turn, to Charli, then Daphne and then to Jackson, and back to Daphne. The silence became awkward, once again.

'Where is your property?' Dominic's question slid into the void, his manner calm and relaxed, his voice neutral.

'Outside Condobolin. Do you know the area?'

'Not really,' Dominic responded. 'I know where it is, though. Not far from Parkes. And Forbes. How did you envisage that Charli would get there?'

This was fascinating! Dominic had inserted himself into the space being created by Jane's leaving and Daphne wasn't saying a thing: she was allowing Dominic to take control.

Daphne was giving up control! I almost had to pinch myself to believe it. And Jane just looked relieved! As though she, finally, didn't have to be responsible for the rest of us.

This was a seismic shift in the family dynamics!

'I thought she might fly out to Orange on Friday afternoon, and we'd collect her from there. There's a flight back on Sunday afternoon. It shouldn't interfere with her uni schedule, although she may have homework over the weekend. I'd expect her to keep up with her studies.' It was obvious that Daniel knew travel options and times, but he was smart enough to invest just enough ambivalence to his tone to make his comments sound like suggestions, rather than fully-fledged plans.

And then, just to astonish me some more, Dominic turned to me!

'What do you think, Louisa?' he asked, and I watched Daphne bristle beside him, her eyes wide with surprise.

'Dominic!' Daphne and Jane exclaimed in unison, whilst I stared at him. Dominic's eyes didn't leave me, but I noticed, in my peripheral vision, his hand move across below the table and imagined that he'd clasped Daphne's knee.

'Why ask *her?*' Charli's voice rang out, and I felt the gazes of the others turn to me.

'Louisa?' Dominic prodded, a slight wry smile *just* curving his upper lip.

I felt Patrick's palm on my thigh, a gentle squeeze in reassurance.

'It sounds like a plan,' I said, finally, my eyes still on Dominic's. 'Charli's wanted this for as long as she could talk, and it's only for the weekend. A taste of farm life,' I added, glancing towards Sam and Daniel. The older man's focus alternated between me and Dominic, his expression shrewd and assessing. 'Charli has a fairly romanticised ideal in her head,' I continued, and watched the outrage spread across her features, consuming her.

'I do *not!*' she exclaimed, heatedly.

Ginny and Michael were quiet, apparently content to watch the show. Sam, I noticed, hadn't said anything either, although he did offer a reassuring smile, and a sexy wink, to Charli, which seemed to appease her a little.

'I can take her to the airport,' I said, and felt the sudden clench of Patrick's hand on my leg and a tensing of his body next to mine. 'I'm flying to the Gold Coast on Friday afternoon,' I said, monitoring my sisters' faces as my words sunk in, their astonishment quite enjoyable to view. 'Patrick invited me,' I added.

'What?' Daphne and Jane chorused again, glancing at each other in surprise at their synchronised responses.

'Well, well, well,' Ginny drawled, her eyes glinting with gleeful satisfaction. 'Our Louisa is spreading her wings,' she taunted, an edge to her voice. 'What happened with you over the weekend?' she asked.

'When did you meet Patrick?' Daphne asked. 'You two seem quite tight.' She grimaced at her use of that word.

'Thursday evening,' Patrick said, before I could answer, his hand squeezing my thigh again, only this time a little higher. 'But Lou and I have known each other for a long time, now.'

'How's that?' Michael asked, sipping his water, the ice tinkling in the glass.

'Louisa and I have corresponded for a number of years,' Patrick said, smoothly, as though this was completely normal. I glanced towards him, warming at the smile he bestowed upon me, and noticed that Dominic, in my line of vision, was quietly assessing us.

'Did you two go out over the weekend?' Charli piped up, her interest in this turn of events evident.

'We spent the weekend at a bed-and-breakfast in the Blue Mountains,' I answered, flicking a quick smile at Patrick. 'It was incredible! The most amazing views from the bay windows. And I hadn't realised what beautiful waterfalls there were up there. You'd like it, Jane. You must go up some time.'

'What! You were gone all weekend?' Ginny huffed indignantly. 'What's with the whole "you didn't come home on Saturday night, Ginny" routine you pulled with me? You weren't home, either. You couldn't have known that I wasn't home!'

'Well, it worked, didn't it?' I responded, a little smugly, shrugging. 'You told me what I wanted to know.'

'Did anyone know where you were, Lou?' asked Jane, her tone laced with concern. Maybe it had only just occurred to her that she had already abnegated her responsibilities for the entire three days.

'I did,' I stated.

'There you are, Snow,' Dominic commented, his voice low and barely audible. He dipped his head, his eyes narrowed as he continued, 'Told you that you all overlooked Louisa.'

'Well, she's front and centre with me,' Patrick stated, his hand gripping mine beneath the table. 'And, if I have my way, she'll move up to the Gold Coast.'

'What!' There went Daphne and Jane again, synchronised surprise, only this time, Charli and Ginny accompanied them.

'I don't know that I'm doing that yet,' I protested into the shocked silence. 'But …' I smiled at Patrick and squeezed his hand, 'I'll go up this weekend and see what he has to offer me.'

Patrick laughed out loud, pleased at my sauciness, I guessed.

'What is it that you do?' Daniel asked.

'Umm. I'm –'

'He's in marketing!' I interjected, saving him from answering. I figured that, if he'd protected his identity from me and his family, he didn't want a bunch of strangers to know his real work.

'And you work with Daphne?' Daniel's question was directed to Dominic.

'I do, Daniel. Not in the same section: Snow's in Metro.' Dominic's answer was concise and I noticed that he discouraged any further questioning of himself by turning to Michael and Ginny.

'How did you two meet?'

'Ginny was a guest at a hotel that I manage,' Michael answered, and I could tell there was more that he wasn't saying by the sudden splash of colour that reddened Ginny's cheeks. 'We got talking and found we had a lot in common.'

'Ginny said that you live in the Bennelong Apartments!' Charli blurted. 'I looked them up. You must be filthy rich!'

'Charli!' Yes, the Jane/Daphne duo was back in business!

'My family owns an apartment there, Charli,' was Michael's softly-spoken response. 'It's not me with all the money.'

'Hotel management?' Dominic's steady voice changed the subject.

'The family owns a string of hotels and dance venues,' was all Michael said.

'I leave tomorrow,' Jane reminded the table, although she was turned towards Ginny. 'Do you promise to explore some options in study when I'm gone?' Her voice was almost wheedling, as though she was worried about leaving Ginny without assisting her in finding a career path.

'Ginny has plenty of options,' Michael responded, startling all of us, including Ginny. 'She's considering training to be a chef, or pursuing other roles within the hospitality industry or charitable foundations.'

By the look on Ginny's face, this was news to her, as well as us, but she recovered quickly, a beaming smile blossoming across her face.

'Is that what you're going to do?' Jane persisted.

'I don't know,' Ginny responded. 'Over the weekend, Michael introduced me to a "Sydney" that I didn't know existed. I'm giving lots of things thought,' she finished, smiling coyly at her man.

'It sounds like your sisters are all on the move,' Jackson finally stated, his hand reaching across to cover Jane's. 'Adventures, all around.'

Jane ducked her head to answer him, but we could still hear her words. 'I don't know that I should leave when everything's ...' She paused, her hand wavering in front of her. 'There's so much upheaval.'

'Jane,' Jackson began, clearly worried.

'You can go,' Daphne interrupted, 'we'll be alright. Charli's only going for a weekend and ... who knows? Lou's only going for a weekend and?' she sent a questioning glance towards me, so I played along.

'Sure, Jane. It's only for a weekend and, who knows? We might see you in Queensland. How long will it take you to sail to the Gold Coast, Jackson?'

'Depends. On lots of things. But it's possible.'

'Charli will be safe with us,' Daniel said quietly, his tone reassuring. 'If she still likes country life after this weekend, we'll see about other visits. But I've told her that she needs to keep up her studies and do well, or all bets are off. She has to finish her degree.' I watched the silent Sam wink at Charli and it dawned on me that the two of them had been playing "footsie" under the table, most likely throughout the entire meal. They may have been quiet, but they'd entertained themselves.

'And Daphne's not on her own,' Dominic added, his low-pitched voice so sexy, I once again understood Daph being enthralled by him. 'It does sound, though,' he said, a deep chuckle resonating, 'that we'll have the house to ourselves this weekend.' He wriggled his eyebrows, his smile at Daphne ... pure seduction! *Oh!* I thought, watching Daphne melt into her seat, a blush burgeoning across her face, her eyes darkening, *he really is hot. And so into Daph.*

'Are you right?' Patrick asked beside me, jolting me and drawing my attention back to him. His grin, though, was playful.

'Yes. Yes, I am,' I said, nudging up against him and squeezing his hand. 'Everything's very right,' I murmured, happily.

'There's dessert!' Ginny's voice rang out. 'I thawed out apple pie, but Michael brought a whole box of pastries. And there's ice-cream. Charli, help me clear the table.'

'Why me?' Charli grumbled, but she instantly rose from her chair.

'I'll help,' Sam said, and it was obvious that they wouldn't be much help: mostly likely, they'd sneak out the back door.

'I'll give you a hand.' This was Michael, drawing Ginny's chair back in old-fashioned courtesy.

And between us all, the table was cleared, side-plates were brought in and two long cardboard boxes, filled with six pastries apiece, were laid along the centre.

It was fascinating, watching the dynamics of our family, which had been stable for so long: Jane and Daphne taking responsibility and managing the household; Ginny planning, preparing and presenting nutrition for all of us; Charli, being Charli, the youngest, most athletic and most exuberant. There was a shift, now, with Jane appearing hesitant and apprehensive – unsure, yet excited – about her new adventurous life; Jackson, a steady fixture at her side, quietly observing and providing ballast to Jane's uncertainty; Daphne, always so stressed and uptight – her mind processing an endless to-do list of details and jobs – mellow in her demeanour and indulgent in acquiescing to Dominic's sway; and Ginny, sitting next to debonair Michael, a newfound sense of confidence and self-esteem replacing her previously rebellious persona, which had its basis in anxiety and insecurity.

Charli, of course, was oblivious to most of this, only displaying awareness that Sam and Daniel held her dream future in their hands. It was reassuring, though, to see the strength of the bond she'd already formed with Sam: their sense of camaraderie, their playfulness, the sharing of their private jokes. And that she saw Daniel as an alternative father-figure was obvious: her care of his health and wellbeing, her quick responses to his requests, the respect she showed his demands.

I half-listened as dessert was eaten, wine glasses topped up, and conversation continued, ebbing and flowing, like a deep ocean wave. The men discussed travel plans back to their accommodation: Daniel offering a ride for both Michael and Patrick, back across the Bridge to the city, in Sam's SUV; Dominic would drop Jackson off at his marina on his way back to Kirribilli. My sisters all agreed that we'd see Jane off the next morning at the marina after a last breakfast together – just the five of us. Daphne and Ginny were running through a checklist of items that Jane could pack, whilst Charli continued to flirt with Sam, the two of them exchanging quotes from films they'd seen.

And then Charli invited Sam outside to see Clancy, who had been gone all evening, disappearing as soon as the house became too noisy and crowded, whilst Jane coaxed Jackson to her room to check her packing. Michael ventured into the kitchen with Ginny, the clatter of plates being rinsed and stacked competing with the jangle of cutlery being scooped into the dishwasher basket, revealing their activities. Dominic wordlessly drew Daphne towards the loungeroom and I noticed that neither bothered to turn on the overhead light or floor lamp.

So, sitting at the table, still covered in a now-soiled embroidered table-cloth, littered with empty glasses and scrunched-up serviettes, there was only Patrick and me left. His hand held mine, his thumb rubbing unconsciously back and forth across the skin at my wrist. I inhaled deeply, turning as the air left me, to offer him a tired, but blissful, smile. He'd been watching me – I'd felt the heat and sizzle of his gaze – and his eyes glittered with sexy satisfaction, a blend of his innate confidence and a smug delight; possibly at how the evening had panned out, maybe because I'd conceded that I'd spend next weekend with him. Or both.

'Well, Athena, the gods couldn't have orchestrated events better themselves. I'm impressed.'

'And so you should be, Iris. It's almost a story-book ending.'

'One we might need to write.'

'You and I?'

'I don't see why not. I probably haven't told you this – and I'm sure you've figured it out – but I've always believed that my writing improved considerably after we emailed each other. You've been a positive influence in my life for years now.'

'Of course, I have,' I said, adopting a haughty, goddess-like tone. 'You've been lucky to have me.'

'Well, he grinned, 'now that I've seen your powers, first-hand, I'm not surprised that I'm a better man for "having" you.'

I thumped him on the upper arm. 'Patrick!'

'I'm serious, though, Lulu. I'd be more than happy to collaborate on a book, or series of books, with you. I felt, sometimes, that we were already writing together, but I'm ready to do it properly, if you are.'

'What? Under Iris Greyson?'

'Probably not. What's your mother's maiden name?'

'Mackenzie,' I answered.

'We could work with that,' he replied. 'Something Mackenzie,' he pronounced, before nodding decisively. 'But now, whilst no-one's hovering and before I leave with Jack, are you going to kiss me, Athena, or not?'

'W-e-l-l,' I drew the word out, taunting him whilst I shifted towards him, tugging on his hand, 'I suppose I could.'

And I did.

A long kiss. A slow kiss.

A kiss to seal a deal.

A kiss the gods would applaud.

And a kiss worth writing about.

Acknowledgements

This series of novellas may have been focused on sisterly dynamics, but it was propelled by the love, encouragement and appreciation of very special friends. In naming them, I risk inadvertently leaving someone out, but I'll do my best.

To Terri, who bought me dinner one night in a south coast hotel and insisted, 'You already tell stories. You can do this. Just have a go!' Your words never left me, even when I thought I was in way over my head. Thank you.

To Trish, Nicky, Michelle and Jenny S, who gamely read my manuscripts and provided that essential feedback and advice that all new authors need. Thank you..

To Penny, I thank you. There are no words to describe the incredible effort you have made on my behalf.

To Pam, Jenny G, Claire, Kay, Georg, Heather and Eleanor, all of whom dropped whatever they were doing to nurse me through this long process of writing a book. You have my eternal gratitude.

To Genevieve, who calmly unscrabbles the mess I make with social media. I owe you big time!

And, finally, my daughter, who continually inspires, motivates and encourages me. This wouldn't have been done without you.

About the Author

Sunny Mackenzie loves romance, especially with smart, feisty women; gorgeous, sexy guys; and stunning Australian locations.

An avid reader since childhood, Sunny is now living her dream: travelling throughout the country in her trusty campervan, with Tom, her Australian Stumpy Tail Cattle Dog, for company.

Sunny is having fun: meeting new people, hearing their stories and writing hot romances for busy women to enjoy!

Contact Sunny

Sunny loves to hear from her readers and she does her best to respond.

Feel free to contact her on sunny.mackenzie@outlook.com or through her Facebook page: Sunny Mackenzie Author.